The Missing Link
And Other Tales of
Ape-Men

also translated and adapted by Georges T. Dodds:

by Jules Lermina: To-Ho and the Gold Destroyers

The Missing Link
And Other Tales of Ape-Men

Selected and adapted in English by
Georges T. Dodds

Edited and annotated by
Paul Wessels

A Black Coat Press Book

Visit our website at www.blackcoatpress.com

Table of Contents

Introduction
Neither Man, Nor Beast...

The purpose of this introduction is not to exhaustively review the theme of Man-Apes and Missing Links, but to provide some context to the works selected by Georges T. Dodds, and suggest other French works of likely interest in the same vein.

Not unexpectedly, the obvious similarities between men and apes have always proved too fascinating for storytellers to resist. The notion that the ape was but an imperfect avatar of man can be found in medieval romances such as *Le Roman de Renard*, a compilation of animal-centered tales from the 12th and 13th centuries in which the character of Eme the Ape is a wise companion to Noble, the Lion-King, and interacts with other talking animals. He and his wife, Rukenawe, have two children, Bytelouse and Fulerome, whom the wily Renard ends up devouring.

The presence of wild creatures spotted by explorers in faraway jungles who might have been either primitive men or apes, was also a staple of so-called "traveler's tales" that, in turn, inspired numerous works of fiction. In the 18th century, Rabelais, Restif de la Bretonne and the Chevalier de Mouhy all imagined various societies of animal-men in imaginary countries located in Africa or beyond.

The character of the 18th century Man-Ape, inspired by the social theories of Jean-Jacques Rousseau and the condition of Natural Man, reached its apex with the hugely popular novella *Jocko* (1824) by C.M. de Pougens (included in this volume), which was plagiarized and turned into a stage play. t took Edgar Allan Poe to present a strikingly contrasted image of the Man-Ape in his classic *The Murders in the Rue Morgue*

7

(1841), in which an abused orangutan ends up killing two women.

The tradition of the traveler's tale was still very much alive, but with a satirical spin, in Léon Gozlan's *Les Émotions de Polydore Marasquin ou Trois Mois dans le Royaume des Singes* [*The Emotions of Polydore Marasquin or Three Months in the Kingdom of the Apes*] (1856) in which a castaway arrives on an island inhabited by intelligent monkeys and becomes their leader by putting on the skin of a dead gorilla.

Although the idea that man and ape were related was not invented by Charles Darwin, his *On the Origin of Species* (1859) provided a theoretical formalization of this evolutionary connection. But this must not be confused with what came to be known as "the missing link." Indeed, the meaning attached to the term itself shifts fairly dramatically within its 250 years of existence. A German biologist, Ernst Haeckel, in a moment of over-zealous enthusiasm for the ideas of Darwin, mistakenly took Darwin's common ancestor theory to be a unilinear and polygenic fact of emergence (the missing link or "stage 21" of his *Chain of the Animal Ancestors of Man*), rather than a multilinear, monogenist account of natural selection.

This fueled the imagination of many, thereby establishing in fiction what could not be supported by fact. Nevertheless, the "missing link" gained a momentum in France through the popular works of Thomas Huxley and Charles Lyell, amongst others, even though Huxley's (not to mention Haeckel's) work on embryology showed clearly that there were very significant differences during the late phases of embryonic development in man and ape. Lyell's *Geological Evidences of the Antiquity of Man* (1863) reportedly inspired both Jules Verne and H. G. Wells. Certainly, the former's *Journey to the Center of the Earth* (1864) and *The Island of Dr. Moreau* (1896) reflect this.

In the absence of immediately available fossil evidence, and due to the competitive historical conjuncture of New Imperialism and the exciting developments in European theories of evolution, the popular imagination sought pseudo-scientific confirmation of the literal *missing link* in the physical existence of black people. This was facilitated by the ancient idea of a "Chain of Being" or hierarchy of perfection from mud to God, of which Haeckel's *Chain of the Animal Ancestors of Man* was a relatively new variation. This introduced a racial competition, racism, into the misinterpretation of Darwin's theory of natural selection, attested to by the idea of a literal missing link in the form of "the savage Hotentot, or stupid native of Nova Zembla." Only the popular version of the "missing link" has survived the test of time, science (and morality) having rejected theories of racial anthropology.

Darwin's work, rightly or wrongly, led to the creation of the sub-genre of prehistoric fiction with Samuel Berthoud's *L'Homme Depuis Cinq Mille Ans* [*Five Thousand Years of Man*] (1865), Elie Berthet's *Le Monde Inconnu* (1876; rev. as *Paris Avant l'Histoire*; tr. as *The Pre-Historic World*, 1879), and, of course, J.-H. Rosny Aîné's classic *Vamireh* (1892), *Eyrimah* (1893) and *Nomai* (1897), which became key works in that subgenre.[1] As the stories collected in the present volume show, some writers incorporated racist theories into their fiction uncritically, whilst others did so to undermine such views through various means of ridicule. Interestingly, a master of the genre, Rosny Aîné, often repeated Darwin's mantra that black people had more to fear from White Imperialism than from any perceived slip on the evolutionary ladder.

From the standpoint of the fictional evolution of the Ape-Man Albert Robida's *Voyages très extraordinaires de Saturnin Farandoul dans les 5 ou 6 parties du monde et dans tous les pays connus et même inconnus de M. Jules Verne* [*The Very Extraordinary Voyages of Saturnin Farandoul in the World's five or six Continents, and in all the Countries*

---

[1] All available in *Vamireh*, translated by Brian Stableford, Black Coat Press, ISBN 978-1-935558-38-5.

9

known—and even unknown—to Mr. Jules Verne] (1879),[2] is a mammoth, riotous and rollicking homage to Jules Verne in which the indomitable Saturnin Farandoul, a young man raised by apes on a Pacific Island, teams up with various Vernian heroes. Whereas Polydore Marasquin was a fake, a man dressed in a monkey skin, Farandoul is a quintessential Ape-Man, predicting Edgar Rice Burroughs' Tarzan. Farandoul, too, is a Rousseauesque character, a "noble savage," born into natural freedom and goodness, and civilization can only threaten to turn him into the same kind of morally-defective, money-grubbing, luxury-loving, war-mongering boor that it has made of almost all of us.

One writer who fully embraced the perceived consequences of Darwin's work as extrapolated by Haeckel, was Emile Dodillon with *Hemo* (1886) (included in this volume). Dodillon was careful to never categorically state that Jan Maas' experiment to create a true Man-Ape hybrid had succeeded. The reader remains free to believe that the title character is only an ape more evolved than others.

In Marcel Roland's *Le Presqu'Homme* [*Almost a Man*] (1905) (included in this volume), the broad influence of Darwin's ideas are also manifest, but relatively unexploited from a purely dramatic standpoint. The consequences of the discovery of a creature who is half-man and half-beast is better left to Jules Lermina with *To-Ho le Tueur d'Or* [*To-Ho and the Gold Destroyers*] (1905)[3] in which a 10-year-old boy is rescued during the bloody Dutch-Aceh War in Sumatra by To-Ho, a member of a peaceful tribe of ape-men who secretly live hidden in the jungle.

Included in this volume are three more, lesser known stories in the same vein: Léo d'Hampol's *Le Missing Link* (1910), Grégoire Le Roy's *L'Étrange aventure de l'abbé Levrai* [*The*

---

[2] Available in a Black Coat Press edition translated by Brian Stableford, ISBN 978-1-934543-61-0.

[3] Available in a Black Coat Press edition translated by Georges T. Dodds, ISBN 978-1-935558-34-7.

Strange Adventure of Brother Levrai] (1913) and Marcel Rol-
and's *L'Echelon* [*The Missing Link*] (1914).

Gaston Leroux' *Balaoo* (1911) is another important work
on the same theme. In it, we meet Professor Coriolis Boussac-
Saint-Aubin, a dedicated follower of Darwin, who returns
from Indonesia with a mysterious servant who is, in reality,
Balaoo, an anthropoid "humanized" by Coriolis' science *à la*
Doctor Moreau. Unfortunately, while Balaoo passes for a human, even studying Law, he remains at heart a savage and
unpredictable creature and kills several people. Worse, he falls
in love with Coriolis' daughter, Madeleine, to the scientist's
great dismay. Coriolis instead forces her to marry her cousin
Patrick. A series of adventures ensue during which Balaoo
redeems himself by being noble, generous, rescuing Madeleine, returning her to her fiancé and departing with a broken
heart to return to his native jungle.

According to Leroux, Balaoo is not a mere jumped up
ape, but a new and heretofore unknown breed of anthropoid,
cousin to To-Ho's or Burroughs' Great Apes. As usual, Leroux attempts to bolster the credibility of his story with pseudo-scientific quotes from the fabulist Louis Jacolliot and a
professor who allegedly spent seven years studying the language of apes. But this very attempt to suspend the reader's
disbelief is what makes Balaoo a truly ground-breaking novel
in the genre.

During the period between the two World Wars, one
work merits a mention: H.-J. Magog's *L'Homme qui Devint
Gorille* [*The Man Who Became a Gorilla*] (1921; rev. as *La
Fiancée du Monstre* [*The Monster's Fiancée*] and *Le Gorille
Policier* [*The Policeman Gorilla*], 1930). What makes it significant is that it used a theme arguably introduced by Maurice
Renard in his classic *Le Docteur Lerne* [*Doctor Lerne*] (1908),
that of a "consciousness" transplant between two persons of
different species—Renard wasn't categorically postulating
actual brain transplants. Magog goes one step further: a villain
who wants to get rid of a rival (Roland) enlists the help of two
mad scientists to transplant the brain of his victim into the

11

body of a gorilla, and vice-versa. Roland's body with the ape brain is quickly locked up in a lunatic asylum, while the gorilla with Roland's brain, initially sold to a circus, succeeds in gaining the trust of his keepers and then proceeds to get revenge. All is put right at the end.

Eventually, the popularity of Tarzan fostered a plethora of French (and other European) imitators, especially in the comics, such as Akim or Zembla, which came with their own hordes of Man-Apes to fight, such as Zembla's Boor or the intelligent man-apes of the secret city of Anthar.[4] Transplants of human brains into ape bodies, popularized by pulps and serials, also found their way into French popular culture such as Maurice Tillieux and Will's *L'Ombre sans Corps* [*The Shadowless Body*], a Tif & Tondu adventure published in 1970. The humanized apes from Pierre Boulle's classic novel *La Planète des Singes* [*Planet of the Apes*] (1963) were the vanguard of other alien apes, such as Max-André Rayjean's *Les Singes d'Ulgor* [*The Apes of Ulgor*] (1979), who were all heralding grim portents about the future of our own species.

Now let's turn back the clock to a simpler time, when men and apes took the first steps towards each other.

Jean-Marc Lofficier

---

[4] Available in a Black Coat Press edition of *Zembla*, translated by Jean-Marc Lofficier, ISBN 978-1-932983-93.7.

Emile Dodillon, (1848-1914) was a French author of the late 19th century. His other works include Les Forgerons de Montglas *[The Smiths of Montglas] (1882), and* Jean Lamy *(1903).* Hemo, *originally published in 1886, is a scathing, radical satire of the mores of the day.*

Emile Dodillon: *Hemo*

CHAPTER I

Jan was the last born of Philip Maas, and Philip Maas was the custodian of the main temple in Rotterdam. Formerly dedicated to Saint Lawrence, the huge building has maintained its Catholic name. It remains the Great Church, with an amphitheatric interior for professing grave things such as are common in Protestant churches, walls cold and unadorned under their whitewash, pews arranged in tiers. In the Great Church, guides, printed or living, wishing to show the "curiosities," describe a half-dozen marble mausoleums and the copper grille separating the nave from the choir. Forced to mention the 1,25 franc entrance fee, these guides would likely fare better were they to omit mentioning ahead of time that there was nothing to see. However, this emptiness was a good reform, as, unlike in Italy or as in former times in Belgium, one avoided the triple tedium of being forced to run between several chapels, to admire one masterpiece and a couple of crusts. When the Joanne and Baedeker travel guides mistakenly failed to incite travelers to the daily use of their gullibility in favor of recommending the packing of flannels, the only result was a daily decline in the gullibility of tourists. As the visitors, aside the lure of the tombs, the organ and the metal work, are never abundant in the Great Church, Philip Maas, the caretaker, seldom added tips to his meager fixed income.

Now his family was large: first, his wife, then, between Adrian his eldest and Jan his last, ten other children. A thin partition divided his caretaker's quarters, in a corner recess of the aisle, into two rooms. With one alcove and a closet that could fill each of the two rooms, they could already barely fit the first child's crib; for the others, Philip had to look in the city for supplemental housing, or give up his position. He rented one of those basements that impart such a distinctive look to the cities of his country, a kind of cave from which one reached the street by way of steep steps between the foot of the house and the top of the sidewalk, and into which the day-dreaming loiterer is at risk of tumbling while browsing along the shops. It was in an alley between the square and the street that housed the city's richest stores. From there, by climbing the stairs and extending their neck a bit to the left, one of the children kept watch on the caretaker's quarters, as well as he would have beside the church, near the door.

The father, as an old man, was returning to his old trade as tailor. Nevertheless, in a basement, particularly a basement in Holland, it is altogether too dark for sewing. Not to mention that this brave little caretaker-man, always with a slight cough, was so vibrant, so nervous, so perpetually in motion, that he could not stay put a quarter of an hour without jumping up suddenly from his rest, like the little devil in a jack-in-the-box. He found employment more gainful and more to his tastes: the raising of song birds.

Compared with the many stores where birds from the islands press the ruffles of their fine multicolored striations against the support rods of their aviaries, motionless as the skylarks skewered and barded by the dozen food purveyors' where innumerable species of parrots chirp and perform gymnastics on the end of the fine chain that holds them, like a galley-slave, to their perch; next to the famous market in Anvers, where showmen and circuses from all over Europe supply themselves in animals of all sorts, Philip, Philip Maas of the narrow roadway to the Church, in Rotterdam, patiently developed a most deserved reputation. There were a dozen cages, hung, on pleasant days, on the bar of the rail surrounding the top step of the sunken entrance-way that led to his home, and brought in, at night or in winter, to the room downstairs. And each held but one bird of drab plumage, but which he knew how to make into an incomparable artist.

To the starlings he gave hemp seed and biscuits; to the robins, a mixture of poppy flour and chopped calves' heart. The heart cost him less than a quarter florin, roughly 0,50 franc per week; the poppy flour, six sous a pound, and he did not even use a pound a month. As the robins, at the time of their migration, tore out their feathers, flayed themselves, tore themselves apart trying to take flight, Philip padded the wires of their cage roofs in cotton batting, and was often forced to blind them. Good and gentle, he hesitated, disturbed at no longer seeing them shake themselves, shift their eyes and puff up their crop in anticipation when he shouted "Attention" to them when showing them their treat, a cockroach—an insect that thrives in moist places. He was only comforted from this horrible operation by hearing them sing better later on, and in selling them at a higher price.

His triumph was the common lark, the grey lark, with the dark speckling of the throat and chest, and with the forked tongue; sober, retaining any music one whistled to it, and quiet at night. He had some that knew the national anthems of all the countries; an Englishman, brought by the child who was on lookout at the Great Church that day, had bought one which repeated *God Save the Queen* like a flageolet of the queen's Scottish guard, 75 florins, more than 150 francs. The robins learned these melodies, but with greater difficulty because of their habit of always returning to the banality of their usual serenades.

With only one child more per year, their living quarters took on the appearance of a rabbit-hutch to the extent that Philip took advantage of the fortune he had made with the Englishman, to annex the ground floor. Thus emerging from a cave, the light of the new rooms was an endless joy to all. The birds themselves sang louder. A number of windows opened

15

on the alley. When the fog broke up, there were summer days during which, unless one had to work, one did not need to light the lamps before 3 p.m. The house was finally ready for honest and peaceful happiness. But then Death entered the premises.

Adrian, the eldest child, was married and living in Haarlem. The others, except the last few, were still in school, working here and there in the city, only returning to the family domicile to eat and sleep. Nearing 20, the youngest son fell sick, lingered awhile, then died of consumption. A daughter, the third eldest, began coughing at the same age, and followed her brother from the heavy Utrecht-velvet armchair where he had sat for hours under a pile of covers, to the cemetery. Then it was another daughter; she did not live much past the fatal age. Then a son. One daughter returned to the status of eldest; when the disease began, terrified, she, one dark December night, went and drowned herself in the Meuse. Her corpse was found the next day, crushed between the sides of two of the many barges tied up at the *Boompjes* docks. Three younger ones, taken on as ship's boys as soon as they could climb the rigging, sought in vain to escape. The sickness boarded with them, allowed them to grow, develop, to think themselves safe, to laugh and cry, even to forget, and, at the fated time took them and laid them to rest forever. Two had died in the East-Indies, at Batavia, the third on the open seas. The poor mother, the least touched, went mad and was committed to an asylum. When the old custodian, long on the brink of death, finally died, there only remained the eldest and youngest sons, Adrian, 37 and Jan less than a third his age, to serve as pallbearers.

The funeral over, the elder took the younger by the hand and brought him home to Haarlem with him. Neither one dared look behind them.

On their way, wishing to break with their past, they opened the cage of the last skylark their father had trained. Disoriented, it perched momentarily on little Jan's finger, tottered as if inebriated with its sudden liberty, flapped its wings, rose, turned, and tore off towards sunnier climes beyond the horizon where the big windmills seem to grind up the fog continually—without even a word of goodbye

CHAPTER II

Adrian's wife was older than he. Widowed, already a mother, she had made him understand the very day of their nuptials, that her late husband having been rich, and Adrian not being so, she did not wish to have any new children who would be beneath, as she put it, their uterine sister, and consequently that they would have no children together. Dumbfounded, the young man could only mutter:

"If only you had told me earlier!"

"What for? It was time enough tonight."

"But I'll make money, I'll work..."

"I certainly hope so, I chose you for that very reason."

Adrian had lowered his head, and never since raised it.

On the whole, Adelaide Brinckleymann was a good woman. A barmaid whom Brinckleymann had married after a country fair, and whom he had put in charge of the Brinckleymann café, she had almost been forced to a quasi-avaricious stinginess. He was an easy-going drinker, gambler, eater and drinker, and not, like most of his race, of a cold and near-melancholic disposition; his bursts of laughter were enough to split a beer stein. As long as the party went on all night, he was always ready to put the tab he had encouraged his friends to build over the day onto his own tab, the ledger of profits and losses. With his potbelly, his widely-set jaws so well adapted to chowing-down that his cheeks seemed horizontal, and especially the crimson blush of his bloated face, Brinckleymann should have lived in the days of Franz Hals, whose wide-ranging and bold genius would have immortalized him, among the marvels of a nearby museum, in the forefront of his banquet of freebooters. The cellar was emptying without

17

the till filling. A few more years would have brought ruin. Adelaide, having brought nothing more into the marriage than her corsage and her work ethic, was constantly careworn. Nevertheless, her first husband dead, dead of natural-causes, of no other sickness than a week of partying, she had promised herself a husband who would take on all the worries, and would keep as quiet as she had.

She could have found no better.

The clientele changed: the old, now fewer since they could not pay up their tabs on a regular basis, were complemented by a more profitable one of merchants and landlords. The establishment kept the name of its founder: Café Brinckleymann, but the new manager, Adrian Maas, appeared more like a servant in his own home.

The good folk, sitting side by side on the moleskin-covered benches lining the walls, enveloped in the smoke of large cigars and long clay pipes, rarely moving but to unfold a newspaper or pick up a glass, their lips speechless, their motions noiseless, resembled a row of well-oiled, silent automatons arrayed behind smoky windows. Adrian served them, often leaning against the door with his towel under his arm, glancing around but oblivious, given that he lived there, to the originality of this Haarlem landmark. The bells and the famous organ pealed out their songs in the church over to the left, but Adrian heard none of it. However, a single sharp clang struck by his wife had him scurrying to see who needed him. One of the automatons wished to pay, or was in need of oil; there was change to make, a stein to fill. Then he would return his post.

When the museum opened, a few strangers wandered past, some countrymen from adjoining provinces, Friesian, whom a stray beam of sunlight would on occasion light up by the forehead-strap and pendant-decorated blinders in a glitter of gold. Dogs, their tongues hanging out, followed the bakers' and herb-sellers' carts. Adelaide rang again. Adrian leaned his elbow on the marble top of the waxed oak counter behind which she sat in state. The great array of windows behind her allowed a view of a narrow courtyard with tiers of red geraniums that conferred a pinkish hue to the nape of her neck and the rims of her ears. He admired her at length: pink-complexioned, fresh, blond, chubby, bearing a vague smile, as if dozing from the rocking of her ample bosom and its endless drone. When she drew him from his reverie, her finger stretched out, her rings glistening less than her skin, pointing out a drop of spirits or the ring left by a saucer on the last table vacated by a customer, he would sigh, and wipe it down.

This love, which the wife's crabby dominance only allowed to blossom on rare occasions, Adrian's simple heart ended up reallocating in friendship upon Saskia, his predecessor's daughter. She believed him to be her father, and every time she, in chatting with her dolls, called him "dad" he would hug her and feel his life was not so bad after all. He missed her more than she missed him when they sent her off to school as a day-boarder. Every morning he would prepare her little lunch-basket, hiding all sorts of treats, which her mother pretended not to see, under her primers. He would see her there and pick her up again at the end of the day.

On his way back from Rotterdam, he was not without some apprehension as to how the imposing Adelaide, decidedly stingy, would welcome little Jan, now their dependant. A last hesitation was slowing his steps across the square, when Saskia, serving a doll's dinner-party on an outdoor table on the terrace, spying them out, left her games, jumped up to hang on Jan's neck, whom she then breathlessly pushed towards the counter, her hands clapping, crying out loudly: "Oh! mommy, daddy's brought a little brother."

The mother did not contradict her, smiled at the lad, and Adrian always reckoned that it was thanks to Saskia's intervention that his wife had not pouted for more than a minute.

The two children grew up together.

The part of the bench along the great array of windows was their little nook, usually empty, for the customers generally lined up near the entrance. They play-acted a wedding, being husband and wife. They imitated their mother and father:

Jan set the table, did the cooking, the groceries, the big jobs; Saskia sat and made tick marks on a chalkboard with the gravity of her mother tabulating accounts on the counter, losing patience with his slow progress, accusing him of being good-for-nothing, then, seeing him heavy-hearted and on the brink of tears, she would quickly give up her shrewish role, call him silly for crying over nothing, sit him in her place, fix the awkwardness brought on by her scolding, and climb up onto her knees on the bench to hug him and force-feed him the better part of their play meal. His cheeks bloated, he hesitated between hugs and cookies, eventually passively accepting both. However, being timid and no glutton, he preferred the kisses, not daring to return to the candies.

One day, Adelaide told her daughter that it was not appropriate to hug little boys all the time. Jan moved off to the other end of the café to sulk, and Saskia, surprised, asked which boy, for in her mind Jan was not a little boy; he was her brother. The mother did not answer, but that night in her room she asked her husband point-blank what kind of future he intended to provide for Jan. Was he addressing the situation? Had he even considered the question? At 14 he was no longer a child. Why continue sending him to school? Given that he was penniless would it not be better for him to learn a trade, a useful job which would allow him to be self-sufficient later on? She recounted the earlier events. Without reading into these games more than was reasonable, she wished them to stop. Any minute now these children would learn that they were in no way related, their friendship could blossom into love, and their separation would then be far more painful than now.

So much foresight dumbfounded the good man.

"My poor little Jan!" he repeated, having indeed never thought of such things. The children were so happy together. Jan was still only 14. He congratulated himself at seeing him playing and laughing so nicely, eating and running so well. A thought frequently tormented him: it was that the others, his other brothers and sisters, died as a result of their closeted life, their wretched roach's life in a Rotterdam basement. Here, in the open air, with the care and food that were lacking there, he heartily wished to save the last-born, the little Jan. Honey, the others, it was only in their 20th year that the horrible sickness...and his little brother was still only...My God! how dreadful, at the least cough...

He was almost sobbing. Adelaide, even-tempered, powerfully moved, comforted him, multiplied her words of support in her good-times voice: He was not thinking. He could not see clearly! He had daguerreotype of the poor brothers and sisters of which he spoke. Well, all were good looking, drawing it from their father—Philip Maas their father—dead of a weak chest. Adrian, meanwhile, had survived and his young brother, Jan, would live because they took from their mother, still alive, if off her head. He need only compare, look at himself, then look at Jan. Look, look, you big puppy-dog, do you not both share the same nose, mother Maas' nose? See for yourself...

Adrian checked. A teardrop was hanging from the inner crease of his left eye. In squishing it to dry under the pad of his thumb, he felt his nose, verified his wife's assertion, and went into the room next door where Jan slept and from whence he thought he had heard a groan. Yes, the sleeping child, his face sunken in the white of the pillowcase, also clearly showed their mother's nose, long, round and pendulous at the tip, the color of unripe prunes.

Jan was not sleeping but had been listening and had indeed moaned plaintively. He kept quiet, pretending to be asleep when Adrian came in, but alone again in the darkness, he opened his eyes and burrowed under his covers to cry at his leisure. So, he had been mistaken until now: Saskia was not his sister. The lie exposed tore him apart. They would send him away. He recalled the need, expressed by Adelaide, for a quick separation, and what was no less heart-wrenching, what she had said about his resembling his brother. He feared being ugly, of making Saskia laugh at him. Remembering, finally, the remainder of the conversation, he understood, without trying to figure out why, that his nose, which he already imagined flushed red in response to Saskia's malice, was, on the other hand, a kind of guarantee of good health. He fell back to sleep, bewildered and not knowing whether to rejoice or lament.

Keeping all he had heard that night to himself, Jan unknowingly took on the habit of scratching his nostrils. The frequency of this gesture surprised Saskia, who teasingly asked him why he always looked like a preening cat. He shut himself up in silence, kept to the shadows, intimidated by the least glance his way, imagining that what he most feared was occurring: that his nose was expanding and reddening by the minute. From then on he bore the humble smile and resigned sadness that were to be his forever.

They apprenticed him to a gardener. At first he would spend his evenings at home with his family, but during the winter he would often stay in a room at his employer's, a small bachelor pad, simple and clean, at the back of the garden atop a storage shed for the greenhouses. As the heater, the upkeep of which was his responsibility, was located in this shed, he enjoyed, on the floor above, a temperature that allowed him to spend a portion of his nights engaged in one of his favorite pursuits: reading books which, little by little, filled the shelves he had built around his room. His master limited himself to jokingly chiding him when he had to call on him several times after a long night. Jan provided him, in a seemingly carefree manner, with the welcome results of a number of horticultural techniques forgotten and rediscovered in old books. The good man, guileless and honest, soon let him sleep, allowing him to work how and when he wished, telling all, with a wink of his eye, that his apprentice would go far, would bring back—who knows?—the Haarlem of legend, where the bulb of certain tulips sold for several thousand florins.

Saskia, having become a beautiful young woman, blonde, pink-complexioned, her bosom giving, like a summer's peach, a longing for a bite, happy with the excellent

22

reputation garnered by the one she continued to call her brother, would greet him with a bright smile, reproaching him for
his infrequent visits. He was smart enough, yet he still buried
himself in those terrible books.

"If only that would shrink my nose," Jan would answer,
smiling. She told him off for bearing a grudge so long, thinking that he was referring to some childish teasing from long
ago, and she insisted, to punish him, that he take her for an
outing every Sunday.

When one day, at the noon hour, sitting pensively behind
the cash register where she was taking her mother's place, she
had, after her customary greeting to him, more quickly than
usual returned to her embroidery and thoughts, he in turn had
laughingly wagered with her that he could guess what she was
thinking about. What an idea! She was thinking...no she was
not thinking of anything, really. Bending over he whispered a
name in her ear, that of Martin Heltzius, the son of a textile
manufacturer, and, seeing her blush and her bosom heaving,
he tenderly apologized. A few days before, Heltzius junior, for
whom Jan had fagged when they were together in school, ac-
costed him, something he never did, and feigning a cheerfulness that the jiggling of his chubby body belied, had him come
to his home, offered him tea and cigars, took him to soak up
the sun along the shores of the Spaarne, arm in arm as if they
were inseparable. Jan, wishing to calm his fears, told him to
relax, that he understood the friendly interest he bore towards
his dear sister Saskia, and would happily pass on a message.
Martin jumped up and hugged him around the neck in the
middle of the street. He was a good boy, one of wealthiest
born of the Haarlem merchant-class. Jan became the two lovers' confidant, not, however, without having assured himself,
with a tactful honesty, that her mother would approve of such
a marriage for Saskia.

In the middle of a flowerbed, having perused the newspaper he had just received, he returned his attention to unpot-
ting some hyacinths, when his master, unfolding the newspaper he had tossed on a bench, asked him what number had

come up in the Amsterdam Orphans' lottery. Jan had not looked. He had some tickets, but had given them to Saskia as a present. The florist insisted this was not the case, that Saskia had only accepted half the tickets if he would keep the other half. He eventually remembered that he must indeed have, somewhere up there in the drawer of his table, among some seed packets, five extra tickets. Once he was done, he would try to remember to go and have a look.

The old fellow, less patient, wanted to see right away, climbed the stairs, turned over the drawers, full of a jumble of things, moved over into the light of the open window, tickets in one hand, newspaper in the other, read, tried to call the one he loved like a son, but could only frantically wave the ticket, held out at arms' length, choking, collapsing in joy against the casement-window. Jan rushed up to help him, compared the ticket with the newspaper, saw that to avoid any error they reprinted the winning number several times throughout the paper, in letters and in numbers, and said calmly that he was lucky, for now he could buy Saskia the long-chain pocket watch she had for so long wished for.

"At least go and tell your parents."

"Not the way I am, no sir"

Then, his hands black with potting soil, his sleeves pulled up, without a tie, in gardeners' boots and apron, he slowly proceeded to wash up.

Before he was even finished, his boss, who could not wait to bring the story to the Brinckleymann café, or to disseminate it on the way, brought back a good part of the city with him, Adelaide and her husband in the lead. The clapping died down and the staircase was creaking under the press of those wishing to congratulate him. Among all those there, including the silent and intimidated winner and his crazed employer, dancing with joy, the happiest was Adrian, who wrapping his little brother up in his arms, could only speak in monosyllables. The floor of the little room was at risk of collapsing. Those who could, got in where they could. Many curiosity-seekers were still coming in to see the newspaper in which it was printed, to see the ticket, and especially to see Jan, the winner of the jackpot, who when poor had only a few friends, but now shook the many hands extended towards him and mumbled some thank-yous, overcome in the end, not by his sudden fortune, but by the emotions of others. Upon the request of those below, he had to present himself in the window frame in the image of a conqueror. The bravos rang out twice as loud in a last burst. Jan, returning to his elder brother, held out his hand to him.

"Well you know, brother, it's halfsies."

"What?"

"You won't refuse me. Accept half..."

"No, it's yours, and yours alone. Not a guilder for me or my wife. We don't need anything. You, you're young."

Adelaide had pinched her husband on the elbow, but not early enough to interrupt his answer. Besides, Adrian was delighted at his own quickness, for he knew and understood that to avoid the domestic scene he now foresaw, he would have hesitated to appear disinterested, however sincere it might be. He further added, in the faint hope of softening his irascible wife:

"My word, little brother, you'll be able to buy the little Saskia a lovely present."

"Ah now, you blabbermouth, we can't hear anyone but you," said Adelaide with the ghost of a smile, "Mr. Jan knows better than you what he should do."

She curtsied, then embraced and invited Jan, now Mr. Jan, my dear Mr. Jan, and went home repeating: "'Til this evening, 'til this evening," at the bottom of the stairs. Adrian followed her. Jan, delivered, went back to his cleaning up. Then, dressed, with several hours to kill, he chose a book and decided to go for a walk. The remarks, the glances, the exclamations, the questions with which each passerby assailed him, his story already spread everywhere, not to mention a group of children who stuck to him like glue, forced him towards an alley into which he entered, in order to take a shortcut. Gossips to the left and to the right, assembled and drawing close to look him over and complement him, formed two rows of ample bosoms between whose happy jiggling he had to proceed slowly and prudently, like a river-pilot entering one of those difficult canals, from which he knew he would never emerge if he unfortunately came under the sway of the canal-bank eddies. This pass traversed, he escaped to the Brinckleymann café.

Quite another surprise awaited him there. Adelaide, turning over the cash to her husband and forbidding him to leave it, immediately dragged him off to the dining area, and there, wham! in a stuttering declamation, the words escaping as if from a release valve behind which they were boiling, she congratulated him again, but also congratulated herself and all of them, for he could, if he so wished, forever assure the family's complete happiness...by marrying Saskia. Jan nearly fainted. She sprinkled him with cologne, and explained: Her daughter suspected nothing as she had been visiting a school friend since breakfast. He was to tell her himself, upon her imminent return, of his newfound wealth, and she, her mother, would devote herself within the next few days in preparing her daughter.

"Never!"

Jan came to something of a confused attention. He thought the girl did not love him. Her mother grumbled that she would very much like this to occur, but a single motion on his part quelled her angry outburst. He said that she loved him as a brother, not as one should love a fiancé... The mother said that as soon as she returned, without hiding anything from her, without prior coaching, she, her mother would ask her. Lord! as much as he adored her, and though this was the first and probably the last time that he would admit it, it was not for his own sake that he insisted on this procedure. No indeed, it is for her, the dear child, who thus surprised would allow her innermost feelings to be apparent. They would see, would they not? The very idea that he might have dreamed of her as his wife would bring her to tears; or rather, no, he swore to himself, she would burst out laughing.

Poorly concealing his uneasiness, Adelaide signaled him to be quiet: Saskia was coming in. Breathless she gave Jan a great big hug. What! Was he not happier than that? Well! She, as soon as she found out, could not stay away another minute, and ran over all aflutter. To think he wanted to give her all ten tickets, today she would have been the one winning the jackpot, 30,000 florins! Now she would go and take flowers from his lovely gardens. She had stopped doing this since she had heard, not from him but another source, that he reimbursed his employer for the bouquets she picked. Was she not a silly girl to ignore the fact that flowers were sold and were to be paid for like any other merchandise?

"Yes, everything is sold," said her mother in an oddly grave tone, as much to interrupt this pointless prattling as to confer some honest counsel. From this tone Saskia concluded that there was some important news, and she quietly listened. Then, furious that Jan was forcing her to act so quickly, but, her voice, even more deliberate, trying to hide the fury which would have given away the fears which assailed her, Adelaide, trying to bore her eyes and her thought into those of her daughter, informed her that Jan, Mr. Jan, did her the honor of asking for her hand in marriage. She should answer truthfully and frankly.

"My hand? What for? Ah!"

And suddenly, with great candor—yes, truly! with great candor—she burst into unquenchable laughter. She, at her age, to be taken in by such a silly story! And her dear mother lending herself to such silly games. For she was truly taken in for a moment. "Fie upon you, naughty joker!" she went on, jumping up on Jan's knees and patting his cheeks; and she, who no longer allowed herself to pull pranks on him...had she said yes! After all, he would certainly be a good husband, were they not almost brother and sister, and had they not loved one another.

Jan, interrupted her in turn, addressing himself first to Adelaide, then to her, while letting her dance on his knees as she had as a little child:

"Well then, has your gamble fallen sufficiently flat? Imagine this, Saskia, that believing you incredibly naive, she bet she could make you believe that I was asking for your hand in marriage. Thankfully, you didn't fall into her trap, for then I would have lost. I, like you, could no longer keep a straight face, and was dying to burst out laughing."

Holding it back too long, he, like Saskia, burst out laughing, even louder than her, laughing to tears.

Adelaide had run off.

"What's she so furious about, losing?" Saskia asked.

"Well, no."

"Well, yes. Didn't you see how she slammed the door? So, what did you win?"

"Why, the jackpot, 30,000 florins."

"I know, I know, I was talking about your bet with mom."

'I promised not to tell."

"Oh, come on, tell me right now, for I'm dying to know."

"Why...why, we bet that if I won, I would be the one to set the date for your wedding with Martin Heltzius. You'll need to get cracking on putting your trousseau together."

The young woman ran off to give her mom a great big hug.

Jan had put aside for her, at the great jeweler's on Bartel Joris St., the watch she had long admired, and then made his way towards a nearby park. Night was falling and he still walked. The street lights, the great signal-lights in the railroad station in front of him, all shone out. Remembering, he lowered his brow and stepped back into the shadows. A light this red had lit up in his mind when Adelaide had so rudely proposed to have him for her son-in-law. Had they both hoped that Saskia, knowing him to be rich, would answer yes? The mother, perhaps, but he could witness to the fact that he had never had such a reprehensible thought, but had always judged Saskia to be what she was, adorable in her ignorance of vile connivings. No, flowers are not sold; yet they are sold. Thus his love had been more than disdained, but rather ignored or unsuspected. Hurt, his pain had a strange, sweet, almost suave quality in seeing that the object of his love had not, even for an instant, done anything to forfeit the esteem he held her in, in the humble and pure altar of his heart. Raising his head, he returned to the city.

CHAPTER III

The day he was handed, upon simply presenting his winning ticket at the lottery offices, 30,000 florins, more than 60,000 francs, Jan, accompanied and advised by his brother, deposited them with a banker in Amsterdam, where honor was as hereditary and solid as his huge fortune. Adrian, on their way back, asked him of his future plans. He said he had decided, most definitely, to be content to live off the interest, without making any attempt to build upon the capital. Fate brought it to him; well then, he would prove his gratitude to generous fate, by showing himself forever satisfied. This was the old family principle of a simple life. Adrian lauded his choice.

Saskia and Martin Heltzius married. The nuptials over, Jan, notwithstanding his good-hearted employer's wish to leave him the gardens, the client-base and the firm's excellent reputation for half the price offered by a young business competitor, untied his florist's apron and dove into what ran the risk of becoming his only passion: books.

Having lived in Saskia's old room that faced onto the square, right in front of the statue of Laurent Coster, he bought the small house of an old French painter who had washed up in Haarlem and had made a living making endless copies, for the small frames of the second-hand market, of Frans Hals' masterpiece, where he grouped the portraits of 19 musketeers around their officer along with his own in the back, on the left, as if the light-hearted master, by placing himself in the background, had counted on posterity, which had not failed him, to bring him to the forefront.

Jan loved the French. As a child, in Rotterdam, he sought them out in particular among the visitors to the Great Church. Their prayers were a bit long; they were asked to pay the admission fee, they would argue about it, they would be brought before the fee written on the walls of the caretaker's quarters, and no doubt remembering Belgium, they remarked that both catholic and protestant always ended having a hand in your pocket. However, they did end up smiling and paying up faster and more generously than other foreigners.

At the Brinckleymann café, he had been, from the day after his arrival, a friend to the old artist who ate there; he followed him to the museum, on his walks, and to his home. The old man would set up an easel, a canvas, leaving him to break open the pencils and pierce the paint tubes, answering his questions in Dutch, in the argot of Parisian studios, and they understood one another perfectly.

He was a sketch-artist, sent over by one of Paris' illustrated dailies when the great lake was being drained, with no family, already older, with no talent, but no longer deluding himself about it. Well over any fevered ambitions or desire to engage in pointless struggles to reach the top, this stranger had grown old alone, calmly, silently, a voluntary exile not only from his country, but from life, yet nonetheless of a gay disposition. No one remembered his name, not even himself it seemed; they called him the Frenchman, and he was held in esteem, loved, greeted wherever he went. While the will left to the city's homeless shelter the little he owned, in particular the receipts from the sale of his home, a request, though not a condition, was attached. It was to hang, in some corner of the museum, a painting of his he had designated, which was found in the middle of a shambles of unfinished pieces. Haarlem accepted the bequest and fulfilled the request. The painting, signed with two initials, was the portrait of a woman—apparently a Parisian woman—before a lovely French landscape.

Jan converted a vacant lot into a garden, extended the ground floor with a greenhouse, containing, as at his former employer's, a circulating hot water heater. A spiral staircase led to the floor above, where two rooms, one long and narrow, where he slept, and another, the artist's studio which he converted into an office, constituted his true residence. He continued to take his meals at his brother's. His home being behind the railroad, in a wedge of land between the river and the canal beltway, he would, at the same time every day, with the short steps of a small landowner, saunter down the shores of the Spaarne to the street facing the square, and then return the same way.

The regularity of his passage cheered up the river folk. Besides these self-imposed outings, he rarely wandered outside his neighborhood, but remained in the lovely park set above the early fortifications, hand behind his back or holding a book, daydreaming, muttering to himself. If one tried to accost him, he would evade one, if one insisted, he would rudely break away and take refuge at home. Given his new state one might have accused him of being prideful, but this did not occur to anyone, as he was too well known.

He would receive books from everywhere: Germany, France…he neglected his garden and greenhouse; his light remained lit until dawn, the glow from the bay-window in his office remaining almost all night, shaded from time to time when he moved about by the great shadow of his silhouette. In former times one might have thought him a sorcerer or an alchemist, but today the good folk whose greetings he barely and only absentmindedly acknowledged, would, behind his back, tap their foreheads with a finger, in the universal sign of a mind gone astray.

His visits to Saskia upon her giving birth tore him somewhat from his stay-at-home ways. Mrs. Martin Heltzius, tied to her business, was forced to place her child with a wet-nurse. The store returned to its former routine, and Jan's visits returned to their former infrequency. At the dinner table he answered so queerly that his brother- and sister-in-law stopped speaking to him. Finally, when an Amsterdam newspaper commented upon the baroque lucubration he had just published, there were no doubts left: clearly, he was mad.

He was devoting himself to natural history.

Had he limited himself to those descriptive domains, such as existed in botany, requiring little more than memorization, underpinned by themselves alone, being immediately accessible to all, he could have acquired some hard and fast knowledge, something whereby his long nights would have contributed important new information to the field of taxonomy. Unfortunately, he had quickly been captured by those generalizations whose careful laying out was the purview of great minds, but of which vague projects penciled in the margins of science were more closely associated with an entire class of harmless, powerless cranks. Jan was certainly among these, thrusting blindly between two well-established pillars of knowledge to emerge somewhere in a morass, off the beaten path, a path which he had at one time trod. Losing themselves all the more, that, their backs were to the goal, they pressed forward, simple-minded folk, crushed by doubt, incapable of being content with mere theoretical estimates arrived at through pure reason. Such an agenda for duly witnessed certainty, for something henceforth undeniable, did not bother them, for discovery exalted the seeker and provided him with the ecstasy of certainty, which once tasted, rendered him insensible to all other pleasures. Their imagination, neither powerful nor expansive was instead smoky, scattered, foggy. Capable only of dreaming, yet not poets, they could not supply their own materials, but found them in arithmetic text, never seeing in science, but what was not there. Naysayers or believers, the seekers of the absolute were recruited among them. They required vast quantities of money and conceit for them to be dangerous, and their attributes being generally contrary to their temperament, the majority, like Jan, remained harmless creatures, innocuous reformers of humanity and healers of its woes: poverty, war, prostitution, vivisection. Their books dealt with everything, and besides ran the gamut from the Sun

32

to the Moon, supporting scripture upon Mesmer's teachings, and true geniuses upon such innocents as themselves. While in medieval times they had their chance to write, on occasion some modern scholar would dig up one of these "Summas," and not wishing to admit to the pointlessness of having exhumed it, they would demonstrate, with footnotes, commentary, prefaces and afterwords, that the author was one of those great forgotten geniuses, who in an age of darkness illuminated the glittering achievements of the future. All this was child's play, as everything could be predicted, mothers and doctors assert, from the babbles of a child or from hallucinatory ramblings.

Jan had named his book: *Hemo*, drawn from the Greek word "blood." Hemo was the name with which he baptized the new-blooded man, the renewed-man generated by his method. The Adam of old was subject to Nature, to the world, but the world would be subject to Hemo. An explanation of the world was then indispensable, for man must know what he must tame, so Jan established immediately and completely his cosmogony.

God, the Divine Spirit exists throughout eternity. No one, not even Moses in the Hebrew Genesis, had ever stated—as Voltaire had correctly pointed out—that anything was made from nothing, or that the Divine Spirit was literally the Wind stirring the Waters. In criss-crossing it, these wind-driven currents filled the universe. At every crossing point, a gas burst forth—oxygen—forever bearing the creative spark, inseparable from God, and whose different manners of condensing led to all the celestial bodies in the universe. The universe was thus God incarnate in all things through his breath; the universe was the Spirit and the Spirit was God; whence arose that mystery which greater number of religions admit to, from the Hindu Trimurti to the Christian Trinity: God the father, creator; his breath, the Holy Spirit; and the universe, starting with man, his creation, his creature, his son. The divine breath which was in everything, which was everything, the overall single causative agent, of which matter and its multiple phe-

33

nomena—life, sound, light, heat, magnetism—are but its objective manifestations, which current science has proven that these supposedly different processes are different forms of motion. This principle which was cause and effect, matter and energy, body and action, creation and creator, universe and God, was electricity. Jan then broached the subjects of transcendental anatomy and physiology, comparing the small blueish veins on a young woman's brow to the Milky Way, tiny veins on the brow of God, tumbling along suns like blood cells. The human brain was a gathering of stars, a nebula link to a central sun: the soul. The soul, as everything else in the universe, was an electrically charged fluid. Adam and Eve's sin was to have usurped God's role in mixing their fluids; they created, but by lessening themselves. Every man was the result of such a reduction in two prior beings, those which had created him, and this loss constituted original sin. Man and woman, brought together, burnt in a supreme collision, sparking love at the sacred moment when the melted portion of their two fluids broke away as a soul of its own. This man and this woman, if they loved each other without reproducing themselves, thus lost part of their electricity, diminishing God by the entire quantity of divinity that they had not passed on to a child. It was the crime perpetrated by Onan and recommended by Malthus, the crime of nations that would perish. And Jan, rising to heady moral speculations, invoked the God within him to purify his lips from vulgar words and maintain chaste his overheated thoughts. Perhaps here, the image of Saskia had arisen in his memories. Anyway, this invocation completed his work. Admitting with a scrupulous honesty his need to undertake further studies, the author begged his philosopher colleagues to wait for the complete exposition of his conclusions, in order to judge the system at once, as a whole. The cornerstones were set, the world explained, man as he was, understood. The true Homo, man as he must be, would be the topic of the second volume.

The philosophers waited.

His humble horticultural work abandoned, Jan tossed out the rarest flowers from his beds to bury maceration vats. Cow and horse heads, entire carcasses of dogs, rabbits, and birds, picked up here and there, were thrown in. The vats exhaled a charnel stench over the ramparts. The neighbors complained. He apologized, and emptied the vats, too early, into the greenhouse. Needing to tear off the greening flesh, to scrape the tendons and ligaments from the still fatty bones, his hands in the rotting matter, his nose hovering over plates in anatomy texts, he was prone to continuous bouts of nausea whose retching clouded over his eyes. Threatened finally, because of the reek pervading his clothing and entire body, of being refused a place at Adelaide's table, he buried the bones and with them his project to mount himself a collection of them. Upon the counsel of his doctor, he went to see a naturalist in Antwerp very skilful in preparing skeletons.

While he did not find what he wanted, for the naturalist only undertook custom work—he discovered something better. The famous wild animal fair was in town. He went wandering through. Around the auction block, the avenues were lined with the sheds, tents and caravans of the menagerie owners, come to renew or complete their personnel, before winding their way through Europe. All the curses of Babel, dominated by the "goddamns" of the great British circuses, coalesced into a single argument startlingly accompanied by all of the creatures' voices, from the ill-tempered gibberish of the parrots to the roars of the wild beasts. The ebony gavel's short sharp strikes seemed to fracture and split apart the enormous mass of noise into thousands of smaller echoes, whose last vibrations fell into silence. A huge African elephant, brought out unfettered, shifted heavily, a back resembling granite rounded and scored by diluvial pebbles, its motionless eyes seemingly maintaining over the crowd it dwarfed, the soft pensive gaze of a patriarch who has seen the worst and overcome it. At the door of the Zoological Gardens, where the parade of buyers and their purchases did not end, was the exit, far from Ararat, of a new Noah's Ark. Jan, after

35

mature consideration, brought back a cockatoo and some monkeys: living forms of nature, no longer the dead remains which narrow minds of no synthetic capacity continue to manipulate.

The cockatoo belonged to the small Philippine species, with a white body, wings and tail, and a red crest. Attaching him to a bronze perch by way of a silvery chain around his leg, Jan did not bother with him, except to maintain a supply of seeds and water. His studious contemplations were immediately taken up by the monkeys.

He had four of them, in three cages: one langur, one Alouatta howler-monkey, and two marmosets. Lining them up on a trestle between the office window and his desk, he would only take his eyes off them to flip through stories about them in travelogues, where nothing would surprise him, his imagination far outstripping the most bizarre descriptions. The squirrel-like marmosets, agile and restless, perched on the crossbars at the top of the cage, their tail, longer than their body, twisted around their neck like a woman's boa, were of little interest to him, even often annoyed him with their high-pitched squalling when they argued over a sowbug or a spider. But the langur, old and morose, crouching with his feet in his hands, his black, hooded face and stiff dirty-white beard lowered, closed his eyes as if remembering the splendor of the Brahman temples where he had leapt about free and venerated. His dreaming took him to the land of the huge Buddhas, of the Sun splitting the bark of the guava trees, beneath which the fakirs let the nails of their clenched fists grow through their flesh for 50 years. The Alouatta, while rather sick, huddled in a corner like the langur, silent, almost inert, the goitrous sac of his laryngeal pouch hanging loosely, thought he heard the frightening cries with which these monkeys nightly terrify the American forests.

Reading those works of popular science where good folk tire themselves out debunking ideas which scientists have never themselves had, he threw himself into tearing down the latter and coming to the rescue of the former, easily addressing, here as elsewhere, the toughest questions. He, who placed oysters with fish, and eels with snakes, would then, with an ineffable degree of ignorance, make categorical statements regarding the field of heredity and the hypotheses of the fixity of species and evolution. Thus, would he say, do alleged scholars place monkeys amongst their ancestors? This vile creature, which spends its days delousing itself in front of me would be among my ancestors! Bah! To the answer so often cited from the French naturalist Edouard Claparède, who assured a bishop that he would rather be an improved monkey than a degenerate Adam.[5] Such opinions struck Jan as insulting, and he mulled over them continuously.

Worse off yet, one night, as he was just about to blow out the light, he discovered a chapter in a zoology text that described the great cynocephalic apes as having a sexual interest in black women.[6] He was haunted with nightmares. In the middle of the night he woke, terrified, feeling—feeling in an

---

[5] The actual saying is: "better to be an advanced ape than a degenerated Adam" and is attributed to the Swiss comparative anatomist René-Edouard Claparède (1832-1871). His father, who was French, found refuge in Switzerland after the revocation of the Edict of Nantes by Louis XIV in 1685. Interestingly, Paul Broca (1824-1880), the resolutely free-thinking, progressive French physician, anatomist and anthropologist after whom the speech production center of the brain is famously named (Broca's area), who opposed slavery, fought against the conservatism of the church, was denounced as a radical, etc., invoked Claparède's saying and held a complex position in the raging debates of his day. On the one hand he defended Darwin's common ancestor of all life forms thesis, which one assumes can only rely upon mongenism, and yet still made a case for polygenism. [Ed.]

[6] A common mechanism in this and the following tales is the projection of anthropomorphized sexuality onto primates, and a racist, comparative anatomical ranking between primates and ethnic human groupings. [Ed.]

indubitable manner—the bastard born of such an unholy alliance tugging on his hair, puckering up to kiss him like a human would, while strangling him with a triple wrapping of its long prehensile tail. Wishing to wipe a sweat born of fear from his brow, he met with a furry hand and almost fainted. It was one of the marmosets, which had managed to spread apart the arched wires of their aviary-like cage. They had taken refuge in the warmest part of the room, and Jan found them curled up under the corners of his pillow. He let them stay, petted them, laughed at his fears, but nonetheless dared not go back to sleep, but rather began to smoke.

Saskia's son, a great big child, now five months old, was out to nurse some leagues away, near a small fishing village served, during the bathing season which was now just beginning, by a number of train lines from the city. He decided to go and give the child a hug, and the better to stretch his legs and refresh his mind, he left on foot in the wee hours of the morning.

CHAPTER IV

The beach, rising in a series of imperceptible undulations, formed at its top a hog-backed dune followed by a much steeper one. Nestled against the second, a score of homes made up the hamlet, all built askew, miserable, sinking, cracked, their ends almost spanning the narrow vale, their doors consequently only on the sides, these homes seemed to have slid down from the top of the slopes, settled there, resigned to their fate, and already half buried beneath the sands that surrounded them. There were a few gardens plots sheltered between a home and the black limbs of a dried up Tamarix hedge, where onions and lettuce grew thinly and did not thrive, even with constant watering. Even the most rustic of plants could take root in this shifting aridity. When the great winds powdered the flat roofs, were it not for the thin wisps of smoke that, in the rapidly quelled air, quickly resettled into a heavy inert layer within the funnel-like vale, rising straight up, as if a motionless column, to swell, waver and dissipate at the elevation where the breezes blew, one might think each house to be a gigantic mole-hill rising from the ground.

The men, all fishermen, spent their days outside this hole, on the sea, where their hard, rough work stretched their lungs. The children, if they managed to get out of the cradle, climbed on all fours to the crest of the slope, then they too would run down the seaward side, in the salubrious air that allowed their growth. But the women and the elderly, remaining indoors, their eyesight eroded by the glittering reflection of the Sun on the white sand, dragged themselves about with withered limbs, worn out with anemia, their chests shaken by endless bouts of coughing, the sand having insinuated itself into the narrowest ramifications of their bronchi and choked them, as it did the sandstone miners, whose watches, notwithstanding boxes double-stuffed with cotton and suet, constantly stopped.

The families succeed one another in lesser and lesser numbers, though the mothers spewed babies from their flaccid bellies like doe-rabbits their litters, and no adults ever permanently left this miserable hovel, all permeated by a strange love of the land which depressed and made them languish and even die under more favorable climates. In this they resembled the Inuit taken from the cold, the hunger and the stark bareness of the Pole, or a colony of madrepores taken from the reef it was born on. The good season was horribly stifling, without a breath of fresh air; the winter one long night under a low cloud ceiling. The only resource, the sea, was close, but miserly with its bounty, always difficult, too frequently in a fury. Calmly it beat against the dune at ebb-tide like a great howling pack; at high-tide the barkers smelled carnage and threw themselves at it in angry but futile assaults; during storms, men feared the creatures' victory, the dune at risk of collapsing, a great rumble rolling over their heads, combining with the chaos of the skies from which the great off-shore birds, lost and injured, dropped.

A few hundred meters away, visible from the vale's wasteland, whose dismal aspect it increased by its startling contrast, was a green paradise, enclosed in flagstone walls and a quickset hedge spread across a hillside which was nothing more than the end of the abundant pastures of the mainland. The trees were, under the influence of the sea-winds, gnarled on the crest, twisted and bare towards the flats, becoming, as they penetrated further and further into the vale, smoother and thinner, their foliage in softly rustling tufts. Long ago, the homes arranged there formed a leper-colony; nowadays vegetable growers lived there in the quiet routine of a simple and profitable existence. They had cattle, pigs, bees, vegetables, fruit, and the rabbits expanded their warrens and multiplied in this ancient dune whose soil had become resistant, yet easy to till.

They had, among other things, managed to transform the bottom of the valley, where there converged, into a concave mirror, the least ray of sunlight, into a true natural greenhouse, and the hiker on the high trails, leaning over the gulf carpeted in vegetation like an oversized bowl, was intoxicated with warm breaths, delicately blending colors, and suave aromas.

It goes without saying that as good neighbors the fishermen and the farmers were close enemies. The adults were content in their rare meetings to glare suspiciously and mutter curses under their breath; the children, more up front, disdained the appearance of a false peace. On the shore, their games were separate; frequent fights tore the clean clothes of the little gardeners, left in tatters those of the little cabin-boys, flattened the noses and blackened the eyes of both. Lucky were they when the parents, drawn by their cries or the tales of the beaten, did not take things into their own hands for one side or the other, and finish the fight between themselves, with more serious cuffs.

Enmity had long reigned, but a serious incident broke the camel's back. The women took in nursing infants, the farmers to increase their prosperity, the fishermen from below to lessen their misery. The former asked for more pay and never bargained; the lovely location of their bright little homes, and their placid and gay disposition provided them a good reputation. Their work at hand, near the hedges, under the shade of the trees, they helped their spouses, wandered about the vegetable beds in the garden, without ceasing to keep an eye on the sleepers in the cradles, so as to be able to rush over at the slightest call from the charming and avid lips. The caring, patience and genuine mothering of one, kept alive a rachitic premature birth, not deemed viable by the obstetrician. Upon arrival, its body was wrinkled and had the appearance of being macerated, looking, amidst the lacy frills, like a museum fetus specimen drawn from its vat of alcohol; it had since become the wildest little demon, laughing, rolling and splashing about in the puddles along the shoreline. The father, a rich textile-manufacturer, was ecstatic. No ingrate, he showered the good woman with gifts which, should she have wanted to, would have allowed her to wait out her old age in well-deserved retirement. Furthermore, he took steps to see that she received a large sized gold medal from the Haarlem Medical Board.

The honor of this deserved reward was reflected on her companions, the most tender, upper class women of the city giving birth to poor, weak little creatures, preferred, notwithstanding their distance away, to have them raised by the farmers' wives, than by the best wet-nurses they might have had at home. They were hotly sought-after, hired eight months in advance. It became fashionable to put new-borns in their hands, even the healthiest of them. Stout-hearted, they knew, while remaining worthy of the fad, how to profit by this; always suckling, they demanded, after each weaning, more love from their husbands, and more money from their customers.

Their competitors, the fishermen's wives, vexed at not being able to present such credentials, decided to do the same anyway, kept their prices where they were, and took on two, sometimes even three infants at once. Of course, they were not able to keep them satisfied, and so, took to bottle-feeding them. It was quicker to fill a bottle than a woman's breast and the milk was just as good, they would affirm; it was better, they should have said, than that which the poor little creatures were forced to draw, drop by drop, from their withered breasts. Soon their trade became rather shady. Factory workers, serving-wenches at country fairs, homeless itinerants, all now stuffed themselves with men, fearless of the consequences, running off to rendezvous without fear of what had at one time held them back a little, coming back with four ears rather than two. They quietly gave birth, brought their bastards to the fishermen's wives, paid three months in advance at a set price, and were immediately relieved of any future worries. Within the first fortnight the child was tossed in a corner, given a bottle never rinsed out and almost always with air at the nipple. Wetting and left stinking in its diaper, it soon looked upon this world with distrust, seemingly knowing that the best thing to do was to leave it, and simply died. The courts, with their habit of sticking their noses where there was a bad smell, soon managed to nose out these more than once-reported charnel-houses of the innocents. The investigation was simple, the evidence was abundant. The most capable of these angel-makers was imprisoned, and all were condemned to end their activities.

Their ancient jealousy toward the farmer's wives grew even more inflamed. They refused the free vegetables which these women, unselfish as are common folk with their prosperity, offered them quite frequently. This help admittedly consisted of cabbage stumps, scraps of food, and useless morsels, for the farmers' wives combined frugality with charity.

It was then that the sickness which declared itself among the children changed the jealousy to hatred. The farmers thought that their children had contracted it from the fishermen's children, dirty, atrophied by a slow hunger; the sickness from below, they called it. The sickness from *above*, clamored the fishermen's wives, who, on this occasion were right.

The affliction, very insidious, began with a light spotting on the chest and especially on the arms. Pink, only skin deep, hardly visible prior to rubbing, the one washing the first infant, stricken, accused herself of having made them appear by washing down the child too vigorously and using rough towels. They were so tender, these little lettuce-hearts, she wrote the mother, telling her of a simple effervescence of the blood caused no doubt by the summer heat.

The mother, an actress from Amsterdam playing at the Kuursal in Ostende for the holidays, received the letter at the very moment she was locking up her suitcases. Even though she had left quickly, she stopped off to visit her son, surprised by the redness which would disappear only to reappear under the softest sponge. She recommended calling the doctor if things got worse, and made her way back to the railroad, the call of her blood relieved by the five minutes she had devoted to family matters. Until the end of the season she gave herself entirely to her art. An impassioned fan taking her away to Italy, she contented herself with sending off a six-month advance, and warning them that she would come by as soon as she returned, probably the next spring.

At the same time that the wet-nurse found aphthae in the child's mouth, she found others on her breasts. She believed them to be fissures as she had once had before, and neither she nor the child seemingly suffering from them, she attached no importance to them. One morning when she was working some distance away, a neighbor, to quieten down the wakeful and crying little one, suckled it in her place, a common courtesy they had among themselves. The neighbor's areola also developed the same cracking, but she was not overly concerned about it. Many children thus transmitted these sores to one another, which moved from the lips, spread out, became raw, pallid, coppery.

To all, these were milk-crusts, common little sores which they greased with the froth from stews, their universal recipe. They got used to it, and only began to worry when some of the youngest, no longer able to suckle, began to waste away.

No one had yet notified the doctors. As the first to call them was liable for their traveling fee, everyone else was hanging back, waiting for someone else to pay. But an abundance of anonymous denunciations reached the district intendant, in which neighbors mutually accused each other of having brought scabies or tinea to the community. The district intendant referred the matter, according to the chain of command, to the provincial governor. The provincial governor, after mature reflection, promised to consult the hygiene committee which he presided over.

However, it was on the eve of the elections for the Upper House. A rather unpleasant candidate threatened to win, which would have represented a horrible failure for the minister in power and his minions. The governor in particular saw his chances for advancement evaporating; so, ignoring everything else, he did his best to direct the spontaneity of the vote towards his best interests, providing the voters with good counsel from behind the scenes, in such a manner as not to arouse their doltish suspicions. He was successful. Leaving the opposition to fulminate, with a strong understanding of modern concepts of liberty, he recognized their right to criticize. He then laid siege to his superiors, striking while the iron was still hot, boasting of his victory, obtaining the posting he deserved. And, named to that post, he left, satisfied in leaving it in the hands of his successor and best friend, upon whom the opposition critics took their revenge by contesting his qualifications and affirming him to be far inferior to his predecessor. For the new governor, taking care of the many files which were in arrears, right from the start, would go a long way towards proving his abilities and diligence.

On holiday, but anxious to get to work, the new titleholder moved into his government offices a week after his holiday was over. He received and made the necessary official visits, then those of convenience, changed the office's personnel, and sent useful circulars to his representatives, asking them what improvements might be made in terms of the respective services they provided, but especially to enjoin them not to reform or modify the wise traditions heretofore enforced. Then, moving on to things of lesser interest, yet nonetheless requiring a solution, he convened the hygiene commission for the next fortnight.

The committee members quickly gathered, but in insufficient numbers to form a quorum. It was proposed to reconvene in a week or so. The elected secretary complained that he was marrying off his daughter on that date, and that one should at least put it off for a fortnight. This time, however, the question entered the stage of a definite inquiry: three members were designated to lead the inquiry: a pharmacist, a veterinarian, and an engineer, second-class, for bridges and canals. In a touching spirit of accord, rather rare, the doctors had refused to take part in this investigatory commission, putting forward as a pretext that if they went there for free, as hygienists, to a village infected by an alleged epidemic, the inhabitants would bank on being able to call upon them in this manner all the time, so that in the end the administration would have encouraged the most foolish and blameworthy of peasant traits, namely, avarice. Was not the primary responsibility of the sick to heal themselves?

The delegates put in a lot of work. Vegetable farmers and fishermen, men and women were questioned, and the names, addresses and professions of the infants' parents, consigned to a statistical databank. Samples were taken from every well, every piece of salted meat and fish kept in the households. The cows, and as a secondary form of animal production the goats, were first examined themselves, then the grasses in which they were pastured, then their stables, which were measured and their cubic feet of volume determined. They were then each milked individually and 20 vials of milk, sealed and labeled, made up the rest of the samples. Plans were drawn up, the scope of surveys required was determined. A monument of science, of understanding and patience, a clear account shedding light on everything, of what had been done and what was left to do, of the results obtained and of those to obtain, the gentlemen's report received in the General Assembly the congratulations of the president, and unanimous praise from their colleagues.

Each one of them insisted, with noble modesty, on the items which remained to be elucidated. The pharmacist admitted that the chemical and microscopic analyses of already over a kilogram of lard and of fish which had been seized had not revealed anything. The veterinarian, a rather wordy speaker, but a scrupulous experimenter, was feeding the suspect milk samples to small rabbits, and formally promised to persevere, though the young animals in the laboratory which he had set up at his own expense in the two halves of a sawn-through barrel had not as yet presented anything abnormal except a quantity of fleas which he thought to be well above average, an observation he made in passing, reserving the right to later draw whatever conclusions from it which might suggest themselves. The engineer, second-class, of bridges and canals, presented estimates for the most urgent expenses, digs to be made to see whether drinking-water wells or fountains were receiving any infiltrations from septic systems.

Without hesitation, the council agreed upon opening a line of credit. It offered to provide its time and energies, without discussion and without asking anything for itself. Was it not desirable for the State not to haggle over the necessary expenditures to continue the studies so well undertaken? But the honorable governor, who had taken on the responsibility of forwarding the request to whom it may concern, did not end up needing to do so. A wet-nurse, who might be excused for having maintained in this backwater town some of the common folk's doubts regarding the administration's vigilance, decided to bring in a doctor who would quickly rule out the wells, the animals and the latrines. There had been much exaggeration; all it was, was syphilis, indeed a contagious disease, but well known and which the honorable governor, thankful of one less worry, did not have to take care of. The sessions of the hygiene committee suspended, the pharmacist left off his analyses of the drinking water for the more remunerative task of making up hydrargyrum pills and salves, and the veterinarian, not without some regrets, drowned the dogs, and returned the young rabbits to their mother's warren.

At this point, eight children, two wives, one widow, and four men (the two husbands of the two wives, and the widow's two lovers) were contaminated.

The families of the uninfected infants were ordered to take them back. Alas! The little Heltzius had shown symptoms the day before. Jan, whose visit, after a night of insomnia, had occurred right after the doctor had left, had been the first to bring back the deplorable news. Saskia took to crying from morning 'til night, frightened by all that was withheld from her, and especially by the prudent interdiction made to her against bringing her child home, or even going to cuddle him.

The disease, now that it had been diagnosed and attacked with all the means that could be put into practice, and that specific recommendations limited its ravages to the 15 people already stricken, seemed to hurry to do the most damage possible to its victims. In some odd injustice, the actress' kid who had brought it to the community seemed to have gotten over it. It also remained benign in the well-fed and well tended children of the farmers, as well as Saskia's which had little more than an inflammation of the throat. It incubated slowly in the humans. But it progressed unchecked in the weak flesh of the fishermen's rough brats; their eyelids and nostrils were stuck together, pale, ichorous; their joints knotted; their cracked lips receded, pursed like the opening of a tightly tied drawstring bag tearing when the pill was pushed between them; blisters grew on the palms of their hands and the soles of their feet, bursting, and discharging their fetid, sanious fluid, their irregular edges joining in a large, purplish sore.

Jan did not wait for Saskia to plead with him before going for further news. Sometimes with Martin Heltzius, but more frequently alone, he arrived on foot, handing out alms and pity. The fishermen, who at first ran from him with the wariness of the poor, now invited him to relax for a moment. One afternoon he took shelter in a woman's house during a violent summer storm. Black as ink, the low cloud cover seemed to have captured a strange light which did not emanate from any distinct sun, and which insinuated itself into the darkest recesses, attenuating and even erasing the distinction between objects and their shadows, bathing everything in an uncertain, static, and dead pallor. Most of the women, before going down to the beach, where they walked about anxiously, listening, watching the waves, trying to discover behind the great swell which the North Sea sent to crash at their feet, their men and elders' vessels, had collected the sick little ones in the same hovel as Jan had taken shelter in. The convalescents slept; one, almost a corpse, showed no movement of the chest; the face of another whom the virus had bloated with confluent tumors looked as though the pustules of a toad were crawling over his face; all were breathing and droning with such monotony as to render Jan sleepy, making him dream, on this doleful day, of the cruel limbo into which innocent newborns expiated some heinous sin of their father's.

The sky cleared up and he thanked the fisherman's wife who accompanied him as he walked along the switch-backed trail over the dunes to take a breath of fresh air and view from a greater height the horizon over the sea. Comparing farmers' homes on the fertile lands to her hovel in a bare sand pit, she spat out spitefully:

"Oh! Those monsters, to think they are the ones that poisoned us all. They accused the infants of having brought the rot of the cities to the beach. Who knows? These soils which only they dare cultivate are indeed rich, but rich with corpses, those having formerly belonged in the leper colony. Traitors, they allowed the old boats which had fed their ancestors to fall into disrepair, for their cowardly mole's life sheltered from the storms. By stirring up the burial grounds and sowing their filthy wheat, have they not brought forth into the air the germs of pestilence which were buried there? Horrors! They taunted us with the white bread of their harvests, which they showed us from afar, but they have eaten leprosy and the pox with it."

Jan calmed her down with a little money and sent her on her way.

He found Saskia's son to have already regained, thanks to the efficacy of the treatment, his initial vivacity and good humor. The doctor allowed the wet-nurse to bring him back permanently to Haarlem, and for the mother to smother him in kisses. But Jan always feared a relapse. He read medical texts, and as the ignorant do not realize that the authors are forced to describe all cases, emphasizing the worst and enumerating them one after another, so too did he not understand that any given individual may only show the least dangerous symptoms at any given phase of the disease. All their lives, long or short, he saw those children which were thought to be cured, but tainted by the foul virus, transmitting in turn this eternal menace to their children's bone marrow. Then he remembered his big brothers and sisters, inheriting their father's consumption, this even worse disease which had killed off 10 of the 12, in their youth, in the midst of happy, healthy times.

Stung with disgust by man's fate, a peculiar pity for the sadness and rancor's of life brought him to blame life itself. What insanity is it that wishes to bring to life creatures doomed to misery, he would say, while he preserved that of a pregnant beggar-woman extending her hand to him. The listeners at the Brinckleymann café would sit and listen wide-eyed at his thoughts on the subject, taking up their conversations again with a wink of the eye and a tapping of a finger on their brow.

"Poor Mr. Jan! His walks along the seaside this summer chased away his bizarre thoughts but since he's been keeping himself cloistered recently, here they are again, worse than ever."

He went back to keeping strictly to himself as he had in the past, of muttering to himself as he walked along with great strides. Even his best friends, Saskia and his brother Adrian, had no conviction in their whispered voices when they defended him from accusations of being mad. Then one morning at dawn, after another one of his many sleepless nights, he got up, leaned on his elbows at his open window, and gave in to his vague desires.

The old French painter, who had smoked so many pipes under the same roof, came to mind without him knowing why.

The exile had seen the seas outside Haarlem upon the horizon under the lingering fog which little by little was drawn away by the Sun; and he saw the spongy soil of the *polders* spread out in vast pastures. Well, everything changes, everything passes, thought Jan, except those great men whose name, on occasion, survives even their works.

That morning, the neighbors and passersby found him finally settled down. He walked calmly, singing to himself, hands in his pockets, no longer waving about madly like a free-whirling windmill. Truth was that after months of experiments by trial and error and further studies, his small obsession had led his visionary's mind, bubbling with ideas, to set a goal for himself: he was going to work at regenerating the human race.

He distributed among his parents and friends his parrot and his monkeys, thus convincing many he had regained his sanity. His books, atlases, and tools of all sorts, packed in crates, were secretly taken to the railroad station. He told his brother he was taking a trip to Belgium, but quickly left Brussels for Paris, and Paris for Marseilles, from where he wrote to Adrian and Saskia not to wait for him for another year, for, given that he was already so close to Algeria, he had decided to visit it. His collection of books, atlases and equipment complete, under the cover of a humble protestant missionary he took ship for the Pillars of Hercules, Guinea, Gabon and the unknown.

CHAPTER V

The cabin, very large and round, had a wall built of woven bamboo and bark, whose fissures are filled with a coating of clay, and for a roof a solid conical structure of narrow, thick planks five to six meters long, which supported palm leaves sown together with straps made from lianas. The hinges and lock on the woven-reed-door were made with knots of similar lianas, and the whole place was painted with white-wash. Matting covered a portion of the floor; the fireplace was in the middle on some stones, and its smoke rose freely through an opening at the top of the roof. The table was made from slabs of slate nailed to three posts driven into the soil, and bore some coarse pottery and some books. Chests, stools, pitchers, mats, pineapple fiber nets, kindling and logs for the fire were strewn on the ground; animal pelts, fish, clusters of fruit, bananas, grapes, cobs of corn, and yaw tubers were drying on the wall, amongst a number of weapons hanging from water-buffalo horns; hung so as to dangle in the smoke were legs and shoulders of antelope and boar, turning under the radiating heat.

The fire no longer flamed, but the heated atmosphere and red-hot coals indicated that it had been burning for a long time. There was no light, other than the reflection of the red coals on the gun barrels, tool blades, and the curved surfaces of a glazed jar.

A man in tattered clothing, chest, legs and arms bare, crouched near the fire, elbows on his knees, face held in his hands. From time to time he rose and on his tip-toes crossed over to a place where darkness accumulated, bent over a low, wide cot built of rushes, leaves, grass and pelts. At his approach, a moan came from the darkness; he arranged and carefully spread the covers as if for someone sick, whispered a few soft, calming words and returned to his place, no longer hearing—the moans having ended—anything but the irregular, halting, rough and sometimes wheezy breathing of the poor creature, his mate, whom even in sleep seemed a martyr.

He lit upon the revived fire a hemp wick soaked in a bowl of oil, drew a stool close to him and leaned a large octavo volume on it. The light flickered in the column of air drawn up by the chimney's opening, but provided sufficient light. It was indeed Jan Maas, little changed; still Jan Maas the meek baby-faced dreamer from the land of tulips, except that he was clothed in rags, that his nose was more prominent between his thin tanned cheeks, and that his eyes, deep and sparkling, indicated a fever. And always, as was the case when he attended lectures, his mind wandered in spite of himself, while his finger flipped through the pages.

The book was a treatise on child birth. Among the medical illustrations which followed one another under his absent-minded thumb, one held his attention. Representing the methodology for undertaking one of the most difficult manipulations with the forceps, it appeared abominable, and his gaze, troubled by a brighter flicker of the fire, believed it to be spotted with blood. He blew out his light as if he hoped it would also put out his fear, pushed away the book, and slipped back into the shadows. "My God, let's hope this case is not the same. Let's wait...I've seen so many already!" he sighed, drawn by these words to review his past.

The long crossing, his arrival at the French mission in the Bay of Gabon, going up the river, the joys and fears, the wild beasts, savages worse than the beasts, fevers worse than the savages, numerous dangers besides that of being eaten by a tribe of Pahouins who had kept him fattened—all these things, though they had lasted months and months, were of so little importance to Jan, that they floated about his mind in an indistinct fog. Adventures whose true yet brief description would have been enough to cover ten explorers with glory were forgotten before the motives he had to undertake them. A walking, talking mummy, he had walked amongst the most fearsome and spectacular of what central Africa had to offer, his eyes turned inward, hypnotized by the intensity of his internal contemplation. Nothing having taken hold of his mind outside those facts or thoughts directly linked to his goal, his memories began with the first encounter with the great apes in their free state.

Having become now the pampered guest of the Pahouins after he had administered large doses of quinine to their sick chief thus saving him from a malignant fever and himself, by a singular cause and effect, from being impaled and roasted, he joined a few of their warriors in beating out antelopes. A very young girl, an intrepid huntress, followed them. Having remained behind to admire her already chubby nakedness in a pond—attention to style, following findings which Jan thought to be new, existing in all latitudes—they suddenly heard her cry out for help. A gorilla was attempting to kidnap her, a huge male, he held her by the waist in one of his arms, compensating for the extra breadth of her hips by using his second hand; with the top of his bent-over phalanges he supported himself against the soil. The young Pahouin's fiancé, boldly running after the kidnapper, struck him from a distance with a poisoned arrow. Sensing himself injured, the d'ginna, such was the name the other hunters were shouting, stopped, softly put her down in the grass and began to rape her, disdainful of the menacing screamers which leapt after him, driven mad by an overbearing desire to satisfy his lust before he died. To drag him from the body of his victim, they had had to finish him off with spears and clubs. Thrown onto his back, the herculean grasp of his arms had relaxed. His lips, in spite of having receded over his canines, seemed rather to flutter for a kiss than to tense for a bite, and his look, rather than the cruel expression which ought to have been imparted upon them by his bloody death, maintained a fluid languor of ecstasy. The young Pahouin girl, with the annoyed gesture with which a European woman flounces her dress, slapped around her kidneys to erase the grass marks, and smiled. On the way back, under her breath, she told Jan that she had not been very afraid, the hairy men of the woods never hurt women; and Jan, still studying their manners, asked why then had she cried out for help. She answered that had she not, she would have been considered tainted for seven weeks, and her marriage into the tribe would then have been delayed.

He thanked God, for thus had he unraveled the tangled mess which his numerous predecessors had accumulated: where they differing observations, simple exaggerations or legends collected among the natives? He guessed that in the attending chaos the office-bound naturalists admitted or rejected certain facts, according to whether they found that they supported current theories or not. He was struck by the weakness of other peoples' frequent accusations of the French being weak-minded; was it not instead among them, that so many scientists, when they presented the results of their most conscientious studies, always feared offending religious sensibilities? Was it not among them that many, to avoid taking a position, joined that school of dishonest cheats in which the positivists boasted of their disdain for the big questions, and of ever coming to any hard and fast conclusions? Weak minds, he told himself in an echo of sermons heard in the temple in his youth, could not grasp that Creation, as one studied it in greater and greater detail, would manifestly reveal the Creator in his inherent justice and eternal beauty. He vowed to himself not to retreat before any new truths, certain that they could not but support his faith. It was for allowing him to so quickly elucidate the question of contact between native women and apes, that he thanked God.

He lived some two leagues from the Pahouin village, in the middle of a clearing deliberately chosen amidst the old-growth forest, the limits of which were unknown to him, except towards the village where it ended among the mangroves on the shores of the Como River.[7]

His new friends had built his cabin in the shelter of a huge fig tree, standing there alone like some great king of all vegetation. They had cleared and planted a wide zone around it, and had offered to organize a great beating out of elephants and d'ginnas of whose terrible proximity they had warned him of, insisting rather that he abandon his project of living alone and continue to live among them. Bearing a sincere affection for him, even revering him, after the cure he had effected on Akayrawiro, their chief, as equal to the most skilled of shamans, these brave folk could not have conceived, given his refusal to eat them, that on the contrary, the proximity of the fierce apes led him to speed up the construction of his shelter. He accepted their services as carpenters and gardeners, but not as hunters, hoping to make them understand that it was not

---

[7] In Gabon. [Ed.]

dead, and not in order to tan their hides that he wanted gorillas and chimpanzees, but living, so he could educate them, help them to climb the last rung of the animal ladder, to finally raise them, not only to the level of the guileless and naive cannibals, but to his, the evolutionary philosopher and fervent Lutheran.

A troop of young elephants destroyed his crops. One night when he was returning from nursing a sick man in the village, a panther lurked about, without however attacking him. At noon, on a day of blazing sun, as he was leaning against the inner wall of his cabin reading he heard above him and outdoors a strange scraping, slow and heavy: a magnificent python, as large as a man's thigh in the middle, was climbing sideways up the slope of his cone-shaped roof, festooning it like a sculpture of barbaric splendor, the jewel-like scintillations of its scales barely muted by the deep shadows imposed by the fig tree. No longer being a novice tourist, Jan did as he had seen the blacks do in similar circumstances; he grabbed hold of the overhanging tail with two hands, tore across the clearing dragging the snake who could now not uncoil itself like an inert and monstrous blood-sausage and smashed its head against a tree-trunk by throwing it like a stone from a sling. To fill his larder he hunted kudus, slender antelopes with the gracefulness of a gazelle, and, with fewer regrets, the Phacochorus, frightening boars which resembled hairy hippopotami.

The rainy season arrived. The floods doubled the width of the rivers, the frequency and intensity of storms only allowed for short outings and prevented any visits to the Pahouins. Tropical storms, where the storm clouds crashed to the ground in a wild cavalcade of leaps and sounds, and spread, even in the daytime, such a nocturnal opacity over the land that neither the straight nor the crooked bolts of lightning could penetrate and dissolve into huge livid flashes, were frequent.

After one such storm, during which he had, for 48 hours, believed his uprooted home to be constantly spinning through

55

the air, he heard plaintive human voices calling him from the edge of the forest. He burst out with happiness. Finally the gorillas had come, the long-expected and mysterious guests, of whom he had not seen a trace since the one he had seen trying to rape the native woman.

This time it was a couple, a large older male and a female, with her lesser size, much younger. She was moaning. She had been caught in the fork of the tree, where they had been sheltering during the storm, after it had straightened up, pinning her wrist like a vice. The male was shaking her around the waist. Immediately, Jan, his gun thrown over his shoulder, climbed the lianas to reach their refuge. At first, the male was content to make, with one hand, the same gestures with which a man might warn away the importunate, then, seeing him continue to climb, let go of his mate, growled, slipped down onto the lower branch upon which Jan's foot was about to alight. While instinctively loading his rifle, the good Jan continued to talk to the other as if he knew Dutch, repeating that he wished him no harm, but rather to help release his mate, and put a tender intonation like that of an indulgent school teacher into his voice to appease an infant's anger. Bloodshot eyes, bared teeth grinding, nostrils flared, the hair on its brow erect, the large square bulk of his pectorals rounding at every breath, the d'ginna continued to advance. Jan, to keep him at a distance, extended the rifle like a stick. In a fury it took the barrel by the end, bit it, and, the shot having gone off by itself, he tumbled down, the back of his head blown off, from branch to branch, into the thick understory, with a unique quasi-human cry, whose imaginary echo, like the last gasp of a murdered man, would later, on several occasions, lead his adversary to wake up with a start.

The female, by her uncoordinated and futile movements, was exhausting herself. Her feet left the fork in the tree, and she spun hanging freely by an arm like some ancient martyr. Jan, even if he already blamed himself for her mate's death, even though he did not shoot deliberately, rid himself of his gun and approached. She clawed him in the face. He petted her, put her back on her feet, lifted her to relieve the tension and ease the pain of her pinched muscles. All this he did with such precautions that she calmed down little by little whilst her eyes followed him and seemed to implore and encourage him. Jan, with a saw-toothed knife widened the cracks in the tree limb with successive notches so as not to further damage her wrist. Freed, she held on to him, wrapped her good arm around his neck, and allowed herself to fall to the ground, her pain such a rapid and capable tamer. Having barely reached the ground, she already could not stand, and fell fully onto her side, moaning loudly. Jan believed her to be more severely injured than he first thought. He carefully felt her limbs, ascertained that besides her right hand being crushed to a bloody pulp, she had a contusion on her left knee. He picked her up and took her off like a mother would her infant.

Nothing disturbed his devotion or his patience. "How are you my little d'ginna?" he would ask her minute by minute, so baptizing her individually with her generic name. D'ginna turned herself over on the bed, silent, sleepy from fatigue, refusing warm, honey-flavored herbal teas. She wanted cold water, her looks and the fingers of her left hand extended toward the water jug indicating this on several occasions. He dared not give her any because of her fever. The knee was improving, the swelling going down under a simple clay compress, a treatment borrowed from the Pahouins, and she could support herself, walking without much of a limp. In vain did he employ all the medical knowledge he had acquired during his voyages or in the books he constantly flipped through. The wound, in this miasmatic atmosphere, ill-suited to healing, took on more and more the aspect of a bad wound, the flesh as if bleached, the pus fetid, ragged tears, weeping and pale, ran deeply through the scattered, crusty boils. A cold turgidity, which kept the imprint of a finger, was spreading over the wrist and forearm. Jan was frightened, having noticed the corpse-like odor of gangrene which he had so often smelled among lightly injured natives who nonetheless died soon after, and had decided to allow, according to the expression of an

57

old surgeon he had known, the "boon of steel" to intervene. Until now he had hesitated. No help. One of his best knives, some boiled batting, a needle and thread were prepared; he restrained the patient in a veritable straightjacket and amputated the arm above the elbow, in the healthy portion, where a series of tourniquets stopped the blood flow, allowing him to delay the ligature of the larger blood vessels. He need not have tied up the patient for she was so low that she barely reacted and fell, after the bandaging was complete, into a torpid sleep.

He watched over her, barely sparing himself quarter hours of sleep. The trauma-induced fever lifted, all fear of complications gone, he took off the bandage, and ascertained, to his great joy, the complete success of the operation. On the rounded stump, free of suppuration and of a magnificent purple, the folded back flaps of skin were knitting, and in the middle, the sawn off end of the humerus now only offering a bare surface to observation. The healing finished, he still continued to apply the dressing and batting to the injured area, a precaution born of tenderness and continued to protect from any shock or abrupt change in temperature, the soft scar tissue, prone to soreness. Her appetite and strength were returning. Eating, moving about with the ill-considered precipitation of convalescents, who seemingly wish to make up for lost time, she gave herself stomach and muscular aches. He had to ration her food and playtime. She growled, even once biting his thumb so hard he collapsed in pain, stretching out on the ground. The remains of the day came in from outside through the door that was ajar. She leapt towards it, sucked in noisily, then, as if dizzy from this breath of fresh air, she closed the door, came back inside on her three limbs, stumbling on her still somewhat stiff knee and swinging her stump about, she lay down next to her savior, put her arm across his shoulders and caressed him softly with the motion he himself had so often cajoled her with to calm the irritation of her fresh wounds and stop her from removing the dressings.

Awakened, he took a few seconds to completely come to. D'ginna continued to rock him with the monotonous and sleep-inducing hum of an unspoken canticle. She licked his hands. Not thinking, he scratched her head like one would a young dog, thanking her for the affection which, for the first time, she was showing him. Suddenly he sat up halfway, surprised by an unusual contact. The darkness was unfathomable. Blushing at sensing himself blushing, ashamed of his own shame, he had supposed the animal's caresses to be without motive. When these same caresses, now so precisely directed that, even chaste as he had been, he could not but comprehend their intention, he ran outside, troubled and silent with disgust.

He quickly recovered in the coolness of the open air. Believing them once again to be the result of happenstance, or that he had a nightmare when he was passed out, he mechanically swallowed a few mouthfuls of manioc and smoked meat, and prepared himself for a night of forgetfulness by stuffing a number of pipes with a Gabonese plant which is more intoxicating than tobacco, a sort of hashish-hemp whose smoke had the added property of repelling mosquitoes. D'ginna was not hungry either, and slept so calmly that he ended up being reassured. Obviously he was overcome with an unhealthy urge. Smiling at his alarm regarding his modesty, he went to sleep somewhat overexcited, rolling from side to side before finding a comfortable position.

Were it empty the cabin would be no quieter.

Jan's bed consisted simply of leaves and grasses swept over; D'ginna's bed, richer by a pile of mats and dried pelts. Exhausted by the night's madness, he barely slept, when, upon the same caresses as before he felt the same excitement as before. It was no longer possible to have any doubt. He lit the lamp and dared not blow it out. D'ginna, returning to her spot and leaning her shoulder against the wall of the hut, was resting as she had during her life in the wild, when she would sit with her back to the truck of a tree in the fork of a tall, strong limb. Her hands knotted under her knees, her eyes closed, she feigned sleep, but the movement of her lips thrust forward like a snout, and arranged in the familiar pout of grumpy children to whom one has refused something, belied this. Jan, walking to relieve his nervous excitement, saw her as he passed back and forth before her, batting her eyes at him in the same way the young serving girls in Haarlem, tried to goad him from his reticence, when upon festival nights he would saunter alone along the walkways of Kenau Park. Perhaps it was a trick of the light wavering under the winds of his comings and goings; for the tenth tune at least, he felt that insomnia and fatigue were abusing his senses, and he returned to his bed. D'ginna softly slipping in beside him brought him back to reality. Should he sneak off to the cold of the tall grasses? He knew too well the treacherousness of such nights, when miasmas constantly emanated from the soil which had accumulated, activated and incubated in centuries of organic matter, the most pernicious of viruses, slow but more pitiless killers than the wild beasts. He was staggering about, asleep on his feet. Taking refuge in his books, the usual cure for his pains and troubles, he came across the modern theories on the origins of man, theories whose complexities and apparent contradictions he had a great deal of difficulty in sorting out, his lack of a bold outlook never allowing him a sufficient understanding of the concepts of space and especially of time so important to such studies. Automatically he turned to examine the false calmness of D'ginna still leaning against the wall. Thus this creature was not his immediate ancestor, as so many frivolous minds would accuse the scientists of teaching, and which the latter appropriately concurred in denying, but descended with him, like two branches of the same genetic tree, from an animal awkward in walking erect and without articulate speech.[8]

---

[8] This was the theory put forward by Ernst Haeckel (1834-1919), a German biologist and evolutionist perhaps best known for his beautiful illustrations of organisms collected in books such as *Natürliche Schöpfungsgeschichte* (1868, translated into English as *The History of Creation* in 1876) and *Kunstformen der Natur* (1904). Unfortunately, Haeckel was prone to wild speculation, and the so-called 21st phase or "missing link" of his *Chain of the Animal Ancestors of Man*,

His imagination inflamed, Jan eliminated the immeasurable time passed and thought of this common ancestor, a four-legged giant, hairy and without speech, unknown and unseen since the Miocene. From one side were the great apes born, which must be those amongst the current anthropoids which would most resemble him; from the other, primitive man, still similar to him, but who would soon flake the flints of Thenay, and appropriating unto himself the Sun, domesticating it for his short-term needs by discovering fire and keeping it alive in the shelter of caves. So D'ginna looked not so different from him; of an inferior but related race. His life among the Pahouins aided in him accepting this conclusion, as soon as it began to emerge as the germ of an idea in his brain. He dropped to his knees under the massive blow of a sudden idea. His arteries carried this excitement through him. Did he not bear the renown, the scientific glory of all his dreams, for which he had suffered so much? The possibility of sexual relations, would it not prove an identity in nature? He got up, drew closer, and believing himself to be acting in the fullness of his free will, judging himself not to be giving in to the excitement of any vile desires, he took D'ginna, now reticent, and married her.

The next day, the experimenter's enthusiasm having waned, he believed his actions to be the result of a diabolical temptation, that he was now forever among the fallen, weeping in regret for his former candor, he ran off into the forest, avoiding the puddles of water where he could have mired himself. But the night, inciting in him troubling memories worse than his remorse, he fought in vain. Insidious doubts assailed him, the monstrous sexual relationship was well consummated, and the poor Jan soon presented a rare case of a splitting of the will. In the day, he tended to the ordinary chores of a new Crusoe, more carefree than he had been in the past, re-

---

whilst inspiring many writers, also gave credence to the racial anthropology which came to inform much of New Imperialism. [Ed.]

membering nothing, indifferent to the tattoo-like traces of D'ginna's howling embraces. As soon as dusk came, like poorly healed wounds of a rabid dog, which reopen and needle him to more ferocious battles, each of the former caresses seemed to spread, to become poisoned; and he would run to his mistress begging her for new ones, deeper and harsher.

He was only cured of this form of sleep-walking one morning while gardening, when he noticed his mate's pregnancy. Picking fleas from the folds of her groin, squatting in the sun, leaning back a bit, her belly in this position cast a rounded shadow so ridiculous that at first Jan refused to believe what was right before his eyes. Floored when he understood, the pact broken, the bewitchment dissipated, his memory now clear, he accepted, as a form of expiation, the reality of his adventure, and vowed he would confess to his crime with complete candor. I shall be dishonored, he thought, but immortal; the good, ignorant, common folk will hound me from civilized countries so that my sight will not taint their women and girls, but in deference to the results that will bring them the experimental solution to the most difficult anthropological questions, the fanatics of this science, in their conscience, in their spoken teachings if not in their written works, would forgive me that which the vulgar would term my filthy bestiality.

Months went by.

The river back within its banks, the trails practicable, the Pahouins arrived to consult him regarding their sick, the number of which increased after each winter season. Still believing him capable of outperforming their shamans, and conquered besides by his goodwill, they spared him nothing, renewing his supplies of oil, honey, corn, fishing tackle, hunting snares for birds and other small game, and happy to finally see his dream of possessing a great ape fulfilled, they congratulated him in having found a pregnant female, knowing, they told him, that when they were in this state their mate would defend them to their last breath. One of their javelins, with shark-like sawtooths, could not have slashed Jan's heart any worse than this complement. He hid his sudden sadness. Having accompanied them back to the banks of the Como and being alone, the thought that perhaps they were right, that D'ginna was probably already pregnant when he had killed her powerful mate, plunged him into such a cruel perplexity that he did not eat or sleep for several days.

For the simple calculation which would remove any doubt, the required elements were all missing. As eddies, chasms and cataracts conceal the direction of torrents, as admiring the marvels of the forest takes away any leisure one might have to pick out landmarks, the disgust, the regrets, the triumphs and delirium of kisses exchanged had prevented him from counting the days. He did not know when he settled in the clearing, when he met D'ginna, when their lovemaking began, at what date he noticed her pregnancy and the number of months since. Had he this information, the main element would still be missing, the gestation period of the African great apes. The best of his books, a well known medical dictionary translated into French, only indicated that they menstruate periodically, a capacity incorrectly assessed by naturalists as being limited only to human beings, and the suppression of which in the woman was a clear sign of impending motherhood. D'ginna never having shown such a flow was thus either pregnant before their intimate relations, or became so immediately after. And in this was Jan's despair at being unable, of these two mutually exclusive truths, to definitely eliminate the first.

CHAPTER VI

For what seemed like minutes, centuries to Jan, D'ginna was bracing herself, howling out in her agonizing exertions, her mouth foaming over, her body twisted into a bow, held up from the bed by only the nape of the neck and the heels. She collapsed. It was immediately clear that this was but a false respite for an animal machinery at the brink of collapse, husbanding its strength for another terrible fit, the foam between her lips continuing to escape, bloody, spuming, and localized contractions sweeping like knots across the muscle mass, leaving behind furrows of hairs erect and vibrant on the skin, as if they were on the vocal cords.

As he was leaning over her to whisper encouraging words, trying to avoid looking at her or touching her, as her fiery eyes would burn into him, and at the least contact she would throw him back with a near galvanic jolt, a cry, a thousand fold sharper than all the others, and which one might have thought to be the rending arising from the release of a soul from its bodily housing, penetrated Jan to his very bones. He had pulled her sideways, on the edge of the covers, and held her knees up and bent over her pelvis, a position he believed to be conducive to the widening of the birth canal. Suddenly he felt his thighs soaked, the amniotic sac had broken. Amongst the shapeless, tepid, pale wastes which followed and wriggled at his feet, and from which wails emerged which made him mad with both joy and terror combined, Jan, abandoning the mother fallen quiet again, untangled, not without difficulty, the new born and undertook the complete removal of the placental membranes and the ligature of the umbilical cord.

Had he there, in his arms, simply a young gorilla, or the feverishly awaited and yet unnamed first and immortal originator of a new race? A pure ape, or an ape-man? Anthropoid or anthropopithecus?[9]

Having wiped it and covered it in old rags, specially prepared, he brought it outside, not wishing to undertake under the artificial light of his lamp the examination upon which would depend his defeat or triumph, his shame or his pride. Beneath the stars, glittering so brightly in a blue so deep that they seemed diamond encrusted water-lilies undergoing the

---

[9] Anthropopithecus was the scientific name for the chimpanzee and meant "man-like ape." [Ed.]

barely perceptible rocking of an infinite sea, he pushed aside the swaddling clothes. A quick look was sufficient to confirm his glory. It was indeed a little human being, his child, his son. Kneeling and shaking, suddenly drunk with joy, his chest set back and his face beaming in exaltation, he raised his son in his two hands and held him out to each of the cardinal points, as if to have him adopted and blessed by all the sky bearing witness.

D'ginna woke with a long sigh of deliverance. He cleaned her bed, changed the wet, soiled grasses and pelts, rolled up in the opposite corner the refuse and dirty objects until they could be sorted, washed, kept or buried. She remained stretched out on her back; he put the little one down beside her, and immediately saw him extend his mouth towards her breasts, take one and begin suckling on it, his cheeks bulging at each suction, his eyelids lowered like a taster entirely wrapped up in his cup, and its tiny hands, already useful, caressing the maternal bosom and pressing upon it to facilitate the flow of the savory stream between his lips. Jan smiled, attentive to the safety in and precision of this admirable instinctive movement, and did not lay down beside the fire he wished to keep going all night, until his mate fell asleep again, exhausted but still hugging to her breast, with her single arm, the satiated infant, who nonetheless would not let go of her.

In order to stop her from going out or even getting up, having read in an obstetrics book how much the good health of the delivered mother depended on her remaining in bed, he did not leave the cabin for several days. The provisions were abundant. Thankfully so, because the wet-nurse, without choice foods, would have been unable to satisfy the glutton whose ravenous hunger was a constant torment. He did profit by it, for he rapidly grew physically stronger, and was soon capable of hanging from his parents' necks.

One morning, holding him thus in one arm and giving the other to D'ginna, weak still, Jan took them to the Zondag-Zay basin, a gigantic bowl at the base of an outcropping of granite, rising in terraces into a sort of natural pyramid resting against a hillside. After each flood, the retreating river would leave behind a pond which the springs of the adjacent slope would also supply. The water remained there, between two overflows, abundant and clear, its evaporation slowed by the powerful shadows of the overhanging outcrops. Given the day he had discovered it, Jan called this place, barely a kilometer from his cabin and unknown before him to the natives, Zondag-Zay, from the two Dutch words for "Sunday" and "lake."

Stepping up the pace they arrived at dawn.

Water striders skated over the lake, the circular ridges born beneath their delicate legs alone troubling, imperceptibly so, the stillness of the surface, whose cobalt hue, darker near the rocks, softened towards the edges into a soft blue. Not a reed, not a moss hung on the rocky walls. Not a sound. A ray of light slipped between the canopy of two trees extending an oval of light to the very depths, a dormer window of golden daylight opened in this huge mirror of blue. Having waded in at this location, while D'ginna was sitting on the bank resting, Jan detached the soft sleeping bundle still hanging from his neck, woke it with a kiss, held it under the armpits, and dipped it into the luminous water.

"I baptize you Hemo," he said.

And extending him to all four cardinal points of the mariner's card, like the night of his birth, and shouting out each time: "Hemo! Hemo! Hemo! Hemo!" he offered him to the Sun, which upon its first contact dried him and enveloped him in a transparent haze similar to the radiant halos with which the painters of the *Adoration of the Magi* surrounded the divine child's cradle. He added:

"Yes, as I decided, when I daren't hope for you in my secret dreams, you will be named Hemo, for the new blood which flows in your veins. Yes, baptized by this water, free from all other contact until now, go, Hemo, grow, true savior of our worn out races, be the founder of a regenerated humanity, purified of all original sin, I mean of all unhealthy traits, through its return to the primitive womb."

As a king in his swaddling-clothes is not cognizant of the future splendors of his destiny and prefers his bottle to the honors bestowed upon him by the Senate and ambassadors, Hemo wailed, extending his lips and limbs, made active by the coolness of the bath, towards his motionless mother. Jan, the ceremony finished was readying himself to join her, when he stopped, one foot in the air, frozen. A real voice, and not an echo, was repeating with a dreadful clamor: "Hemo! Hemo!" Jan leapt out of the Zondag-Zay, held the infant to his chest and put it before D'ginna who was alarmed at his sudden movement, but as indifferent to the vociferations as if she were unable to hear them at all.

Mandrills were filling in the upper tiers of the pyramid. Having his back to them, entirely wrapped up in his role as John the Baptist in the Jordan, Jan had not seen them; frightened at first, he laughed at his fear and soon understood the calm maintained by D'ginna. From where she sat she had seen them arrive, and used to their jabbering, she was not surprised. Having come down little by little, they lined themselves up on the other side; the females entering the lake would dip the curled up feet of their infants, and raising them in their fisted hands, howl to the four winds, accompanied by the males who sedately crouched on the shore waiting for them.

At this disgraceful parody, Jan, in a fit of anger, lost the indulgence of disdain, put Hemo down on the grass, loaded his rifle which he kept across his shoulder, and fired in a rapid uncontrolled motion into the middle of them. One dead tumbled under the water; the troop, for whom it was child's play to leap across the great crevasses and to climb the irregular terraces, disappeared as if by magic onto the other flank of the rocky outcrop. Alone, a large stout one, no doubt the leader such troops have, pretended to be brave, approaching along the shore. D'ginna, of a species akin to his own, was, generally speaking, no great surprise to him. But before the Dutchman, upright on two legs, his face pink, the poor cynocephalus, looking positively timid, embarrassingly brought to bay, after, it is true, having assured himself that all his subjects, having fled in a cowardly manner, would have nothing to jeer at. Now, annoyed at seeing Jan redder in the face from an urge to laugh than his former disgust, he wished to show that he too bore other colors than the hideous blue off his wrinkled cheeks, and turning his back, he went off slowly trumpeting in a deep baritone, and raising the stump of his rudimentary tail, so as to allow one to long admire, between the violet calluses of his flaming red rump, the bright crimson of his scrotal sac.

Jan and D'ginna took other walks, but the Zondag-Zay remained their favorite.

In the afternoon, the nocturnal mists having dissipated, they traveled in the forest, undisturbed. They were at ease among the palm trees, their terminal limbs ending at such great heights, impenetrable to rains and to light, so that all other plants were choked out beneath and that the smooth trunks, propylaea opening upon the infinite, framed to all sides vistas of bare colonnades. They were crushed by the low ceiling of the colossal baobabs, whose branches, fallen back to earth, formed, under the most blinding of light, dark labyrinths seemingly dug out amidst the mysterious greenery. They were caressed by the swinging of the lianas in the undergrowth or about each tree-trunk, with countless morning-glories, orchids, bignonias, vines, and passion-flowers springing forth, climbing, twisting, disheveled and taking on every shape, every color, every aroma. Here Jan would harvest large quantities of a type of mango whose seed crushed into a paste was as good as cacao; excellent oils which could be made to pour down from the least incision into a wide variety of trees; kola nuts which bound so tightly to the lingual papillae that they become insensitive to unpleasant flavors and made one think brackish water was fresh; ginger, nutmeg, vanilla, cardamom seeds so aromatic that they were termed seeds of paradise, gamboge, elimi resin, rubber. He avoided the terrible ranks of the venomous plants, some misleading by the smiling hypocrisy of their pale nuances and suave aromas, but most on the contrary marked in such a manner as to warn the traveler ahead of time, with their succulent, hairless, verdigris-colored stems, sweating death into ampullae, tumors pock marking them like the back of a toad, with eczema and dartre eating away at them like chancres of some secret disease, and with their huge flowers, calices yawning scarlet maws with poorly excised fangs, adhering like the lips of a lurid pus-filled wound, swelling out into muzzles ready to spit out their venom, their phlegm a tainted mucus, their skin peeling off like that of lepers. A mere atom drowned among the triumph of rising sap, before virtually identical sister species of *Apocynum*, one secreting a delightful honey, the other a narcotic milky latex beneath the eternal indifference of a Sun which cooked to a tee poisons and balms, incubated and hatched crocodile eggs in the mud and those in the 50 bird nests suspended in the radiant sky on the midrib of a single banana leaf, Jan understood the disheartening triteness of human endeavors before Nature personified, and tired, intoxicated, ashamed of working, he would mold himself a bed with grasses and would loll in it, curled up in a ball, as if frightened of dissolving into the enormity of ambient life.

D'ginna, languorous after her childbirth, usually left him to go back into the cabin. Even when she accompanied him all the way, he continued to take care of Hemo alone, since the time when he had entrusted her with him to pick some grapes, and she had moved away, forcing him to search for an hour before finding them. Having climbed up into a clump of fig trees, baby at her breast, she had not responded to his repeated calls either by signal or by noise. When, attracted by the happy drone of the suckling infant, he had found her motionless and silent in the middle of the freshening dusk spread over them by the abundant silvery foliage, she had purposefully hidden herself with all the care of a hunted creature. Had she wished to escape? From the ill-tempered manner in which she received his harmless scolding once upon the ground, to her stealing longing looks into the far distance, he believed so. Overcome by a great sadness at this discovery, he vowed to keep an eye on her and never again leave her alone in charge of Hemo.

Inside, outside, on the matting, on the mosses, she seemed quiet, eyes half-closed, finding no fun in games, in the amusing, noisy boisterousness with which Hemo would regale the cabin and neighboring area from morning 'til night. Those first babbling words which resonate like ineffable music in the heart of a mother, the first gesture in begging to be given a toy which a mother senses intuitively, the first steps she encourages, backing up little by little, luring the child with the promises of refreshment at her breast and a warm bosom between her arms, all of these left D'ginna indifferent and in no way altered her sleepiness or her boredom. She only moved to scratch her own itches, and the little one was only deloused and washed by Jan, who was quite capable of all these tasks, father from head to toe, and even so much so that he was only that.

Haarlem's incorrigible dreamer, the fanatical theoretician of progressive evolution, the discoverer of Eden, the rejuvenator of humanity, the Adamite ancestor were all dead, and D'ginna's mate no less so. He no longer took care of her and would in good faith have denied their lovemaking had she suddenly been gifted with the power of speech and had spoken of it. Forgetful of the past to the extent that today, prolonging their midday nap because of an impending storm, he rejected her from the bed where she came to brush against him, perhaps tempt him, asking her with some impatience what sort of bee was in her bonnet. Like those old men, who at the happy age of lost virility wish to get rid of their mistress in order to devote themselves to the adoration of the son she bore them, adopting him as sole heir to name and fortune, so Jan, even if ensured himself of never being unpleasant with her, to never deviate from the strictest propriety, his attitude belied his words, and nervous yawns would complete a smile with which he attempted to correct the inflexibility of his resistance to her nonetheless frequent flirting. Completely separated from her, he even secured himself against the recurrence of any such desires by building himself, near the crown of the roof, a kind of small loft, with a hammock from which he could draw up the ladder and so completely isolate himself. Every night he went up alone; during the day he played with Hemo.

One such day, when they had capered about a great deal and the little one, thirsty, held onto the hammock with one hand and waved the other towards his mother crouched below, Jan brought him down, and a little tired, went back up for a nap.

The slamming of the door woke him. He bent over the side of the hammock.

The cabin was empty.

Leaping to the threshold at the risk of breaking a leg, he saw D'ginna with Hemo, already two thirds of the way across the clearing. Five minutes later and they would have been in the forest, and most likely lost to him. For there was no mistake: turning every ten paces, and tearing off at great speed as soon as she saw herself being pursued, she was trying to escape.

She was nearing the woods, leaping from side to side to keep from being observed. Was she frightened by some snake, the terror of all apes, or did she reflect upon the fact that her lone functional arm, beside the burden of Hemo at her neck, would make the climbing of trees too difficult, and the lianas would only tangle her up and lessen her chances of escape? She now seemed to no longer hesitate and headed straight for a point where the cover gradually thinned, giving way to open country. Jan had never explored the limits of this blind alley of the clearing, which D'ginna knew full well from their walks together. Hoping to better lose him there, she boldly moved forward.

They arrived somewhere in that open country which was unknown, at least to Jan. The terrain was broken by a series of bare knolls and grassy slopes. Behind the ridge a steep slope, then, as far as the eye could see, a swamp, a veritable forest of reeds.

The water, not having the necessary depth to support crocodiles or hippotami, slept in thousands of irregular puddles, the remains of a huge lake sunburned away. Spread out in soft curves were marshes so large that the ripples upon them seemed to form the beginnings of currents, which took on, beneath the undulating vegetation, the appearance of slow sinuous rivers, disappearing into dark places edged in peat beneath the magnificent spherical umbels of the papyrus, marvelous reeds, genuine little trees whose sharp-edged triangular stem was adorned, three meters up, with great downy white feathers.

Standing on the ridge momentarily before further pursuing D'ginna into the marshes, Jan made one last appeal to her, promising to forgive her. When she ignored him he cried out in despair and regret for not having his rifle on hand, for he would have fired. He then moved forward, stepping on the mat of roots so as not to sink into the mud, hanging on to the gigantic gladioli, whose sharp lanceolate leaves cut like barbarian blades. The innumerable flocks of water birds were barely disturbed and upon seeing the fearlessness of the creatures Jan, notwithstanding his fevered condition, recalled that Darwin once observed a similar setting on his voyage to the Galapagos, a countryside not heretofore visited by man. Rank upon rank of ibis stood up like pickets on their spindly legs, their heads scarlet, softly fading rose on wings and neck, twisting eel-like into hieroglyphic contortions. They aligned themselves along the shore with the black ducks of the golden brown wing-quills, and the kingfishers with their metallic green-bronze reflections. Above, pelicans, their goitered mandibles above the swan-like crop, perched at rest upon trees burned by their guano and whose dead branches bore the empty skins of snakes left behind at their time of molting, now floating like mummy wrappings shaking their ruby dust and old gold scales. Higher still, bald vultures flew about hovering in the yellow patches of mist.

He was about to reach her.

A stream separated her from a soot-colored soil turning blue in large dull wet patches and cracked like a compost heap too long exposed to the Sun. She felt around to see how deep it was, sinking to her knees, and to get herself out more quickly she gathered what strength she had left and stepped over onto the other side. What seemed a fairly dense soil was nothing but horrible muck. She nonetheless continued to advance; Hemo piggy-backed on her shoulders as she slipped along. The two banks of rotting matter on either side of the furrow slowly closed up and leveled over. The silt lost more of its consistency, becoming so soft that little wavelets skirted over it; she continued to push forward, now up to her waist, drawing herself up forcefully amidst a spattering of mud which threatened to both drown and poison her. Jan, after a single step, was forced to throw himself quickly out of the horrible quick-sand; he watched her, trembling, his teeth chattering even though he was streaming with sweat from every pore beneath the crust of mud which covered him.

Now the poor wretch could no longer walk, no longer slip over the surface, but rather swam in a lake of muck, mouthfuls of which stifled the cries of terror coming from her mouth. Her head had disappeared more than once, when she believed she saw a solid rock a couple of strokes away; an agonizing moment and she was able to touch it. It was the corpse of an elephant, no doubt a victim of the last flood. While the Siberian ice preserved such corpses intact for thousands of years, the tropical sun, powerful incubator of rot which hastens the recycling of matter, had already made of this a disgusting piece of carrion whose flanks rippled under the thrust of worms. D'ginna climbed, but the hideous raft tore away under her grip; sinking little by little, and knowing herself to be doomed, she no longer fought, no longer attempted to escape, but turned instead towards the kneeling Jan and lifted Hemo out towards him as far as she could reach. Having quickly taken off his clothing, Jan tied together two great bundles of reeds which he tore up by the handful and which in turn tore up his flesh. He used the bundles as a pair of life-buoys to support himself from sinking into the quick-sand. D'ginna was almost totally submerged except for the top of her head and the arm supporting her dearest responsibility above the level of the marsh. In her final act of motherhood,

73

she threw him the child with the miraculous accuracy of a mother on the brink of death.

Back on solid ground, safe along with Hemo, Jan's over-excitement got the better of him and he passed out. When he came to, he saw himself naked, filthy, and it took a few moments and much rubbing of his eyes in order to remember. Hemo, sitting calmly beside him, was stroking and looking through his hair. The Sun was going down. Upon the marsh nothing moved but clouds of mosquitoes. Likewise, nothing could be heard but a deadened clamor of fright like the voices of those buried alive emanating from the long, dry, hollow bamboos transformed into mysterious organ pipes by the dusk breeze.

CHAPTER VII

The rainy season was back: 30 to 35 weeks of rain, two thirds of which came as hurricanes and torrential downpours. The cabin, warm, well sealed, took on the reek of a slaughterhouse and tannery with meats smoking in the rooftop, two pelts destined for carbatines rolled up, fur side out, in one corner, as well as water buffalo and antelope killed the day before. Jan cut out clothes and shoes from other pelts which he would then assemble during the long evenings of this season.

Hemo slipped down from the hammock in which he was swinging, dragged a pelt over towards the fire and settled there, sucking on sugar cane stalks and tossing them on the coals once dried of sap. They were at first blackened, suppressing the flames and giving forth thick smoke, then they would catch and crackle in a shower of sparks. He stretched out fully and fell asleep.

Interrupting his tailoring, Jan stared at him so fixedly that one would have thought him to also be asleep, were it not for two big tears rolling down from his staring eyes. He remained many hours examining him thus, for months he had been wondering if the creature before him was or was not his son, was a human being or a little ape; but this was the first time he cried, his thoughts never having taken such a cruel turn.

Doubt had not assailed him all at once.

His native friends' assurance that they saw in Hemo a young d'ginna which he was attempting to tame, rather than eat, had nothing to do with it, for to this he saw the counter-point in an instance recounted by one of the greatest natural-ists of modern times, where he had drawn a picture of a new-born monkey, only to have a woman who had recently given birth claim she saw the features of her little boy in the portrait. In the moonlight he recognized Hemo as his son, all his old fears evaporated, and he was exultant and joyful, psychically intoxicated with the certainty of his paternity. Nothing re-mained of his past. Quivering with pride he now lived only in the present, but his brain, after D'ginna's death, so long over-excited that it was a miracle that it had not been overcome by apoplectic shock, naturally cooled down. Alone with Hemo, always cuddling and kissing him, he could not help but see the physiognomy, the behavior, the whole being, rather than con-tinuing its upward progress, beginning to stagnate, even to regress towards increasingly maternal traits, growing worse and worse as time went on. Little by little, during these rainy days of reclusive, forced indoor confinement, his uncertainties grew. He consulted his books and observed Hemo in the hope that some idea, some remark, a clue, a mannerism previously unseen and suddenly discovered would force him to either admit him into his family or reject him as purely animal in Nature.

In two columns labeled "Hemo-Man" and "Hemo-Ape," facing each other in a copybook, every piece of evidence sup-porting one or the other thesis was tabulated; the two columns remained basically equivalent in length.

Hemo was two years old, smaller in terms of height and more burly than most European children of his age; but such traits vary so greatly on an individual basis that one cannot conclude much from them. If his brow bulged outward, and his eyebrows were prominent, the belly had a protruding navel which one might think about to burst open like an abscess, the Pahouins were the same, their noses were even more flattened. How often, in his proudest moments, wiping D'ginna's son's nose, had he believed himself to be wiping the characteristically elongated nose of the sons of the Maas' of Rotterdam, one of those noses like his own, at which Saskia used to laugh so heartily, out there beyond the desert, the oceans, at the Brinckleymann café, in Haarlem! Hemo hardly has a chin, but neither do a great number of Christians, his rounded ears with the outer edge of the conch rolled inward, like those of men, were closer to these by their lack of mobility, than those of so many monkeys met in the tropical forests, including amongst others, the galago lemur which, when he spied out their narrow snout among the foliage, Jan always took to be an aerial hare, a sort of strangely perched sentry.

The heavier hair grew quickly. Matching everywhere the pattern seen in man, the hairs were upturned on the forearm—a trait Jan knew to be of particular importance. This trait had led to the belief that the common ancestor was in the habit of sheltering himself from the rain by crossing his hands over his head. The orientation of the hairs towards the elbow in front would offer a preferential path for the water to run off, and so become hereditary. The hairs were black, heavy on the nape of the neck, few at the joints. So, not counting those men in every country in whom a probable atavism confers a hirsuteness such as Hemo's—for example, the famous Krao from upper Laos, whom the first scientists in London hesitated to categorize as a woman or a she-ape—are there not entire races renowned for the extreme development of their pillosity, for example the Ainu of the Kuril Islands and Amur River delta, who, according to Lapérouse, Broughton and all the navigators who followed in their wake, seem to literally be covered with a bristly fleece?

The wrinkled face, the hands and feet having remained hairless were suntanned. Jan observed, after many others, the

strange commonality of skin color between men and apes in-
habiting the same climes. As black with D'ginna as it is with
Africa's black natives, so it is a yellowish-red in Oceania
among the Malay as with the orangutan.[10] Similarly the gorilla
and black man have an elongated skull, the orang and the Malay a short skull.[11] Feeling Hemo's then his, Jan discovered
that they were similarly constructed, and within the two extremes.

The noblest organs of this face, the eyes, separated by a
thin nasal septum, directed forwards, bright or dimmed when
some surprise wrinkled the brow, were imminently human.

The extremities of the limbs were so to the same degree,
except that on the hands the first two fingers, the index and the
middle finger were less distinctly separated, and on the feet
the thumb was opposable and the sole of the foot not curved
into a pretty arch. But this similarity of the limbs still meant
nothing to Jan in terms of anatomy, for he knew that most apes
presented those traits; that the expression quadrumane had
been expunged from present day science; that rather than
comparing the ape's foot to that of European man, compressed
within shoes and for thousands of generations only employed
for walking, one should compare it to that of other races, and
one would see them as flat as the other, and both with an opposable and prehensile big toe, which other races demonstrate
by handling tools equally well with feet or hands. He knew
that while other anthropomorphs resembled man, the orang,

---

[10] The orangutan (genus: *pongo*) is here given its modern English spelling. Elsewhere, or when cited from French or anti-
quated sources, it is given as *orang-outang* or *ourang-outang*.
Also sometimes referred to in antiquarian literature as
Wurmb's Pongo after Baron Von Wurmb (?-1781) who established the *pongo* in the taxonomical order of Primates. Huxley
referred to him as the "very intelligent German officer." [Ed.]
[11] Needless to say, one of the many problems which finally
managed to dismiss the "missing link" from serious scientific
credibility was its *de facto* racism. [Ed.]

especially by its brain, and the chimpanzee by the bone structure of its head as well as its teeth, the gorilla underwent its evolution primarily in terms of the structure of its limbs. Jan remembered having first chosen the orang in his Haarlem laboratory for his future experiments, based on its advanced intellectual faculties and its habitat in the Dutch colonies; however, since there was nothing which evolved more slowly than the skeleton, and this Oceanian great ape had an extra bone in the wrist, he had rejected it as a more distant cousin than its Gabonian counterpart. And as he reflected on the large effect brought on by a small cause, he stated: "One less small bone in the orangutan's carpal region and it wouldn't have been D'ginna I married."

Hemo took his first steps like a child, the feet pointed inwards and only touching the ground along their outer edge.

If he wanted something he could not reach, he pointed to it with his finger, whined like a child wishing to suckle, struck the ground with the palm of his hand to draw attention. If one refused him this request, he sulked, face scowling, mouth thrust forward in a sullen pout, arms linked over his head by interlaced fingers. Then, when truly angered, he screamed, lips retracted, throwing his arms about left and right, and rolled on the ground. If one annoyed him, he turned his back, making the hand gesture common to all men wishing to chase away the importunate; if one tickled him, he smiled, eyes sparkling, eyelids creased, the commissure of the lips drawn back in a satisfied purr. If something or other amazed him, his eyebrows were drawn up, his entire physiognomy took on the expression of bewilderment taken on by an actor who played the dimwitted servant. Presented with an unpleasant smell, he sniffed, shook his head, blocked his nose. Jan left birds loose inside the cabin to entertain him, and he would feign sleep, blink his eyes while they approached unsuspecting, then pluck and torture them with the wicked pleasure of a young boy when he caught them. He never cried, but as the lower monkeys and many other animals cry, even tears cannot be admitted as a privilege reserved to man.

Thus he resembled a child of his age, no more nor less than them. He did not present, or at least Jan did not see in him any specific trait, which drawing him closer to man or differentiating him from any other pure-bred gorilla, would supply an irrecusable proof of his immortal bastardness.

Jan had discovered in the books in which he sought the principal distinctive trait of humanity, that a baboon dissected by Galen had served as the basis of his anatomy. Since then, as they progressed in their studies, scholars had recognized that between men and the great apes the leap was less abrupt than that between these larger apes and the class of apes immediately beneath them. This held true for the intellect, the emotional baggage, the inclinations, for the soul, in a word in all ways as with the body. This was, of course, as long as one compared the chimpanzee or the orang to the nearby Pahouin or Dayak and not to Rembrandt or Newton, following the mistakened belief of those who cited as specific to man his religiosity, his capacity for self-awareness, for linking cause and effect, while no doubt ignoring that the Hottentot had no more interest than the mandrill in those who comment upon Plato and Hegel, and that in this regard more than three-quarters of the world, including Europe, is populated with Hottentots. Between the intelligence of the many savages with whom he had lived and that of D'ginna, his even more intimate friend, Jan would only admit to small differences in quantity, not quality. If he allowed that savages had a soul, albeit one still in Limbo, as proud son of the janitor of the Great Church of Rotterdam, he would affirm with equal energy the existence of D'ginna's soul, and with great pleasure, given certain memories. While he was a theoretician rather carried away with the concept of progressive evolution, seeing a golden age in the future and not in the past, he compared the universal assent of races, which he had heard invoked in the past, to the belief of all indigenous people that the apes with which they had daily intercourse, had the same origins as they, belonged to their own tribe in primitive times, and had been chased out for their laziness and depravity; a belief, the young Jan added, just

79

warming up, identical to that of the Catholic writer who, thurifer to both pope and executioner, places science and civilization in the garden described in Genesis, and considers, during his evenings in St. Petersburg, the savages to be degenerate branches, broken away from the social tree.

At least, if he did not have what he was looking for, Jan knew what he must look for. The most characteristic capacity of man being not only that of language—the majority of animals, perhaps all, having one they understood and by which they communicated quite well—but that of articulated speech. If Hemo displayed it, then the experiment was concluded. Again, here the range of abilities was very wide: from Spinoza's most sensitive hiatus to the Australian aborigine whose language only included a couple of hundred words; from the aborigine to monkeys' rising clamor during their games or their disagreements. There was no need for Hemo to discourse like Demosthenes or like an honest businessman advertising his damaged wares. No! Let him articulate, like the most humble of savages sound to which he attached a specific meaning, let him acquire speech, the principal prerequisite for conscious thought, let him speak then and the proof will be irrefutable.

Jan reproached himself the silence he had kept almost constantly since D'ginna's death. Never hearing a voice, how would Hemo develop his own? Those deaf at birth were they not also dumb? Little boys, be they French or Italian remained mute when with a mute, and would at best resort to the sort of indistinct prattling which would draw from a mother a kiss upon the lips like unto flowers noisy with the sound of tame bees.

He then chatted incessantly, did not ask for or hand over an object without carefully enunciating its name, pretending he was not paying attention when presented with any gesture, until it was accompanied by some babble or other. The child, impatient to reach towards a fruit, towards his fruit and drink, got angry, made a great fuss, and his squalls thrilled Jan, to whom they seemed more complex than his earlier cries.

Besides that, he sang: ancient Dutch ballads by Cats the storyteller, Fockenbroch the macaronic, or the peasant Cornelius Poots, tales of country fairs, battles with the English and Flemish, waking no memories in Jan other than those of the nice old lady who would mutter them by his bedside. A more modern one by Tollens, about some sailors' victory over the polar ice, he could not begin without remembering his father, good old Philip Maas, serenading the first verses to a parrot for an entire year with a fit of coughing after every verse, so that the bird, coughing in the same manner, sounded like a polyglot with a cold, adding to refrains pertaining to Holland the sneezes of Poniatowski. Presenting concepts quite at odds with what he expressed, Jan's features and words, along with his appearance and his sense of social hierarchy were in such poor concordance that even a student more attentive than Hemo would have been confused. Happily, he usually would hum children's rhymes which reminded him of Saskia's beaming face as a child. An involuntary smile became so commonplace to him that by force of smiling he soon was blessed with only clean thoughts and happy songs.

Fearing that a virtually uninterrupted reclusiveness would be detrimental to Hemo, who, so it seemed to him, was losing some of his vivacity, he took him for a noontime walk when the rain allowed, not too far from the cabin, so that they could come back in quickly in case of a storm. The magnificent forest, perpetually green, sheltered them well, but Jan feared the ambush of fevers more pernicious than ever hiding beneath the strong aromas of reawakened sap. Between the stones, recently flooded cavities teemed with fish. In these fresh waters, blessed with the warmth of an incubator, the fry, drawn away by the river, hatched in mere minutes. The temperature in these climes was always moderate and free of sudden fluctuations. Jan fished, and got Hemo used to what he caught, where at first he refused to touch the flopping creatures. He wished to rid him gradually of the fear of reptiles which he had inherited from his mother, such a fear that amongst the entire race the sight of a snake paralyzed them and they allowed themselves to be bitten when they could easily have moved aside. Hemo, certainly more educatable than certain urban street urchins whose rickety frames and idiocy, caused, alas, by lingering hunger and alcohol, took pleasure in this game. Boiling over with impatience, leaping on the pike, he would grab everything, adults and fry, and enjoy squeezing them to see their gills gape open. They fished with igongo, a lovely leguminous plant whose leaves, when torn up in the tiny pond, poisoned the fish, or rather, put them to sleep, for they remained fine to eat once one took them belly up from the surface where they lay stunned and yawning. Jan had to stop Hemo from going into the deeper recesses in order to catch the smaller fry. His cries of happiness during these moments of freedom differed so much from his raucous, angry cries or mutterings when in a bout of sulking, that Jan, the dreamer, wondered whether sounds so simple yet so diverse might not be a step along the path to those interjections and onomatopoeia which must constitute the basis of any truly primitive language. Had it not been shown that the vowel *a* tied to a given sound, such as *ba, pa, da, ta,* and thus constituting the easiest sound for the child to vocalize, signified, almost everywhere in the world *father, mother*?

A storm kept them trapped inside for several days. The locked door was windowless, and daylight only barely filtered through the narrow slits between it and its frame. Hemo was very bored and he found no pleasure in his favorite games. Crouched near the fire, almost in the fire, stationary, listless, he barely ate, chewed on sugar cane, irritated his throat by breathing in the smoke, coughed, always dying of thirst, always wanting to drink something. If he shook off his listlessness it was to circle around like a wild beast in a cage, to measure out on hands and knees the messy indoors, following the curved wall, which he would strike with his elbow as if he hoped to move it outwards, or to cut a window out of it. Then he stopped before the door, lay down flat to see the outdoors beneath it. Jan was worried. He had tried everything, in vain, and did not know how to distract him. He noticed with great sadness that the poor little contabescent had become silent again, had again regressed, no longer making a sound or uttering a word, even to complain, and did not even sigh. Jan knew that it was best to find him a friend. A child, a little Pahouin of his own age with whom to play, with whom to spend long hours of forced inactivity, this would indeed render his recovery so likely that to not make such an attempt would be barbaric. Unfortunately, for this to occur, he would have to wait for the dry season. His native friends would then come and offer him, of their own accord, a portion of their first hunt. He would ask them for one of their young children, certain that they would all be at odds as to who first would give over their own to the gentle and agreeable white shaman. With a few more fishing expeditions, Hemo could perhaps manage to ride it out. But it was not two or three weeks of delay, but rather four months, four! Thousands of times longer than was needed for consumption to sap Hemo, to sap him unto death. Jan decided to anticipate the situation by going to visit the Pahouins.

Helmeted, dressed, shod in freshly greased boots, axe strapped to his hip, rifle under his arm, a bag of supplies, food and bullets on his back, and Hemo, carefully covered, bundled up in woolens, carried piggyback, he closed the door behind them. A series of quagmires followed one upon the other, and he took his first break in order to cut himself a pole with which to probe them. Hemo, in a livelier mood, chattered above his head and drummed on his chest with his heels. Jan slipped, fell to his knees, walking almost bent in half under his mule's burden, rose again, often mired in water up to his hips, would fall again, amusing the little one no end, who smacked his lips more loudly, searching, his appetite renewed, in the pouch which Jan had taken from his shoulder and handed him intact so he could choose at his leisure. Jan heard him bite down and chew on something for a while, then sensed him become a dead weight falling asleep under the rocking gait. His back nearly broken, groaning, Jan held back a moan lest he woke him. Laid low by hunger and fatigue, wishing to eat in turn, he looked about him in vain. Hemo, having sated him-

83

self, had lost the pouch containing the remainder of the food, holding on to a bundle of corn cobs. Of these he refused categorically to share even a single grain, howling and grinding his teeth when they were threatened. Admiring the little one's determination in defending that which he had every reason to think belonged to him, Jan took another bite of a kola nut he always kept on his person, lit a pipe full of marihuana to reenergize himself, and moved on. The smoke annoyed Hemo who tore the pipe away, burning himself on the bowl in the process, and whimpered until a hug and a song consoled him.

The rumble of the cataracts announced their proximity to the river. Night fell. On the road since dawn, not wishing to risk passing through the marshy thickets along the banks, in the impenetrable darkness unbroken by even the brightest of summer suns, they camped in the shelter of a sort of cave formed by an overbeetling rocky outcrop, not much bigger than a cupboard, which Jan selected over others given its contrary orientation to that of the wind. Laying with his back to the outdoors, protecting Hemo who had fallen asleep in his arms after crunching up the corn, Jan stocked the fire, necessary in all seasons, not so much against the cold, as against the mosquitoes and carnivorous ants. In the morning, the little one wished to sleep some more, and Jan had the hardest time calming him down. Jan walked while rocking him in his arms. For hundreds of steps he had to jump from root to root, around the flooded trees, so as not to get mired down. At other times he had to climb to the top of one of these trees to map out his way. The Como had tripled in width. The breakers made a frightful din like the rumbling of thunder tearing the skies asunder; frothing whirlpools sparkled in the sun carrying down entire forests, in a single second torn from their centuries-old haunts and still festooned with flowering lianas. Two Pahouin hunters of hippopotami and manatees, on a small island, were keeping watch. Jan drew their attention with two shots from his gun, which he fortunately had loaded before Hemo had lost his ammunition. They recognized him, untied a canoe, and with the ability and boldness of consummate paddlers, they passed through the reefs, torrents and thousands of pieces of floating debris which threatened to capsize them.

The village was celebrating.

CHAPTER VIII

At the beginning of the overwintering, they had fought against the Bakalay, who inhabited the lower reaches of the river to the west, over the possession of some poorly cleared areas, when upstream, to the right and to the left were limitless savannahs, more fertile, more arable, and entirely unclaimed. The true reason, this land claim being but a pretext, was that each tribe wished to, at their neighbor's expense, stock their larder of human flesh.

Victors, the Pahouin warriors had brought back a dozen prisoners to the quartering enclosure, while their spouses, who from afar had supported them in their combats, ran onto the field of victory where, of simple tastes and not yet having acquired a refined taste for aged meat, they ignored the dead, to finish off, carve up and bring back those of the wounded, which remained presentable. The kitchens were smoking, stews bubbled, steamed dishes hissed, roasts browned, and all day the children peeled vegetables for seasoning an orgy of Bakalays served with carrots. Poor elderly anemics regained their adult vigor; the rickety were cured; sad little girls not yet married because of their ballooning bellies, gained enough energy to evacuate in one fell swoop, great bundles of tapeworms with which they had been stuffed.

Until the moment when, in public meals cunningly scheduled so that the guests would avoid having their indigestions come too soon one after the other, they were served as the *pièce de résistance*, the prisoners were submitted to a progressive fattening, well taken care of, and kept in constant confinement. Chained by the neck in the back of the council hall of the greater dignitaries, they were released, under the watch-

85

ful eye of numerous guards, so they could stretch their muscles; they were forced to amuse themselves, to gambol about, to laugh, under penalty of the rod; they were washed, shaved, anointed all over their bodies with palm oil, as well as their little mates, and they were only brutalized in their best interest. One of them, lacking in dignity in his role as royal cattle, refused all food, seeking to lose weight and pull one over on the cooks, was slowly cooked alive so he would not lose any further weight. Even his tribe mates applauded his fate. Honorable players, they would have as victors relished some Pahouin meat; defeated, the Pahouins would do the same. Resigned to the will of Amara-Widdah-Booloo, the great serpent which laid the world, and whose knotted coils moved about the Sun and Moon, the Bakalays sang, stuffed themselves all day, vainly competing to be the best fattened on the banquet table.

Akayrawiro, the chief Jan had cured of the fever, still reigned.

Jan had already often damned the practice of cannibalism, in particular during his first passage among them, when, about to be eaten, he had pleaded with all the ardor which someone with a less ardent temperament would have devoted to such an intensely personal issue, began a dialogue in which his limited grasp of African languages forced him to supplement three quarters of his words with gestures, elevating himself to an eloquence of the greatest pantomime. He had stopped one day seeing Akayrawiro, his most faithful listener, listening and applauding him, while picking clean, with his teeth, a leg of man. Calmly the king had answered his reproaches.

"Certainly, my dear white shaman, it is a poor habit, but it is of such ancient date that to abandon it would show a lack of respect to innumerable generations of our ancestors who passed it on to us. Tradition, old fellow, tradition! And in respecting tradition, you see, everything is knitted together and linked. I grant life to my enemies, this would seem an insignificant detail, wouldn't you say? But then who knows if tomorrow my own subjects, that is my goods, my inheritance, my merchandise, would not blame me for using them as I saw fit, would not regret that I gave them as cat food to my favorite lion Irro, who will not deign to eat anything else? Do continue your discourses, they interest me—unless you'd like to share my humble breakfast...What! let me lose my throne if I can only understand your fear. From the moment I kill a Bakalay, have I not forgiven him for the crime of being a Bakalay if I eat him myself rather than leave him to Hoo-Too-Vah, the eternal, the loner, the immutable, the infinite?"

Jan asked about this awful Hoo-Too-Vah, and the chief concluded:

"Hoo-Too-Vah, He who is. In the Heavens, on Earth, everywhere. The one of whom even the Bible, the white man's book you have been reading to me, exalts the sovereign grandeur; the king of kings, the uncreated, that is to say born from nothing..."

"Too-Hoo-Vah: Jehovah!" Jan cried out, deeply moved.

"No, Hoo-Too-Vah, the one who is without navel, without feet, without eyes, without ears and without a mouth, born of all creation, always like unto himself, going everywhere, seeing, hearing, devouring all..."

"Why yes, Jehovah!"

"No, Hoo-Too-Vah, god of the maggots."

Remembering the adage on morality or rather morals which vary according to the latitude, not knowing besides how to answer the native's question as to why the white man perceived a difference between eating his dead enemy or leaving the worms to eat him, Jan fell silent, less so to avoid future discussions than to avoid the prime minister's unending obsession with having him honor him by marrying his wife for the duration of his stay among them. All he had gotten out of them was that while he was present his friend Akayrawiro would no longer surrender himself, nor let any of his subjects surrender themselves to such delicacies. So he demanded that day, having caught them preparing the manducation of the last prisoner: the village was alarmed, the pots and clay jars lined up

87

before each doorway, the stake erected in the middle of the main street. Akayrawiro apologized, the white man's visit was unexpected, how were they to hide the feast from him? The worst part was that he could not put it off, as the women had invited a number of friends. But Jan was no longer listening: overcome with a saintly furor in seeing the Bakalay stupidly watching the preparations of his own cooking, he ran forward, untied him, and pronounced him freed. The other, never having seen a white man, remained stunned for a moment, assuming him to be an invited guest at the banquet, was terrified at the prospect of passing through the stomach of this pale monster. He jumped on him, bit him deeply on the hand, on the shoulder, and would have bitten his throat out had Jan not, losing his composure, struck him down with a blow from his axe. It was the first time he had had any trouble with a savage; it seemed to him a poor omen for his continued work. He cried upon hearing the famished cries of the crowd accompanying the cooks taking away the corpse, and he cried harder upon receiving the congratulations of the executioners upon his skill; they only suggested that in a similar circumstance he should not strike the skull for it damaged the brain, a choice morsel.

Happy cries from Hemo, playing with a group of children from which he only differed by his slightly more intelligent features, drew Jan from his lamentations. Believing himself to already be smelling the odors of the fierce kitchens, he wished to leave the village as quickly as possible, and stated the purpose of his trip. The assembled elders smiled, had the young girls paraded before him, and he was forced to once more explain that he was not asking for a wife for himself, but a playmate for his young...ape, he alleged, hesitating to renounce D'ginna's son. A child? A little boy no doubt? And the elders laughed uproariously, declaring themselves to be flattered that he had finally adopted their manners. He blushed at their disgusting insinuation, and moved off with Hemo. Akayrawiro asked him to sit down again; no one wished to offend him; they were all laughing because all felt great pleasure in advance at allowing him to choose in their seraglio of both sexes. They were mistaken, but all in good faith, and their white cousin should not hold it against them. And the good king, commanding the chief among his favorites, one always ready to play the role of being indispensable, to gather up a cohort from the families' sons under his watchful supervision, made a sign to the elders, tapping himself on the forehead, indicating that they should ignore the white man's poor manners: the white friend has enough qualities that fashionable society can cut him some slack.

One of the great dignitaries arose and kowtowed deeply before this sound observation. Akayrawiro had for the good of his kingdom, and the needs of the next war, just cast off half of his progeny into the army, at the rank of colonel. Who would then, in the Pahouin nobility, supply replacements? Why, did this great dignitary not have on his knee, at this very moment, his last born son, which he dragged everywhere in the hope that the king would notice him; in his paternal foresight he was gripped by the fear that Jan would strip him of his favorite and unknowingly cause irreparable damage to his ancestor's honor. To get off cheaply from this quite conceivable turn of events, he rushed off and brought back one of his daughters for the white friend, the little Kaylinkah.

Jan was effusive with his thanks and left, Hemo in one hand, Kaylinkah in the other.

The Pahouins accompanied him on the way back, helping him across the river and through the marshes, then returning quickly for a Bakalay dinner.

From then on in the isolated cabin there was constant commotion, high spirits, and an endless liveliness.

Hemo was no longer the same. He who yesterday sulked sluggishly when presented with any sort of meal, could today not hold himself back at the table. Finding everything tasty, he stuffed himself, and like a schoolboy hoarded his dessert to finish during recess. Between the three daily meals, at every moment one had to be ready to prepare them a slice of bread and jam, to hand out fruit, or to pour them something to drink.

They moved and upset everything. The first one to stop remained prey to the other's teasing, so they only settled down when fatigue overcame them both simultaneously; even then they were inseparable, and wherever they happened to be they dropped in one another's arms, and Jan, at the risk of waking them and their racket, would pick them up and put them to bed as one.

At first, in spite of Kaylinkah's constant prattle, Hemo's language skills showed no sign of improvement. But by dint of listening to him, Jan discerned that his many vocalizations were reproduced in an identical manner when circumstances were the same, that an undeniable logic guided his comparisons when he designated several objects by the same sound. He uttered genuine "hee, hee!" and "ah, ah" sounds when presented with anything shiny: the morning sun, the lamps which allowed him to see clearly and continue his games, the coals which warmed him, the debris of a broken mirror which he picked up. Thunder and gunshots made him utter the same "hoo! hoo!" sounds, and anything which surprised him lead him to exclaim "oh! oh!" Along this path Jan went from discovery to discovery, and the intelligence of this little bit of a man almost floored him. When Grumpy, Hemo puffed up his cheeks and blew "f, f, f," on a wisp of down to indicate that the wind had blown in a similar manner over his hat. The next day, having released a little bird which Jan had managed to find for him, he blew once again, "f, f, f," crying and showing his empty hands. Kaylinkah would ask the names of the plants they picked in the clearing, and Jan, to answer her, consulted his guidebook to local flora. Hemo would tear up some grass in turn, grab the huge manual of botany, open it, pretend to be looking for a page, put his ear to it, wait gravely for the book to speak, but the book, alas! kept quiet, so he would toss it away, annoyed. On another occasion, rolling on some pelts spread out to dry, his sudden surprise was made manifest in such a way that his gesturing caught Jan's attention. On his knees near Kaylinkah, who was resting on her back, Hemo made a detailed examination of the pretty girl's body, then of his own, underscoring by noisy "oh! oh!" the anatomical details which he discovered to differ, wishing then to continue his investigations on his father, who, to keep him away had to flick him on the fingers.

That night Jan's dreams changed.

For a long time, since his doubts as to Hemo's origins had originated, the perplexities which haunted him every night brought him D'ginna's ghost. As soon as he fell asleep, the only door to the cabin solidly closed, she entered, came up to his hammock, squatted on his chest, identical in aspect and pose to the grimacing demons of nightmare in old prints, but even more hideous in form and feature as the most Medusa-like of monsters improvised by the black fancy of a Goya or a Rops, for she came forth from the marsh which had swallowed her up, her fur plastered down, a shroud of mud on her decomposed corpse, with growths and tumors crawling beneath, finally bursting open in infectious maws.

Awakened, dripping with sweat, thinking her ichor had dribbled on him, he accepted the horrible vision as a just remorse. Yes, D'ginna reproached him for ignoring her once she had delivered; had not the contempt he had shown her contributed to her running off and then to her suicide? The ardor of their passion had so often united their two souls as one! Supposing he had merely been ungrateful towards D'ginna, had he not acted like a selfish coward towards his other mistress, science, to which he had pledged himself, and to which he had promised eternal fidelity, even if this fidelity brought him derision and accusations of criminal behavior? Was it not indeed a case of drawing himself away from the experiments he had conceived and consented to, rather than one of abandoning the poor D'ginna at a time when delivered of her fetus which he feared to be a bastard, she had remained pure, tame, solitary, and finally ready to supply him with a child whom no one could have contested the paternity of, the genuine Hemo which no other male, this time, could have claimed as their son, his hero, his miracle, his god, his immortal half-breed? On this slope of regrets, rather than a D'ginna turning green in

91

the stinking muck, he saw once more the one he had known before, a wounded creature whose gestures were weighed down by weakness; the convalescent whose big eyes, until then dull, were fixed upon him in the soft alacrity of tender gratitude; the lover so burning with desire that upon their bouts in the dark, the black pelt seemed to sparkle, to phosphoresce, and render the surrounding shadows luminous. Delirious, he could well close his eyes, and re-cover his pallet with fresh leaves, but the reignited sparks penetrated his eyelids, his arms caressed emptiness, his whole body tingled, flogged with the nettles of remembrance.

Today, better dreams complemented his hours of rest, coddled his hopes, and left him in a warm nervous excitement, allowing him to better taste the calm of night.

In some bright obscure paradise of the adjoining woods, where an intense release of aromas made the flowers steam and sing; better yet, in the very center of the clearing, far from the curtains of lianas, at midday, on the sand, between the implacable and dazzling bare ground and the sun spread over the immensity of the cloudless sky, he seemed to see Hemo and Kaylinkah, drunk with the sap of their youth, naked, copulating, with no more vile modesty or shame than awesome Nature, which enveloped them, placed in the other matings, infinite in number, of its plants and animals. He gave them his blessing, and soon, gobbling up time, blessed and married their little ones, then their great-grandchildren, who swarm in families of simple, pure giants, forming a people at whose feet the others all together appeared as an anthill. They built cities in the others' squares to enclose old growth forests, sent out their sons and daughters to the world which saluted their coming to save poor, shattered humanity by infusing it with some of their new blood, their strength, their candor and their goodness.

Sitting in the hut, the sound of the two little ones around him, or with summer returned, when holding their hands during a walk, he often continued this dream, forgetting his usual concern with Hemo's linguistic education, and remained silent for hours, rocking on his stool. When he took along the two children who skipped and ran themselves ragged at his side, it happened that he, as Moses must have done when leading the Jews to Canaan, turned around to see if he was followed by the peaceful army which he already believed himself to be leading, not to conquest, but to the salvation of the worn down old world.

Forcing himself to get back to the task which he correctly considered to be his most pressing duty, teaching Hemo to talk, he set himself a task. Every night he read aloud for an hour and forced him to listen. Fairy tales were lies of an allegedly religious nature with which one was in the habit of stuffing the imagination of youngsters, placing such an impression on the malleable minds of civilized children that this nonsense was never entirely erased from their memory. Sooner or later it sharply resurfaced, even in their death throes, when the sensible ideas developed later on disappeared in the inverse order with which they were acquired, the latest ones first, the first ones next. Jan wished to spare his student this problem suffered by so many philosophers, falling back in their old age to the superstitions which they had fought all their lives; he never taught him these errors be it even purely for entertainment purposes or in poetry. Rather than torture the Bible with attempts at rational explanations, he hid it entirely from him, agreeing with the preacher, who, denying himself the right to choose amongst the miracles, entreated his brothers to thank God for the evident generosity which he had manifested for their weak-mindedness, in having Jonas swallowed by a whale, when instead he could have had them believe the whale to have been swallowed by Jonas. He told him no more stories, as he only knew a few legends anyway, resolved, besides, to trying to make him understand, to supply him with cornerstones to build a solid base of understanding for any future studies with those concepts whose truth was no longer in doubt.

He spoke to him of the vast Earth, its great rivers and deserts, its poles and its tropics, from its abysses to its Himalayas, turning upon its equator and about the Sun. About the Earth turned its own satellite, the Moon, dead down to its geological activity and concealing beneath the suavity of its borrowed light all the gloomy horror of emptiness; he told of the other planets, of the enormity of Jupiter, of the mysteries of Saturn. All of them, from Neptune the eldest to Mercury the youngest, like Earth, spinning upon themselves and about the Sun which created all of them, and which in turn rotated upon itself as it traversed absolute space at a velocity of 200,000 leagues per day, towards a shore as yet unknown, around another more central sun, star of the constellation of Hercules, of Perseus or even Halcyon, the brightest of the Pleiades. Every star was a sun, ours but a single speck in the Milky Way, and the Milky Way, that agglomeration of solar systems which all the generations of humanity, past, present and future would be unable to number, but a narrow projection in motion through the infinite. His mind unable to grasp the complex concatenation of lunar, planetary and solar orbs, man came back down to Earth, and on this speck of dust found himself, a mere mildew, a nothing, which standing erect on two legs contemplated the universe, dividing it into two parts *me and the rest*, believing the *rest* to exist expressly for him, for a him who did not even have his own *self*.

He spoke of the plant kingdom, from the microscopic to the gigantic, from the athlete's foot fungus to baobabs and sequoias; he spoke of the animal kingdom, those in existence and those which were extinct, in a word, of life, from its appearance on the primitive landscape—that is, from the Precambrian, including the problematic Foraminifera of the Laurentian strata, and the algae which gave rise to beds of graphite mixed within the same strata, the oldest on Earth—to the creature which incarnated it in sovereign form, man.

He spoke of matter, of the Force of which all other forces, including the soul, were but modalities, all emanating from the warmth of the Sun, true father, supreme creator of that which had lived, lived now and would live, such that in the final analysis, present day man, almost returning to the religion of his savage forbears in the most remote of ages, saluted the Sun as sole God. And the good Jan fell back into his daydreams. The quantity of matter which made up the Earth, if one ignored the negligible input of meteorites, was as invariable and inalterable as the amount of force, since matter and force were inseparable terms. The portion of this matter and force circulating within living things, necessarily limited, must be divided to a greater and greater degree with each rise in births. Did this not explain from a material perspective the wearing down of the human race as the number of individuals rose, and from a dynamic perspective the growing rarity of genius as the surge of mediocrity increased? Did this not explain why wild plants and animals disappeared under domestication and cultivation, as did inferior races upon contact with the civilized races? To these questions which he asked himself, the good Jan remained silent, and listened to Hemo snore.

The latter, like most schoolboys, sitting still with his cheeks in his hands, seemed to listen when the teacher was watching, but scratched his head, rubbed his eyes, sucked on his tongue, stole a glance at a fly buzzing by or at the sparks crackling from the fireplace when his teacher's back was turned. Finally, like all schoolboys, he could not stand it anymore and fell asleep. Jan, who never had the heart to wake him would carry him to where Kaylinkah already lay sleeping, and taught him only during their outings.

In the presence of the objects he showed him and spoke to him of—pebbles, flowers, birds—he managed to hold his attention upon those elements of natural history with which he wished to begin his education. He took advantage of every encounter: having gone bathing in the Zondag-Zay, he remarked to what degree a group of cynocephalic apes, crouching on the rocks, exposed the errors of certain modern scholars, sitting-room explorers too quickly discounting the geographers of antiquity thus denying what could easily be understood. For example, would apes seen thus, with no neck and their body bent over below their shoulders, not resemble the fantastic Blemyes described as having faces in the middle of their chests? Were gorillas not the satyrs of which only the face was human? And the Ogipans, with a man's head on a goats body, whose existence was so commonly accepted that Pomponius Mela did not bother to describe its features,[12] contenting himself with confirming that they were indeed those attributed to it, was it not a she-ape in the process of stripping fruit from the garden?

It was upon his return from one of these visits to the Zondag-Zay that Jan felt the first symptoms of malaria. Rather than determination to continue his work and the vivacity of his limbs, of the clear-headedness which the pure waters of the lake usually conferred upon him, he began to tremble, to have cramps, almost drown, this former expert diver from the port city of Rotterdam. He managed to reach the bank, dressed and made his way back quickly. But even upon trails basking in the sun, or cooking before a great fire he had built, he could not overcome the chill which dogged him day and night.

He was surprised to have remained for so long untouched by this fever, endemic to the region, even forgetting about it and believing himself to be immune. One easily accustomed oneself to good health, the true state of man. This was in contrast to the views of some misanthropic individuals who, already bewildered at the very threshold of the anatomy rooms by the infinite ratios of gears which drove the animal machine, were amazed to see that it did not break down at every moment; that neither was disease the law, nor did euthanasia occur by accident. They did not think that if this fabulous machine did not work well it would still have lasted, that it would have broken down completely and not adapted itself in a different manner, that in the latter case they would still be

---

[12] *Tum primos ab Oriente Garamantas, post Augilas et Troglodytas, et ultimos ad Occasum Atlantas, audimus. Intra (si credere libet) vix jam homines, magisque semiferi, Aegipanes, et Blemyes, et Gamphasantes, et Satyri, sine tectis ad sedibus passim vagi, habent potius terras, quam habitant.* [De Situ Orbis, Book I, chap iv].

amazed by the state of its final organization, were it entirely different from what it was.

He did not treat himself right away, hoping once again to recover without any help; but the chills, the insomnia, the lack of appetite would not leave him, and he had to resort to the medicines which he was saving for his Pahouin friends. Quinine cut off his fever, but unfortunately his supply of arsenic was exhausted, and the anemia which followed persisted, always serious under such debilitating climates. Soon he was unable to get up, and after long hesitation was finally forced to have both his children, for Hemo would not let his little friend go alone, contact the village. Their trip in this season would pose little danger, by the river they would certainly find some fishermen who would get them across and lead them; and so it happened. As early as the next day, Akayrawiro himself, his ministers and his most trusted shaman hastened to the cabin, led by the two brave little messengers.

CHAPTER IX

Jan wished to be treated at home. The shaman, upon a sign from Akayrawiro, was formally opposed to it, stating with some dignity that he would never, under such circumstances, take responsibility for a such course of action, when a basic element of the treatment was to distance the patient from any marshy land, placing him in clean, dry, healthy fresh air. Jan, forced to agree with him, was taken on a stretcher into the royal hall. As soon as he was there, and they had proceeded at a quick trot, the shaman, upon a second sign, declared that this location was no better, the mists were still too thick; what was needed were the true mountains, for example, the isolated and fortified palace where his Majesty retired when he himself was sick.

The good Akayrawiro did not hesitate, immediately ordering the warriors who bore the stretcher to get on their way, and following on behind with his servants, ministers, physicians, seraglio, slaves and priests. His people, thus abandoned, cried out, trying to hold him back, tortured with sadness, prostrate at his feet. He calmed them down with the abundant application of a cudgel and a hippopotamus-hide whip, upbraiding them for their ingratitude. How was it that his white cousin cured him, saved him—the Sunbeam—for them, the dregs, and yet they could understand that he must in turn sacrifice himself for his white cousin! It was almost enough for him to give up in disgust his reign over such brutes. They apologized, greased their wounds and contusions, and the procession, having slowed for the moment, picked up the pace.

The countryside where they were headed was only two leagues away but a gorge, impassible in their dugouts, formed an elbow which doubled the distance. Sheltered from the sun by the esparto mosquito netting which formed a canopy over the litter, softly swaying under the porters' careful cadence, Jan remained in a dull torpor of which he was conscious and which he tried to overcome, but was unable to shake. As they approached the village, the river circumvented, the dying echoes of a gun battle nonetheless made him jump. He bent over to question someone, and realized that the royal caravan, triumphant at first, now seemed to be in a disordered retreat. Worried, he asked after his children. A porter, in answer, showed him, far ahead, the party of chiefs. Besides a rearguard of slaves, the litter ended the procession. Jan assumed that Hemo had preceded him, and broken by his slight effort, fell back onto his pallet.

It was indeed, in the distance, the echo of rifles, and amongst the ranks, a disordered retreat.

Now, in spite of the sharp slope of the trails, all were running silently: warriors, cooks, musicians, holding up sabers, kitchen utensils and tambourines to stop them from clashing, breaking or resonating. Jan, jostled hard, holding onto the edges of the litter, feared more than once that he would go for a header.

Finally they arrived. The king absorbed in affairs of state, now seldom came to his country retreat; the dozen or so huts making up his palace had collapsed little by little to the ground. They hastened to rebuild one, in which they housed the patient who was now exhausted, delirious, almost unable to speak and moaning constantly.

"What can he possibly want?" the king asked his ministers.

"Your Majesty, we, as yourself, do not know; perhaps Kaylinkah and the ape."

Hearing this, Jan gathered up his strength and stammered:

"Yes, yes, my children, Hemo and Kaylinkah, Hemo! Hemo! Hemo!"

The king smiled and deigned to lower himself and pat his cheeks in friendship.

"Why, sure as the devil, cousin, you had me worried there, naming as your children that little girl which is not of you, which perhaps you have not even married, and that animal. I was wondering if you hadn't entered into some sort of secret marriage, that you might not have had a genuine son which I would have been loath to leave behind. For, you see..."

The entire sky was turning red at the point on the horizon which his august finger was indicating.

"Fire," exclaimed Jan.

"Yes, fire, fire in my capital. Oh the monsters, how fortunate you are that you saved my life. Otherwise I would not have been able to stop my subjects from taking out their vengeance upon you and yours, upon your hideous white brethren."

"White brethren? What?"

"But your fever..."

"No, no, I beg you, tell me."

Akayrawiro explained.

Neighboring kingdoms had, over the last several days, told him of the approach of a troop of white men. These whites, in great numbers, an army of no less than six or seven people, not counting the natives they borrowed from each successive region they went through, were coming, not like Jan up the river from the sea, but from the other side, the east, and they must have traversed Africa in its greatest and most mysterious breadth. If one impeded their progress, tried to bargain with them with respect to supplying them with food, shelter or other assistance, if one tried to lead them astray, they fought and won, took what they wanted, drew information from even the most ardent of patriots by showering them with compliments and gifts. He thought that having Jan in his capital would facilitate his relations with these pale-faced devils. While he was getting along with his household and his loyal nobles, he had nonetheless preferred high-tailing it out of there. The change in climate which Jan's sickness required was an excellent excuse, one could not have come up with a better one. His people, towards whom the greatest secrecy had been maintained, would deal with it as they could. He was quite happy to be safe. Even the fire, which could be seen from where they were did not bother him; it proved to him how wise he was to absent himself. Indeed, if the town was burning it was because the people tried to defend it. Present he would have had to fight, either with the white men against his own subjects, or with his subjects against the white men; either way would have been dangerous, very dangerous, too dangerous for he whose sole ambition was to live to a ripe old age so as to devote himself longer to upholding the love, prosperity and glory of his country.

Crack! Boom! It was his throne, two drums stacked one upon the other, which had burst under the gestures which accompanied his eloquence.

Thus the white men, Europeans no doubt, his countrymen perhaps, would have passed near Jan, in the depths of Africa, without him having a chance to shake their hands. A meeting with them would have, the poor exile thought, at least tided him over until his work was done. And this stupid king...

"Wretched coward," he cried out, "why have you brought me along? Is it so I can attest to your cowardice?"

"It is the way it had to happen, since I wished, in avoiding the situation, to make it appear as if I were accompanying you. Why, think of it in such a manner, in the eyes of my people the business which brings me here is one of devotion to you. I followed you, I did not go back."

Jan's thoughts returned to Kaylinkah and Hemo. Would Akayrawiro have forgotten them? The king remained patient, and again answered.

"Why yes, besides, my capital is crawling with little girls like that, even fatter ones, entirely at your disposal. As for your little gorilla, notwithstanding that you seem to attach some undue importance to having him, we'll find him again. As for Kaylinkah, that's the name isn't it? you don't care one way or the other if it's her or another..."

"Or another!" Jan repeated incredulously before fainting.

They left the village to settle some ten leagues further away, in the opposite direction, so as to throw off the white explorers if perchance they had had the intention of having themselves led towards the court by the villagers. They camped in the forest. The meat sizzled. Mouths followed each other in rapid succession on the spouts of the large jars bearing the supreme delight of palm wine and rancid termite oils. Wild music got even the most tired among them moving, raised the drunkenness of the drunkest two-fold, as fires kept the beasts at bay. Every night, in the smoke, more exciting than the drink, the furious beat of the orchestra, or the aromatic herbs thrown on the fire to keep away the ants and flies, were the dances, running, whirling frenetically, in devilishly lascivious embraces, uniting every rank, every age, every sex in every sort of laughter, sobbing, kissing, moaning, in every wild, indulgent behavior, ending only in the morning, when the young, the adults and the elderly collapsed in hideous piles about the collapsed heaps of coals, whose last flickers, like the bulging manganese-glazed surfaces of Etruscan brown-clay pottery, were reflected outward from the sweaty curves of

101

piled up bodies, arms barely relaxed, their anger not yet fully expended.

Soon however, the security forces announced the departure of the white men. The king reentered his liberated capital; imposed taxes which would help compensate those who had shared his hardships in exile; had those plotters who had led the defense and now bore a certain embarrassing glory impaled; softened the mob with great feasts organized in honor of his return; and busied himself trying to satisfy Jan, who was still asking him about Hemo and cursing the weakness which nailed him to his pallet, preventing him from finding out on his own.

Alas, all the accounts agreed. All the villagers interrogated stated that there had been six of the invaders. Calm at first, the king's absence, which they claimed to have foreseen, still irked them. To punish him they had lodged in his own huts. They had one of their own black servants beaten for his negligence in having caused the fire during the very first night, to show that it was his fault, not theirs, and had pitched their tents in the open space. Stupidly, they freely handed out guns, cloth, and glass trinkets in exchange for bows, spears, headgarb, and pelts, rather than taking what was theirs by right of conquest. In vain was their barbarity concealed, for the next day it was revealed: they refused the young women, looked over everything, dirtied with black scrawlings a beautiful white material which they called paper, picked useless flowers, and finally, horrors! they broke, inside the temple of the 20-headed, 100-limbed God, and replaced it with their own fetish, the representation of a man on a cross, with only one head, bent over and crying.

As for Hemo, the pale devils had taken possession of him as follows. Yet another of their stupidities: able to acquire him for nothing, they paid for him with a magnificent revolver. Having seen him playing in the street with Kaylinkah, they were very much pleased. Why, some wondered, do the white men all have such a passion for d'ginnas? Might they be, with their faces as hairy as the apes, themselves the apes of their own countries? Hemo, no doubt believing so, allowed his legs to be bound, and expressed no anger until they tried to tie his hands together. He fought, screamed, bit, and finally leapt upon Kaylinkah's shoulders, who ran off as fast as she could. The ferns protected them for a while. A white man, losing hope of catching them, took aim, but afraid, lowered his weapon; a Pahouin then took down Kaylinkah with an arrow, took the living d'ginna and exchanged it—see here—for this brand new revolver.

"Vile wretch! it is then you who slaughtered my poor little Kaylinkah!"

"Not exactly. Having fallen near the river with my arrow in her lower back, she cried out for help."

"And you didn't run to her assistance?"

"Why, yes, to retrieve my arrow!"

"And Kaylinkah?"

"What do you expect? She might have remained alive, but crippled. But don't feel bad, she didn't suffer much. She was screaming so loudly that the crocodile soon heard her. One bite took her to her grave. Well now! enough chatting or I'll be reprimanded. Lord, cousin to the king, please grant that I may leave you now. The nobles are astir, and I am the one to cook the stew."

The nervous collapse which tortured Jan for a full hour had, overall, a two-fold benefit: he was cured of his pernicious fever, and a sort of crack opened in his mind through which the remembrance of his difficulties, his aborted work, his vanished glory were lost. He no longer complained of them but in a vague manner, accidentally, as if sympathizing with the misadventures of an old friend. He hiked around, devoured his meals, slept—he the eternal dreamer—12 dreamless hours, silent and only opening his mouth to repeat the last words of the Pahouin who had told him of Kaylinkah's death: "grant that I may leave you now." Akayrawiro, in spite of his indulgent nature, ended up finding his behavior rather dull, and in a spontaneous moment, such as even the most considered of leaders has, he ended up granting him his wish, to the joy of the courtiers, jealous of his friendship with this vile white man, but to the chagrin of the people, who, with their base mundane concerns, were taken with affection for this sort of crazy man who never did them any harm, protected them from soldiers, and babysat the infants whose parents were off in the fields or hunting.

CHAPTER X

With his luggage packed, a notebook and a few fruits wrapped in a kerchief at the end of a stick, Jan Maas tied on his bark leggings, and left with an air of resignation; the good king, regretting his quick decision to leave, forced him to accept an escort of ten sturdy men, veterans of extended expeditions, who knew how to prepare for such things.

Half a league away, to these warriors were added another 30, encountered along the road where they were working off their taxes. In vain did Jan object to their accompanying them; with their sickles they hewed a sort of shield upon which they hoisted him with a portion of his luggage, handed him a fern-frond parasol, and took him away at a brisk pace.

The pleasure of being useful was not their only motivation. The explorers who had taken Hemo had preceded them along this same road, tearing asunder obstacles. The fiercest of regions, terrified, would open up their gates, chicken coops, and silos at the approach of this second caravan, which they thought was a continuation of the first. Jan, on his throne, appeared as a bold white chieftain. Happily taking advantage of the circumstances, the Pahouins, to better abuse the neighboring tribes, spoke with authority, ravaged crops, torched villages and raped women; and if Jan, shaking off his torpor tried to calm them down, they answered the inhabitants' pleas by saying that the pale-faced chief was ordering them to ravage, burn and rape even more. At each stop, a fresh orgy, and those taken from each location, in turn, joined the takers in the next day's skullduggery.

Jan threatened the killers with his rifle; they might well have strangled him and thrown him to the crocodiles, but his presence among them was their safeguard, his pale face the flag before which all disagreements were silenced, any attempt at defending a village or hint of revolt was brought to its knees. They contented themselves with shrugging their shoulders at his reprimands, whistling derisively at his morals, and grating into his soup bark of the icaja bush, whose strange narcotic effect kept him in a mummy's sleep for several consecutive days. Once, the dose being too large, the poison had the opposite effect; instead of falling asleep, the poor Jan, shaken by a terrible drunken frenzy, rushed among the dancers and behaved so lewdly that, though at first amused, they quickly found his behavior more embarrassing than when free of drugs and enjoining them to behave sensibly.

Bakalay, Fawn, Bulu, Shaykiany, and Mpongos augmented the numbers of the troop by some ten-fold, creating a great moving horde, stretched out helter-shelter, blazing tangled trails through the old growth forest. The stragglers and laggards had not finished sacking one place, when those in the lead were already receiving gifts from the next village, the inhabitants having run out to meet them in the hope of buying themselves off from being pillaged. Jan no longer left his litter. The clever Pahouins kept him prisoner within it, served him, prostrated themselves to him like priests before an idol, and, in order to maintain the preeminence of their companions, boasted of his strength, declaring him to be a powerful missionary from the white civilization, who had chosen their tribe as allies, and did not deign to entertain a direct interchange with them.

Day by shortened day the dark bacchanal nonetheless advanced, finally reaching the estuary of the Gabon. The river dwellers, less gullible given their frequent contact and traffic with Europeans, smelled a rat, searched the litter and unmasked the leader. Finding the one they thought so fearsome in such a pitiful state, the Bakalay understood that they had been duped by the Pahouins; the ancient hatred was rekindled and argument then fighting broke out, which opportunity Jan availed himself of to escape from his protectors.

On the shore of the river widened into a sea inlet, he came down from the awful Calvary which he had climbed upon his arrival in Africa. Already alone back then, carrying munitions, his cartridge belt, his coat, a well-stocked pharmacy, bearing weapons and especially having faith in his work, confidence in the future drawing him forward, insensitive to the cruelest agonies, laughing at the greatest dangers, certain that the hour of his death would not toll until he had accomplished his mission. Comparatively speaking, he was now sick, worn out, had lost everything, and though still disdainful of the savages, the beasts and the climate, it was because he was getting farther from his goal, returning to the disgust of a mundane life, and he knew that the tomb was never ready for the poor cowards who pined for it like him, for they had been left with only one certainty: that of the ultimate mercy of death.

And in a sign of ultimate derision he saw the Nature which surrounded him stricken with the very death he sought in vain. The mangrove zone: neither breeze nor sunbeam penetrated the immutable night of the motionless coppery green canopy. Beneath its prop roots, hideous black crabs stirred the mulch like a horde of monstrous spiders. In the steamy air the slightest noise reverberated as through a solid medium, and when they disturbed one of the rare nests in the branches, the raucous, lugubrious, strangely extended cry of the turaco sounded like an invisible finger tearing the thick shroud of fog. He ate the crabs and the filthy oysters stuck on the rotting roots which emerged from the waters. Having fallen into a bottomless marsh, he hoped at last to never rise again, when the nuns of a nearby French convent, spying him from the dugout in which they were fishing, paddled from midstream towards him. Their devotion, their practical experience in treating the fevers prevalent in the region quickly rid him of his symptoms. He thanked them in their tongue, which he re-membered from his youth at the side of the old Parisian pain-ter who had taken up residence in Haarlem, and these good folk, thinking they had saved a countryman were all that much happier. They continued to lend him a hand even when, unde-ceiving them, he confessed part of the truth, that he was Dutch and a naturalist, but keeping quiet with respect to his experi-ments on animal hybridization. His severely compromised health precluding his further stay among them, their superior paid his way on a mail-ship headed for Marseilles. From France it would be easy for him to get home.

After Port Gabon[13] the ship put in at Saint Louis.[14] Jan remained aboard, keeping to himself for the entire crossing. As silent and isolated in the dining room as in his cabin, his favorite spot was a corner of the between-deck lounge; with his elbow on the back of a bench, he could follow, through the narrow opening of the portholes, the ever changing passage of the coastline, now near, now distant. What he saw of it in this manner sufficed, he neither shifted his head to follow a partic-ular point beginning to disappear to the rear, nor tried to antic-ipate what new shores would present themselves towards the front. In front of the Bay of Arguin,[15] a group to whom an English tourist, as voluble as the English are when they wish to be, was telling of the wreck of the *Medusa*, rushed onto the bridge to sound the horizon open with their glasses, and a Pa-risian clapped as if, in his sights, he had rediscovered the magnificence of Jericho. Jan stayed put. At the edge of the great desert, which began at the White Cape, the more placid, the curious, driven to distraction by the monotony of the show on the right, lost themselves on the other side in a contempla-tion of the immensity of the open sea, awestruck as if they could breathe the heady aromas of the West Indies and Mex-ico. Still at his porthole, he took pleasure in his solitude. These

---

[13] Port-Gentil, Gabon. [Ed.]
[14] Coast of Senegal. [Ed.]
[15] Banc d'Arguin, Mauritania. [Ed.]

300 leagues of unchanging cliffs lulled him into a soothing forgetfulness from which he seldom awoke, except to envy the land spread out behind the endless rocky ramparts: the bare Sahara, almost as lifeless as a lunar landscape, flatter than the ocean, without a wisp of grass, without a sound, without movement save for the tigering of its surface by a cloud as it moved in from offshore, and having barely made an appearance, dissipated in the vast shimmering of a mirage. He would like to walk there. In the silence he would be free to proclaim his despair. Or better yet, no! he would not trace even the narrowest of furrows for his bed, he would lay down upon it, his face up, eyes wide: it would not be enough for all this sun to eat away at his retinas, to search his chest, to dry his tears and warm his anguish; not enough of all this death to symbolize the one he felt in his soul. At Cape Noon, a milestone the ancient navigators had not crossed, he sighed a goodbye to the last of the granite upon which the ceaseless surf of the waves struck. But his imagination, once again free to roam, was his solace. Beyond the slim past of the Babylons, Memphises and Troys, whose histories did not appear much different to him than the stories told in yesterday's big city newspapers, he followed the geological eras back, and turning towards the ocean, looked for the Atlantis of Tertiary times which cemented together two worlds and carried a torrent of silt in huge rivers whose deltas one could recognize in Spain by the very thickness of their silt deposits.

A few days later, in the small Marseille hotel where he waited for the money he had requested from his relatives in Haarlem to finish his trip, he continued to daydream in this manner in his room beneath the roof. At night, the street which narrowed between the double row of whitewashed facades became a chalky ravine upon whose cliffs, in a long ago epoch, he dwelt; the tramway passing below, its two large headlights lit, was a mastodon with huge eyes; and if the car stopped to let off a passenger, he imagined the animal crouching, ridding himself of one or another of its excrements, which hardened into coprolites in the ensuing centuries, enough for the scientists to reconstruct the intestines, the stomach, the teeth, the head, and finally the entire original creature.

Having received his money, his clothing purchased, he went to the railway station. An employee showed him, upon his humble request, to a car which would not be too full and wherein one could be comfortable. Only one other passenger, but what a passenger! what luggage! Jan could well push himself into a corner and pretend to sleep, but the packages overflowed onto his knees, pressed into his hip, and their owner forced him to listen to his adventures, the battles he had recently fought with the lions of the Atlas range. Bing! bang! the rifle shots, the roars of the injured beasts, marvelous stalking in the dead of night, the leaps, the battles, the horrors of thirst in a dried up *wadi*[16] transformed into thickets of cacti and gladioli, whose spines were like darts and edges like sabers. Jan heard, saw everything, suffocating, barely occupying a quarter of the space in the corner of the compartment, where the frightening gestures with which the intrepid hunter accompanied his no less frightening accounts, pushed him, brought him to bay, flattened him.

"So friend, where are you coming from, yourself?"

Directly interrogated, Jan, who had remained silent throughout, was forced to answer.

"From Gabon."

"From Gabon! And this is all you are bringing back?" With a laugh that could crack the window had they been up, the friend weighed with his hand, dangling from the nail of his little finger, the kerchief which bore the entirety of Jan's possessions, a spare shirt given to him by the nuns in Libreville. Jan, embarrassed, picked up his pitiful bundle and sat upon it to hide it. The Provencal, a good man in spite of his bragging, fearing he had hurt his feelings, ended his playfulness and adding "my good mans" one after another, took up once again his bing! bangs! and exuberant mimicry. Jan's ears were buzzing, the blood was going to burst forth under the din of this

---

[16] The Arabic word for valley or dry riverbed. [Ed.]

voice wherein the death rattle of lions, which it had provoked, rumbled. At this moment the conductor announced: "Tarascon, Tarascon!" The mad hunter, having reached his destination, ran to the carriage door, into the arms of all of Tarascon's delirious citizenry, who, clapping excessively, awaited his return.

"Hurrah for Tartarin! Hurrah for the lion slayer! Hurrah for Tartarin of Tarascon!"[17]

Tartarin, for it was Tartarin, the immortal Tartarin of Tarascon, was hard pressed to escape the crowd's enthusiasm, pulling out pell-mell his packages into the right of way, giving Jan an embrace, saying goodbye to him as if he were an old friend. Would they ever see each other again? Alas! Who knows? Back in his native lodgings only long enough to equip himself with new weapons, Tartarin would soon get back in the car, but this time to go poke his rifle at the terrible bear of the polar ice, the monstrous polar plantigrade, in Switzerland.[18]

Paris, Brussels, and Jan finally breathed in the peaty smell of the polders. Even though it was December, the red cows, their long horns smoothly curving with their tips to the front were still in pasture, excited by the cold, and looking even more gluttonous than in the summer, as if the light sleet spangling the grass blades was dusting them with sugar. Against the background of the sky, which seldom changed in any season, the same brownish mists still drifted about, rounded smooth by such high altitude winds, that the windmill vanes deployed everywhere seemed only to capture their lost

---

[17] Alphonse Daudet. *Les Aventures prodigieuses de Tartarin de Tarascon.* Paris: Dentu, 1872. Alphonse Daudet (1840-1897), a French novelist aligned, though not without tension, to the naturalist school. Tartarin of Tarascon was a naïve and boastful character appearing in three of his burlesque novels. [Ed.]

[18] Alphonse Daudet. *Tartarin sur les Alpes. Nouveaux Exploits du Heros Tarasconnais* (1885).

wisps and then turn backwards. In the canals the long, flat barges, the *trekschuiten*, harnessed to a horse, still made their slow way, barely rippling the dark and ever sleepy waters. On the level rails the same solid cars rolled smoothly on, filled with smokers, but where not a single traveler tapped the ash from his cigar anywhere but in the small wooden box, nailed for that very purpose to the lower portion of the window frame.

"Haarlem! Haarlem!" In front of the station three cabs were lined up, their three drivers solemnly aligned in a row, offering themselves to the occasional tourist. Along the streets the children were playing, and Jan, who walked alone, having forgotten to warn them of the time of his arrival, shivered for the first time in a long while and hastened his sleepwalker's steps, believing he recognized in certain of the childrens' cries, an echo of Hemo's rowdiness.

He headed to the closest place, Saskia's home.

Martin Heltzius' store was open and merchandise over-flowed from all its shelves, but it was free of any customers or boss. He knocked, he rang. A five to six year old child, his fingers red from cold, ran up from the garden where the children made up two opposing sides and bombarded each other with snowballs.

"Do you wish to buy something sir?"

"Are you then the salesperson, son?"

"Oh! No, sir, I just keep an eye on the store. If it's to buy something I'll go and get my dad or uncle Adrian at the Brinckleymann café. I say my uncle, but he isn't really, he's my grandmother's husband, but not my grandfather either. I call him my uncle Adrian, because I love him very much."

"And your mother?"

"Mommy is at the church, praying for another uncle whom I don't know, who will be back one of these days from...from...I don't know, from far, far away."

"Do you not know this other uncle's name?"

"Why yes! He is my uncle Jan. And mother wanted to name me after him. My name is Jan too."

111

Jan cried. Given his two large teardrops, his leanness, his arched back, his bundle, his leggings, his walking stick, his pathetic exterior, the child, moved by a certain thought, asked if he had come to beg for alms. Indeed, his mother was not in, but she always gave to the destitute, and he could give in her stead. And drawing a copper piece from his pocket, shiny from having been rubbed by the marbles he kept there, he extended it to him, timid for not having more.

"Here my good man, don't worry, my mother will give it back to me."

Jan hugged and thanked him. No, he was not begging for charity, or at least not for money. Let him tell his mother and father that a friend wished to speak with them, nothing more, a friend who has been far, far away.

The child was already trotting off towards the café, when he changed his mind. One could read on his worried features his parents' injunction to not go far from the store, and his hesitation at leaving the stranger there alone. Looking him over once again, with one of those childlike gazes which skim over the surface of things yet nonetheless unravel their thread, appearances and posturing for the gallery having no hold on their innocence, and trusting the tender meekness of his features, he ran off again, this time for good.

Jan's hand, resting on the counter, touched a newspaper. He picked it up. *The Amsterdam Gazette*, several days old, but still in its wrapper.

Dear sheet! thought Jan who unfolded it unconsciously. He no longer remembered how many years ago, but it was from it that he had learned of the drawing of the Orphan's lottery, and of the fortune which suddenly fell to him. Had he not won the jackpot, what would his life have been? A digit greater or lesser in his ticket's number and he would have stayed, cultivating tulips, his universe limited to his flower beds, D'ginna unknown to him, he would not be beset with that sadness, his memories of Hemo, which might kill him, kill him all the better by burdening him with a secret which he could never rid himself of by speaking of it.

Hemo! Who had whispered the name? Through what strange coincidence had his lips pronounced it, while his eyes read it, no devoured it, on a back page of the *Gazette*? Written as plain as day, almost on every line, here indeed were the two triumphant syllables: Hemo! Hemo! Hemo! He spelt them out, his sight clouded, mumbled them in a choked voice, and suddenly rushed off like a madman from his cell, out of Martin Heltzius' store, returning to the train station, just in time to catch the express to Amsterdam. For there was no doubt. Hemo, D'ginna's son, Kaylinkah's playmate, the native of the Pahouin country, his pupil, and perhaps much more than his mere pupil, was in this city, or at least was on the date on the newspaper, in which he reread over and over again an article entitled: *Peter the Mattress-maker*.

CHAPTER XI

NEWS REPORT FROM THE AMSTERDAM GAZETTE

No more is it *Peter the Mattress-maker* that our headline should read, but *Peter the Assassin*. Last night we were no longer on the theater beat, but at the Assize Court. No longer tearing our white gloves applauding the actors, we have soiled them with blood handling a corpse. Indeed, last night, blood soiled our magnificent Palace of Industry Theater.

Since we are not critiquing a play, but recounting a true crime, there is no need to obey the laws of stage propriety by holding back on the emotional scenes, or delaying the outcome until the end. So then, the outcome, here it is, right away, in all the simplicity of its horror: last night, in the middle of the show, before the eyes of the public, one actor murdered another. For we must not deceive ourselves, this was no accident, it was murder, and premeditated.

I leave it for you to judge.

One will remember that a troop of English pantomimes were making their debut at the *Paleis voor Volksvlijt* a fortnight ago; our dear readers can find the exact date in our newspaper's back issues. We were the first to note this troop's immense success, thanks to a singular act, one of those *great attractions*, well designed, we must admit, to draw a crowd. The main role was held by a young gorilla from Gabon. The leads had also given us a complete rundown on the strange animal, and we will remind you in this regard, that these details were reproduced by a number of our colleagues, without one having the decency to cite the *Gazette*, from whence they had taken them.

Let us then repeat for those who might have forgotten, that this ape had been brought to Europe by one of the sailors who had escorted Sir Thomas Stayel, the illustrious English traveler sent to Africa by the Society for the Abolition of the Slave Trade. Jonathan Doyce—such was the sailor's name—with a broken revolver which was no longer good for anything, had bought him near the sources of the Como, one of the upper affluents of the great Gabon River which flows into the Atlantic just above Senegal, from some Pahouin savages in whose village, if one can term a jumble of noisome huts a village, it lived a domesticated existence.

Had these Pahouins been raising this young quadrumanous beast so they could devour it, rather than their own children, in leaner days? This would seem to be the case. Farther upstream, Sir Thomas Stayel had discovered hideous mounds of cooking wastes, which the pen refuses itself to describe, within which the bones of men and chimpanzees putrefied together. Alas, how slowly does barbarism retreat before civilization! How many more lives like that of Sir Stayel, entirely devoted to progress, will be needed to bring light to the very confines of the world where the deepest darkness reigns! *That is the question*, we shall, along with the illustrious explorer, repeat in the language of Shakespeare and Byron.

We know that France exerts her protectorate over those regions of Gabon where the gorilla's habitat is situated. Nonetheless, the Paris Natural History Museum only owns one specimen...stuffed. Hence did it try to acquire the one it knew to be in the possession of the English sailor. Jonathan Doyce would consent to part with it, but—who would blame him—in drawing the greatest profit possible. Unfortunately for the Paris Museum, the budget with which it operates did not allow it, in these circumstances, to compete with the circus owners, and the ape was finally awarded to some English clowns, who, his education completed, undertook a tour of all the great cities of the continent with him. Having disembarked in Antwerp, they had already drawn applause from Belgium, when they made their debut in Amsterdam.

Hemo, such is the name of this unique actor, the same name he bore among the savages, however that may be, the name, given first billing on the posters displayed at the *Paleis voor Volkslijt*, sold out the hall every night. We have analyzed, in this very column, the pantomime he played. We stated that it was what one might suppose such a thing should be: an excuse for extraordinary gambols.

Pierrot the Mattress-maker, such was the title.

Hemo, that is the ape, included in his role as Pierrot the functions of mattress-maker and of Colombine's husband. Colombine was played by the ravishing Miss Betty. The Harlequin with whom, as always, she always hoodwinked Pierrot, was William Ochter, the most stunning clown, bar none, to ever have donned the traditional and elegant red and black diamond-patterned costume. As soon as Pierrot's back was turned, he came to laugh and frolic with his mistress, drink and eat with her Pierrot's wine and paté. The latter quickly guessed what was going on between them. He watched them, caught them, and threatened Harlequin, who answered him with a hail of blows using a washerwoman's beater.

Pierrot locked up his wife. While he worked on one side of the stage, one could see her pining in the lonely house which filled the other side. He combed out his mattresses; when they were finished, he rolled them up, tied them up and brought them inside; Harlequin slipped into one of them, after having distracted him with a call from offstage; completely unawares he brought him into his shop, such that the two lov-

115

ers, Harlequin having quickly left his hiding spot, caressed each other on the mattress prepared and brought in by the poor husband.

Upon hearing their kisses, Pierrot caught them again. This time there was a mad chase, such an emulation of grimaces, of contortions, of tumbling between Harlequin and Pierrot, that one could no longer tell, between the two, who was the ape and who was the man. They scuffled about on the second floor of the house, in the trees in the yard, on the roof; they tumbled down from prodigious heights, turning several times upon themselves, and bounding off faster than ever.

Harlequin finally escaped, and Pierrot, aching all over, limping, pondered, trying to figure out how he had gotten into his store, sounding the walls, checking the shutters, the door, with the bewilderment of a screamingly funny grotesque. Upon seeing the untied mattress amongst the others, he blinked and tapped his brow with his finger to indicate that he had understood. In the following act, when Harlequin was sneaking his way in again, he pretended not to notice anything, but, once the mattress was rolled up and tied, rather than dragging it into his home with the others, he drew it up to the bottom of a tree, and ran him through with several thrusts of a sword. The trick was simple, but very cleverly executed; Harlequin as one will have guessed, had disappeared through a trap door in the flooring; bladders of dark red wine designed to be burst open by the sword bubbled forth a stream of blood, and Pierrot would smear his whiteface with it in one of those exaggerations typical of the English stage, which, as we know, never holds back from presenting the public with the most trivial and repugnant reality. Harlequin, offstage, imitated the cries of a pig being slaughtered; as in the best developed of melodramas, the women were all atremble. Not yet appeased, Pierrot took up the bloody mattress and like a reaper might his wheat, he beat it mercilessly, sat on it, trampled on it, and finally unrolled it to admire his work, to wallow in his vengeance.

From the basement, Harlequin had slipped in his place in the mattress a flattened, life size portrait of himself painted on an inflatable gold-beater's skin. The crowd was in stitches. Colombine, drawn by the joyful cries of her fierce husband, was almost unconscious as she tenderly ran her fingers over her lover, reduced to a pancake. So when policemen passed through at the rear of the stage, she ran after them to denounce the crime.

Having remained alone, poor Pierrot began to shake, seeing himself judged, convicted and hung, and previewing the noose about his neck, he kicked about, croaked, his tongue drawn out by the sudden jerk of an irremediable snap. But suddenly his face changed, a glimmer of malice came over it; he loosened the slipknot which he imagined was already about his neck, sighed deeply like one asphyxiated now reborn to life, ran home, came back out with something hidden under his smock, and having made sure he was alone, he raised it in triumph. A bellows! It was a bellows of which he fitted the nozzle in the nose, the mouth, the ears, even in the lower back of the inflatable man, with such a drollness of motions that it covered for what was the rather risqué nature of the last joke. There were indeed a few shocked "oh! oh!," but these were quickly drowned out by the laughter upon seeing the inflatable figure growing round, its arms and legs spreading apart, and Pierrot putting it back into the mattress with endless precautions so as not to deflate it. When the police officers, led by a Colombine in tears, proceeded to investigate, it was, of course, the real Harlequin who, back in place, rose up better than ever, between the two spouses whose amazements during the proceedings, were equal but pleasantly contradictory: the wife, thrilled, the husband dumbfounded. Harlequin showed the police officers his close-fitting vest pierced by the sword; and Pierrot, handcuffed, was taken away, but not fast enough for him not to see his supposed victim and his unfaithful Colombine pay out to one another their arrears in kisses.

From this pantomime like unto so many others, the gorilla created a strange work of art through the intense expression of his features, and his frantic capers. Let us cut to the quick. As much as our readers have had a hunch, so we are certain: it was in the act where Pierrot runs through the mattress with the sword that the murder occurred.

The crowd, gayer, and more tumultuous, was packed into the hall even more densely than on the previous nights. Let the reader forgive us a word of backstage slang: it *gave* itself wholeheartedly to the actor.

Pierrot, the Ape, Hemo to give him his true name, had never shown such verve. A single one of his leaps took him right across the scenery; he shouted like Othello, the first time he discovered Harlequin, and looked at him as if he wished to devour him: one could hear his fangs grating. The waves of applause followed one upon the other without end. Given the meager week in the theaters, nothing drawing us elsewhere, we had come to occupy our seat for a second time. We can say: "I was there." Thus, we were approaching the scene with Harlequin in the mattress.

"The business scene," such as the illustrious Parisian speaker who deigned to honor us with his remarks, if we daren't say his friendship, during his recent trip to our beloved Amsterdam on the occasion of the Exposition—M. Francis Quarcey—does indeed thus qualify as the most important scene, the scene where the intrigue is knit. We know that his theories on the theater have contributed to him being categorized among the master writers of his country, at least as much as his *Le Roi des Dunes*, that marvelous novel which ignorant and jealous reviewers (these alas can only be found in Paris!) said was plagiarized from *Rolla*, a ridiculous Italian poem. And this reparation is only right, so have we assured ourselves in the numerous, yet all too infrequent conversations which he has allowed us to profit by—we mere pupils—conversations whose recollection remain among the highlights of our already long literary career. For M. Francis Quarcey, whose modesty will be vexed if perchance his eyes come to peruse these few words, joins the tactfulness of a Pascal, to the profundity of a

118

Béranger,[19] and we understand why his countrymen have awarded him the flattering yet deserved name of La Bruyère's[20] grandson.

Those whom, like us, had attended the first show, noticed a few changes in the details, but without attaching any importance to them.

Until now Pierrot had only tied the mattress containing Harlequin in the middle, with a loose piece of twine. Last night, on the contrary, he tied it at both ends, tying it tight, thus creating a huge bolster, solidly sealed at both ends. He believed it to be a complication designed to better conceal the disappearance of the clown and his replacement with the life size inflatable simile. Then, rather than leaning it against a tree, he propped it up at the other end of the stage, near the wall of the house; we supposed that the trap door had been moved. Finally, when he brandished the sword and lanced the mattress with even fiercer blows, and the mattress gave a start as if shaken through the frothing of red blood, we applauded with greater warmth what appeared to us to be an improvement on the old trick. O! fatal error!

Poor William Ochter, the clown, was indeed wrapped up like a dumpling, imprisoned in a sack. It was indeed him, in the flesh, which the sword was relentlessly running through. It was indeed his blood that was flowing. And when, after an uproar, at first indistinct, was heard backstage, came the cries of the entire cast of actors, walk-ons, stage-hands, and firemen, frightened and frantic, completely forgetting to lower the

---

[19] Pierre-Jean de Béranger (1780-1857), a popular songwriter of the time, credited with reviving the French chanson (song) with intelligence and sentiment. [Ed.]

[20] Jean de La Bruyère (1645-1696), French essayist and moralist. The allusion is presumably to the reputation La Bruyère had following the publication of his masterpiece, the harshly satirical study in manners, *Les Caractères* (1688). This work was revered for its sharply poignant style of composite suggestion as opposed to direct expression. [Ed.]

curtain when they unraveled the horrible bedding, it was no longer a mock-corpse, a dead-man-for-laughs which appeared before the speechless and as yet uncomprehending audience, but...

We shall not describe this butchery. We are among those who respect the reader, not of those whose pen takes pleasure in laying out all the gruesome facts of certain events, to dissect the wounds, to count the pustules, to search through revolting remains which no longer bear a name in the speech of good folk.

Harlequin was hiccupping out his agony, and was even more upsetting than the normal figure of someone dying, the painted face's last convulsions loosening the paint, the white of pearl and the rice powder in large flakes.

The crowd, before the curtain finally lowered, was dumb with fright. On the stage, now invisible, the hubbub grew. Suddenly, it ended, and from the room, on the contrary, burst forth a single awful cry.

Hemo, divested of his black headband, of his white shirt with blue tassel buttons, his clown-pants, his laced yellow boots, in a word, of all his Pierrot togs except his floured face, had climbed, with the help of the scenery supports, to the upper rod supporting the curtain, from which he sprang, once again the great wild ape of the old growth forests, toward the top of the room, towards the vault lost in shadow, among the jumble of arches, right-angled joints, iron beams and girders supporting the huge glassed over roof. And through this dizzying escape, which might have seemed a minor episode in such an abominable tragedy, he took with him, holding her to his hairy chest with one arm, who? Colombine, the poor little English actress, miss Betty, unconscious, almost dead, and whose head, the long braids of which she had loosened, and her limbs, all dangled motionless at every leap her fierce abductor made.

The firemen quickly gave up on pursuing him, and the troop director thought better than to bring him down with a pistol shot. Would Miss Betty not likely be killed by the horrible drop that would result from bringing down the assassin? The authorities proceeded with reason by first having the Palace evacuated. All the doors and windows bolted, an entire squad, armed with ropes, planks and ladders took to the chase; a terrible chase, whose outcome the growing, anxious crowd outside awaited. For the story had already spread through all the city. Among the groups of people, comments were exchanged, they generally agreed to lay the blame on the chief of police. What was he thinking, allowing the English pantomimes to have, on stage with them, a supposedly tame beast, but whose true ferocity, alas! was no longer a topic of discussion. Besides, doesn't it seem to you that, recently, our leaders...

CHAPTER XII

As soon as he had finished reading this article, where the editor of the theater beat, flattered to have for once been one step ahead of his colleagues in the field of politics, and seeing his prose rise from the newspaper's back pages to the headline, had filled the four columns of the front page, Jan started reading it again, while unconsciously rocking back to front and then front to back, as children do to hasten the forward and backward motion of a swing.

Night was falling. Standing upright in the middle of the car, he continued his reading under the light. When the train stopped he could not stifle a cry in response to that of the employees calling out "Amsterdam," throwing his ticket at them, jostling the most hurried of travelers, he left the station and headed towards the Palace of Industry.

The box-office was not open. He wandered around the square, reading posters announcing a concert followed by a ball. Prey to a growing apprehension he asked left and right, from police officers and from passersby, who yawned in indifference at his haggard look and choppy speech. In the vestibule of the Palace, a boutique owner informed him that, since the night of the murder, the pantomime show was no longer playing; the administration, under orders, had immediately revoked any contract with the English troop; the morning edition of the *Gazette* had still not reported what had happened to the infamous ape; as for the clowns and dancers, a gentleman can easily get news of the latter—added a smiling old gossip, her hand extended—by visiting the alleyways near the Rokin Canal. Were the gentleman a stranger to the city, she offered to lead him there. He paid her for her information, but refused her company.

Besides, he had no need for a guide; however timid his life as a young man, this had not saved him from hearing, long ago in Haarlem, the old fellows at the Brinckleymann café, sing the praises of the alleyways in question, and to compare them, in joyful whispered confessions, to the Ryddeck in Antwerp.

Kalver-Straat was the busiest street in Amsterdam. Along its two rows of store fronts, the butcher's markets sparkled, their windows without a speck of dust, their hams seemingly of freshly varnished mahogany, the scarlet wrapping of the tongue patés livening up the immaculate whiteness of the pyramids, grottos and rock gardens built of lard; at intervals a café presented a contrast, its first room dark and without any other light upon the curtain which separated it from the restaurant proper than that of the glowing end of cigars upon the lip of smokers preferring this isolation in the shadows to the gaslight and sound of billiards from behind. He made his way up as far as the Dam Plaza, turned around and changed sidewalks, now following that which ran parallel to the Rokin Canal. The boutique owner had been correct in indicating the alleys to him; after a number of coarsely painted and gaudily rigged out chubby-cheeked girls, who insisted on pushing him towards some vague half-open doors at the street corner had embarrassed him, a young woman brushed against him, and whispered in passing: "G'night blondy, you're lookin' good." He recognized in her, notwithstanding the impudent tone of her French, that she was a young Englishwoman.

"You wouldn't happen to be Betty?"

"No, Betty, that ain't me, that's my sis', but it's the same thing."

She slipped her arm under his and drew him towards the canal as she answered him. Both of them, in a tacit agreement, avoided the most frequented places; he felt her trembling against him when they crossed police officers walking their beat or doing sentry duty. On Warmoes St. she stopped him before a darkened passage. At the end a doubtful light trickled down from the first floor, illuminating as best it could, but rather worse than best, a spiral staircase. However, upon their approach a door closed, everything turned black again, and she had to lead him by the hand.

A coal heater gave off an asphyxiating heat. Lighting a candle of which she allowed a few drops to drip on the mantelpiece so as to stick it there, the woman brought the fire back to life with a few kicks to the bars of the grate, then impatient and as if to warm herself up faster, she began to dance, to pirouette on her toes around the table, the only piece of furniture in the narrow room besides an iron cot with sordid bed linens and a chair upon which Jan let himself drop.

After the fog outside, the kiln-like temperature dried up his throat. He was made nauseas by the noxious odor of greasy cooking left over from what one could only surmise had been pastry scraps cooked in beer, mixed with some yet more disgusting odors emanating from the toiletry implements spread out over the floor: soured washbasins of frothing water, jars and vials of rancid pomade and of brilliantine which had lost its bouquet. In short, not having eaten and long consumed by fever, he had to hold his head together with two hands to gather the thoughts he sensed were slipping away. Some old dancers' skirts, in yellow satin decorated with fake pearls and painted-glass jet, unsown and nailed right into the only window's wooden frame, served as drapes, but prevented any air circulation. He wished to open the door on the landing, but the little one refused to do so; some creaking of the floor led him to ask if someone was not spying on them; no, it was nothing, just one of her brothers listening to see if she was home. To reassure him she bolted the door and pulled the bed over against it.

Thin, pale, a rash on her cheeks, coughing, her shoulders drawn together by a bodice of tacky velvet with threadbare braiding, she took up her dance again, paused to look at him, and suddenly unclipped herself, sat on his knees, and tapped him playfully on his cheeks and under his arms. Jan only then realized that she had misunderstood his intentions, and drew back; she thought he did so because of the rather unappealing look of her yellowed undergarments. Embarrassed, her eyes lowered, sighing, coughing harder, almost sobbing, she apologized for her poverty.

Her family had had a string of bad luck. They had spent their advances on their costumes as soon as their engagement at the *Paleis voor Volkslijt* had been confirmed. Such profitable conditions! The premiere, such a success! With her elder sister Betty, they had brought some lovely bargains from Paris, where they were part of the scene on Richelieu Street and at the Royal-Palace, until their parents had called them back to begin this European tour which was to make them rich. What a bizarre dream their father had had to acquire that hideous ape and to have imagined turning him into an actor!

Upon hearing Hemo's name, Jan remembered the object of his visit. He had come to have the whole story told to him, the details published in the *Gazette* being insufficient. First, what had been done with the ape?

A fist pounding and a rough voice shook the door.

"Darlin'!"

"Dad?"

She opened up and debated with a large man on the threshold. Until now she had spoken in French, but now she and her father spoke English. Still, Jan understood them well enough to grasp a few snippets of their conversation, amongst which the word "reporter" was frequently repeated. The man came in: a sort of monstrous dwarf whose strength must have been Herculean, wider than tall, gap-toothed, shaved, with reddish brown brush-cut hair resembling a calfskin skull-cap, with jowls hanging to his shoulder blades, mutton chop hands, and feet so wide, beneath his spindly legs and knock-knees, that one would have thought them to be webbed. His moleskin vest thrown on with nothing underneath so constricted his chest that his flesh protruded out in great rolls from between the buttons. Even had he not been staggering, his face and small, bloodshot eyes would have been sufficient indication of his inebriated state. In a stupor, grumbling at the tiresome task of having to answer the reporters' endless questions and repeating the story over and over again, he muttered to Jan, whose thinness and clothing he disdainfully measured up, that he should have at least come to him, the troop's director, and not waste the time of his lazy daughters, who needed no encouragement to loiter about. Jan offered him, awkwardly, as he feared offending him, a ten florin gold piece. It disappeared by sleight of hand and the dwarf, his features and words softened, asked Jan to join him in the adjoining room, the current one being his daughters'.

Barely larger, this second room only received the false light from a peephole in the partition of the hallway during the day. But right now a kerosene lamp was hanging from the ceiling by a wire. The empty chimney had, in lieu of a wind screen, a piece of packing cloth held on the mantel by a rudimentary kitchen utensil, plates, bottles, rusted pots, in one of which a bottle stood upright, allowing some hard liquor to seep out of its cracked bottom. A narrow cast iron stove, with a long, elbowed chimney pipe, roared red hot, supporting a large pot of potatoes. On the cots, piles of rags which were children were stirring; the mother in the middle of them was feeding the smallest whose irritation at vainly suckling on the flaccid breast was rising; a skeletal boy in a clown suit was standing reading beneath the lamp. The reek, the heat, the thickness of the sweat and fetid breaths were such that Jan,

125

inured to the Pahouins' huts, nonetheless leaned on a wall so as not to collapse.

His tongue loosened by a full cup of liquor drawn directly from the pot on the mantelpiece and swallowed in one gulp, the director, having chased away with his foot, as one would a nest of vermin, the infants on one cot, lowered himself into a weightlifter's squat, invited Jan to join him and lamented his dog's life, past, present, and future.

In order to provide for his needs and those of his family, he only had his take as a mountebank lifting weights on the street. On a rainy day, no curious folk out, not a penny in his cup, he had considered, rather than coming home to clamors of hunger, to take a header into the Thames. The posting of an advertisement for the sale of a young gorilla by a sailor back from Gabon, gave him a brilliant idea, which a large sum, wired for and received two days later from his eldest daughters, dancers in Paris, allowed him to accomplish. He bought the animal, a bit dearer than he might have liked because of an agent of the Paris Museum who kept outbidding him thinking he could compete with the purse of an English entertainer.

As much as Jan insisted on knowing immediately of Hemo's whereabouts, the director kept drinking shot after shot and rattling off his clap-trap story, an arranged translation which he spouted between pauses. Once, however, he interrupted himself. His "Darlin'," right in front of him, was warming her hands by the stovepipe, but he had not yet taken notice of her. Brandishing his fist at her, he asked her what she was doing there.

"I'm a-warmin' meself," she answered, completely indifferent to his threat. His fist striking her on the back with a hollow thud, she did not move any more than before. The father said nothing, but forcing her to stumble down the stairs under a hail of blows, sent her to her job on the street. The door having barely closed, the girl came back in, just as calm as ever, looked for her mantle on the cots, slapped one of her little brothers who was curled up in it, then leaving it to him, went back to the landing, when a bout of coughing bent her in half so violently that Jan interceded on her behalf.

"Stay Darlin', the man's done changed his mind."

At Jan's gesture of denial, she sighed, disappointed, having for a minute hoped she could stay warm. The father, moved to pity, comforted her with a glass of liquor. She drank it and left, resigned, while he described how Hemo had been trained. Skilful in the training of all sorts, this was his proudest achievement; he named and boasted of each progressive phase with an abundance of technical terms. Jan, getting carried away, asked him to make it short; then, paralyzed at the fear of giving away his secret, he resolved to shut up and listen; in all the verbiage he would manage to sort out the truths which would be of use to him.

"Listen to me, as fer tellin' ya where the ape's at, I dunno, or rather I ain't sure. Prob'ly at the Zoological Gardens."

Jan suddenly lit up and got up to run off there, when the other convinced him otherwise. "Dammit, hold up a minute!" He missed having company. Besides, the displays were closed until the next morning, but Betty would be back any minute now, and she would have had some news during the day which she would be happy to pass on to him. While he waited, if he wished, he could read the proof that the ape was taken among the savages, Pancks will lend him the book. At these words the clown handed him a book, whose illustrated pages he flipped through. It was the authentic account of Sir Thomas Stayel's voyage. Understanding written English better than spoken English, Jan found the passage where the author related in a few lines, with the man of action's disdain for long exposition, his meeting of a young tame gorilla living in king Akayrawiro's capital; he tried to tie him up, a little savage girl freed him and ran off with him. He hesitated to use his rifle, given his membership, one he bore most proudly, to the Society for the Protection of Animals, fearful of injuring the ape and only wishing to bring down the thief. While he mulled it over, a savage, promised a gift, aimed, so skilled with his bow that he transfixed the black girl through and through, without

127

even grazing the creature sitting piggy-backed on her shoulders.

Had Jan been harboring the slightest suspicions, the concordance between this account and that which he had formerly heard from the very mouths of the Pahouins', dispelled them. It was only out of curiosity that he waited for Betty, to meet someone so intimately involved in Hemo's melancholy adventure. Steps made the stairs creek. A rough voice swore in the darkness, that of a man Betty was bringing to the room with the iron cot. The father prayed that Jan would be patient a bit longer, then went and scratched at the door, a discrete and agreed upon signal to have the girl speed things up. The man, to which she wished a good night, left her and stumbled down the stairs. She came in, handed over a wad of cash to her father, who presented Jan to her as a generous journalist who wished to ask her some questions. She exclaimed with a tired shrug.

"Well damn it! this is turning into such a bore."

With such a clear command of French, she was able to explain how she had acquitted herself of the mission of gathering information her father had entrusted her with. The police were considering whether Hemo should be tried as a common murderer! Here was a lovely chance at ridicule that few would pass up, she was surprised when they did not persevere. Seats at the trial could sell for more than they did at the theater. Without being snoopy, she would give her eye teeth to be there on the day the judgment was handed down, to watch Hemo, the accused, surveying the magistrates. As intelligent, good looking and strong as he was, and they as ugly as they were, one could bet that Hemo would take them for some inferior brothers, apes like him, but of some degenerate species.

In short, he was in the Zoological Gardens, chained and hidden away, but as soon as the public's memory of the dramatic events died down, as soon as one no longer feared a public outcry, he would be afforded the relative liberty of a large cage. They, for now, should relax; a secretary, a charming boy whom a common friend had introduced to her, had received her in private audience, and would forward them a large sum in compensation, which the father could cash in at the central administration.

At this outcome, though expected, they were overcome with joy. The clown danced a jig, the kids on the bedrolls squawked their hoarse cheers, and the one that was suckling on empty purred in hope as his mother switched him to another breast. Darlin', back in haste, completed the scene. She was out of breath. She had dragged into the dark alleyway a police constable, whom she had thought to be a john. He would have arrested her had she not slipped through his fingers. In Paris, in such a case, one could scream and put up a fight, and passersby, who were always on your side, would berate the officer and force him to let you go. By comparison, here people were so stupidly thick that one wondered if they would not side with the police.

The father comforted her with a kiss on her brow, and to celebrate the entire family being reunited, promised to buy a seed-cake, if Jan would consent to buying a few bottles of pale ale; the café on the corner sold some that was excellent. Jan accepted and emptied out his pocket, happy to be able to chat with Hemo's last friend.

Betty was only too glad, having been mistaken as to the interest she had aroused. Half laying on a mattress, her head held up by a plaid rolled up as a bolster, her legs stretched out and her feet leaning high up on the stove pipe, she confessed, between puffs on her cigarette, to things which she had heretofore kept secret.

The clown's murder did not surprise her, actually she had almost been expecting it; and if she only admitted it now, it was that the case having been closed she no longer feared that she would be harassed, or that her admission could be used against her, to accuse her of not having done anything to prevent the calamity which she suspected would occur. It was unbelievable, but a reporter—is that not the case?—was used to hearing all sorts of things. Well then, the truth: the ape was in love with her, and jealous of the clown.

Like an actress or an orator who has uttered some powerful lines and listens for the crowd's response, she paused. A shudder or a murmur of indignation would have pleasantly tickled her perverse fancy. But Jan, after the painful alternatives of his suppositions regarding Hemo's origins, did not even give a start. Betty, disconcerted, wondered if she had a common man or a refined one with peculiar tastes on her hands, put her elbows on Jan's knees, to better gauge his impassiveness, and in a pique of self-esteem, in an effort to compete professionally, continued, giving greater detail to her story, particularly upon hearing her younger sister needle her that she was wasting her breath.

In her opinion, her father's pride in Hemo's education was not legitimate. Only she managed to win him over, for the poor beast was simply going to kick the bucket before she began to nurse him. Blows, caresses, even holding back his food left him indifferent; always shivering with cold, he would stay entire days motionless and silent on the bench which had been built for him over the stove, not even pulling up the covers which were placed on his back. His lips and around his eyes paled, his four little hands grown thin, he pulled his hair out like a mangy dog, panting feebly; a veterinarian whom they had consulted did not require a long exam to draw his diagnosis and predict his coming demise; Hemo, apparently was becoming consumptive, like most animals of his species transplanted to Europe. He was beginning, besides, to cough in little dry bursts, such as, you see, seldom leave Darlin', our little daughter whom the doctors say is seized with a similar sickness.

Thankfully she immediately took a liking to him. Curled up, his chin on his knees, sitting up in spite of the most blazing fire, or during his fits, his chest with sunken ribs bulging out, his mouth agape in an attempt to draw in the air he was missing. He drew close to her, came down from his shelf and held his arms out as he watched her. Tired of rolling on the carpet, in a gesture easily understood in thirsty children, he pointed at his nurse's bosom. She picked him up under the arms and led him playfully around the room. Just like a wheedling child, he held on to her, crossing his hands on her shoulder, placing his cheek against hers, his eyes half-closed in contentment, and jumping on the bent arm with which she supported him at the least lagging in his walkabout. Such a great sadness would then overcome her, so that she reproached herself for being strict with him, and this would fade until sleep loosened him from her neck.

He recovered.

The father's training scarcely went beyond the typical tricks which the circus riders taught the lowliest of carnies: being drawn apart between the top of two ladders, archery, cup and ball, dominoes, gun play, sword play with sabers and bayonet. It was she, more ambitious, who imagined trying to turn him into an actor. One of her lovers altered, according to her directions, the script of an old pantomime play. The other players required were recruited, the troop organized, her student, as early as the first rehearsal, knew his role better than anyone else, but then also showed himself to be more jealous than the stupidest of men. Everyone laughed about it, including William Ochter, the object of this jealousy. Only she worried about it, and then only to herself; she would also get angry if anyone brought it up in front of her. Did they take her to be a she-ape?

This William, her lover in the play, had become so in private. Not that they loved each other, but it was difficult to live together as they did without such a thing happening. Besides, the men, the poor devils, made so little; they would be rather penny-pinching, would they not, to refuse them what they could not buy elsewhere? Will, a very good-looking boy, was a great favorite of the young ladies of the casinos and skating parties; quite intelligent, he kept himself for a better match, and would only stand still on stage for the opera-glasses of the wealthy bourgeois women. He reasoned correctly: these were the most generous, but they demanded that their favorite not run around. In sleeping with him, they simply acted as good friends; they allowed him to wait, without risking his health with the streetwalkers, so that what filled his tights could be appreciated by some honest women.

Whatever the case, Hemo was jealous.

And to do as much as confess, she admitted to be deserving of a few reprimands. Since everybody laughed about this jealousy, she, who didn't laugh about it, should have been more careful. But see! Even the best take pleasure in having a man languish; who in her place would have resisted, especially when the man languishing was an ape. The joke was so funny! If she kissed William, Hemo closed his eyes as if not to see her, and, as if he could not control himself, growled, blew out hard, tugged on her skirt, and made faces that would put a smile on a coroner. If William kissed her it was much worse, he no longer growled, he threw himself against him, pushed him away, and ended up grinding his teeth, to the point of making him retreat. "Filthy creature!" stormed William, ending his caresses. Once when he left her open-mouthed, waiting in vain for his kiss, in jest she took an angry tone. "Let Harlequin go to the Devil, he doesn't know how to protect Colombine." It was stupid, but it nonetheless vexed the clown, who came up to her and took her in his arms. Pretending to be fighting him off, she called for help. Hemo then leapt on the poor man, knocked him over, and stomped on him so violently, that she was forced to order him to let go, and repeat the command several times and even strike him, he who would usually obey her least signal. Will then wished to take vengeance upon him, to kill his...indeed, yes, his rival; she calmed him down and made a solemn promise never to play that game again.

All of this, already somewhat bizarre, became altogether so on a certain morning, or rather a certain afternoon. Some men had taken herself and her sister out the night before to dinner, and had kept them out until breakfast the next morning. Darlin' having something to do in town, she had gone home alone. Will gone, with the whole household, for a walk, the house was empty except for Hemo. She stoked up the fire, and very tired, she went to bed. The night's champagne and truffles, and especially her beau, a very nice beau, but older, had gotten her all excited. She tossed in her sleep, the sheets fell away, she felt herself kissed, snuffled, on her eyes, her lips, her breasts. She knew she was not dreaming of the older man, his kisses were too different. Wonderful in their awkwardness, she guessed in them a well-built cherubim fearful of pushing things too far, the poor innocent one, and so as not to trouble him or further intimidate him, she kept still, and even though she was awake she kept her eyes closed, almost. All of sudden, a storm broke, that stupid William tore Hemo from the bed like an idiot, and where, at first, she was disconcerted, she was then convulsed with laughter, until she had to jump down to separate them, for they were giving themselves up to a genuine duel, the brave ape opposing his fangs and nails to the brutal clown's knife. From that day forward, Harlequin watched Pierrot as much as Pierrot watched Harlequin. To maintain the peace she had to avoid both of them. But the theater drew them together. The crowds would have had to be awfully dumb not to notice that the ape and the clown, Pierrot and Harlequin, were not playing a part, but really despised each other, throwing each other around in earnest, and that the screams which escaped her were not all in feigned fear.

The newspapers, seeing an easy story, only scrutinized the details of the murder, not of their background.

Betty, her throat dry after such a long tale, nonetheless added an account of her memorable vaulting, in the gorilla's arms, through the rafters of the Palace of Industry. She would remember it all her life. The newspapers say she had fainted. She had when he grabbed her and launched himself upward, but soon reawakened and immediately understood that she was running no risk. He held her so tightly, yet so tenderly on his vast hairy chest that during the wildest leaps she thought herself merely swinging from a richly appointed hammock, elastically woven in horsehair. He kissed her ears with such heated breath that she still wonders whether he was not then, in his language and with his ape's tongue, whispering words of love to her. And when, cornered by 20 firemen, stagehands,

133

soldiers, pursuing him with a forest of poles, stakes, ladders and scaffolding, he put her down safely in a recess in the wall. Taking a last look at her so full, so long, so drowned in regrets, shattered hopes, in youth betrayed, that at the moment he charged towards his aggressors and provoked them with a grinding of his teeth, signaling his readiness to fight, she could not keep quiet and cried out, her hands extended: "Hemo! Come to me! Come back! I love you."

The soldiers finally took hold of him, loaded him in chains, dragged him away, and the uproar muffled her voice. Had this not been the case, she would have been mercilessly jeered at.

"Not me, my girl, not me!"

It was Jan, who could not keep quiet either. Oh no, he would not laugh at her for speaking of Hemo as a human being. Bent over her, he grazed her brow with his lips, fevered by the thought she might not have confessed everything, that a false sense of propriety held her back, that she had guessed Hemo's nature, that they had shared hours of intimacy, decisive, demonstrative of the equality of the two races, or at least of the similarity of their two races to the point of confusion. He brooded over her with great affection, amused himself by curling behind her ear the wild wisps of her fine hair. She thought she had conquered his cold facade and with a scornful pout she called her little sister an ignorant scamp, incapable of inspiring anything in a serious man. But she laughed in her face, Jan showing himself so serious indeed that he was heaving like a good man to whom one might propose an incestuous relationship.

The father kept an eye on the goings-on between them, though apparently absorbed in his reading of Sir Stayel's voyages. He burst out in curses, and both asked him simultaneously,

"What is it?"

"There is that it's just bloody disgraceful," he turned towards Jan, taking him to witness. Reopening the book which he had a suddenly slammed shut, he read the episode of a

meeting between Stayel and a slave caravan, the Arab mer-
chant placidly upon his donkey while his servants whipped
long lines of wretched blacks in wood and iron shackles
whose edges skinned them alive. And as if the misery of the
blacks had recalled this white man's misery to himself, he
finished his beer and cakes, and cursed his daughter's laziness.
Let them beat it, since they were too stupid to please a distinguished guest. The theaters were letting out, the streets filling
for the last time that night. Their buns would be history if they
didn't improve on the evening's take!

Jan blushed, searched through his pockets, found not a
single guilder, and apologizing for his departure, followed the
girls down. At the bottom of the stairs, as they were going
back to the Dam Plaza and Kalver-Straat, their usual hunting
grounds, he went his own way.

CHAPTER XIII

His rash desire to return to the site of the most recent
events in Hemo's life led Jan back to the Palace of Industry.
The festivities were at their height, the bay windows, the
glassed-in cupolas blazed with light, burst with music, and the
rays, those echoes of happiness contrasted so painfully with
the poor man's state of mind, mournful, silent, sad unto death,
that as soon as he arrived he ran away. But the same desire
guided him again, going across the Amstel he headed for the
Zoological Gardens. Over the wall, a tree limb appeared to
him as an arm reaching out and lowered itself to grab him on
his passage; upon the deep sighs of some great beasts in their
nearby lodgings, he cried out oblivious to his own actions:
"Hemo, Hemo, is that you?" and, surprised by the sound of his
own voice, he ran off into the distance.

He wandered about the sleeping city, by preference along
the alleys and canals. The few who were still out late took him
for a drunkard, because, his head on his chest, staggering with

weakness, he did not see them and so jostled them with his elbow. The rich folk coming back from an evening's entertainment went out of their way to avoid him; a homeless man, his nose to the wind, followed him, took a hard look at him under a street light, but given his pitiable state believed it useless to feel inside his pockets.

He had not slept since his departure from Marseille and had not eaten since the day before. The fault was not in his not having money, even rich he would no more look for a bed or dinner, no longer feeling hunger or fatigue. His body to him was simply a worthless rag; only his brain worked, and with a life force that much more intense than fever, which general wear and tear had amplified, pushed ordinary sights into a realm of delirium. The least impression transmitted to him by his senses, a reflection, an odor, a whisper, led to sequences of mad analogies, bringing forth memories which condensed into hallucinations, and which he perceived as present, coexistent, no longer ordered in their proper place in the past. In the same minute he was 10, he was 40, he was 1000 years old, and he contemplated, modified, perfected, admired his old dreams, now fixed, solidified into visible and tangible realities.

The places and the night melded together. Exhausted, he crumpled to the ground on the edge of the dock, among the loads of cargo.

Around him was stacked merchandise from all over the world, wooden crates in pale pyramids, bales and bags in shapeless piles stuffed under coarse canvas covers, barrels one on top of another in uniformly stacked fortifications whose tops stood out in rounded waves, unlike a pile of coal whose crest showed a jagged profile. One might think it a dead city of collapsed buildings, some having remained partly standing, and one would situate it in the tropics or in the fjords, according to whether the draughts blowing through the maze of apparent ruins brought warm aromas of a shipment of spice or the harsh aroma of Norway spruce, and if the strong odors which always masked others blew in heavily, the empyreuma of tar and the stale mustiness of fish, it would still recall the sea.

She was in basin facing him, her sides braced against the docks.

Other ships were filling her; all the sails were taken down from the rigging and folded away. The masts were raised in a bare, polished forest. They seemed to form, their lines streaked pale across the night with the horizontal and oblique tangling of the yards and rigging, a gigantic web supporting with the thickness of its links the less dense tissue of the great patches of darkness piled up behind. Different colored fires opened here and there with huge eyes of red hot coals, sulfur, emerald, and were enveloped in the fog with purplish halos, of which more than one, lighting at intervals some carved and gilded nymph on the prow of a ship, revealing a livid and floating drowning victim, which the shadows that played about its recesses when the ship rocked seem to surround with greenish hair. A transatlantic liner, proud, concealed its massive cathedral. Nothing stirred. Not a sound. Suddenly, at the rising of a breeze, everything oscillated with the same rhythmic roll, some flames died out slowly at the swashing of the water, pulleys creaked, mooring cables strained briefly then slackened, chains rattled against one another, the canvas covers snapped, and the sides of the ships which came in contact with each other cracked like great spindles. Once again it stopped and one could only hear the harsh grinding of rats nibbling on garbage, the roar of a steamer starting up its engines for departure, a strident whistle-blast, and occasionally, on a big barge, the flat deck of which was barely dented by the roof of the cabin, a guard dog did his rounds and howled.

The Moon was rising on the other side. Clouds continued to interpose themselves in its slow ascension, tiring it. At first wide, swollen and of a heavy crimson hue, by the time it reached its zenith, where it waited listlessly, it was no more than a collapsed, empty, pale mask against a ceiling of darkness. During a short lull, she lit up again, came back to life

137

with new blood, giving back to the vast slumbering lands under her influence a bit of the redness of life. Her gaze cast into the shadowy abysses, changed them into black velvets upon which ancient scumble of phosphorus paste turned blue, and myriads of tiny waves on the surface of the water were crested with ephemeral glows.

She continued her course, and the battle with the clouds was enjoined again. She went down towards the sea while they emerged from it. Livid, far over the waves, they emerged as granite islands bordered at the base by a narrow bar of horizon, while their compact masses, as if solidified, proceeded from the fathomless depths of the sea where nothing could intercept the breath which pushed them. The ridge atop them was crowned with shifting crenellations, arrows, gigantic towers which endlessly collapsed and recreated their nightmarish architecture. The silence of their collapse was not the least of the horrors, the silent storm suffocated one with fear, as if, presented with the lightning bolts of cosmic chaos, one waited endless minutes for the final peal. And the Moon, in the middle of these fuliginous blocks which endlessly rose and disaggregated, grew bloody in the parting of the cracks between them, waned, cadaverous and half eaten by their smoky fringes, was then completely eclipsed beneath their opaque curtain, drawing along in a spectral dance, with its many, rapid intermittences, everything of Heaven and Earth.

The lurkers drew nearer to Jan.

The different states of calmness and well-being which existed over the lowly haunts teeming with restless needs and vices, led to the welling up of, along with the rats from the vacant lots and sewers and bats, those human larvae which traversed back and forth through the sleeping city. Like those beasts of prey, vermin or jackals, whose voracity was deceived by the meaty smell of certain harmless flowers, they made their way towards Jan, who seemed to them, motionless and alone, a lost derelict, at the disposal of the first one to smell him out.

First, a woman. Through the inky night and the dock's thousand obstacles, she moved toward him, shook him, believed him to be drunk and searched him. Nothing, and the poor woman's weak smile turned into a heart-broken grimace. Where to work at such an hour? They drove her out of basements, from the most abject of hovels, because of her far too pungent rags, of the cancer which ate away at the middle of her upper lip and exposed at the base of her nose the stump of three bluish teeth, teetering in their bleeding alveoli. Others preceding her, she believed, must already have stripped the good drunkard with the fine clothes. After having tried in vain to get his overcoat off, she resigned herself to her bad lot, slipped in against him to borrow some of his warmth, turned her face toward his so as to be ready for the kiss that luck might bring.

A naked beggar sat down to his left, so thin as to make his joints crack, while on his neck and arms, the veins, dissected and hardened by alcohol, stood out in knotted bundles. Then, of all of them the most wretched, two children drew near. Brother and sister, they held each other's hands, furtive, suspicious, on the look-out for the police of whom they have an hereditary fear, but nonetheless innocent and who would remain so, even when later they were thieves and murderers. For it was the city alone that was guilty, which abandoned them to every perverse contagion and to ravenous hunger, the seed of crimes for the so-called future justice of the courts and prisons. Instinct revealed to them their true fellows in this regimen of misery; they avoided Jan and crouched between the knees of the ragged fellow and the prostitute with the confidence of homeless dogs.

A light rain, having threatened all day, now whipped, ice-cold, across them. Their backs to it, the group drew closer. The kids were racked with bouts of coughing which tore their chests apart, turned their faces purple, and whistled in their throats.

Indifferent to the bad weather, the half-naked old man burned over every inch of his tanned skin, like a lamp wick without oil. For he had not had his full ration of alcohol, and his frame growing free of alcohol was curling up in horrible contractions, and, sucking the inside of his cheeks, he drew a thin stream of blood which he swallowed growling: "Gimme something to drink." The woman scratched her itchy labial chancre, needled by the cold. She thus increased the unbearable burning, lamented, dug her nails into the palm of her hands to stop herself from tearing her face off.

Jan, at the children's coughing, the fetid breath of the drunkard, at the poor creature's pain, remembered his older siblings who died of consumption, the epidemic among the suckling infants in the fishermen's village, and his generous ambition to fight against and conquer the afflictions and destructive vices of the species. He had gone out, without hesitation, not even drawing back before the worst accusations of obscenity and lying, placing over all else the putting of his theory into practice, right up to his choice of wife, not some Gabonese or Hottentot savage, but poor D'ginna, whom he no longer thought of since his return to Europe, through scruples, which at this precise moment, seemed to him more like cowardice.

Why had he not told Betty everything? Had he not vowed to sacrifice himself to the end, to deliver his good name to choruses of boos, to opprobrium? But Betty would not have understood. Besides, why harp over regrets? Had he not reached his goal? Was not Hemo nearby, and would he not see him in the morning? Who cared if the ignorant, the brutish had not seen in Hemo any traits which might have led them to suspect irregularities in his genealogy? Was that sufficient proof that these traits were absent, had they not instead already drawn naturalists to investigate them, scholarly authorities whose doubts would become convictions, as soon as Jan confessed to them the frightful love which they would be forced to absolve him of, forced as they would be to glorify the results?

Betty's adventures were the beginning of a proof, and the strange passion she admitted to having shared, she must have been driven to by an undeniable, secret instinct.

He was discouraged, yet was on the verge of triumph. The theft of Hemo by an English sailor, his voyage, his sale, his arrival in Holland, his internment in the Zoological Gardens, in the country and location where he himself had aspired to submit for examination by the stunned academies, all of this done miraculously, should this not give him a certain faith in the future, showing him that he had been favored by the mysterious fate without which the best laid plans of men came to naught?

These thoughts and thousands of others whirled around in his mind to the rapid rhythm of his carotids.

Jan thought to himself that one sentence spoken by Hemo would have forced even the greatest dolts to pay attention and would have already caused a considerable stir everywhere, but that overwhelmed with his new life whose every detail must appear a prodigy, tied up, jostled, perhaps struck, the free child of the virgin solitudes must have isolated himself in a fierce silence. Besides, those words that Jan, mad with enthusiasm, used to hear him stammer out, who knows if, tired of repeating then without success, the first days of their separation, in the hands of the Pahouins' or the white men speaking a different language, he had not forgotten them, but that tomorrow, recognizing the beloved and patient voice which taught him, he would not suddenly recover his ability to speak, to cry out in happiness and filial tenderness in defiance of the incredulous mob.

And the mad dreamer, as always setting foot right in the middle of his dream, saw the crowd break open the disgraceful cage from whence Hemo harangued them, and knelt before this human being mistaken for an ape, as if before the victim of the most extraordinary, most cruel error. And he heard himself hailed as the scientific heir of his countrymen, the embryologist Swammerdam and Leeuwenhoek the microscopist who discovered zoosperms; he saw his name inscribed next to theirs, in the immortal list to which the Lamarcks, the Darwins and the Haeckels had risen. Back in his small house in Haarlem, he would complete at leisure Hemo's education, supported this time by the goodwill and counsel of all the world's scholars, now become his attentive correspondents and frequent visitors. As Hemo grew and adapted himself to his environment, any trace of motherly influence would diminish, while that of the father would increase. Hemo would lose most of his hair, by the same process of evolution which, before birth, rids the child of the woolly fleece it wears during its first months *in utero*, and which are the last vestiges of its ancestral simian hairiness. Hemo would marry, reproduce, marry off his sons, and perpetuate himself in numberless generations who would soon deny him, considering any allusion to their origins an insult, and would end up discovering a solar myth in the union of their forefather Jan with D'ginna.

Jan smiled at this ingratitude of his offspring and forgave them in advance. He had done his duty; if he was successful in retarding the bastardization of the human race by infusing it with the pure scarlet of new blood, he demanded no recognition.

After a short respite in the light, his thoughts turned more towards the darkness, thinking that heredity never abdicated its rights. Progress marched onward, which had the principal effect of undertaking selection in reverse, to bring the strong to debauchery, to the celibacy of army life, to war, to the overwork necessary for the continuous rise in demand which typified civilization. It also saved the weak, the sick, those with birth defects, by exempting them, giving them social assistance, opening its hospitals to a growing army of rickety children and as if throwing out the baby with the bathwater, abandoning the healthy street urchin. Through Christian charity it soiled its mittens trying to rehabilitate fallen young women, leaving without a job that could support them those who had not yet fallen. Ah! civilization... Along with a French doctor who had told him of some of his visits to Pacific islands infected by European sailors, Jan intoned: "Civilization: sy-philization."

Still prey to his obsession, he now saw his descendants, Hemo's descendants, struck down in turn by physical and moral wretchedness. Science had conquered leprosy, the plagues which in medieval times cut down entire nations like a scythe, and would overcome scourges just as dreadful yet more insidious which still struck at the source of life: consumption, scrofula, cancer, neuroses, alcoholism. But, science, who would conquer her?

Outside of measurable time, the last men appeared to Jan. They had completely subdued Nature, its every law had been enunciated. Convinced of the truth that only life was real, and that life was only a short passage in a certain state of aggregation, each one of them practiced the ultimate wisdom which could be summarized, in the last analysis, as one of enduring as long as possible in the momentary state of time and matter which it represented. Joy, sadness, vice, virtue, desire, lust had been so many causes of wear over the past centuries. All the mysteries dissected, weighed, even the scientist's curiosity was dead. Upon being born, even the cretins knew everything. Why would they budge? The Earth, modified to their use from Pole to Equator, was everywhere identical, and it sufficed, to know it as it was anywhere, to give a quick circular glance around the point where one had remained fixed.

The vertebrate man no longer existed except as skeletons which hung beneath museum tags. His body was atrophied little by little at the ever growing profit of his mental capacity. It was the reign of the Pure Cerebrals, crab-like creatures made up only of a brain and a few organs, the excessive division of physiological labor having continued to perfect, in each individual, such and such special adaptation at the detriment of others, so as to give this specialized organ, under a reduced volume, all the possible power and ability to discriminate. Straight away, without the help of ancient instruments, the astronomer resolved all the questions regarding nebulas;

the physicist read telegraphic missives by the vibrations in the wires; the musician needed only to listen to hear the roar of comets through the ether; Don Juan, with a single kiss shot from the tip of his fingers, fertilized his 1003 lovers.

It was the penultimate era, that of the blossoming of the mind after an irremediable collapse. The lack of balance between the thought and the action grew still; in the same way that man condensed himself into a brain, so the brain condensed itself into a single cell, a recreation of Haeckel's amoeba from which every organized creature was born amidst the Laurentian seas. But life is a cycle, the cycle is closed, and as the primordial cells evolved through every animal form to reach man, the last disintegrated into the simple elements, returned to mineral dust, and finally, it was thus, with regard to the human race, the end.

What good would attempts at regeneration be, he asked himself, if it was not to put off the final degeneration for a few million centuries, a mere split-second in the infinity of time? Just so, the wretched who had come to sit near him had slipped off the bench, had snuggled up to each other in a shapeless group, and he took their faces, their only feature visible in the opacity of night, for those human larvae he had earlier visualized. They would have fallen in his dream, into the mud, and under the play of the Moon which hid and unhid them, they hopped as pallid toads at his feet. He got up, stepped over them, and took his sudden disgust for his former hopes out onto the dock.

Suicide was something which best distinguished humans from other animals. How did those who maintained any hint of faith in any individual immortality, resist the temptation to experience it right away? What would they risk? Beyond the grave cannot be any worse than what preceded the grave.

And he was probably going to decide to throw himself in the water to elucidate this question from some other place, when some distant rumors made him draw himself up. People were running through the streets, and their cries where getting louder as they approached.

"Fire! Fire!"
"Where?"
"In the Zoological Gardens."
"The Zoological Gardens?"
"Yes, in the monkey enclosure."

CHAPTER XIV

The enclosures for the wild beasts were laid out in two rectangular areas on the right and on the left of the huge half-moon shaped cast iron and steel cage. They were paved with bitumen, had a water basin in the middle, and a gigantic perch in the form of a fake tree whose thick limbs were debarked oak trunks. A trapeze and some rings hung from the domed roof. The floor, in freestone, was divided regularly into shelters to protect the monkeys during the night and the bad season. This cage, as yet unfinished, served, as it waited for its future inhabitants to frolic about it in almost complete freedom, as the contractor's storage area. A long service hallway stretched out behind, allowing cleaning, ventilation, heating, feeding, and also access for visitors with special passes to visit in the winter, when the front grillwork was closed up.

It was in these new constructions that Hemo had been imprisoned after the tragedy at the Palace of Industry. The honor of the hangman's noose and guillotine demanding that they be reserved for human criminals, the authorities were content to keep it quiet; the public furor appeased, perhaps he would be allowed to live and once more be exhibited. Well, in 24 hours they had not only forgiven him, but he became the top attraction at the Zoological Gardens, even all of Amsterdam. Hotel pageboys, guides and carriage drivers would mention him to tourists even before the Art Museum. The *La Ronde de Nuit* was no longer the only object to hear, from 30 feet away and before anything had been seen of it, the oohs and ahs of admiration on command. They lined up. Treats

145

rained down on his litter. He did not touch any of it, not even the hazelnuts he usually adored; not even at mealtime. The administration, whose fortunes he doubled in doubling the attendance were worried, consulting his former masters the English pantomimes, who, well paid, diagnosed correctly that he was languishing with boredom, not being used to such isolation.

An orangutan couple lived in the next cell over. Three months off a ship from the Malaysian colonies, they were still ashamed to have fallen in the Dayak hunters' treacherous traps, but understood the pointlessness of delayed anger, enviable in the dignity of their defeat, they kept quiet, and motionless among the woolen blankets with which they formed a veritable cocoon, only their faces sticking out, like Peruvian mummies wrapped up with their knees against their chests. On visiting day, when the umbrellas and canes of the rubberneckers forced them to move, the male would turn his back, draw his mate over to him, protect her in the soft fur of his reddish chest, wrap her up in his overlong arms, shield her from their vile taunts and almost from their view. She would begin to cough from the consumption which kills them all, in spite of all the care given them, under the healthier climates of Europe, a remarkable fact given that they were native to old growth forests pumping for all eternity over the stagnant waters of a spongy soil, venomous mists sweating forth beneath an implacable sun. Resigned to her fate, she circled with her arm, like a child its mother, the neck of the veterinarian who slowly picked her up to look her over, and only weakly resisted the brutal keeper who would roughly rub her ribs with tincture of iodine, filled her carelessly with prescription drugs, applied vesication ointment, and even, if no one was watching, spat on her and struck her, furious at his low wages for such an irksome task. And from the point when, the male seeing her beaten for no reason, had launched himself to her rescue and had received a heavy kick in the stomach, which had left him laid out and howling in pain, she stifled her least discomfort and offered herself at the boor's feet, letting him tear the skin off her or strangle her on the pretext of bandaging her or having her yawn so he could toss some pills down her throat.

To cure him of his boredom, Hemo was placed beside them, at the risk of having him contract the tuberculosis whose contagiousness was yet only admitted by the theoreticians, those whom people with common sense call empty-headed, until they themselves, constrained to accept a new idea, affirm disdainfully always having known it to be so. Hemo first pulled a good prank on their keeper. Having noticed that in the presence of the overseers he always pretended to be as patient as he was mild, he pinched him in the calf one morning once the veterinarian, his consultation ended, had walked away. The individual slapped at him; he dodged it and began to execute a thousand contortions of despair, to scream like a burn victim, to hold his jaw as if it were broken, all with gestures and looks of fear so clear, so precisely targeted, that the doctor, having run back, understood that the keeper was abusing them, called him a dirty coward, an idiot, and had him fired. Hemo lavished his hand with expressive caresses as he used to with Colombine, clearly indicating that he understood his charitable intervention, his actions brought on by pity. Then, Hemo got rid of the curious, especially the nasty little urchins whose compact hordes succeeded one another before the bars on general admission days, by surrendering himself to a series of manipulations so obscene that the administration's sense of decency led them to close up the shutters. Finally, he taught the patient how not to swallow the pills given her; she seemed to accept them, but concealed them in the recess of her cheek, spitting them out when the keeper had left. Naturally, she was no better or worse; if anything she gained by it. Believing the first treatment to be ineffective, they began a second; instead of grains of arsenic to upset her stomach, she received rations of good quality liquor; and the ruse which had hastened this pleasant change did not cause any problems, since her sickness was incurable.

Even though the veterinarian had long known that a taste for alcohol was amongst those which the great apes, like savages, most readily borrow from man, the poor creature relished the liquid in such perfect beatitude that he took upon himself the pleasant task of serving her, to see her half close her eyes, smack her lips and curl up her tongue in anticipation, crestfallen when upon entering he hid in fun the bottle in his coat. As gluttonous as her, the other orang and Hemo would end up each getting a spoonful themselves. It was then that the keeper looked upon the flask with such strangely covetous eyes that the veterinarian, in handing it back to him to put away, made sure to take note of the content level in the bottle, and to smell its strength.

She soon no longer had the strength to rise. Besides her glass of liquor she would take in nothing else, lying on her side for days on end, her arms crossed or, when her mate tried to perk her up by playing, extended them, one under her head as a pillow, the other below on her charms, like the Medici Venus. Her nails were curling more and more into claws. The arch of her ribs seemed to flatten, and along her protruding spine, spots long in contact with the floor lost their hair and excoriated, began to bleed. They brought her a mattress of kelp, a second blanket, larger, warmer, and the gesture was lamentably human when she tucked this blanket beneath her, shivering at the least breath of air, shaken after the least effort by bouts of coughing which left her breathing raspy. She died. A boy loaded her into a wheelbarrow, to take her to the amphitheater where the naturalists' aides waited. It was indeed a body, not some sort of carrion. To bend the stiffened body, the boy had to push with his foot on her lower belly. The head, thrown back, rubbed on the wheel, and upon the chest thus bent back, the breasts showed two little cups of bare flesh, streaky, with purplish nipples, while the larynx's resonating chambers lay flattened on her neck, like the flaccid pouch of a goiter.

Hemo, who always carefully studied the comings and goings of the staff, grabbed the key which the amphitheater boy had left in the lock, with the ring attached to it, hid it in the straw and sat on it. The boy, his wheelbarrow delivered, came back to look on the ground, to search through his overalls, hesitating for a moment, and decided to only lock up with the bolt, supposing that the keeper had picked up his keys. The latter came to the same conclusion when coming to stoke the heater for the night, and Hemo, hearing him going off, remembering the English clowns, danced a jig in front of the orangutan which had remained motionless and stunned since the body had been taken away. But having lost the habit of such exercise, he quickly tired of it; sitting then near his fellow ape, he stared at the thin streaks of the pale dusk which filtered in through the shutters, saw them slowly disappear, and, as soon as he judged that night had fallen, headed for the door, slid his hand between two bars, pulled the bolt, and slipped into the hallway.

A few night-lights hung from the ceiling, their flat wicks giving just enough light to allow him to stay in the middle of the path. The wild beasts which were already sleeping, not recognizing their keeper, stirred; at the bars, claws ready to grab him were stretching out, great bulks were rising to their feet, strongly sniffing the air, like the puff of a working steam engine, growling; finally the disturbed creatures went back to some forgotten bone from their last meal. Hemo thus seemed to wake, from cage to cage, the sounds of great maws, and to light pairs of dull eyes into living carbuncles.

His little walk assured him he was sole master of the place. At the end, from the door through which the last lamp in the hallway sent a light which, too feeble to outline itself on the black of the growing medium, melted into an indistinct reddish glow, there came the heavy atmosphere of a greenhouse saturated with the humid warmth and smells of vegetation reminding him of his native country; he drew it in, thrilled. The only things lighted were the tree ferns from Brazil and New Zealand, some with an upright stem, covered in what resembled scales, left behind by the ancient attachment point of leaves, the others with their middle fronds curled up in a fiddlehead and hairy like an animal's tail, along with a giant screw-pine, immediately climbing and lost in the

149

heights, allowing its long striped leaves to hang down into the uncertain light which washed out their color and left them like so many motionless tapeworms. At the edge of the shadows, a shelf of cacti bristled with needles, twisting prone stems into a tangled nest of snakes. And beyond that many other shapes waited in ambush for Hemo who guessed at their presence in the darker clumps distinguishable in the greater darkness, his fears restraining him from going any farther.

In front of his shelter was a sort of store-room, a large cupboard containing the maid's equipment. All he needed to do to gain access to the flask of alcohol, when he came back, was to lift the catch. He took three-quarters for himself and poured the remainder into the orang's dish, who, not educated by Miss Betty, did not know how to pour drink straight down his throat, scooping it in his hand instead. Tipsy, but not satisfied, he searched some more, finding in the messy pile of objects a carboy of oil, which he tilted towards his lips, and dropped so abruptly in suddenly drawing away from it in disgust that it broke into pieces. The nauseating liquid spread through the small drains used in washing out the cages and the hallway, soaked into the pine flooring and litter. When Hemo bumped against the long fire-iron which he had seen the keeper use to rake up the coals, he grabbed the tool and in his imitative rage rummaged around in the heater with it. When the first bits of hot coal fell outside the heater, trails of fire immediately sprung up everywhere.

Between the two furrows on either side of the hallway, he dragged the orang, stopping only to turn in glee towards his work. The burning oil, which the slope of the drains directed towards them, was catching up to them; a large vestibule offered a closer shelter to them than did the greenhouse. They pushed at a pair of swinging doors, and thought themselves free. But they were only in their previous palace, huge, and with no way out. Furious at this failed escape, Hemo took vengeance in a cruel inspiration. He went back into the hallway, pulled, across the line of fire, the bolts of four of the cages that had been closed no better than his, and running back to his companion, at the top of their huge perch, waited to cheer on the ferocious battles and all of the spectacle which, with the help of chance, he had so ably prepared.

The first victim of his malice was a poor little chevrotain[21] which had been isolated from a family of eight to ten individuals for his own protection, one of his legs was already broken, from the unappeased rancor of an old buck whose lovemaking he interfered with. The new layout did not allow him to be put anywhere else, leaving him neighbored with a panther who, in spite of several dividers being interposed between their cages, scented him, and whose mewing kept him pinned to his litter, trembling, taking up as little space as possible, his limb wrapped up in a splint as well as his others bent under his stomach. Forgetting his fear, he came along, limping before the bars of the monkey palace; his doe was already answering him from far away in the park when he expired, his flanks and neck torn open by the panther.

Two lions next door did not bother moving except to turn their backs to the fire and resume their sphinx-like poses. A calming of nerves flattened their hindquarters; they rejoiced at their ease, calm except for a few twitches of pleasure at the base of the tail, and did not extend their nails, to face the danger and leap, in bounds of several meters, right into the greenhouse, until the heat became unbearable. Upon their roaring out, as if at a signal, all at once the hallway rang out with the cries of all its denizens, with all the howls of a sinking ark. The fire, as if fanned by these cries of terror, burst out more violently. The large cage in turn was on fire, where everything seemed to have been set out to facilitate the fire: the contractor's equipment thrown in haphazardly, sheets of flooring piled up in a corner, wood chips left over from carpentry covering the ground, scaffolding poles and platforms leaning on the perch, pots of colored paint and barrels of thinner and oil for the painters. And if, in the hallways, the fire smoldered without one being able to see much from outside, here it

---

[21] A species of the Tragulidae family of deer. [Ed.]

formed an open-air pyre that lit up the surroundings, scattering its sparks over the sleeping creatures scattered about the gardens. Aviaries became animated like a chicken coop at the approach of a fox. From the edge of their deep pool the sea-lions, believing themselves back in the land of the aurora borealis, dove happily to rise back up every minute and, just above the surface, saluted the sudden wavering glow with short barks. Blinded by the smoke, the panther left its meal, followed the inside of the bars, sometimes drawing up against them, the black velvet of his coat gaining the luster of magnificent moiré patterns, as crimson as the blood which still dripped from his chops. And in all the walkways, help was arriving, at the sound—sinister in the night—of the trumpet and drums.

Upon seeing the panther, the museum's employees cried out that the big cats had escaped, and were panicked into headlong flight which had at least one tangible benefit: it left the way open for the firemen. One of the latter, immediately close enough to the beast that it could hope to strike him with its claws, threw an axe at it through the bars, missing it, but, getting closer, the fire and its fury bringing it back towards him, this time he split its head open to the neck. Another, resolved to get into the hallway, which he thought to be the seat of the fire, by way of the yet intact greenhouses, cut, his safety light in one hand, his pickaxe in the other, an easy breach in the windowed structure, only to be confronted by a lion's mouth, before which he drew back. The cowards had not overstated the danger, the big cats had indeed been released.

The officers pushed back the curious and met briefly. They just had to keep the fire from spreading, and to stop the beasts from taking their carnage or at least their disorder into the city. Cordoning off the area, men with rifles cocked, fingers on the triggers, were ready to bring down the surviving beasts should the walls collapse. At the same moment terrible cries drew everyone's eyes to the top of the monkey enclosure. It was Hemo and the orang who had been forgotten there. Asphyxiated no doubt, the latter tumbled down, bouncing off the bars, and in spite of the fact that they were heated to a brownish red, clenched them and bit them in pain, leaving behind torn shreds of his hands and lips, howling lamentably until the very moment he entered, finally dead, the blazing mass where his flesh sizzled, his skull exploded, and where his large, fierce body was soon no more than a mass of blackened axle grease stinking of melted fat.

But Hemo, whom the orang had held onto, had had to knock him out with a punch to the face in order not to follow him, still had not given up. The perch, half burnt away at the base, was weakening so he took to the arches and cross-braces supporting the top of the building. Swinging down the trapeze which the masons, whom he had disturbed in their handling of their ladders, had attached by means of a lozenge of wire to the structure supporting the glassed over ceiling, and sliding straight along the horizontal bar, sent it careening like a swing. The flames were almost touching him, but the wind from his rocking to and fro blew them back, to the front, to the back, farther away at each successive and faster pass. He appeared above them and amidst them like the demon which emerged invulnerable from the bubbling cauldron in which witches reduced aspic and toads, the roots of euphorbia and mandrake to an unguent which they applied upon the Sabbath. The crowd, recognizing him, called out his name, when a bizarre scene suddenly quieted a thousand voices at once, the scene of Jan Maas arriving from the docks, pushing aside the guards, falling to his knees before the monkey enclosure, his arms extended towards Hemo, crying and calling him his son. And the sympathy of a sincere pity soon replaced the laughter and mockery which had at first risen at every hand. As soon as they saw how thin he was, how haggard he looked, how downtrodden and fevered the stranger was, and how he tried to force his way through the ranks of the firemen, who held him back, they knew him to be insane. For what party had the devil that night let the animals out of their pens and the insane out of their asylums? Two men dragged him off. A poor angry sheep, in tears, he pleaded with them, begged that he be allowed to save his child, since the firemen themselves refused to do so. And as if feeling him to be so weak, posing so little danger, the hands around him would loosen, allowing him to throw himself back on his knees and cry out anew: "Hemo! Hemo! My son!"

At this distinctive voice, Hemo stopped short on the trapeze, jumped to the bottom of the cage, and in spite of the smoke which choked him, in spite of the sparks which lit up his fur in little bouquets of oakum, in spite of the coals he crushed beneath his feet, he too knelt, his arms outstretched towards Jan, and sobbed in genuine sobs, crying real tears, until, out of breath, he was forced, in order to breathe and to regain his trapeze and get it swinging again quickly. But now no one was in doubt that these two wretches, the madman and the gorilla, knew each other, and the question of knowing where and how their friendship was born was the topic of every conversation. One could not suppose Jan to be an old employee of the circus which had brought the creature to Amsterdam; he was not English, and from the language he spoke, without an accent, they could not deny him the attribute of being one of their countrymen, even if he had not out and out said it. For now, here he was telling the whole story, his family in Rotterdam and Haarlem, his trip, his dreams of regenerating the human race, the Pahouins, and finally, ashamedly, he told of his tropical lovemaking, of D'ginna and the birth of Hemo. The apparent bestiality of this type of monomania surprising the men somewhat, they drew back in exaggerated disgust, while the greasy throated gossips lowered their eyes and demanded all the gruesome details.

It was then that Hemo, whom none had heard proffer the least sound since his departure from Africa, not even the Englishmen who had long educated him, not even the spectators who had seen him murder the clown and escape with Colombine into the theater's rafters, intoning a strange concert, brief and strident cries from a coppery throat, guttural muffled croaks, prolonging the same note as the wind through the deep recesses of a marine conch, the tremolos of a tongue rolled up

154

against the pallet. Jan, in ecstasy, heard in it a speech expressed almost entirely in onomatopoeia, but which he understood, and consequently which all could understand, and which finally supplied that proof so long hoped for, the indisputable proof of the success of his experiment: Hemo sang, Hemo spoke, Hemo was thus born of man, was thus indeed his son.

Hemo, for Jan, improvised a hymn to the glory of fire, a superb recapitulation of a number of lectures and teachings which Jan had lavished upon him in their hours of common solitude.

Having little faith in chance, Hemo did not believe that the discovery of fire was the result of lightning in the forest primeval setting, a fire in giant ferns having dried up under a sun larger than the one which appeared today, or by the striking together of dead branches in a hurricane. It rather probably occurred during some terrible winter of the Ice Age. An alpha male among the males, among the males of an era lost many thousands of centuries in the past, extended his arm bearing a club cut from a tree trunk, over the women he preferred, over the children he had had by them, over the elders which bore him and whom before him, when they no longer could follow the shifting camps of the tribe, he killed, over the orphans whose fathers had been smothered to death by the great cave bears, or gutted by the four incredibly rigid and sharp tusks of the mastodon, and stated: "This share is my share. Beware all who try to lay a hand on it!" And the human family, thus barely constituted under primordial justice and consecrated by force, defeated by the eternal cold, was in its final agonies, and would die.

The cave which it inhabited, chosen for its depth, opened halfway up a hill by a narrow entrance which overhanging rock made even smaller. Racing brooks; rivers so slow that ripples from cross-current winds led one to misidentify the direction of flow; great lakes whose limpid surface the great stag took for a stretch of sky fallen to earth, and where, thirsty, he would, in admiring his four meter wide antlers, forget to drink; torrents the steps of whose cascades seemed an atomizer of light; all these now but a chaos of ice, piles of jagged blocks, their tumult congealed in place and hardened into silence. Around them, neither the mountain nor the plains had, under the universal shroud of snow, any defined shadows, distance and elevation being confounded. The whole Earth was leveled by a sepulchral whiteness, barely tinged, deep in the abyss of night, with a blue metallic sheen.

Their skin slashed on the edges of the ice; the callosities on their feet crushing the rounded pebbles of granular glacier snow; their nails, like genuine claws, scratching even the smoothest of the slippery surfaces; sinking to their navels and sometimes even completely disappearing into hidden crevasses, the men were headed to the forest in a tight file. The father was in front, erect and spreading wide his hairy chest to protect his elders behind him from the squall which had taken them unprepared. The hollowness of their eyes, their cheeks, their hypochondriums, indicated months of famine, and the frightful emaciation that stripped the very meat from their bones, brought out the husky nature of their skeletons. Their veins and tendons stood out like taut ropes, their joints were knotty masses, and their spines resembled the angular backbones of the hyena. Naked, a stone axe in their fist, a spear on their shoulder, their hair full of pellets of ice, two steady streams of steam as their breath exited through their nostrils, between which gleamed their sharp chattering teeth. The last hope which led them out to the hunt rose as they approached the forest; the red sun set in a pale sky seeded the understory with shifting gleams, which they took to be the eyes of wild creatures watching them. And they sped up, straining their pace and voices, throwing their weapons by the wayside to lighten themselves, drunk with lust, believing already that after the fierce embrace of starvation they would eat and drink their belly-full of fresh meat and warm blood at the very breast and neck of the monsters whose glowing ambushes they could make out. The men's hunger defied that of the monsters.

In the forest where they rushed, loosened from the treetops by their passage, chunks of ice lapidated them; they found, rather than the eyes of carnivores, the cold purples of dusk pouring over the ground through the low branches, they heard only the echo of their own cries. Exhausted, failing, they leaned on the fir trees, and beneath the sweat which chilled their backs and the rest of their bodies, they felt a tightness around their hearts, their joints stiffening, as if they were being petrified alive.

However, the women, the children and the elderly, having remained behind, crouched down in a single group to share their remaining warmth. No longer having even their animal-hide or bark clothing to chew on and appease their hunger, they sucked on the gravel they had picked up at the base of the moraine and clasped their hands around their middles. A girl, Adah, leaving the shapeless group, sat away from the others, her legs stretched out on her bed of moss and dry leaves. Her love for the strongest of her brothers, now hunting with her father, drove her last hopes. Before dying, she dreamt of flaking him a flint axe sharper than all those found among the natural chips of rock split by the frost or broken off by avalanches. Holding the rock she had chosen upright between her knees, she struck at it with another, work which she had already begun outdoors, without noticing, as here in the shadow of the cave, the sparks which were ejected from the striking point and which she vainly attempted to catch. She believed them to be day-flies suddenly born around her, or the drops of a mysterious, previously unknown blood which escaped from the secret heart of rocks which one broke, leaving no more trace than the lightning- or meteor-like blood spatters. Now warmed up, she struck harder, only pausing to rearrange the pads of moss which helped her to better stabilize the stone whose edges she sharpened, between her shaky thighs.

Drawn up suddenly in a jerk of her back and hamstrings, she dropped her tool, shook the sprigs of moss warmed by their contact with her maiden's lap, and which the sparks had lit. Bent over the dancing redness, which from the mattress spread to bundles of bark-based twine and scattered tree limbs, she wanted to catch them, put her finger in them, crying out

157

more in surprise than pain at the slight burn. She quickly taught the elders, the women, the children, who were now awake, amazed, and fearful, to bring their benumbed limbs near the young god which manifested itself in bringing them warmth, light and joy, and all the life of the bright sun of their lost summers. Fire was discovered and men, having come home without killing anything, paralyzed with cold and thinking they had nothing left to do but die, lay down near it and were saved. In Adah's honor the young women were consecrated to serving the hearth. The adults now pursued their prey until they reached it and to wherever it took them, and prolonged their lying in wait well into the night; they no longer feared getting lost; back there the coals glowed red to guide their return, and the smoke rose and flew in the breeze, as if to carry afar the amorous thoughts of the keepers, the proof of their vigilance, and of their tranquil state. During the rests which came with stormy weather, the elderly who no longer slept, along with all the rest, free of dull tedium in the warm and well lit shelter, inventors of future arts, fired pottery; strung shells to adorn themselves with bracelets, necklaces and hair decorations; carved, onto slabs of ivory and schist, fabulous beasts which then existed: elephants with manes, bears with bulging foreheads. Emptying the leg bones of the Dinornis, a bird before which the ostrich would look like a crow, made a quiver, boring holes into smaller ones made musical instruments, sculpting stag and reindeer antlers into staffs and whistles of command for the chiefs, into dagger handles and barbed harpoons.

Finally, at a second memorable date, fire gave man, now become the king of creation, the first and best servant to his sovereignty.

As the ice receded slowly toward the poles, restraining their empire to their immutably dismal regions, the seeds of flora and fauna which were spared rapidly multiplied in the liberated areas, and the fight for survival became so harsh that the family of man had its development more at risk, amidst the irresistible thrusts of life, than when it laid about its caves amidst the apparent death of creatures and things. Humble grasses like Sigillaria, which children's steps now cut down in tufts, grew up as great columns, losing their green domes in the clouds, and which the anger of a herd of rhinoceros no more unsettled at their base than a swarm of ants. Fires set by man freed him from the encroachment of the forests, but his huts built, when he should be enjoying the sun and breathing a little easier, it was still only by surrounding himself with logs that he guaranteed his safety from the ceaseless animal attacks, that he purged the cinders of his clearing of the even more deadly reptiles and insects; and if the circle of fires burned low, he saw behind them another blaze approach, almost as bright, that of the wild beast's eyes watching him.

A woman crying out as if she had been gutted had the camp leaping to their feet one morning. A mother had entrusted the fire she was pledged to maintain to her daughter named Adah in remembrance of her great ancestress. When she came back to find her, she discovered her asleep, rolled over, and alongside, almost on top of her, an animal with frothy and bloody, shear-like canines. The whole tribe gathered round to see, but in place of the carnage they expected, the child was playfully pulling the fluffy tail and pointy ears of the beast, and the latter not only did not get angry, but licked the cute little hands and begged for their caresses. Then, turning her snout without otherwise moving towards the clubs already lifted over her, she showed in all her appearance and especially in her long imploring glances which begged for mercy, such a humble and submissive meekness, that rather than striking her, the clubs spared her, as perhaps she spared the little body she had at her disposal. A she-wolf or jackal, one of diverse genus, she was bitten all over, one of her hips was crushed, she had a wide tear on her flank, and the blood which flowed from her lips came from her own wounds which she continued to staunch. Besides, she was gravid, and this state as much as her weakness explained why she took refuge near the fires, the only way she could escape the attacks of the larger carnivores. Out of curiosity regarding what would come of her, they washed her and bandaged her; the little Adah, under her neck-lace of winkles which slapped her face, and laughing through it all, leaned on her as a companion, and refused to let her go, her arm around her neck, the mother took them both along. The litter having come to term, wolf cubs and children nestled together on the same litter and play-fought over the she-wolf's breasts; and soon, both, grown up, having the same needs, sharing the same passionate interests, loping along in unison on the trail of some prey, guile, patience, speed, courage, strength, all the power of man multiplied ten-fold, a hundred-fold by the first faithful pack to help them out, by the dog for-ever become man's liege-animal.

At this point in the story, Hemo was thoroughly excited. The roar of the lions in the heavily damaged greenhouse, as they were being shot, served as an appropriate accompaniment to the savagery with which he exalted the pride with which primitive man must have flared his nostrils when, upon the signal of a blast of horns, the first dogs lost their series of bites and rabid baying at the throat of elands, boars and aurochs, and delivered their still quivering flesh to the hunger-driven sharing of the flint and obsidian knives. And in singing he continued to swing, not being able to stop lest the flames en-velop his legs.

The lions dead, the firemen who no longer feared en-countering any further large carnivores, all by then cooked or asphyxiated, entered the hallway from the greenhouse, where they attacked the fire in the hottest of its foci. The nozzles of their fire hoses were spewing forth water in great streams, when the barrels of oil and thinners which the painters had put away in the monkey enclosure blew up in turn, feeding such sheaves of flame that Hemo, suffocated, dropped from the trapeze and was swallowed up by the heap of red hot coals, his final shriek answered only by Jan, who fainted in the crowd and was taken away.

"What, somebody injured?"

The good folk to whom everybody who met them asked this question, answered that it was simply a stranger, a poor madman who claimed to be related to monkeys, and which the police commissioner ordered to be taken to the asylum.

The last of the curious gone, the night which had been interrupted now became thicker and more silent, though still somewhat disrupted in the eagle's aviary by the frightened rustle of large wings spreading out in response to the unusual sounds, and, in the basin at the rear of the gardens, by the raucous barking of the sea-lions, still believing in an aurora borealis, and continuing to salute the smoky red which remained in the sky above the ruins.

CHAPTER XV

Jan Maas' identity easily established, the asylum notified his family. His brother Adrian, the old widow Brinckleymann, Saskia his step-sister, and Martin Heltzius, all came in from Haarlem the same day, recognized him and took him with them against the better judgment of the director, who wished to see him submitted to a medical examination before releasing him. Hearing Jan name them all, inquire about the health of each of them, of their occupations, their financial situation, remembering obscure details of their common past, which they themselves had forgotten but which the precision of his words and memories helped them recover, they thought it the director who must be crazy.

However, Saskia and her husband were both very much surprised, when, having asked him what had made him rush off when he had barely arrived home, he initially hesitated and then answered that a newspaper, which he happened to find at hand, had proved to him the presence in Amsterdam of the best, of the most faithful companion of his years in Africa, and, his anger concentrated, his sobs poorly concealed he explained that this companion was a young ape, which he had the right, even the obligation to immediately reclaim from the ever-cursed people who had taken him.

The director then said to him, in a very natural manner, that his friendship for this lovely animal, this gorilla which the English clowns had been forced to give up to the Zoological Gardens, where he died in so singular a manner that night, could easily be understood. Was Hemo not his relative? His...?

"Alas! Sir, he was my son," sobbed Jan.

"So then you had knowledge of, you understand me well, I say...knowledge of...his mother?"

"D'ginna! Yes I knew D'ginna"

And this time Jan allowed his tears to flow. Adrian's wife and daughter no longer knew what sort of face to put on, Martin chuckled heartily, and Adrian, drawing the sick man to him in his big arms, hugged him, and cried out: "My brother! My poor brother!"

The director was no fool. He authorized his departure; but before, thrilled to be able to lay out a bit of science with no medical intern there to shrug his shoulders, he drew the two women and Heltzius off to the side and explained to them, gravely nodding his head, that the brain was a kind of piano, with a keyboard made up of thousands of keys, and that madness often consists in only one of these being out of tune, and thus people seemingly quite rational to the layman are indeed found mad by the psychiatrist, whose experienced finger presses the sensitive spot, knowing how to detect the broken note. Let them surround the poor boy with every precaution and always somewhat suspicious of him, given that his monomania of believing himself the father of an ape and thus the former—how can he express this—husband of a she-ape, indicated most likely some strange aberration to his reproductive instinct.

These recommendations offered in wisdom were met in a similar manner, and the family thanked the director.

During their return, Jan could not so much as look out the door of their train carriage to see some forgotten landscape without his brother gently restraining him from behind, like a father his dizzy child. Intimidated, but as always not wishing to complain, he sat down again. The big Heltzius would then drum on his ribs with his elbow and say: "You joker, you damn joker!" and whisper in his ear: "When we're talking man to man, you'll tell me all your jokes, won't you?" with concealed winks that Jan no more understood than the actions of his brother who was being excessively careful with him, thus annoying him a great deal more. As for the old widow Brinckleymann, their gazes barely came to cross each other before she would pout in profound aversion. To change the mood, perhaps to rekindle an ancient fondness, he wished to hold the hands of Saskia sitting across from him; the gesture and the shriek with which she drove him off betrayed such fright, that the other travelers in the coach, suspecting him of some inappropriate behavior, all turned their angry faces towards him. Even a respectable matron of some 50 years, with mucus hanging from her truffle-nose, judiciously reflected aloud that it was horrible that those of her sex must be exposed to certain lewd individuals; and, a few minutes later, seeing Saskia, who, somewhat embarrassed at her outburst was smiling at Jan, she added that besides, such dissolute people were well acquainted with those to whom they chose to address themselves; she, had never been attacked. But Jan, remaining still, pretended to sleep.

Once off the train, Adrian, blinded by brotherly love, and reminding them that they were one family, begged them all to reveal nothing of Jan's bizarre ideas, to say nothing of what asylum they had found him in. A family would be rather stupid not to keep to itself, as one family, as much as possible, the stain of one of its members.

His wife loudly demanded to be heard. "There is this. How can Mr. Maas repeat 'one family, one family?' Jan is of the Maas family, yes, but not of the family of the two, widow and daughter of Brinckeylmann, and not any more of the Heltziuses, don't you agree my son-in-law?" She put the emphasis on "my son-in-law," to clearly recall to her second husband, who had not said another word, that Martin was her son-in-law, but not his. And to disengage herself from any responsibility in events that were to follow, she confided her fears to

163

her friends as early as the first night; if it was entirely on my shoulders, she said, I would have taken him on, as I often repeated to my husband, insisting that he bring back the poor devil, despite the burden he represents; but, you see, according to the asylum's director, the most inoffensive looking madman is necessarily a constant menace, his psychoses can erupt at any moment, under the most diverse and unpredictable of circumstances. In making such a solemn admission regarding persons of this nature, she had overcome her pride and felt it her duty to at least inform her most intimate friends. These good folk comforted her, and so that their relations not be strained, and so that her unfortunate brother-in-law not become the object of idle curiosity, they promised her to keep the secret.

The next day all the city knew about it.

Jan lived a tortured life. In the street, the children gathered around his footsteps, calling out to one another to follow him like a mask, or, if he sent them away with some anodyne scolding, they would ambush him at every milestone to shout: "Beware the madman! Beware the madman!" They would then run off laughing, jostling passersby and rubberneckers drawn out on the threshold. Women pointed him out to one another, young women looked at him sideways, pushing each other, stifling their laughter. At the museum, the guard never took his eyes off him, and drawing near every time he stopped in front of a piece, repeated an injunction to not touch anything, telling him to move on, as if he always expected him to deface the canvas.

Through the double windows of the shop-front and of the inner verandah of the Brinckleymann café, he could see his step-sister at the counter, her large bosom overflowing onto the marble having to hold her and her crocheting up, her rump filling the width of the chesterfield, her ample figure dozing open-eyed. With a stereotypical smile for the clients on her face, she offered, unwittingly pink in the cloud of pipe smoke, the image of a majestic idol of congealed fat, calmly and without disdain accepting the usual offerings of incense. His

164

hand on the door handle, this fat trembled, her mouth was pinched, the gaiety of her complexion faded. He nonetheless entered, building up all his courage: her eyebrows became furrowed, and her features dropped as if the tobacco smoke had settled on her like jaundice. The customers, disturbed in the normal silence of their digestion, whispered. He sat down. His step-sister sighed, turned her eyes up to the ceiling, and finally left, having closed her accounts ledger with a sharp smack, an invariable sequence of events after which her brother brayed, in a whimpering voice, that it would be best if he went back to look after himself in his room.

This room was in the Heltzius' house, on the first floor, facing the garden. If he closed himself up to read, the maid would interrupt him until Saskia herself would have to go up and berate him for trying to make himself sicker. Saskia also forbade him to go and pick up the children at the baby-sitters, a pointless interdiction since the little girls, terrified, would burst into tears as soon as he touched their hands, and the eldest, the boy, refused categorically to be seen with him, because his friends would then laugh at him. In the store downstairs, he would not have penetrated into the place for more than a few minutes when he was shoved out, a buyer having arrived, while in the kitchen, the kitchen-maid would badger him, complaining that he was always in her way. If he took refuge on a bench in the garden, Saskia would again bother him, asking him how he expected to get better if he was always day-dreaming. He should instead get about and do something. To obey her he tried to take walks outside the city, but fared little better. Sitting one day, for example, very calmly on the edge of the smooth waters of a sleepy canal, he suddenly felt himself picked up from behind around the waist. A farmer thus dragged him off to his house, locked him up without even answering his bewildered questions, and ran off to get Heltzius, who brought him home like a truant child, having him run ahead, berating him for wishing to drown himself and bring down all sort of trouble on the family. Given time, he'd do something that would have them regret they allowed him his liberty. And from the outskirts to the house, everyone on their way told each other how he was already under the water when they dragged him out.

The next day he found some peace and quiet a little further out in the country. But upon his return the police were waiting for him. A little girl, having been victim one night in the woods of an indecent assault, public rumor had formally accused him, and he would have been arrested had they not discovered at the same moment, a stranger, an Englishman, who truthfully admitted to having acted with the consent, dearly paid, of the mother. Long after this day, poor Jan, whom the insulting suspicions had crushed, kept hearing the cries of the pack of gossips gathered during his interrogation, and threatening to break into his home to punish him immediately.

Newspapers from Amsterdam calmed him down to some extent, plunging him back into his old obsessions, and teaching him that Hemo's corpse, barely singed by the flames, had been dissected in the greatest detail. In spite of a century of research, one of them said, it was good nowadays to seize upon such opportunities, of which none will deny the extreme importance in these sorts of studies. One has again not found the existence of any significant differences in anatomy between man and this Gabonese ape; he has two feet, two hands, and the term *quadrumana* coined by the Frenchman Cuvier[22] is clearly inappropriate; the circumvolutions of the brain, except for some insignificant differences are the same; in a word, the gorilla approaches the Hottentot bushman as closely as the

---

[22] Georges Cuvier (Jean Léopold Nicolas Frédéric Cuvier, 1769-1832), a French naturalist and zoologist. Cuvier only applied this now obsolete classificatory mechanism, a term first conceptualized by the remarkable German physician, physiologist and anthropologist Johann Friedrich Blumenbach (1752-1840). The Latin *quadrumana* refers to "four hands," such as found on apes, and *bimana* to "two hands" as found on human beings. [Ed.]

bushman approaches civilized man, another Frenchman, Bory de Saint-Vincent,[23] considered the bushman to be a transitional form between man and ape. There remained the question of articulated language, but would it be extending logic too far then to hesitate at categorizing those born deaf and dumb...

Alas! Jan remembered having gone over these points and many others in every which way, when he was searching for proof of his paternity. Since the autopsy did not show the least unusual characteristic, he concluded in a flash of lucidity that D'ginna had been pregnant before their relations, that Hemo was in no way a part of him, and that only his fever had made him believe that this true ape spoke intelligible words the night of the fire. Finally he realized that the dangers he faced, the suffering, his lost youth, his dreams of glory, could be put out of his mind like water under the bridge. Well then, so be it, he would resign himself to this, but not without first satisfying a last fancy, which was to give a last goodbye to Hemo's skeleton, displayed, according to the same newspapers, in the comparative anatomy galleries. And without mentioning it to anyone, he took the train to Amsterdam.

At first he wandered from room to room, around the one he knew to be his goal, as if to increase his desire by a voluntary delay. One of these galleries brought on bitter disgust, there, labeled jars bearing fetuses preserved in alcohol were lined up on shelves, displaying the innumerable and multiple forms of hideousness of all the monstrosities, larvae more frightening in the reality of their repose than when they swarmed onto a nightmare-ladder, their greenness as if spread out and diffused in the cold light of the tall bay windows seemed to mottle the light, changing to the light of a vent-hole. In another, the arsenical smell of stuffed birds revolted him, but caught his eye with their bright colors. Then, on both sides of a narrow vestibule, glassed-in cases devoted to bats frigh-

---

[23] Jean Baptiste Bory de Saint-Vincent (1778-1846), a French naturalist (botanist), explorer, and soldier who developed an influential system of racial classification. [Ed.]

tened him again. Examples of their numerous species, arranged in every pose, rotted there slowly. To distance himself from the great specter of a vampire bat, spread, a meter wide in wingspan, as if in flight, the fangs sticking out like halberds[24] beneath its nose, he drew nearer a group that was uglier still, the kalongs of Timor, arrayed in their natural sleep position, their marten-like heads bent downward, their angular wings completely enveloping them, such that they resembled the monks long ago condemned to suffer hunger and thirst for having drunk at the black mass, who were then hung by one foot, with their robes accentuating the bony protrusions of their emaciated bodies, and whose gibbets one would have seen lined up in the background.

The sequence of the mammals was begun with these bats. To the right and left of the entrance to the next suite of rooms, the bony frames strung on iron rods followed, one after the other, what a mere layman would see as an inextricable tangle. Completely in the back, in the middle of the walkway, widened into a round-about, Jan recognized Hemo, without consulting the notice. The skeleton was erected in a normal posture. His two feet nailed down to a waxed oak platform, he further supported himself by the curled up underside of his right hand's phalanges, while the left hand, raised up, held onto a branch which came off horizontally from a tree trunk beside him. Prepared with great care, the matte whiteness of the bones was brought to life by the yellowed polish of the natural ligaments left on the joints. He was huge, his rounded rib cage capable of serving as the framework for a forge bellows, his mouth bearing a wonderful grin, the ridge of the eyebrows still shading the eye sockets. As from the bottomless urn of a great river, his coxal region, almost as big and harmoniously curved as a man's, could have eventually issued forth generations until they formed a people. And Jan admired the solid base, and thought that action must be a pleasure for mus-

_____

[24] A spear fitted with an axe circa 15th- and 16th-centuries. [Ed.]

cles endowed with such leverage, an action for which he himself bore only antipathy. At this hour, more than any other, the
gallery had no other visitors to stop him from sinking back
into his reveries.

Unaware in this situation that he perhaps was experienc-
ing the remaining fragments of his parental pride, in his prolonged contemplation he hypnotized himself, until his wobbly
legs forced him to sit down. The harsh daylight spread out in
the middle of the polished floor, sprinkling with gold dust a
steel bar, a screw head, the edge of a varnished table, but was
chased from along the walls by great swaths of shadow rolling
out their transparent airiness, crepe curtains beneath, where, as
the paleness of the bones was projected upon them, Jan saw
the skeletons grow and move about.

Having long practiced the teachings of the Bible, Jan recalled from afar the readings of his childhood, the Valley of
Josaphat, that valley of carnage where Joel summoned the
reborn nations to listen to the lion-like roars of the Lord. Jan
believed himself to be witnessing a sordid parody of the Last
Judgment. Indeed it was not the dead rising from the universal
putrefaction, trying to hide their wounds and their vices from
God on his throne of clouds, trying in a supreme and derisive
hypocrisy to thicken about their rediscovered flesh and soul,
the folds of the shroud and of repentance; it was the skeletons
which he had examined, of beasts existing or extinct, detaching their feet from the pedestals, slipping down from the half-
open cabinets, ridding themselves of their supporting struc-
tures, jostling each other in confusion, rushing forward, pranc-
ing, climbing onto one another. An elephant with an ostrich on
its back, frogs standing on his tusks, walking on their hind
legs, those in the front carried on the shell of a fossil glypto-
don,[25] with which early men sheltered themselves; about the
seven cervical vertebrae of a giraffe, all those of a boa were
wrapping themselves; mice, cats, dogs and bears chased after

---

[25] A now extinct giant mammal of the Pleistocene, and relative
of the armadillo. [Ed.]

one another, while off on the side, an assemblage of heavy bones which had been a lion, its head buried inside the rib cage of a sheep, but unable to bite because its lower maxillary, which, its copper staples rusted, had unhooked itself, hung chattering in anger. These skeletons expressed the same fears and hungers that they expressed, struggling in a ridiculous continuance of interspecies competition as it had been, but supplying not the last of the episodes of the parade which Jan saw march by beneath his eyelids and in front of Hemo. For all of them, the hunters and the hunted, the executioners and the victims, the cruel and the meek, the giants and the vermin ended up coming to bow before the great ape, who, with the phalanges of his left hand, anointed each of them with a quick and disdainful benediction.

Since they then disappeared, the comedy seemed to be coming to an end, when the door at the back of the room opened. The two leaves of the folding door opened themselves without a creak against the doorframe. Beyond, instead of the vestibule through which Jan had entered, an arched canal, a half-full sewer stretched out, stretched out to the point of narrowing down to a point imperceptible from the other end, and the only lighting allowed one to plumb the smooth spread of its walls arising from the pale life of its waters. Indeed, these waters, while they at first glance seemed to stagnate and give off a fetid stench, like a motionless and deserted cesspool, supported creatures which in leaping from the surface spread a lunar-like reflection upon it. Jan, noxious, suddenly felt his heart clench and fail him, as he recognized these creatures which he had been unable to distinguish at first, as the fetuses of monsters escaped from their jars.

There were those that flopped about like fish, some that looked like geckoes, which climbed with the stumps of their rudimentary limbs, or with limbs emerging worm-like from their bellies, and dropped from the curved arch where they had left a glistening mucous-laden trail. However, they did not produce in their fall any more than a soft gelatin-like rippling of the surface. Glimmers, bleached and dull, but variable,

170

greenish, sulfurous, of the pale lilac hue of cyanogen[26] flames to the pale blue of steel, left Jan no need to compare them to the phosphorescent infections which certain storm-driven tides washed up on tropical strands. The light seemed to spread with the pestilence, as if these embryos were anxious to spotlight their putrefaction. And perhaps the most hideous was that they did not exhibit that vague allure of life where the squirming of larvae animates corpses but, instead, their own joyous activity.

Jan wished to escape, but it was too late. The water was seeping into the gallery; in order not to get his feet wet he had to draw them up with two hands crossed over his knees, and even then the fetuses stuck to his legs, unclean leeches which he detached in epileptic spasms. They all then headed for Hemo, but instead of saluting him and disappearing, they wrapped themselves around his tibias, his femurs, in two uninterrupted columns which filled up his pelvic region. More were coming up; to fit them in, the skeleton grew in every dimension; his pelvis became a vat and this vat a charnelhouse spreading like a nebulous soft roe, which drew from the abysmal depths of the darkness new things which Jan recognized in turn as the bats from the first glassed-in displays. They hovered and perched on Hemo's head, now as wide as his pelvis, and there watched, through the disjointed sutures, the inside of the skull where the foetuses, continuing their ascension along the vertebrae, penetrated through the occipital. The bats then seized upon them at their arrival, and swallowed them without bothering to tear them to pieces, almost pumping their unnameably denatured meat into a sticky, juicy, macerating porridge.

The last glow thus extinguished, Jan felt on his brow the glancing touch of sticky wings and the sharp bite of tiny teeth on the fat of his arm. Satiated, would the vampires suck his blood to wash down their disgusting treat? As he drove them away, a tender voice reached him. It was still broad daylight.

---

[26] A poisonous, pungent gas which burns with a purple flame. [Ed.]

His brother Adrian begged him to calm down, sponged off his bristly face which was clammy with sweat, and pinched his arm to draw him from his lethargy. Martin Heltzius accompanied him, and a third individual which Jan did not remember ever having met, though Martin presented him as a friend. All four left the gallery, passing back through the hallway with the bats, where Jan could not hold back a shiver of fear, and which his brother, who assisted him in his still torpid gait, noticed and asked him about. He answered that it was a silly dream he had just had, already forgotten, but in which these vile beasts played the main role.

"Ah! You hear, sir," Adrian then said to the stranger, "he was dreaming, merely dreaming, and that happens to the healthiest among us. It's that, you see, my poor friend, that you certainly surprised us when we came upon you. Your back was hunched, your legs pulled up, and you were swinging your arms over your head like a windmill."

The stranger remained silent and impassive, but Martin lightly shrugged his shoulders.

Outdoors, Jan, struck by the reddened eyes of his elder brother, questioned him in turn. It was clear he had been crying. Over what? Was someone sick at home? It was Martin who, when they all got into a carriage and left the museum, reassured him; no, everything was fine in Haarlem, they were only a bit worried that morning upon discovering his sudden disappearance; but the scattered newspapers in his room, in telling of the public exposition of Hemo's skeleton, allowed them to easily guess where to find him, especially since at the train station they questioned the very employee who had sold him his ticket to Amsterdam. And with his usual cordial demeanor, pretending to interest himself in what he knew interested Jan, he insisted on discussing the skeleton.

"So, how did you feel seeing that big devil of a skeleton? I bet you gave each other a hug, that you talked of your adventures in the land of the savages and that you were both homesick for those lands and savages, especially for those native women, now weren't you, you little prankster."

172

But already surprised by his brother's behavior, who with a finger on his lips and big tears in his eyes was indicating to him he should keep quiet, Jan was even more surprised when the carriage stopped far from the train station. The stranger got out first and invited him to follow, while his brother, to whom he appealed for an explanation, drew him to himself by his neck and repeated through his kisses:

"Forgive me my poor Jan, my poor beloved, forgive me. I didn't want to do it, it was the others..."

"Let's get it over with, gentlemen, let's get it done."

And the stranger, untangling the two brothers' arms, took hold of Jan, and closing the carriage door, shouted to Adrian and Martin who had remained in the carriage, "Goodbye, gentlemen," and "Go on!" to the driver, who turned around and went off at a trot.

Jan was put back in the asylum.

He did not move for two days, laying on his stomach, his head up on his elbow, in the middle of a room padded from top to bottom, refusing to answer. He did not sleep, even though his meditations had the intensity of a hibernating sleep. He was left alone. The morning of the third day, he opened his eyes to the incomprehensible maneuvers of people his keepers claimed were nurses, and who, when they forced a long, hard rubber stick between his teeth, seemed more like awkward contortionists trying to impale him backwards.

As he struggled, the men asked: "Why will you not eat with good will?"

"Simply because I was thinking of other things," he confessed in good faith, sitting down to savor with as sincere an appetite as was his confession, the fine stew which was offered him. While not convinced by his good humor, the nurses were no less happy to see their work ending in a friendly manner; they were convinced that the doctors were wrong not to immediately allow more violent measures. "Until proof of the contrary!" they muttered, taking along the esophageal probe.

It turned out to be the only unpleasant incident in his new life. His two days of thought had not been lost. This peaceful serenity which the most fortunate rarely ever have complete, were it only to have the almost indestructible germ of doubt as to its duration, he had it, along with the certitude that it would be forever. From a material perspective, he felt a great relief at no longer having to worry about a place to live, food, clothing, relationships or money; to be able to isolate himself from landscapes, his surroundings, his neighbors, to do or not do like everyone else, to warm himself in the summer, to wander about at night and sleep during the day, to talk aloud to himself; to no longer be interrogated, the butt of criticism, or what is worse, to those marks of respect or sympathy to which one must at least smile politely; to close oneself off and ignore the face or the backside of a passer-by. It might indeed be absurd to suffer no more than the pricking of needles, rather the myriad little nothings that make up daily life he had nonetheless suffered. He considered his incarceration as his emancipation, as complete as it was unexpected, and the fat Heltzius could have, to bring him there, saved on his malice; he would have come on his own had he known the calm and solitude he would find there.

"Everything works out in life, as long as one waits," he would say.

Thanks to his brother's generosity, which he warmly thanked him for with all his heart, he enjoyed a small suite and a portion of park all to himself, in the paying customers' section. His keeper, once he had assured himself that it was pointless to watch him, only came by to bring his meals. He was also allowed to walk around in the huge common courtyard where all the lunatics classified as posing no danger to others were. He noticed with pleasure that these good folk, if they harbored their madness like the well-behaved outside the institution, at least had the advantage over them of leaving their neighbors each to their own; but any human figure having become insufferable to him, he remained in his corner of the garden, where he sometimes accused himself of being self-centered and lacking in charity, but to then absolve himself in considering that his presence, here or there, would be of no help to anyone.

So why get into trouble?

Always finding a practical reason, he judged that one did not require such a great deal of space to stretch out one's limbs, and so he shut himself up in his room so as to continue more comfortably to ponder the questions which were familiar to him. Why bother going anywhere? It would only be to see; assuming one could go anywhere, and one could not go everywhere at once, and especially, especially! one could not go at all times. The same eyes could only view but a ridiculously minute portion, compared to the eternal and capricious metamorphoses of Nature, rays, reflections, colors, topographies, plants, forests, oceans, clouds, skies; and he who could not see all of this in himself saw nothing. In the same way we do not touch, taste, smell, or hear more than a fraction of the available immensity of shapes, tastes, odors and sounds. One might as well then close all these windows of our senses, which only allow us to communicate with such a miserably small part of our environment; and, reducing the beast in oneself as much as possible, concentrate entirely on one's soul, which alone could imagine, reproduce and compass all the phenomena of the universe in their doubly infinite dimensions of space and time.

Drowning so pleasantly in illusion, he would blush in modesty, embarrassed to remember his crazy old ideas. What stupidities had he dared publish after his early readings, the good boy-gardener of yesterday, who, before having assimilated the elements of science upon which he had gorged, had belched them forth barely digested into a filthy magma? And his attempt to regenerate the human race, that blossoming of vibrios[27] which stir themselves for the duration of a lightning bolt! And his wish to leave behind a famous name! Fame... leaving his name...to whom? To what? When the scoria which already stain the surface of the Sun meld into one opaque

---

[27] A type of bacteria responsible for, amongst others, cholera, septicemia and seafood poisoning. [Ed.]

layer, the Earth, immediately reduced to a block of ice, will have no more rivers, no more seas, no more winds, no more exchange between air and water; it will come back to life with short and rare intermittence, by the heat which the center of the Sun, still in fusion, would send it, dislocating from time to time its crust to shine again briefly; oh! how little then would those dominant names, Jesus, Cesar, Shakespeare weigh upon the pale and trembling lips of the last man, holding his be-numbed hands out towards the abolished aurora, from this dead Earth still spinning around a black sun, in a night which would get darker, all the stars being suns that would also die, and the pale smoke of the nebulas being the last to bring light to the few points remaining in the complete darkness.

He no longer moved, no longer opened his eyes, no longer needed light. Someone fed him some food or other. Cauterized with platinum rods heated to white, which were applied to his spine from the nape of the neck to the lumbar regions, and which made his flesh sizzle, he sensed only a few recollections of a world exterior to his own, to which he no longer belonged, except to perceive in his internal visions an unutterable serenity. In the angelic paradise where he dwelt in ecstasy, he pitied the doctor and his assistants who moved around his bed to operate on him, as unfortunate shades not yet afforded the gift of his restful state. They rolled him around in a wheelchair. "Where am I going?" he would sigh in a single breath. "Outdoors in the air, to stop you from molder-ing away on your sheets," the nurse spat back in a gruff tone, which nonetheless charmed his ears like the chirpings from a nest.

And his blind man's eyelids guessed of the light at the limits of his dreams, silvered by a warm beatitude. Jan, having become without knowing it the most divine of gods, Buddha, congratulated himself for at last having attained supreme wis-dom, which consisted in preparing for the supreme emptiness while merely existing in the realm of life.

Marcel Roland (1879-1955) was a French writer, famous for his naturalistic works published in the prestigious magazine Le Mercure de France. *Roland was first and foremost a* feuilletoniste *for newspapers. He is mostly remembered today for his proto-science fiction novel,* Roman des temps futurs *[Novel of Future Times] (1911), about the rise of apedom to supplant humanity,* Gulluliou, ou, le Presqu'homme *(1905),* Le Déluge futur *[The Coming Flood] (1910),* and La Conquête d'Anthar *[The Conquest of Anthar] (1913). Other genre works include* Le faiseur d'or *[The Gold-Maker] (1913-14)* and Osmant le rajeunisseur *[Osmant the Rejuvenator] (1925). He also contributed to the notorious* Journal des Voyages, *with* Le Serpent fantôme *[The Phantom Snake] (1919).*

Marcel Roland: *Almost a Man*

CHAPTER I

Alix Forest crossed the garden, entered the small drawing room by way of the verandah and, pushing open the workroom door, called her forewoman:

"Miss Julienne!"

Before a tall, narrow mirror she began to uncoil her ample squirrel pelerine and remove her large, plush and unique mushroom-shaped chestnut-colored hat. She then collapsed on a corner of the chesterfield, her feet stretched out towards the radiator. Just then Julienne came in, exclaiming:

"Mr. Murlich, your cousin, has arrived!"

"You apologized on my behalf? You told him I very much regretted not being able to make it to the train station, because I had that urgent errand?"

"Yes, miss."

"Poor man! I'm going to go and greet him. So, has Lucy done the honor with the back guest house? He wasn't late? Did his trunk arrive with him?"

"His trunk! Why it was an entire shipment! Several trunks, suitcases, and packages. And then, they are two."

"How's that...two?" replied Miss Forest surprised. "Is someone with him?"

"Why yes, another fellow."

"Why! What's he like, fat, tall, short, slim, blond or brown-haired?"

"Well, you know, Lucy and I barely glanced at them."

"That's intriguing, I must say. Another fellow? Well, whatever, we'll see about that later."

Alix quickly raised her hand:

"Do tell, Julienne, while I think about it! But with whom could my cousin Wolfram-Pierre Murlich possibly have arrived, confirmed loner that he is? You know, I had, on the way, a spark of genius for the Balsamore dress...all in mushrooms my dear!"

The forewoman nodded, winding around her index finger a thread taken from her sleeve.

Alix continued.

"Eh? In a marvelous orange, crinkled silk boleti. Is that some idea? And you add a black velour belt painted in the same pattern. Can you picture it? I have it in my mind's eye, I could sketch it for you."

Finally, Julienne answered:

"But Bertha Balsamore will never accept such a thing, she simply won't hear of anything with mushrooms, and certainly not in something she'd be wearing on stage!"

"Ah!" replied the seamstress with a defiant cock of the head, "she'll be forced to wear them! Did I start this fashion for nothing? Myself, I think such a bodice would make an impression! But here we are chatting; I was forgetting my dear traveler! I'll see you later; my idea, think about it!"

She took up her pelerine, and in the same motion both young women turned their back on one another, the one to reenter the workroom, whose door in opening had allowed a laugh to filter out, the other to go down into the garden. But as Alix went out, already enveloped in the brisk cold of a January morning, she spied her cousin Murlich, approaching a few steps away.

He had changed little over the years: losing a little weight, his features becoming somewhat coarser, but still full of good humor, his skin tanned through his travels, a small, prim and proper man, with a graying beard and blue-tinted glasses. He walked upright, looking modest in his dark clothing and his soft felt hat. When they were before one another, Alix bent over to kiss him on the cheeks. Happily, they held hands for a short moment. Murlich exclaimed:

"You know, I barely recognize you. What a fine young woman you are now! To think it's been almost 11 years since I last came! You were still in short skirts."

They made their way to the drawing room.

"Ah! Good cousin, how was your trip?" asked Alix. "Let us sit down, why, you must be exhausted, get rid of your muffler…there!"

"I had an excellent trip. I left Basel last night, slept in Belfort, where I had a meeting with someone. This morning, I got back on the train at six, and at eight, I was in Paris, not a minute late."

"You'll excuse me, won't you?" replied Alix. "Imagine, this very morning I get a frantic call from a client, asking me to come to her home."

"I know, I know, Alix dearie, it's not important at all. With a car there is no problem. But in France you have very fast trains: two hours from Belfort here, that's some pace. At home in Switzerland the electric trains are still so slow, so slow compared to yours!"

"And how's your health, cousin?"

"Good. At 58 one can't complain."

"You're looking younger! And your eyes? You had written me that they bothered you?"

"Pretty much cured, thankfully. Only there's these nasty fevers, still a few fits now and then, still…But you haven't told me about yourself: what have you been up to, what's happening in your life? How you've changed!"

With a well intentioned but scrutinizing look from behind glasses, his mouth hiding an indulgent smile tinged with irony under a pendulous mustache, the scientist looked at Alix. Her rapid movements drew rustles from the silky material of her skirt, where citrine-hued agarics lent vague spots of pale yellow to the grayish material. Her full 26 years had not altered the gaiety of her thin mobile face, irregular but not ungraceful in its features. Her artistry was revealed by a slip of brown hair which fell across her flat brow, shading her eyes. Certainly, the transparence of her ears indicated an anemic condition, but by a constant biting, which had now developed into a tic, her lips kept a healthy redness.

Alix spoke very quickly, always seeming hurried, fevered, like someone who is perpetually late. She recounted, in short choppy quips her current life, how she had rented this house with a garden, to better accommodate her sewing business. It was necessary. The population's nexus of elegance was there, right in the middle of Auteuil, far from the noisy financial, legislative and judicial districts. The industrialized city pushed back, day by day, the inhabited regions, changing Paris into 20-storey row-houses, modeled on an expansion of the design of old barracks. Ah! it was such a shame, this need for uniformity, this decline in good taste which extended to all things, in an unhealthy obsession with practicality, and which was even felt in the world of fashion. The lovers of beauty in dress were now few. These days people preferred to buy clothing that met with a common standard, in bulk, from National Store outlets, supplied by a hundred garment trade businesses. For the independents who sought to bring greater dignity to their craft, the fight was getting to be difficult: but, she couldn't complain, she was successful in her chosen field, her profits had risen as well as her notoriety: she launched new lines and had orders, maintaining her individuality and making money, was this not the true achievement of the modern way? She was quickly becoming famous in the designer community. Just yesterday the magazine *Art and Fashion* had devoted an entire article to her, in the future, with her mushroom-themed innovations, her name would completely dominate the industry. For, while those jealous of her could well jeer, it was quite a find, this decorative use in fashion design of a long ignored element of the terrestrial flora.

"Why, cousin, you who are a naturalist, is it not your opinion that a number of cryptogams can rival in freshness, vivacity of hue, and elegance of form with the flowers? So then, why not?"

Murlich, smiling faintly with indulgent nods of his head, one by one examined the young girl, the mushroom-hat tossed on the armchair, the double-panes of the door and windows, through which were drawn the shivering lace of the bare trees. And while Alix spoke, he remembered the frivolous, carefree girl she had been until the day when conflicts between her parents had initiated her into the miseries of life. Very young when she thus lost her mother, a woman who thenceforth no longer existed in her life, she had been raised by her father, whose keen wit, open mind, sensitivity and taste for independence she now possessed. So when M. Forest had died, Alix, at 20 years of age, had been equipped to live independently.

"But," exclaimed the young woman, sinking her fists into the cushions of her large couch, "here I am boring you with my stories and not talking about more interesting subjects! You know I was completely engrossed! I read your presentation to the Zurich Congress; it was incredible! How did you manage to attain such a remarkable result?"

"Simply with patience. My observations at the Basel Zoological Gardens had led me to suspect that simians of certain species, apes especially, possessed a number of vocalizations, sounds, thanks to which they could understand one another. But in captivity these animals' behaviors were somewhat altered, so it would have been difficult to observe them as thoroughly as was necessary. It is then, as you know, that I

181

went to study the language of the simians on-site, in their own haunts. Ah! I worked for ten years all over the place, in the Sudan, in Madagascar, in Sumatra; everywhere I went I was able to ascertain that the great apes are indeed endowed with a true language, more or less developed according to the family. But it is in Borneo where I had the greatest success, with a tribe of Wurmb's pongos. There, I observed, from the steel cage which served to isolate me from my hosts' activities, a very high level of civilization."

"Of civilization?" interrupted Alix.

"Yes, of civilization, and a complete language which, after many patient efforts, I managed to learn more or less. Besides, you know all about this. We can speak of it at greater length, later."

"Professor Murlich," whispered the young woman sincerely, "I really admire you."

The scientist, softly nodded his head:

"I'm not particularly remarkable, child, I simply satisfied, along with my taste for travel, an old wish to clear up the matter of these over-neglected creatures, which the great Hetking, a century ago, called our future sons."

"And your first presentation, have you fixed a date for it?"

"In a fortnight, roughly; there're a number of people I have to see, and besides, I'd like my friend to have time to get over the excitement of the trip."

"Your friend?"

"The ape I have raised; he is here."

"You have brought him here? Ah! so he's the second traveler," exclaimed Alix. "I thought you were to send him directly to the Museum?"

"That was indeed my intention, but truly it would be difficult to separate myself from him. I thought he wouldn't inconvenience anyone in the guest house you reserved for me, so I brought him with me. Nonetheless, if this will disturb you..."

"But no, but no, you did well to do so, you will show him to me, won't you? Is he wicked?"

"On the contrary, very docile and not cumbersome, well-behaved, a perfect gentleman. He can even speak. He must be brushing off my clothes. We'll show him Paris, this young man."

"This young…"

"A boy! Barely 13. I had him very young. The hunters hired to capture him for me, in a stupid act of cruelty, killed the mother who sought to protect him."

"Oh! poor creature!"

"Perhaps you saw a photograph of this, some six months ago, when I brought him back from Borneo, where I had educated him."

"Yes, I think so, in some Swiss journal. What's his name again?"

"Gulluliou."

"Gulluliou?"

"It's pongo, meaning in English: son of doves" he said, smiling. "Gui-lu-liou, it's a bit like cooing."

"Most curious! And you speak with him."

"And he almost as well with me. You'll see, he's not even missing the power of speech, I tell you."

And, as if following a chain of thought, Murlich added more softly:

"This creature has every characteristic of man, but is only a beast to us!"

There was a moment of silence; Alix remained motionless and thoughtful. From the workshop on the right, far away laughter covered the whirring of a sewing machine; outdoors, in a light fog, a streetcar passing the corner of Lateral Boulevard rang its bell. The sparrows flew off twittering from the grillwork which bordered the sidewalk. For an instant Murlich and the young woman, in the close warmth of the drawing room, dwelt dreamily on what they had just now evoked. But Alix refolded her legs which she had spread out on the carpet, and rose nervously.

183

"What if we were to go and see him, huh?"

"As you wish, child, but it is awfully messy where I am, I brought a great deal of luggage."

"You'll have time to fix all that. I'll tell the chambermaid. Mind the cold, cover yourself!"

They went out into the garden. It was large and open. The tasteful two storey house though recent, smiled beneath its green and blue crockery trimmings. Ivy embraced the base of the house and the limbs of the virginal vine clung to the verandah's iron and copper banister, and thickly overgrew the clear-paned windows. At this hour a chilly sun appeared, extending its thin veils of gold between the naked branches of the chestnut and lacquer trees, warming everything to the lukewarm temperature of one's breath. The guest house was in the back, behind the house, on the other side of the entrance gate, with its back to Lakeshore Road. This street took its name from the fact that it skirted the remains of a lake which had been dug in the middle of some rather extensive woods. These had stretched as far as the city, but were now carved up and surrounded, thus forming the rich districts of Auteuil, Boulogne, and Neuilly. Only a square portion had remained, of which the lake, filled in little by little, was a part.

"Have you looked through your windows which face the street?" asked Alix. "You have a lovely view: trees everywhere. Only at this time of year, they are seldom very green."

The door of the guest house was open, and the sound of trunks being dragged and chairs being moved about inside could be heard.

"Listen to him," whispered Murlich, "he's cleaning up. He doesn't waste any time!"

Alix felt vaguely worried. She needed the scientist's perpetual smile to comfort her.

"Will you then present him to me?"

"Why certainly, and he will thank you himself for the warm reception you have given him."

"I'm not altogether reassured. Go in first, eh! No, hold on, call him out here, I'd like that better."

"Gulluliou!" Murlich called out loudly in a strange guttural voice.

The noise on the first floor stopped. Something heavy made the stairs creak. A dark, wide, hunched over form entered the frame of the entrance hall, then emerged onto the threshold.

"Here he is," said Murlich.

A little bit taller than his master when standing, Gulluliou had placed on his head, adorned with long black hairs, a red cotton bonnet. His tawny brown, hairless face bore two prominent and constantly blinking eyes, as if they feared the light. The nose was flat, the muzzle slightly projecting. The ears partly disappeared beneath his hair, but could be imagined to be small and stuck closely to the skull. A goatee framed these rather dazed and sad, but not overly bestial features. His neck was protected against the chilliness by a muffler, and a greatcoat covered his robust and gangling body. His long arms, in large apothecary's sleeves, hung like pendulums. Beneath a worn pair of pants one discovered feet shod in boots whose loose laces interfered with his bowed pins.

The ape remained motionless, examining the stranger.

In the numbing air, his short breaths rose in little clouds of steam. He coughed. A sparrow's chirping on the roof worried him and drew away his eyes.

"Gulluliou," enunciated Murlich in pongo, "t'r tirru Kneuh'r!" Turning, he translated under his breath: "Say hello to the lady!"

A wave crossed the animal's face, it was unclear whether his shivering arose from the cold or from his will being severely tested. His eyes seemed to grow, a ray of light moved fleetingly across them. A breath filled his lungs. His arms moved. His right hand gripped the bonnet which he removed from his head. In an extraordinary voice, both soft and rough at the same time, trembling with puerility, the ape spoke:

"*Tirru, Kneuh'r!*"[28] he answered.

---

[28] "Good day, Madam!"

CHAPTER II

In the cozy verandah extending from the small drawing room, Alix worked in the bright daylight of the bay window, filtered to a pale green by the plants. With a clear ring, the electric clock which controlled the time throughout the house, tolled 2 p.m.

Miss Forest was sitting on a very low hassock, her long legs crossed under her dressing-gown. Nearby, in a bin, a pile of little yellow rectangles shone with a raw brightness in the winter garden's tinted light. In a regular motion, the young woman's hand dove into the bin, drew forth one of the pieces of crinkled silk, and with a needle tied it loosely in a delicate conch shape, tossing the mushroom thus generated into another bin. All that could be heard was Alix's breath as she concentrated on this fairy's work. Occasionally, too, the sound of a drop of water striking the bottom of a rocky basin in some dim corner could also be heard.

Outside, the street noise from beyond the garden was smothered by the pallid softness of new fallen snow.

Lucy, the chambermaid, half opened the door:

"Mr. Maximin asks if Madam will see him?"

"Why certainly, have him come in here, Lucy," she answered without moving.

With a familiar gait, Maximin came in, approached the young woman, and, having shaken her hand, sat down in front of her, tossing his hat, gloves and velour cape onto a piece of furniture.

"Well, my dear poet, what's new?" asked Miss Forest.

Maximin shrugged his shoulders:

"Ah! I came to see you because I was bored, I don't know what to do with myself. I've been like this since this morning. It's really bugging me!"

"I bet you've been rehearsing?"

186

"You said it. And Balsamore was horrible! I could have beaten her! When such women get it into their heads that they don't want to perform, well, you know!"

In a gesture which pulverized an empty space, he completed his sentence, adding:

"It would take very little for me to take her out of the role!"

Alix stopped sewing for a moment, and glanced over at Maximin:

"Take her out of the role, are you mad? It wouldn't have been worth the two months of work!"

She tried to find some comforting words. Could he have come up with any better actress to play the role of the Nature-sprite? As if good actresses grew on trees! This one at least, notwithstanding her bad temper, was talented and experienced, she had performed a great deal abroad in the most favorable of countries. And one shouldn't, in an act of desperation, excise a vital part of a theater troop recruited with great difficulty. "Have some patience until the première, afterwards, things will go along by themselves!"

"I know, I know," muttered Maximin, "and it is this thought which sustains me; without that!..." Blond with blue-grey eyes, and a scraggly beard dropping down from a face creased by worries, the musician-poet Maximin appeared far older than his 30 years. His thin hands told of his aristocratic origins. They were constantly in motion, white birds delineating in the air his many and impalpable dreams. He suffered and rejoiced in any number of mysterious things, but his refined intelligence drove him rather to suffer from it. He had published misunderstood books, and music that no one, except a few dilettantes, had heard. He would say, laughing with a melancholy air that he did not belong in his century, that he should have been born many years before, at some rather vague time when men could still form some attachment to images of the unreal. His temperament shifted back and forth like all nervous types; resigned one moment and wild at another, but his anger never went beyond a lovely gesture or a delightful bit of verse. While he wasn't arrogant, he liked himself well enough to indulge in joys which only he could appreciate. He had few friends, of which Alix had long been one. They held each other in esteem. The young woman found in him a counterbalance to those contemporaries of his which she despised. She found in him a poet, a choice wit, a male presence, an attractive charm.

In a minute of silence, Maximin watched the seamstress' nimble fingers. One by one, the little orange funnels continued to rain down in a carpet of watered silk.

Alix smiled, waiting for him to speak:

"Stupid me," he said, "isn't that Balsamore's costume you're making there? The one you were telling me about?"

"This is it. Do you think it will be nice?"

"Such marvelous style. And so natural. Let's hope she'll want to wear it!"

"She'll want to. She can't refuse such a costume. Here, look at the sketch!"

On a table with wrought-iron morning-glory-inspired legs, she looked for the sketch amongst a pile of others.

"Can you see her on stage, your Nature-sprite? In the third act, appearing before the man in this smashing tunic, made from the forest's most humble plants? Why now, I've thought of something, why couldn't she be holding, like a parasol, a huge mushroom?"

"Ah! No, no, not a Mushroom-sprite!" muttered the poet, without further commenting on Alix's strange mania.

He added, dreamily:

"The third act, I've reworked a lot of it since I last saw you. You'd have to attend one of the rehearsals. It's that damned Bertha who made me change half of her lines. But now I think I've gotten a good grasp on it, that act of mine! I've got it pinned down."

Maximin, as was his habit, was getting fired up.

"Ah! You'll see. On stage perhaps you'll like it! You understand, I mostly wanted to make a statement with this play drama or fantasy, whatever one wishes to see in it, a work which carries a punch. And if I composed the music for the Third Act, it was so as to attain the full emotional range I am capable of. Because, this time, someone is going to have to back down, the public, or me. With all these essays and books, I have not been focused enough. True art is expressed in the theater. We no longer have theater, literature, poetry; our era is one of speculation on scientific matters, not matters of ideals. Do you believe in a humanity with no ideals? They make me laugh!"

Alix had stopped sewing, and listened. The artist was now getting carried away, caught in a whirlwind of his thoughts, thinking loud, his hands aflutter:

"People today know the value of money, but not that of a dream. They have forgotten their origins, lost in the origins of Greek and Roman art. The United States of Europe don't want to hear that amongst their distant forefathers was the man who carved the Victory of Samothrace, or wrote El Cid. A starry-eyed rhymer is ill-suited to today's world, one can agree to this, but…"

His voice which had lashed out, softened in hopeful pity:

"But I'm confident, the scientific era has been going on for a while, why should they not make room at their table for poets, scholars of another world? You well know, darling, you well know, I have been working on this production of my Triumph of Man for years. Alas! I don't know if I will be able to waken among us what may remain of a taste for fantasy, for art, for what extends beyond mere existence. I'm not entirely self-confident, I'm not sure if I've managed to create my work as I conceived it, but it will finally be produced! Produced, produced on stage, with scenery, as poets were 200 years ago! And the orchestra I have gathered with great difficulty will play my music, and perhaps then will they listen to me!"

Joy radiated so intensely from him that the young woman, as widely open to emotions as her independent sense of taste allowed, didn't dare express her thoughts, or speak of her fears. Was not this play, specially designed to represent *the Triumph of Man*, a risky business for the poet, as well as the

189

producer who covered the initial costs? How would it be received, what fate would be reserved to the bold whose attempts she applauded? People were no longer accustomed to theater, art was dead, entirely forgotten, something reserved for a few aficionados and the archeologists.

But with her flighty thought, Alix gave herself up once more to her admiration of Maximin, to wishing him success.

"Your play," she said, "is unified in its three acts, it will have an impact!"

Upon a gesture which suggested his fevered enthusiasm had already dropped, he nonetheless still enjoyed reviewing his favorite thoughts. Maximin replied:

"Yes, perhaps, I do feel that. Man appears in the first act burdened by the weight of his errors and atavistic superstitions that is the past. In a second act, having freed himself, he falls under another yoke, that of icy, methodical reason which is the present. Finally, its third act, the future which I have dreamed of as the complete artistic expression through music, poetry and staging, where Man, guided by the Nature-sprite and the Prince of Dreams, rediscovers his true voice and joins with the Woman to redeem the world through love. Yes, I do believe that within this narrow frame I have packed in sufficient good things, along with some things of beauty. Ah! I can't wait for it to all be over! If on opening night, with free admissions of course, we succeed, our cause is won."

Alix, struck her knee nervously with her fist:

"And we will succeed! First of all, Balsamore will be stunning in her role. All the others as well. You have quite a cast! And the décors! The old-growth forest in the last act gives such an illusion of depth and breadth. It's marvelous!"

Maximin approved with a gesture.

The young woman had returned to her work; watered silk mushrooms dropped anew into the bin. Upon the warm pallid silence of the winter garden, all that could be heard were the soft sounds of Alix's hand pulling through the needle, and quickly wrapping the mushroom stems in silk thread, and, on occasion, the delayed drop of the water striking a stone in the basin.

Lucy came in, bringing a tray of tea which she placed on a corner of the table.

Alix served the poet:

"Would you like some cactus liquor with it?"

"Why, certainly. It brings on lovely dreams. I like it."

"Oh! me too!" reinforced the young woman.

They enjoyed the warm drink to which a few drops of the liquor had been added. Two clouds billowed forth from the blue stoneware cups humidifying the air.

"An opium cigarette?" Alix suggested.

Maximin shook his head:

"No thanks, not today, I'm too nervous. Balsamore's to blame for it all."

They stopped talking. The blond man watched his friend, who, bending over, picked up the pile of orange corollas, letting them drop in a silky rain. For a moment Alix's eyes met the poet's, and both felt an unexpressed awkwardness: Alix sensed that Maximin would again broach the subject she had forbidden him to raise with her. He loved her, he had told her one day; she had no doubt. She too, a mere woman, would not have been loath to love him too. If such a thing had been possible in her case, it certainly would have been the artist she would have chosen. But she could not, steeped, no, conquered by too great a sense of independence, to even accept the concept of love, of a mutual fettering. She wished to be contented to enjoy all the pleasures of life, without for a single moment infringing upon her liberties in any manner. In a fear of committing an assault upon her solitary soul's fate, she refused to give herself to anyone. They no longer spoke of such things between them.

To say something and break the awkwardness which weighed upon them, Maximin expressed a sudden thought:

"But your cousin, professor Murlich, has arrived, has he not?"

"Yes, the day before yesterday."

"I saw that in my newspaper."

"What, is it already known?"

"All Paris must know."

"If you wish, I shall present you to the professor."

"Why, sure. Will he stay here long with his famous student?"

"Two or three months. Classes at Basel University take up again in April, I believe. Will you attend the seminar at the Museum? It should be quite curious."

"Perhaps, but when all is said and done, is this ape all that interesting?"

Shaking her head, Alix replied:

"Oh! far more than any man! I'm sure you'll be terribly interested in him. Today my cousin is presenting him to some of his colleagues."

"I'll attend his presentation," declared Maximin.

They were silent, Maximin, in front of Alix, savoring the charms of the resulting silence.

In the greenish transparency of the air in which the stems of the hothouse plants stood, the tea continued to steam from the cups. They entirely gave themselves up to the sleepy hold of the cactus liquor. The bell for the entrance gate which opened into the garden barely disturbed them. Through the double-paned windows they saw Murlich, followed by Gulluliou in similar attire, passing obliquely across the crackling gravel of the path, through the cold fog.

It was a brief view. Silence once again fell upon the verandah, interrupted only by the intermittent lip-like sound of the drops of water falling to the bottom of the rock-lined basin.

CHAPTER III

A fortnight later, the huge amphitheater of the Museum was packed with a disparate crowd: scholars, the bourgeois and the workman, men and women, all illuminated in great globs of light and shadow by the huge electric fixture suspended from the center of the dome. Arranged in tiers, this whispering crowd buzzed in expectant silence. Here and there the anonymous landscape of people, shifting like a calm sea, had their interest piqued by a red scarf, a bald head, the glare from a pair of glasses. For almost two hours the crowd satisfied the same intense curiosity which brought it to the conference in Munich, to the showing of Gulluliou. Preexisting opinion had been fed fresh impressions. This talking ape had shaken from its routine a society for whom science could no longer supply any surprises; everyone's reason was found wanting. In a century in which the human brain thought it had supplied its last efforts, where gears had replaced muscles and sinews, where the artisan himself was reduced to using his thought processes to guide a piece of machinery, one had judged unusual a professor from Basel's offer to prove the appearance of intellectual parentage between man and ape. One had come to witness this with a skeptical curiosity.

It was 10 p.m. With few interruptions the crowd's interest had been maintained. There were even some signs of approbation, some applause, when, to begin his presentation, Murlich went over the story of his many travels, his attempts among many different species of ape, and how, having arrived in Borneo, he came to spend time among the pongos, as well as how he managed to study these dangerous animals.

The orator described to the stirring crowd the large iron cage, a sort of forest home, linked to nearby buildings by telephone, fax, and wireless, equipped with recorders that preserved the most delicate nuances of intonation in the pongos' voices. Thus had he managed, after some trial and error, and using tame animals, to surreptitiously observe the behavior and language of the tribe amongst which he had forced himself to live. After a few months, the apes were sufficiently familiar with him that he could go out, wander freely, and speak with them!

193

After these preliminaries, Murlich had finally had Gulluliou brought before the crowd, dressed in an impeccable dress-coat from which the shirt front burst forth in an icy white. The ape, light beam pointer in hand, covering and baring himself in turn, saluted the audience. He stood very firmly on his legs, his body comfortable, but with the same worried batting of the eyelids, the same sorrow locking his lips in a look of resignation. He then sat down near the chair, where he was seen to serve himself a drink, to pour out some tea and sugar, and savor it in a seemingly distracted and aristocratic gesture, as some long ago prince might have. Especially, he managed to answer with some flexibility, precision and intelligence all the questions which Murlich and his many assistants asked him. These experiments which irrefutably demonstrated the reality of an ape language caused a great sensation, even a certain commotion: the proof of an intelligence superior to that previously assumed to exist among the apes did not go without disconcerting some people. Nonetheless, the facts were clear. And the crowd, amongst whom a few had translated their disapproval by repeated exclamations of hush!, had applauded each of Gulluliou's responses.

It was now under a growing nervous tension that Murlich, in his calm voice which firmly accentuated each word, continued his presentation.

"You yourselves, ladies and gentlemen, have seen that Wurmb's pongos, which indeed seem to be the apes most closely related to us, have the capacity to express their feelings in a series of articulate sounds, a true language. This simple fact, now established, is monumental given all the sorts of information that can be derived from it.

"First of all, a question poses itself, that of the animal's physical conformation. We indeed know, as I mentioned earlier, that at some point in time not far removed from our own, science believed apes to be incapable of speech, in the exact sense of the word. And, given the particular layout of their vocal organs, particularly the small area afforded to the tongue, science had been correct, at least at that time. Certain anatomical specimens in our collections, some 80 to 100 years old, attest that these animals which interest us were indeed not so constituted, or were poorly constituted to make use of speech. However, we have just seen them today capable of speech!

"Well then, ladies and gentlemen, what one must conclude from this is the following: this species has undergone in a progressive manner, for at least two centuries, a series of physical modifications; or rather, these modifications have been occurring for many generations, but it is only recently that we have been able to take note of the level of development towards which the species was heading.

"One must assume that the slow transformation of the encephalon, a little more developed, a little richer in convolutions at each new stage, led to a rise in psychic activity, a need to translate and exchange increasingly numerous and complex ideas. The transformations of the vocal organs and buccal cavity followed, allowing for the use of speech. I remind you at this moment of Nirdhoffer's scholarly studies on the progressive reduction in prognathism among the chimpanzees; a further element in support of our thesis.

"Thus, a brain capable of reasoned thought, a physical conformation compatible with the requirements of language, a reduction in the facial angle: these simians prove that among the apes an undeniable evolution is occurring towards a higher state."

At these words, a prolonged movement was heard in the assembly. But Murlich, paying them no heed, continued:

"However, ladies and gentlemen, notwithstanding the fact that these apes have managed to express their thoughts by way of a language, which is the highest mode of expression, one might have some doubts as to whether this was an irrefutable symptom of the superior state of which I spoke before. By objecting, for example, that Gulluliou and his fellows simply react in a hard and fast manner to emotional stimuli, which they then translate in a variety of ways, all purely instinctive. The anthropoids would then only possess a subconscious, sufficient to allow them to designate certain objects or sensations by onomatopoeia, through cries, even by articulate sounds, but all this in a mechanical manner, the way a drop of water always makes the same sound when falling in the same place, as gears of a winch do at any given moment. One could go on with further examples.

"Certainly, such a theory has little to support it, to say no more. It has nonetheless found some defenders." A new wave of restlessness moved the audience. In his ever calm voice, Murlich continued:

"However, ladies and gentlemen, independently of the question of language, other important factors concur to establish the apes' progress, and, in this regard, I believe that I have personally acquired definitive evidence. The pongos' behavior, which I studied from close up and followed very closely over many months, convinced me that these animals, if their strictly physical makeup had improved in the direction of becoming human, so had their intelligence and social skills. I'm willing to agree that the mud and branch huts built by the pongos may have been designed in imitation of homes they may have seen, although their huts were built deep in the forest, far from any population centers. I'll even admit, if you like, that these animals have borrowed from man the habit of surrounding their hips with a skirt of woven leaves, and of protecting the soles of their feet by attaching strips of bark to them. But how can one not attribute a spontaneous origin to the fact that at sunrise, the entire tribe gathers on some high ground and sings in a monotonous voice a kind of hymn to the Sun? Where would they have seen this?"

Some significant snickers had greeted Murlich's last words. He continued, interrupted every now and then by a strong restlessness:

"Let us not laugh, ladies and gentlemen. On the contrary, it behooves us not to neglect such a strange occurrence, which is uniquely troubling if one remembers that humanity went through a long period during which it devoted itself to these same superstitious practices, which nowadays seem ridiculous:

196

worshipping first the elements, then imaginary beings to which they erected temples.

"Ladies and gentlemen, understand: I'm not saying that a similar tendency is an element of progress, I am simply drawing a parallel between it and the period of our history I have just discussed.

"Furthermore, the accession of these apes to a civilization, yes, to a civilization which while perhaps embryonic remains nonetheless real, is a purely natural and logical phenomenon. It is nothing else but a startling confirmation of the law enunciated as early as 2055 by the immortal Hetking. A law unfortunately little known today. Hetking included, as you know, all of Nature in a vast cycle, or better yet, to a great ladder upon the rungs of which species climb, pushing off others in an infinitely slow process. This occurs in such a manner that when one of them has reached the top and stayed there awhile, it begins to drop, as the next one takes its place. "Hetking's Law[29] stands as a sort of counterpart and comple-

---

[29] This fictional creation is probably a hybridization of the mystic/occult idea of a "Golden" or "Hermetic" Chain, the medieval, philosophical idea of the "Great Chain of Being," and Ernst Haeckel's "Chain of the Animal Ancestors of Man" which is then unfortunately proposed to be a "counterpart and complement" to Darwin's environmental adaptation thesis of natural selection. In fact, what it does is substitute adaptation with competition, putting a spin on the term "survival of the fittest." It is then a short step from this view of Nature as competitive and hierarchical to the transposition of these terms on to the components or forms of Nature themselves. Hence the ape-man links the ape to the human on the basis of shared "race" characterized by competition and hierarchy, and mutatis mutandis, the existing "races" of humankind itself are now in competition and conflict over (human) status. In 1950, UNESCO issued an emphatic and widely supported "scientific critique and moral condemnation of the notion of race"

ment to that which was postulated by the illustrious Darwin, when he established the basis of his 'natural selection.' I will only call up in passing the great gifts of knowledge contributed to us by Darwin. If he only glimpsed part of the truth, he must still be considered one of our great scientific precursors.

"First, against all dogmas, against all the prejudices to which his era was subject, he dared establish, on a solid unshakeable footing, the simian origins of man. Man had arisen on Earth after millions of years during which the species evolved, from the primitive Monera which had become algae, Infusoria, worms, fish, batrachians, reptiles, up to an ancient lemur, with a tail, then into a tailless simian with a human anatomy. Then came the Pithecanthropus, the ape-man, not yet endowed with an articulate language, but penultimate link of a chain which has the cell at one end, and our civilization at the other. Finally, came man.

"Darwin went no further. He was certain that man constituted the final form of animal life having reached its full physical and intellectual development. But, along with those of his era, he believed that this human, once obtained, created a barrier and taking on the attributes of a species, it stood up against the field of evolution.

"One had had to wait a long time for Hetking to come along and, on the contrary, state that the evolution of orders, families and genera did not stop there, but rather that it was eternal. Certainly, the human model represented achievable perfection, but this is no longer the domain of a single species. It will be that of all species in succession. It is towards this achievement that all of Nature strives, dies, and is reborn in all its aspects, in its infinitely diversified stirrings. It is to possess this ultimate rank, humanity, that all the forces of the universe are in motion. In this admirable conception of man, extended to all complex organisms, and no longer limited to a privileged category, do you not see the solution to any number of prob-

---

(Claude Lévi-Strauss) suggesting that the term "ethnic group" be used instead. [Ed.]

lems which those of the past had vainly and confusedly examined?

"To the endless vibration of matter agglomerated into organisms, to their slow transformations, Hetking assigns a goal, a raison d'être. He defined the ideals of a Nature ever striving for the best.

"Why such constant battles, mutual rending, swallowing up of the weaker by the stronger, this great war between the infinitely little and the huge, the bacillus and the giant, ongoing from the very beginning? Our philosophies remained ignorant before this mystery and could only supply mumbled answers.

"Hetking explains everything. Thanks to him we know and now our knowledge of the facts proves it to us, that every species, in rising on the ladder of creation, carries in itself the seeds of its own destruction; that that which allowed its progression, then causes it to backslide. Turned against itself, the Darwinian law will ensure that, for the eternal cycle of Nature to perpetuate itself forever, it will one day yield its superior status.

"Well ladies and gentlemen, we are atop the ladder."

Here, the audience shuddered in a new swell of discontent.

"Our individual and social development has reached its summit. We can rightly be prideful of having both subjugated other animals, and the forces of Nature. But perhaps, in the near future, might we not be pushed off by this fateful law?"

At this moment the crowd's restlessness became so great that the rest of his sentence was lost beneath a muddled hubbub. Maximin and Alix, situated in the first rows of the crowd had already flashed questioning glances on one another. Maximin said softly:

"If he continues along those lines, it will turn out badly. These idiots don't understand. He hurts their pride, an unpardonable crime!"

"Poor man, he is nonetheless extraordinary, don't you think?"

"As a man, I will gladly accept his theory, as I believe Nature holds a number of surprises in store for the narrow and conventional science of today. As a poet I can only deplore the fact that an unlimited future cannot be afforded to our race. It is true that the works of man shall not perish if they are worthy of survival!"

Alix, she too enveloped by the tense atmosphere, said in shrugging her shoulders:

"They claim a monopoly over civilization, and scream like wild beasts!" However, Murlich had managed to overcome the rumor. He now displayed Gulluliou, who, sitting at his table with a worried and resigned look, turned his head slowly.

"Look at this simian, ladies and gentlemen, you have heard him speak, I can attest that he is possessed of more than a simple automatist, that he obeys true feelings, that he knows how to coordinate them, that he is even capable, with the help of his memory, to distinguish between doing good and evil, once he has been told only once. We are thus in the presence of a true sense of morals, inferior, it is true, but which nonetheless indicates in this species a huge step along the road to progress.

"I could, ladies and gentlemen, cite a number of facts in support of this intellectual improvement, on the heels of a physical improvement; and now, with respect to the psychological phenomenon of the association of ideas, there comes to mind one detail which proves that this phenomenon occurs just as well in Gulluliou's brain as in that of a man. For the two weeks since he has been in Paris, on several occasions Gulluliou has been struck with amazement at the many spectacles the capital has to offer its visitors, but nothing perhaps had a greater effect than a view of the Seine, furrowed by thousands of electric ships crossing one another in every direction. Then, to designate this sight, do you know what word he came up with, what word he created? Here it is in pongo: *Ourang pfluitt*, which means bird-tree. Indeed, all the boats are trees to him. He has assimilated by a strange association of ideas the boats which go about on our rivers with the tree trunks he saw carried by those of his country of origin, and to add to this designation an element of speed, he found nothing better than to add the word, bird. Is it not strange that such an animal is capable of so reconstituting, if not in its entirety, at least in his conception, a meaningful expression which used to be used, in the age of steam, for certain boats, a term I found in a description of the Paris of old: the fly-boats?"

As the crowd's restlessness continued to build, the naturalist understood the need to shorten his presentation:

"There is, I believe, a detail which sufficiently supports my thesis. Gulluliou, in being capable of coordinating his thoughts with their representation, has taken a step towards humanity.

"In many regards he is human or quasi-human [each of his words was now met by an uproar] by his general appearance, his language, his habits, even by qualities of the heart [snide shouts]. Yes, ladies and gentlemen, Gulluliou, a true child since he is barely 13 years old, and notwithstanding the precocious development of his body, Gulluliou possesses, along with his faults, all the qualities of the heart of a child: a great innocence, a propensity to confide in those who are familiar to him, to give himself up to them to protect him from the least danger, a sensitivity rendering him compassionate to any sadness, a compass he shows in stopping all his games and remaining silent [new snide comments]. This may seem surprising, but nothing, ladies and gentlemen, is more true. Besides, this tendency to altruism, to getting along with others, to an even temper and mild behavior are, if one can judge from the examples I have witnessed firsthand among the pongo, a racial trait. The pongo tribes, families and households live in perfect harmony, protect each other in any circumstance, and are concerned with the fate of their offspring.

"I would mention in this regard my student's capture, taken when he was very young, some ten years ago. The hunters had, notwithstanding my explicit instructions, riddled his mother, who had tried to protect him, with bullets. I then wit-

201

nessed this: the poor beast, seeing me a few steps from the spot where she had fallen, tore the infant you see here from her breast, and held it out to me with a supplicating look, as if to entrust him to me. And at the very moment she was dying, this mother, shedding human tears, found the strength to proffer on several occasions, the word: *Allok*, meaning in her language, *the child*."

At these words, spoken in a voice quavering with emotion, a more accentuated rumor ran through the crowd; there was some discrete applause. But immediately, from a corner of the hall, a low catcall, and more laughter rose; clearly his detractors were located there.

The uproar became generalized and Murlich was unable to hold back a cry of impatience.

"Ladies and gentlemen," he cried out, "in a century of intelligence and truth, nothing which relates to a soul's expression, even that of a beast, should ever be scoffed at!"

This sentence, into which the speaker had put all the emphasis he was capable of in the word "soul" applied to a simian creature, released a storm. The race was rising, claiming privilege against those who dared to claim these same privileges for animals. The crowd would not have it, could not understand. They were standing, angry brows moved about in waves. Bespectacled gentlemen, scholars in disarray, shrugged their shoulders, motioning as if to leave. Others argued with great animation, their lanky arms flailing about like marionette limbs. Over these controversies salvos were exchanged. The gang of loud-mouths continued to kick up a shindig. Murlich, at the podium, waited, trying to calm his student who was beginning to lose his nerve under the mounting hubbub.

A few minutes later, under the blue haze of the huge central lighting fixture, the hall was abuzz with voices shouting out impassioned comments. Finally, a relative calm fell. An old man, perched on a bench indicated that he wished to speak:

"Ladies and gentlemen," this undoubtedly illustrious individual coughed out, "I would ask the honorable speaker...I would ask him that he present us with an immediate, conclusive proof of the intellectual development of these apes. A proof other than that of language, of course. Then we shall be convinced."

"Bravo, bravo!" voices shouted out.

"I accept, ladies and gentlemen," Murlich answered from where he stood, but what proof do you wish?"

In the middle of the hall, a man rose, holding a roll of paper his wife, who sat beside him, had just handed him. With a foreign accent, he stated:

"This is a copy of the Schweiziger-Revue, where I saw the photographs…[his wife prompted him]…Gulluliou's capture, with the death of the she-ape. Show it to the child, see if he recognizes the scene."

An enthusiastic response. The idea was accepted by all. The magazine was passed from hand to hand to the podium where Murlich, who had understood, cried out:

"But, what you ask of me is so cruel! To show this poor animal the scene of his mother's murder! O! ladies, gentlemen, you cannot wish such a thing. Find something else!"

New sneers denigrated such scruples. A young lady with very short curly hair spoke up in a sharp voice:

"Go ahead, there's no danger that he would understand!"

Near the speaker, friendly voices advised him:

"Do it, to convince them!"

Clapping burst out loudly from within the crowd, encouraging Murlich. He took the picture. The crowd was silent, their attentions directed towards the group made up of the man and simian, one standing, the other still sitting, his face worried, his eyes blinking. Great dark shadows on the rear wall spread in gigantic silhouettes.

Murlich was seen to emotionlessly hand over the magazine to Gulluliou who took it two-fisted. Murlich signaled him to look at it.

Close by, the crowd remained quiet; an involuntary dread tightened around their chests, made their heads throb in the heated atmosphere. From where they were, Alix and Maximin felt they were witnessing some dark crime.

Gulluliou looked at the picture; suddenly he let go of it, raised his head, turned two or three times from right to left. His features were drawn, a hundred creases lined them. Then, his features relaxed, he joined his hands together and before all the lights this grotesque and pitiful child in the pillory of his collar, gave out a little moan.

The crowd shifted uncomfortably. Gulluliou brought his hands to his face, which he suddenly hid. The crowd stifled a sigh. Between the simian's black fingers, one could see something sparkle. In the profound silence which ensued, the crowd remained motionless, breathless with emotion.

The little ape had recognized and remembered. And he cried.

CHAPTER IV

The four walls were painted in light colors; muslin drapes framed the window. In one corner there was a low cot whose tight covers displayed yellow and red stripes; necklaces of stones and shells were hung here and there throughout. A tall dry palm branch was strung up over the hot air duct, which made it sling back and forth, as it once had in a warm wind. There prevailed the bare, virginal atmosphere of a child's room—of Gulluliou's room.

Gulluliou, sitting lazily, one arm dangling, stretched out the other to Dr. Darembert, who, feeling for a pulse, nodded his head and asked Murlich:

"Has he been coughing long?"

"Doctor…"

"Why, yes…he's running a temperature." He leaned over onto a chest taken with a fit of wheezing. "Some obstruction on the right."

"Doctor," said Murlich, "I began to notice his coughing some eight days ago; but I didn't think it would last."

"Where does it hurt?" he asked Gulluliou, in pongo.

The ape, whose fever-glossed eyes awoke, showed his back. The doctor nodded once more:

"One has to beware of winter weather with such creatures. It might only be a bad cold on the lungs. I'll write you out a prescription, downstairs. But, as you know, one must be very careful!"

"Don't worry, doctor."

"Have him lie down right away, he should amuse himself sitting up, with the temperature he's running. And let him sweat, give him steaming hot herb-tea."

Murlich had repeated the doctor's instructions to Gulluliou. When he told him to lie down, the animal weakly shook its head:

"Triouou,"[30] he whispered.

"No, it's now! Let's go, hurry up, we are waiting to see you laying down before we leave."

Gulluliou signaled his dissent. His hoarse coughing resumed.

"Why do you not wish to?" asked Murlich.

Gulluliou did not answer, but looked over at the doctor.

"Would you believe it," said Murlich, "he's shy to do so in your presence! He does not want to undress before you!"

"Well, I'll be, my dear professor," answered the other, who like many of his contemporaries did not lack in exclusivism, and had only recently recognized Gulluliou's remarkable intelligence, "you don't really expect me to think that your ape, however highly evolved he may be, could exhibit such a strong sense of modesty!"

"Well, see for yourself!"

Gulluliou had risen from his chair in a skilful motion and was spreading out his nightgown. Then, when everything was ready, he came back and sat down, looked at the two men

---

[30] "In a moment."

once again, as if to say: "What, you're still here. Can't you see I'm going to go to bed, so leave!"

"Well then, so be it, let's leave him alone, if that's what he wants!" declared the doctor with a skeptical smile.

He extended his hand to the ape, who bent over to shake it. They left the room and went downstairs.

Murlich gloated over his triumph in silence; every day brought a new confirmation of what he had attested to the week before in the museum's amphitheater: Gulluliou was becoming more and more civilized, more and more a human being. He had once again, in the presence of a critical witness, shown proof of the delicacy of his feelings.

Ah! admittedly, he could not yet, with his rudimentary vocabulary, translate into words all that went on in his humble soul, but that which his voice was unable to express, his eyes did. Murlich had learned to read those eyes, constantly hidden by the blinking of his eyelids, but whose dark waters were stirred by inner eddies. Murlich had taken on the fascinating task of unraveling the tangled skein of Gulluliou's soul. In watching the blossoming of this ape when exposed to humans, he was filled with the pride of a partial creator. Like an artist, he loved his creation, dreamed of its coming completion, already seeing it upright, complete and perfect. This was why, in the week during which the ape had been coughing, Murlich had become more and more worried; and, fearing finally that it might be the start of a serious affliction, he had asked Darembert, the noted chest specialist, whom he knew, for a consultation.

"Well then, doctor," he asked in the small sitting room, "you have hopes that it will not be serious?"

"Ah! One never knows, you know. If it were a man I was dealing with, I would say yes. I'll give him a shot of serum."

"Antituberculin?"

"Yes, and I would swear by it. But this is not the case; would he suffer such a shot? Furthermore, would the toxin work in such a creature?"

206

"But, doctor, tell me frankly, do you think he has tuberculosis then?"

The other, the corners of his mouth lowered in a pout which augured poorly, answered:

"Hmm, for now it is not sufficiently progressed to make a determination, but I think it can be nipped in the bud if one takes great care. I reiterate, beware the winter weather! When the animal shall be capable of going out, cover him as warmly as possible."

"He wears a fur coat."

"Good. Besides, I will see him again before that. And, especially, be sure to overfeed him. He eats meat, does he not?"

"Very little, doctor."

"He must eat some. And every two hours a granule of hydrated albumin. As for the rest, follow these instructions to the letter."

He had just written out the prescription, and handed it to Murlich.

"So," the latter insisted, "you don't think it necessary to give Gulluliou a serum injection? Even if he doesn't need it, I can't see that it can do any harm. It would reassure me."

The doctor, bantering, smiled with his shaven mouth:

"It's understood, I'll bring my bag tomorrow; you are a father, and you are concerned for your child's health!"

Murlich was very serious when he replied: "Why yes," in his soft, deep and friendly voice. "What do you expect? Given all of my values I have imparted to him, I see more in him than merely a vulgar beast; he is a kind of son to me. Besides, he is so affectionate and so innocent: a true child!"

Above them, muffled by the floor and carpet, Gulluliou's coughing could be heard.

The doctor, notwithstanding his poorly hidden skepticism had remained thoughtful before Murlich's spontaneous and heartfelt declaration.

"Come on," he said, "go up and see how he's doing. I'll see you tomorrow. I'll give him the injection, don't you worry, we'll get him through!"

Murlich, once alone, returned to his student's room. He saw him stretched out in the narrow bed, only his eyes peeking out. The ape was not sleeping. He watched Murlich come in and make his way over to him, standing at his bedside.

Neither Gulluliou nor Murlich moved as they considered each other in the silence of their mutually mysterious and un-fathomable affection, seemingly reading in each other's eyes the futility of speech in understanding one another.

Gulluliou remained in bed for almost a week; the fevers had been difficult to overcome, all of Dr. Darembert's know-how had been required to stop this bout of bronchitis in its early stages. Plaintive and shivering during this period, he had been nursed like a human being by Murlich and Alix. When the naturalist had to go out for errands or other necessities, the young woman remained at the patient's bedside, encouraging him to drink herbal infusions and potions with a sisterly hand. What struck one with the animal was the resignation with which he suffered. Finally the cough quieted down, and he was less tired by the weight on his chest.

Darembert believed that the injection, given as soon as the first symptoms had manifested themselves, had been able to stop its progression. He allowed Gulluliou to get up. The ape spent a few days on a sofa, in a large quilted dressing-gown, near the window which opened on the garden's bare trees. A succession of picture books went through the conva-lescent's distracted fingers. His greatest joy was a doll, which Alix, his devoted friend, brought him one afternoon. On the pongo's long dark hand the doll swung, stiff and pink. He named it Minnili, after the name of a little bird from his home, thus named for its call. For hours on end, the Son-of-Doves rocked Minnili, with all the paternal tenderness in his simian soul.

Visits distracted him from his days of boredom in the half-light of late January. Since the seminar at the Museum, the public's about face had made the ape almost famous, and an acrimonious discussion of his case and of Murlich's doctrine had been carried out in the newspapers. The excitement born that night had propagated itself, the supporters now equaled the detractors, and all that had been needed for the animal to acquire the right to claim itself human was a few tears. Murlich brought his friends to the pavilion in Auteuil. Maximin, who had come to know the naturalist had also wished to meet Gulluliou. The poet saw in Murlich a capacity for speculation which bore a dreamlike quality, and which he felt comfortable with: they became friends. But Maximin was more and more overwhelmed with his play's rehearsals, which were not going altogether well, and by all the negotiations to rent a hall in which to present it. He was only able to visit the convalescent once, promising that he would attend the premiere of *The Triumph of Man*, announced for the 10th of February. Gulluliou had a week to wait.

The ape spoke little during these indolent days. He did not like to play under the light of the lamps, and as soon as the twilight came, wan and snowy or under worsening rain, he let Minnili sleep in a chair, got awkwardly into his dressing-gown, hunched over like a little old man, his arms hanging to the carpet. At night, Murlich and Alix remained with him a little while. He was content to watch them, but each in a different manner: with a dull but confident calm in the case of his master, and with a stranger, more piercing look in the case of the young woman.

Once, having remained alone, she had become uneasy about this look, about these wild, haunting, yet good-natured eyes which stared at her. But it was over in a flash; Gulluliou, like someone who made an effort to control themselves, had taken up his doll again, cajoled it between his chest and his bent arm, singing in his guttural voice an old tune which his mother had no doubt taught him long ago:

Minnili, Minnili, the little
Bird hops about the branches,

And tick, tick goes his little tail
With his little wing that beats…;
Tick, tick,
Minnili, Minnili,
Little friend, sing me again
Your song!

In the corner the great palm leaf shifted heavily back and forth above the heat duct, as if still animated in the manner it had been in its native climes. Gulluliou watched it distractedly for a moment, put the doll down again, and drew his long body up from the sofa to go to bed.

CHAPTER V

The last line had rung out, echoing from the twilight-drowned stage to the entire silent crowd. Sparse applause greeted the curtain coming down, and immediately, from the orchestra to the cupola, the sound of voices abuzz.

Maximin left the edge of the fore-stage from whence he had watched all of the first act of *The Triumph of Man*; he turned to his friends, who extended their hands to compliment him.

Alix Forest was there, almost pretty under the lively glow of the stage-light, the very delicate skin of her pale neck emerging from the neck of her russet-brown dress, where huge white umbels recalled the young woman's strange obsession. On her hat, covered in dead leaves of the same color as her dress, a scattering of tiny mushrooms rose in a flexible tuft. With her perky yet refined smile, she immediately expressed her joy over the lovely verses whose strong harmony still stirred them. Murlich, who was there too, in the back, silent, applauded discretely, as it behooves a man of science who is not entirely indifferent to poetry. At the back of the box, Gul-luliou, motionless, watched, searching for answers in Murlich's demeanor with hesitant eyes. Suddenly he understood the meaning of Murlich's actions, his palms were struck together, timidly at first, then in a mischievously rough and childish manner.

But Casot-Dorlys the critic, tilted his flushed face, and allowed a glowing review to pass his thick lips.

"Admirable," my dear friend, "and so well played this act of yours."

Maximin surveyed the crowd at length, and shook his head:

"Let's hope it fills up, there're empty seats!"

"But people are still coming in," said the critic with a burr. "Don't worry, you'll have a full house for the climax! Ah! Maximin, the Arts owe you such a beautiful, such a great night! Soon you shall triumph!"

Alix said:

"It's already a success!"

The poet's nervous hands were shaking.

"The battle is not yet won. There should be more people. I'll go see at the ticket office. Besides, the people need only come in. Albani was good, wasn't he? He was made for the role."

"Oh! remarkable," added Casot-Dorlys. "His voice is warm and sonorous, just the voice for your verse! Does Balsamore play in the second act?"

"Yes, a short appearance," answered Alix in lieu of Maximin who was temporarily distracted, "but it's mostly in the third act that she gives it everything. And you'll see the wonderful set!"

In the hubbub which rose towards the great light fixture, the critic said excitedly:

"It will be a triumph I tell you!"

Casot-Dorlys, a big man of some 40 years of age, radiated good-natured joviality and sincerity. His strong uncanny taste for art had tied him to Maximin, with whom he shared the hope of waking the minds of his contemporaries. The admiration he professed for the poet, was entirely reciprocal. For

211

if Casot-Dorlys, hands on his hips and features alight, proc-laimed Maximin's genius amongst the groups, Maximin was not without making a great deal of Casot-Dorlys' critical sense. He was, in a different manner than Alix, another person in which he confided.

Taking up his hat, the poet said, in a very fevered state:

"I must at least go over there for a little while. Will you come along, Casot?"

"Yes, yes, certainly. Pardon me, miss, duty before every-thing! We're off to get the troops warmed up!"

Maximin turned towards Alix and Murlich:

"At the next intermission, we'll go backstage together, shall we not?"

The two friends slipped into the hallway where the main hall sent the overflow of its conversations. The attendance included middle-class people and the author's invited guests for whom this evening had long been a matter of passionate discussion, and amongst whose families bourgeois values had not yet entirely stamped out other feelings. As well, there were random spectators, people who had been passing on the street, craftsmen and employees, those whom the lighted marquis had attracted, and who had come in, having nothing better to do and because it was free. The latter, in a stunned silence, wan-dered about like fish out of water. They had not been the ones applauding before, those had been the tuxedo crowd. But the general public, they alone would make the play a success, if they understood it. Maximin knew that his verses must wake sleeping embers within them, or the play would be a failure.

They moved along, their passage interrupted here and there by friends and acquaintances. Very loudly, Casot-Dorlys praised the play left and right, so all around would hear. He flashed victorious smiles, waved his short arms about as he spoke, in rapid fire sentences, of the wonders of the acts to come.

"You'll see, you'll see, yes a factory set. O! truly grip-ping! My dear Maximin, allow me to present you to an admir-er."

The poet moved on quickly, thanking and greeting people. For a moment, his friend stopped to exchange a few words with a colleague, Gribory, a critic as slim and jaundiced as Casot was round and pink. Maximin went on without him as he was in a hurry to reach the ticket office to have one foot on the sidewalk, to see if people were coming in and if the hall was filling. He need not have gone so far, as a press of arrivals pushed him back; he returned reassured. People were coming in the large door which led directly into the hall, bright with its fresh gold ornamentation and red balconies.

As he wondered whether he would have time to go on stage and watch over the installation of the set, he once again ran into Casot-Dorlys, who had just left off with his colleague.

"Well then," the playwright asked, "what did Gribory have to say about me?"

"O! One never knows with him if it's fish, flesh, or fowl. He has no opinion; he wants to see the whole play before pronouncing himself."

"He's right," admitted Maximin.

Casot, with his usual sanguine enthusiasm, burst out:

"Why, yes, he is right. But he's never been one to allow himself to admit to being carried away over anything!"

Maximin dismissed it with a gesture; one would see tomorrow.

Around them people moved about hurriedly, the intermission was finishing. They returned to the front of the stage, where, from a distance, Alix was showing Murlich, in the boxes and on the floor, the marvelous impact of the style she was launching. Here and there mushrooms were sprouting up from the fabric of skirts and bodices, hairdos heavily decorated with their various hues. The young woman, beneath Gulluliou's fixed stare, named off her client list to Murlich who smiled archly.

Before a now full house, the curtain released a burst of fresh air from the stage, where, representing present times, stood a great glassed-in hall. Machines shook it with their silent motions. Man was there, creator of these machines,

213

through which his muscles were spared all work, all physical exertion. Busying himself solely in the planning of other machines for other tasks, immersed in his cold mathematics which nonetheless led to a solution to his problems, he remained unfulfilled, unconscious from the get-go as to what was missing. Finally he saw clearly and cried out his need for an ideal:

What to do now? I have seen everything,
None of the ancient civilizations' secrets are beyond my grasp,
I have discovered the key to their bygone mysteries
O! Earth, my science could recreate thee!
Yet, the greatest enigma resides within me,
Ah! to know all, to compute everything!
What then, when I reached the bottom of this abyss?
My heart will be no less oppressed,
My brow no less beating itself against the walls of my prison.
Where reason, my blind jailer, would hold me.
But to escape, the birds have their two wings,
The torrent drops alone from the eternal peaks,
The forest can rustle beneath the caresses of the wind,
And I, how shall I be free?
[The Nature-sprite's voice]:
By dreaming.

In a while, a blue light filled the rear of the set, presaging a new dawn, and the Nature-goddess, played by Berthe Balsamore, showed herself for a moment, announcing the anticipated redemption. The curtain fell on the upward motion and smile of this lovely woman, whose blonde hair shed a sunny cheerfulness over the stage. It was so well received, this time, as to augur success. The applause continued, woke long dormant echoes in the hall. Maximin, waiting in the wings, thrilling to every verse, to every movement of his characters, felt that all the awkwardness with which the night had begun was dissolving away, was evaporating under the breath of his poetry. The fever which had held sway over him for days rose under a certainty of success.

He had immediately signaled to his friends to meet him backstage. Casot-Dorlys was ecstatic. Alix, still shaken by the strong feelings evoked in her, joined her congratulations to those of Murlich, who declared with kind affability:

"I see, dear sir, that we share the same vision of man's triumph; you leave the best part to Nature!"

Maximin was content to smile. The critic spoke:

"But Nature is a great crucible in which the most complex of elements are assembled. The scientist can frequently lend a hand to the poet!"

"You in particular, Mr. Murlich!" said Maximin, nodding his head towards the ape.

Gulluliou had bundled himself up in his fur coat. Since his bout of bronchitis, greater precautions had been taken to avoid a relapse which the doctors foresaw would be very dangerous. There were few moments when Murlich was not concerned about the ape's state of health. He must constantly be on guard to avoid possible ill-advised situations, and to attend to everything. That very night, it was by way of an exception that he had consented to allow him out. It took the long anticipated opening of Maximin's work for the naturalist to relent somewhat on his strict rules.

Gulluliou had never been so happy; all he saw was new: the lights, the hubbub, the colorful hall, the curtain exposing another equally large space where people came to speak and talk to one another at length, with gestures by which he could almost understand, even without the words, to build in his imagination a complete story adapted to his understanding of the play. At last, the curtain went down, the hall was suddenly lit up again, and people were getting to their feet, clapping their hands together: awestruck moments, a succession of scenes which had Gulluliou's eyes and mind aflutter!

As the group of friends made their way through the corridors, the crowd, in a sympathetic curiosity, recognized the

215

ape and his master. Murlich, not without some personal sense of irony, remarked to himself how little separated jeers from praises, the whistles from the bravos, that the two were too similar for the distinction to be of any significance. Maximin, praised from all sides, thought of Murlich: the first victory to the scientist, the second to the poet. But was Murlich not a poet of the sciences?

They finally reached, many opened doors later, the greenroom; Maximin immediately met Albani, imposing and powerful in his neutral colors, an ageless and timeless personification of Man.

"It's all right, it's all right, isn't it?" asked the actor.

"Yes, yes, I think so, the last act carried it."

The actor and author stood before each other, both very excited. As those who accompanied the poet were nearby, Maximin only shook hands with those actors who were present, apologizing:

"I will see you all later, I must see Balsamore. Is she up there?"

"Yes, yes, in her dressing room."

"Come," said Maximin.

They slipped into a hallway that gave onto a staircase and went up one floor. The dresser obsequiously welcomed the author and his entourage. This was the floor for the leads, the stars. Emanating from the doors of three or four large and rather sumptuous dressing rooms the weak smell of grease paint and oils saturated the air. The party was a rather strange one: Maximin and Casot-Dorlys, Alix, and Murlich with his ape, proceeding in that order.

At a turn they spied through a wide-open steel door the stage drowned in the twilight of a night ship with the props upright like sails filled by air draughts and entangled ropes shooting up to the flies. The quick peek dissolved; Berthe Balsamore, in a mischievous voice, greeted them from the depths of her dressing room where she was painting her eyes in black before a mirror.

"Do come in, dear!" she yelled out to Maximin.

But when she saw that he was not alone, she turned to them pleasantly, her shadow brush in hand.

"Oh! I'm so sorry!"

"It's an invasion," said the poet, "I have brought along some friends."

"How marvelous to see you! Do come in and sit down. Good evening. Miss Forest, be a dear and move that out of the chair. Good evening, Casot!

Murlich, very much disoriented by her indifferent attitude, and Gulluliou whose uneasiness overcame his joy, were both presented.

"You know, pet," the actress declared, "I've never played Paris before, but I can tell you for sure, it's a hit! Although you owe me a great deal. I fed Albani one of his lines, didn't you even notice?"

"Why, no," answered Maximin a bit embarrassed, in front of Alix, at the familiarity of her tone.

But little was Miss Forest listening, for she saw but one thing; Balsamore's gown, the precious gown now complete, flamboyant with all its silky-orangey mushrooms. And from thence emerged, like the pistil of an enormous tropical flower, the actress' heavy shoulders, and her golden locks.

"Do admire me, Miss Alix," Balsamore said upon noticing the girl's gaze. "Are you pleased? It's better than the first try, eh? We did well to make those alterations, otherwise I wouldn't have worn it!"

But Murlich was in turn tested. He tried, before the opulent and scantily clad 30-year-old actress, to maintain an air of amused reserve though the strange room, both washroom and small drawing-room, overflowing with a jumble of fancy dresses, slips, negligees, of drawings and photographs, of vials and pots, was somewhat disconcerting compared to the cold and ordered layout of the laboratory. Gulluliou lowered his head a bit, like a child intimidated by a stranger.

His serious features, with the creases of a man of a certain age, his full beard, amused Berthe no end. When Murlich stated that the ape was 13 years old, she wished at all cost to take his hand, to make him get up, to see him walk, his legs somewhat relaxed in his black pants, his feet dragging in polished boots.

"Why, Maximin, you ought to write something about him," she exclaimed. "Here is a form of humanity which you hadn't considered!"

"Mr. Murlich is considering it in our stead!" the poet declared, thinking absent-mindedly of vague objects his hands were manipulating in the air.

Casot looked at the naturalist.

"There it is indeed, the triumph of man, your generosity extends all the way to the ape! Is it not right to say that she speaks the truth? Is it not so, Gulluliou?"

"Yes," answered Gulluliou.

It was the only French word he knew as yet, and he would interject it all over the place, when he heard his name spoken. Sometimes it turned out well.

But the actress, who with the help of her dresser, had finished lacing over her bare ankles with pink sandal-ties, begged Murlich to speak to his student in her presence. Just then, Maximin, whose worry had reached a fever pitch at the approach of the third curtain-rise, interrupted them.

"I think it's time we leave, the intermission must be over."

"Well, see you later my pets. Mr. Murlich, will you allow me to go and visit the young man? Truly, I would have liked to hear him talk…see you later!" Her voice was marked with a certain tenseness as she addressed herself to Maximin. "If the crowd isn't asleep, I won't be afraid, but must have their help!"

The poet said, with a chill:

"I will applaud when you come on stage…Good luck!"

"And you too, old fellow."

As the others were already in the hallway, Berthe stopped on the threshold of her dressing room, a finger raised:

"The prelude has begun," she said.

218

A nasal warning followed a slamming of doors, the murmur of voices arguing, some laughs: "On stage for the third act! On stage for the third!" Meanwhile, between the walls, rising from the inner staircase, spreading through the building, a distant harmony arose, coming closer and closer, like some mysterious fluid. And Maximin was taken by the powerful emotion that the music which he recognized as his own, was now being heard by a large crowd of people. He drew along his friends behind him, heading for the hall. They quickly passed the great metal door, open on the darkened stage, where the set was now installed, waiting only to be given life by the lights.

Above them, on every floor the same warning rang out: "On stage for the third act! On stage for the third!"

They returned to their places in the fore-stage, overlooking the orchestra; the room was listening attentively under the growing sway of the first bars of the music. Maximin, breathless, listened.

It was the entire scope of the drama which he wished to reflect with the magic and richness of the orchestra. The previous two acts were recalled, Man rising little by little from a darkness of ignorance and blunder towards greater truth. A plaintive confusion, sketched out by the deep notes of the double basses and cellos, then taken up in muted tones by the violins and violas, which allowed slow, monotonous notes to drag out. Battles were undertaken, light striving by fits and starts to bring day, tearing asunder the moaning veil of the human night, the flutes high-pitched modulations weaving their lacework on the primitive canvas. These fused in to sudden interrupted bursts. Slowly, arduously, the battle continued; the moaning of violins was followed by a syncopation sustained by the quicker tempo of the violas. The storm rumbled with its magnificent and powerful strength, striated with flashes of incendiary high notes. Suddenly there arose, after a moment's silence, the mysterious oboes' melody. These indicated a dawn motif, soon propagated by English horns, veiled by the bold clarinets. And this major theme thus constituted, the

219

whole orchestra took it up in successive tones, ringing in a sort of deliverance. Upon the trill of the stringed instruments, the brass instruments emerged, building their ascending sound in pomp and circumstance.

The whole crowd let out the breath they had so far held; Maximin felt his face grazed by a wing whose touch made him weak-kneed, sensing himself at the pinnacle of artistic happiness, he realized that the crowd had been subjugated. He had to retire in the back, near Alix. He felt the young woman's hand searching for his, squeezing it. In the fore-stage, everyone was speechless as the curtain rose.

Casot-Dorlys shifted his stance with a sigh, Murlich half closed his eyes, kept a secret watch over Gulluliou, whose attitudes continually piqued his scientific curiosity. He had watched him all through the prelude, worried how the novelty of orchestral music would affect this strange creature, and amused himself in transposing his sensibilities onto the animal, and in representing to himself its varied impressions.

Gulluliou, at the first chords of the violins, had had a quizzical look, his head shifting in a silent query to his master. But, the phenomenon persisting, he had shifted his attention back to the orchestra, particularly entranced by the movement of the bows and those of the conductor.

A confused awakening of the senses.

A man who moves his arms about, like the puppet made to walk by pulling on its strings...

It makes noise, very loud noise...

Men who move their arms about make a very loud noise, which lasts a long time...;

Oh! how they move about their arms, and how the sound goes on for a very long time, so long that one's ears ring and one's stomach is queasy, and one cannot breathe...;

As if there were a great typhoon in the guava trees: one hears the wind whistle in the branches, and...;

Minnili, the little bird has sung!...;

Minnili, Minnili, why does he sing through the big storm? Master is not afraid...

The men who move about their arms and those who blow…;

Master is looking at me…;

The noise, the ears, the heart; the noise, the ears, the heart. The heart stops, the noise gets louder, the machine rises, and now it is light again!…;

But, but…; Mother!…;

Minnili! Far…; far…;

the clouds, the Sun!

With a raucous, stifled cry, Gulluliou stood up, his chest heaving, wide-eyed, his hand extended. For, on the stage, he rediscovered all the elements of his forest, alive with waving palms, virginal in its tangles, lianas dropping from the trees like twisted serpents. The entire tropical forest, vast and deep! And this was sufficient to immediately bring back to the ape's dark soul the aromas of his youth, so many scattered memories, nearly forgotten, and which returned! And as it was so close, he wanted to go there, to run there once again; Gulluliou wished to go into his forest. Standing with the black suit tight about his hunched over waist, his neck in the carcan of a detachable collar, he forgot his human condition, his lacquer of citizenry and sought to leap forward and reach the stage.

But it was over in a flash, Murlich had risen too, had guessed what was coming and prevented it. With a few words whispered in his firm but tender voice, which the animal could never resist, he calmed him down. The others had barely had time to notice. It happened when the crowd was silent, taking in the verses which Balsamore, who had just come on stage in her stunning robe, was reciting to them at the top of her lungs.

The act went on under the sumptuous rhythm of the poet's stanzas. The crowd, their artistic sensibilities now brought to the desired state of exaltation, were so vibrant with sincerity that Maximin himself was surprised. This night, begun under the cloud of doubt and nerves, was ending in a rush of triumph. Besides, Maximin had trouble hearing the rest of his play; listening to the prelude had overwhelmed him; he had relived one by one too many powerful feelings, a crushing sense of fatigue was mixed with his sense of victory.

He had retired with Alix, behind their friends, in a small sitting-room where the lights were dimmed, and not saying anything to one another, they waited, listening vacantly. The act was finishing; already a portion of the crowd had risen to acclaim Maximin. Casot and Murlich, when the curtain fell, leaned over to applaud with the electrified crowd.

They were unable to see Maximin, who, after long gazing at the young woman, and taking hold of her wrist, sought to possess himself of her mouth. In the burst of glory which arose, no one knew what was occurring at the back of the forestage. The poet was using the energy left him in this gesture of conquest.

But Alix had disengaged herself suddenly, the blond beard had grazed her cheek. Very pale and chopping her words, she said in a very soft voice:

"It is unconscionable to thus defile such a moment! Leave me alone!"

And she saw Gulluliou, who, half turned, watched her with the same strange, fixed gaze which she had already noticed on a number of occasions. It was tinged with sadness, and fathomless resignation...; Alix was moved by it, and feared that she had understood the expression in those haunting eyes. In her mind she linked Gulluliou's silence with the poet's boldness. She was shaken by a sudden start, that of the free and virginal woman. She wished to lash out at the one who had thought that her independence would succumb to the night's excitements. Pointing out the animal to Maximin, she added:

"That monkey is laughing at you!"

Maximin hunched his shoulders, his lips tightened like fists. In the hall, the cheering continued, the curtain had risen on three occasions, the clapping and ovations were crushed beneath the ceiling where the great candelabrum was shaking. Casot ran towards the playwright:

"Do come, they're asking for you, they want to see you."

The poet, stiff from his unsuccessful passionate outburst, moved to the edge of the fore-stage, so that their outpouring could finally confirm his fame.

He could make out, in a haze, to his right, the footlights behind which all the actors stood; in front of him, to the left, hands clapping and mouths open. Such was glory. He felt both its grandeur and its fragility. Tomorrow his name would be in all the newspapers, his work played, published, interpreted. It would have its supporters and its detractors, one Casot-Dorlys would place him on a pedestal, a Gribory would no doubt vent the bile of his kidney condition upon him. But at last the task was accomplished, this evening perhaps marked a stage in the evolution of the art. A stage...perhaps...he didn't know, he couldn't think, he could barely distinguish between the jeers and the applause.

He held before his eyes the vision of Gulluliou spying out his erstwhile actions, and very precise in his ears were Alix's cruel words:

"That monkey is laughing at you!"

CHAPTER VI

February was drawing to a close. In the house on d'Auteuil, life for Alix, Murlich and Gulluliou went on as usual. They seldom saw each other during the day; the seamstress, very busy on all fronts, threw herself into her work; her cousin busied himself with Gulluliou who, after a second presentation at the Museum, had become the most popular of apes. The creature was beginning to learn a few French words, and a certain exchange of ideas was now possible between him and his hosts. Every night during dinner, Alix had great fun observing the developing *Parisianisms* and innocent wonderment of this child of Borneo transplanted into the great capital.

223

Gulluliou grew in mind twice as fast as in body. Given his experience with men, the happiness of his youth had almost vanished, without him however becoming silent or morose. But he bore a certain nonchalant gravity, quite frequent among the blacks.[31] His health remained fragile; a long hunched over body, sometimes shaken by a worrisome weak, dry cough. The doctor had warned Murlich that the antituberculin serum he had injected some time before, would not take effect, should it be needed, for at least a month or more. Murlich then waited, not without some apprehension, limiting his student's activities as much as possible, not allowing him any overly tiring walks, or any exaggerated efforts. And his overfeeding continued: twice a day Gulluliou took a dose of protoplasmic extract, some Darembert granules, raw eggs which he swallowed with delight, and raw meat, which greatly disgusted him. However, clearly the climate did not favor his development. In order to distract him and allow him to endure the winter season, he was told at great length of the coming of spring, of the house in Basel where they would soon return, where he had his own room filled with souvenirs of his homeland and of his early childhood. Gulluliou listened, indeed answered, and then his gaze would always shift towards Alix, with the meek steadiness which had already so often struck her. But now the young woman could not help but associate this strange gaze upon her, with her memories of the night Maximin had infringed upon their agreement regarding matters of love. She remembered the suspicions she had fleetingly entertained; was it not in such a manner that, long ago, the poet had himself, during a long awkward silence between them, looked upon her? She shrugged her shoulders at such a parallel: a simple coincidence, something which particularly drew Gulluliou's eyes to her, an overly showy color, the sparkle of a piece of jewelry.

March arrived with its downpours, great gusts of wind shook the trees in the garden, the privet and laurel bushes, and

---

[31] See previous footnote on racism. [Ed.]

notwithstanding the double doors ran through the house and pavilion. One day, Alix received a visit from Maximin. They had not seen each other since the showing of *The Triumph of Man*. The poet was now famous, but Alix had long shown herself intractable with respect to forgiving her old friend his indiscretion. However, after a heartbroken plea for forgiveness, she consented to see him again. Truly, he was missing from her sensible and methodical virginal existence.

He sat on the verandah near the young woman as had been his habit before. They spoke together of literature, of follow-ups to the play, of the poet's other projects: Gulluliou never came up. It seemed to both Maximin and Alix that the other was fearful of this event being evoked. Such a feeling seemed ridiculous to both of them, as they carefully hid this from each other. Yet it was on this very day that Gulluliou was to show himself to be a true man, in such a miserable manner, that Alix would remain touched forever.

As Maximin was leaving, on the threshold of the outer hall, in the half-light of a bulb enclosed in a violet-streaked ceiling fixture, beneath a raised piece of tapestry she suddenly caught sight of the ape. He was still and silent. He was allowed to wander through the different rooms, and having heard a noise, he had simply come to have a look. Once the visitor had left, Alix considered scolding Gulluliou for his indiscretion, and searched for the right words, when he, with a sad look, pointed at the door. Using two of the words of his meager French vocabulary, he said:

"Come…he come!"

The reproach was almost human in its intonation. An idea flashed through the young girl's mind, confirming what she suspected. Gulluliou, this 13-year-old creature, formidable and immature…this Gulluliou was in love with her…Contempt, anger, and a sort of mad gaiety came over her all at once. To be loved by an ape as she was already by the poet, was it not the most terrifying of fantasies? Loved by Gulluliou! How ridiculous, Gulluliou jealous! This was too unexpected, too extraordinary, too unnatural!

But, after a period of silence, the animal's voice rose again. He was closer to her, gazing at her with an imploring look, hands together, stating:

"You good…you beautiful!"

He drew closer still:

"You good…you beautiful!"

Alix backed away, touched by fear.

Was he going to touch her? Such a fear overtook her. A certain sudden lucidity showed her the danger. She was in a corner; to reach the door she must cross Gulluliou. She did not dare. She would have called out for help, but her throat tightened in silent anticipation, for she saw the beast rising in the ape's eyes, saw the flame of the brute's wild instincts rise little by little in its eyes.

So this was what he had been planning for so long, what had sucked the life from his body, what made his eyes glow in an unquenchable fever. This was indeed love! How monstrous, to be loved by an ape!

The house was empty, the workroom deserted, Murlich busy in the garden pavilion.

"You beautiful, you good, you beautiful, beautiful, beautiful!"

Gulluliou repeated these few words mixed with words in pongo in a low, muffled voice. The huskiness of his voice betrayed the call of ancestral voices at the very source of his race wishing to be reborn. He approached her, but she backed up. In her terror she could no longer find the buzzer on the wall which would have summoned someone. She ended up being backed into a corner.

The ape came to her, proffering awkwardly delivered, incomprehensible words. Their tone became fiercer, his teeth at times grinding between jaws now more preeminent than was usual. Beneath his loose clothing, arms and legs were tensing as if to leap.

Alix felt the animals short strong breaths on her face. There rose from him an odor of musk.

Gulluliou put his arm around Alix's waist and drew her to him, unable to escape this belt of nerves and sinews. The hideous mouth, the wet-lipped snout, pressed upon the woman's lips. Slowly he pushed her to the floor, petrified, incapable of the least defensive gesture. When she was stretched out, he bent over her, a moving shadow, mingling in the half-light with the soft, thick carpet.

At that point she seemed to pull herself together and with a sudden burst of energy found the strength to grab his wrists. She was so weak before this unbridled beast. Still, she fought.

The filthy kiss nauseated her, and the more she fought, the more she realized she was lost, that she could no longer prevent anything. The ape growled and had again overpowered her. She closed her eyes, her hand before her, her legs bent under her. A last ditch effort before the rape…

She waited…

Suddenly the great black, hairy, snaking arms which embraced her, unknotted themselves. She felt herself free, was standing up in an instant, looking around. Gulluliou was in front of her, his head lowered, his limbs shaking. Something mysterious was going on inside him. He seemed bewildered, his eyes vacillating like candles under an invisible draught.

Then, abruptly, he moaned softly and fell at the girl's feet like a broken puppet which collapses to the floor. His chest was torn with deep coughing, sobs gurgled in his throat. He cried, his body shaking.

"Alix, Alix, you good, you beautiful!" He was no longer anything but a pathetic rag of a thing, miserable, ridiculous, a heap of collapsed flesh from which arose the anguish of love.

The man was victorious over the ape.

CHAPTER VII

Gulluliou was constantly feverish now. The doctor came to visit him frequently, allowing his rising concerns to show.

"Not only has the serum not worked," he said, "but the condition I had told you to expect has declared itself. It's that bad cold he's had for two months that has caused all of this. I had nonetheless thought him out of its grip."

The Son-of-Doves was again taken with a stubborn dry cough, which shook his long bouts of dozing in the recesses of his chair. He was placed before the window of his room, the windows closed but the curtains raised, and from there he watched the progressive development of spring on the budding trees.

One day, towards the end of March, in order to offer a little distraction to Gulluliou and to get him out of the house where he was fretting with boredom, Alix suggested that they attend a sitting of the House which was due to discuss the famous Sahara Railroad scandal. Murlich nearly jumped out of his skin at the mere thought of it. "Why even perfectly healthy people catch the flu there! And how would Gulluliou survive that, the poor wretch? It is crazy to think of such a thing!"

"But," replied the young woman, "what tells you, dear cousin, that dear Dr. Darembert, as famous as he might be, is not wrong about him at present...And besides, whether or not Gulluliou is consumptive, don't you think it better anyway that he have a gay and varied life, rather than be locked up here? Gulluliou is still solid on his feet, he eats very well; it's not because he coughs a bit that you're going to keep him imprisoned. On the contrary, it is because he is sad that I ask you to entertain him. Yes, he's bored, this animal is dying of boredom and nothing else...that's what's giving him a fever!"

She added, to convince the hesitant Murlich, that Gulluliou, carefully bundled up, would risk nothing in seeking such entertainment. He could be driven there in a car and be brought back in the same manner. The galleries at the Legislative Palace were spacious and easy to access, the room heated, the air purified by an excellent ventilation system. And such a sitting of the Legislative Palace was something he had never experienced. Had Murlich even been there before?

The scientist had to admit that he hadn't.

228

"So you see," Alix concluded, there are a number of good reasons! We'll have good seats. Vandrax who is speaker of the House promised me so."

Murlich finally agreed to try it. Besides, the doctor, whom they consulted the next day, while recommending the greatest precautions be taken, had no formal objection to such an outing.

"However, at the slightest sign of him getting overly excited," Darembert lightly struck the top of his left hand with his right, "to bed!" And he said to Alix, "It is a hazardous treatment you are starting here, I would not allow it were he a man!"

It was the young woman's opinion that what Gulluliou suffered from the most was solitude and silence. Her anger at the events during which the pongo had so brutally confessed his passion, but which she had kept to herself, had turned to pity. Only the physical disgust of the kiss received from those black lips now remained. Her heart forgave him. Since then, Gulluliou had been nothing but docile, and most even-tempered. If truly he loved, if this love implanted in the creature's troubled consciousness was indeed akin to human love, how acutely then must the near-man be suffering.

And Alix dreamed of bringing him back to health by exposing him to a variety of sights and sounds, whereby his youth would allow him to recover.

On April 8 at 4 p.m., the great debate over the Sahara Railroad scandal was in full swing.

Erected on the same site as the former building destroyed in the revolution of 2074, the Legislative Palace was just as large. The council-chamber could hold, besides the 1200 members, some 2000 spectators. The members' seats were stacked in tiers and arranged in a semicircle at the back, along with the speaker's platform surrounded by a visitors' gallery. The chamber's layout and dimensions reminded one of the amphitheaters of antiquity.

When Murlich, Gulluliou, Alix and Vandrax's secretary, who served as chaperone arrived, the speaker, in vibrant tones and with gestures typical of a short sanguine southerner, held the floor. His beard shaking, index finger extended, threatening in turn the ceiling, the right, the middle, the left, he straightened up his stocky frame, rolled his r's, and gave himself entirely to the fight.

"Citizens, the time for procrastinating is over...this country demands you step forward and act. The House must prove that a commonality of perspective exists between it and democracy, that they can count on one another. I would ask the minister what guarantees of security he would now make to European businesses operating in our African provinces, given how illusory his former guarantees were...I ask him if a bunch of swindlers and cheats will, with complete impunity, be allowed to line their coffers with the European Union's capital."

Cheers and applause drowned out the orator's voice. The centrists and the right were the ones applauding him. But a rumble of barking cries, curses and whistles arose. At the back of the great narrowing of the chamber the 600 leftist members were on their feet, and with their outcries, the pounding of their fists on the desks, they tried to stop Vandrax from proceeding.

The interruptions crisscrossed: "Cheats yourself! Talk about swindlers! Enough! Those are fighting words! Liar!" screamed the Leftists while the 500 members of the opposing party continued their applause. Finally, Vandrax, his arm extended, turning to face his adversaries, reopened his mouth and bellowed on slowly:

"Your anger, citizens, shall not overcome my stamina! You will hear me out anyway, whether you wish to or not. This debate, which in vain you have, by means fair and foul, tried to delay is of too immediate an importance for us to drop it again before getting to the bottom of it...I said that the swindlers and cheats..."

The thunderous rumbling, which had only let up slightly, rose as loud as ever, accompanied by the other party's opposing vociferations. The already stormy session promised to get worse. In the gallery, Murlich whispered to Miss Forest:

"This is outrageous. And they call this debate!"

"Oh!" smiled the young woman, "this is nothing, they're only getting started. You'll see later!"

And she added, in response to the scientist's surprised look:

"They come to blows in almost every session. What can you do, that's politics! You know, politics is the backbone of the European nations, but France is the country within the Union where it is best loved. Three quarters of the population seem to live for nothing else; every year an entire month is devoted to legislative elections. A month of genuine civil war, where all the passions are reborn with redoubled strength…especially since the women have the vote. Supposedly there was a time when they didn't vote, when they were not allowed to involve themselves in such things."

"Certainly," replied Murlich with approval, "it's not that long since they enjoyed the same civil rights as men. It's only been for 20-odd years in Switzerland."

Alix answered:

"Anyway, I never vote myself. It's like those women who run for office, do you think it's natural for them to do so? That's ridiculous! If only you saw them these poor female members when they are all gathered in one room. One might take them for parrots at the Museum of Natural History: what a cacophony!"

"Indeed," worried Murlich, "how come none of them seem to be here? I see only men."

"They must be in some Committee session," continued the young woman, "they'll arrive soon. There are 100 or so, a small proportion of all the members, but they stick together!...Yes, don't you think all those people would be better off staying comfortably at home, placing their interests into the hands of only a few? We are a strange people, we believe ourselves to be happy because we read daily, in 500 different political gazettes, that there's been more fisticuffs in the House."

"You are," said Murlich, "a people with a taste for fer-ment and independence; and sometimes good things come of it. One mustn't forget, child, that your country was the one to spread the social net which exists today. It was one of the ear-liest republics, it helped in the formation of all the others, ad-vocated their unification, and finally, has always set the exam-ple in terms of progress and emancipation. It's natural that you be enthralled by politics, for it runs in your veins, it courses with your blood. You have been the vanguard of modern civi-lization, and have remained in that role. It is almost in spite of yourselves that you have gathered the ideas, spread them, knocked them about!"

"Especially that we knock them about. You, cousin, look upon our race as an external observer who sees an overall pic-ture, but from close up it's another story."

Murlich, pointing to the hemicycle, addressed Vandrax's secretary, who was following the debate raised by his employ-er with obvious interest, and asked him:

"So there are still three great schools of thought, as there were in former times? And what are their respective points of view?"

"Why, sir," the young man answered, "it's difficult to figure out!"

"However," Murlich insisted, "under former regimes, one could easily distinguish their platforms, based on their party affiliation. Thus, under the 3rd French Republic, so rich in parliamentary highlights, history tells us that the Commons was divided into three parties, whose political platforms were well defined."

"Oh!" the other answered, "we have none like that. A party's platform changes every day, according to the question being debated. Today, for this Sahara business there are those who support the Minister and those who support Vandrax. Tomorrow it will be something different. You do understand that there are no longer republicans and monarchists, nor..."

Murlich, smiling, interrupted:

232

"Obviously such labels would no longer be meaningful, given the agreement which exists on the form of government."

"Consequently," Alix said, "you see that it is when the least reason exists for politicking, that the greatest politicking goes on. Our members' ancestors had very different issues to deal with, issues which no longer exist: cults, war, the navy. They were only 500 to do this. Ours only busy themselves with internal matters, 1200 of them are at it, and they still find a way of fighting amongst themselves."

"The Frenchman's belligerent intensity," the naturalist concluded, "finds its natural outlet in parliamentary sessions. It's logical."

His attention was diverted by Gulluliou, shaken by violent coughing. He immediately gave him a cough drop, anxiously patting him on the back. The ape panted, somewhat dazzled by the daylight that came through the windows, and by the restless multitude before him.

They returned their attention to what was happening at the front of the amphitheater. Vandrax was still at the podium, he stood courageously, his voice fighting to overcome the crowd's powerful rumble, and the rhythmic sound of the desks. A thick haze, was hanging over the assembly, inciting the hot heads, of which one was searching the nooks and crannies of the room. The orator shouted out:

"I ask the honest parties in the Commons to sanction this nation's judgment by their verdict. Will the Minister of Labor then dare to come to this podium to once again attempt to deflect public opinion? He'll not be able to do it! Light will be shed on everything. My supporters and I are ready to sustain the debate. The government's servile accomplices cannot quash our cry of alarm."

Again, the whistles and insults rained down on Vandrax. For an hour now, he had been fighting the storms which rumbled on either side, and had only been able to develop a tiny portion of his question. Suddenly he flew into a rage, shook his fist at the left, screaming:

"Ah! You crooks, you will not let me speak, but I will speak nonetheless!"

This was the signal, from every side the ink-bottles arced across the room. The entire assembly was on their feet in a tumultuous and chaotic state. The tiers of seats, from top to bottom, were awash in invective, and the members threw at each other anything which came to hand. Meanwhile, at the podium, twisting in every direction, alternately straightening up or leaning over, he bellowed:

"Bunch of scoundrels! You fear my words. And you who hold the title of Minister of Labor, Perrette, dirty thief and speculator!"

"Thief yourself," fumed Perrette leaping from his majority seat onto the orator, seizing him by the throat.

For a moment, the two men fought to see who would throw the other from the podium. Above them, the president was content to remain in cover and to frequently set off the great horn nearby, which had replaced the old bell. But already each group within the Commons was flying to the support of their champion: the right to Vandrax, the left to Perrette.

"Ah! Now they're getting to the point!" Alix exclaimed as she looked towards Murlich. "Huh? What do you think of that?"

In the deafening din, among the bursts of shouting, and the bellowing of the horn, the dumbfounded scientist replied: "This is unheard of! Unheard of!"

Vandrax's secretary had long since slipped over the gallery's banister, to go down through the tiered seating, to the middle of the arena. He made the thumbs-down sign beside his master. The melee was now generalized, people no longer fought in defense of Perrette or Vandrax, but for themselves, to allay their personal grudges and express their distaste for one another. Isolated duels were increasing in frequency with many such conscientious pairs beating on each other between the benches, with only their legs and arms sticking out.

Beneath the impassible bust of the Republic, the president overlooked the proceedings, scoring the blows as if it were a vote. Finally, when a last blast on the horn had no effect, he quickly took off his hat, his suit, and pulled up his sleeves revealing that he was an athlete. Bulging like knotted ropes, his strong muscles ended with his huge fists which hung down beside him. He climbed down with an escort of bailiffs, and began to clear a path, leaving a trail of broken noses and black eyes. Behind him, his phalange of bailiffs cleared the way, picked up the wounded and directed them to the adjoining infirmary. This happened quickly, only the front ranks on either side suffered much, the others disengaging themselves quickly. Perrette had to be taken off, Vandrax having broken three teeth from his dentures. The president of the council, against whom many of the people's representatives had obstinately continued to fight, had his clothes torn to rags. As for the furniture, its fragments littered the floor. Thus had bomb fragments, in the age of wars, been strewn over the battle field.

But both sides of a double door had opened on one side of the chamber. A muddled group entered the chamber and opened their session. Their uniform clothing, pressed short pants showing their black stockinged legs, portfolios tucked under their arms, gave the House's feminist contingent the look of a bunch of aging schoolmarms. Ignoring the recent blows exchanged around them, as if nothing in the world was easier, they spread out over the tiers, they held forth and argued, adding their shrill voices to the more virile hubbub of the dwindling battle.

Everything seemed to be calming down. The president, back in his seat, solemnly put his suit back on, waiting only for a sign that relative calm had returned to the assembly, to reopen the proceedings, when a terrible, unbelievably raucous cry rang out. The great amphitheater's walls seemed to multiply and allow this inhuman cry to persist.

And Gulluliou appeared halfway between the gallery and the rostrum, standing on an empty chair. For a moment he paused, hesitant, then with lightning speed he tore the clothes from his torso, tossing them into the stunned crowd. Covered only by his pants, he leapt, clearing several rows of seats. He roared out his cry again, and leapt again.

However, he had been recognized; terrified voices exclaimed: "Gulluliou! The pongo, Gulluliou!" And they fled.

Back in the gallery, others were shouting. Murlich and Alix, were drawn to their feet in bewilderment at the ape's sudden frenzy, at this bout of madness. No one had seen him run off; suddenly beside himself, excited by the spectacle of the fight occurring before him, he must have taken advantage of a moment's inattention.

All was lost in the hubbub which pervaded the room. Gulluliou sprang forward again, reached the rostrum, which had been evacuated in the blink of an eye, and found himself, thrusting out his chest adorned with reddish-brown hair, swinging his long arms, thrusting forward his muzzle which a joyful laugh split from ear to ear, in the very spot in which Vandrax had lately been so eloquent. There was an epic moment; the entire assembly, men and women alike, were standing, shaking in fear before this furious beast. They waited to see what Gulluliou would do; the general hubbub had been followed by a heavy, anxious silence.

They saw the ape fill the water glass that stood nearby, and drink, though not without a thousand contortions. Then he stood still for a brief moment in order to take up a pose, and in a guttural and piercing voice, he shouted: "Ceeteezens!" He struck the desk with his fist, leaned out, then back: "Ceeteezens!"

A single word, remembered because of its frequent use, punctuated every gesture…"Ceeteezens!"…Finally he picked up steam, roaring out his name amidst a great guffaw of laughter, as if he wished to present it as a victory banner to those who watched him: Gul…lul…iou!"

But suddenly the parody took on another form. The nervous shock the creature had received, and the fact that he had stripped himself of his clothes, mimicking the president

236

removing his suit to go down on the floor, could imply nothing less than a sub-latent thought of fighting. The speech represented nothing but the preliminaries. Gulluliou rocked forward, extending his fists towards his imaginary enemies, creating a stampede in the assembly. In one motion he swept the podium clean: ink-pot, paper, pens, glass, water jug...everything went flying. This notwithstanding, with the look of a warrior marching to the most holy of crusades, he leapt to the floor, moving forward with the appearance of a wrestler. Woe to him who stood in his way; Gulluliou, wishing to play his role to perfection, would have floored him with a friendly slap!

But the place had emptied out, the exits were closed, the gallery evacuated, only a few members on the upper tiers, still jostling one another, trying to quickly find a way out, and a few bailiffs trying to put together the semblance of a barricade.

In the distance, through the walls, a cadenced noise of troops could be heard; a detachment of the Civic Guard was arriving.

Meanwhile, on the battleground, someone was coming down towards the ape: Murlich. A fixed gaze coming from behind his blue-tinted glasses, speaking only the name Son-of-Doves, the scientist went to his student, striving amidst his personal turmoil to keep the necessary tone of authority in his voice. They were in front of one another. The pongo, naked to the waist, arms hanging, legs bent, ready to bolt again, turned his head for a moment and made as if to escape. Murlich felt as if he was losing him, that the soul which had been stolen from this body was lost to him forever.

But a clear voice had just arisen, and in turn called out: "Gulluliou!" The ape looked across to the gallery at the back and recognized Alix. His eyes flickered, fixed in a melancholy glow. To the brute's instinct, quasi-human intelligence succeeded.

Tamed, Gulluliou allowed Murlich to put his hand on his shoulder, and seeing that he was undressed, crossed his arms to cover his chest. He reverted to a man once more; his halting, wheezing breath betraying his weariness. A bout of hoarse coughing took hold of him.

The same night, Gulluliou spat up blood; he was consumed with fever. Immediately upon his return to Auteuil, the doctor had been called. When Darembert arrived, already aware of the events through the afternoon's newspapers, he shrugged his shoulders like a churlish man who has been disturbed for no good reason.

"What the blazes do you expect me to do?" he said. "You amuse yourself allowing him to kill himself, and then you come looking for me!"

Nonetheless, he remained at the patient's bedside; no one slept in the house that night, each in turn sitting up for a portion of the night. Everything was a mess, the elder Murlich's strong constitution was shaken by this unexpected turn of events. His clear-sightedness made it impossible for him not to be anxious. Alix, disconsolate, blamed herself for bringing on this situation; but the scientist did not begrudge her this, his experience having taught him to bow before the whims of destiny.

CHAPTER VIII

The next morning, Darembert returned. The fever had not gone down, and despite all the potions and herbal teas, the bouts of coughing were increasingly frequent. In the drawing-room downstairs, the doctor had a long talk with Murlich, warning him that the situation was extremely serious, especially since Gulluliou was beginning, after a short return to lucidity, to slip back into a state of delirium.

Darembert was truly perplexed as to what to do to treat such a condition. His science applied to a man would undoubtedly have effected a miraculous result. But in the case of an ape, notwithstanding medicine's already advanced understand-

238

ing of the anthropoidal physiology, it was difficult to be confident of oneself. Darembert, gruff and frank, did not conceal
his doubts and fears.

"We are virtually colleagues, are we not? I can tell you
anything. Well then! We're going through a bad bout, a very
bad bout. I would have kept him alive, I don't know how long,
if he hadn't acted so irresponsibly! Hadn't I made my recommendations clear in any number of ways: the greatest prudence was required, and no excitement! That crazy adventure
in the commons was the straw that broke the camel's back.
We are, my dear professor, before a body which has been
completely sapped—do you understand?—by a sickness that
was only progressing very slowly, but has suddenly flared up
under the shock!"

Murlich bowed his head:

"It is destiny," he muttered.

Upon these words, the doctor, who had just sat down to
write out the recipe for a potion, looked at Murlich and
shrugged his shoulders heavily.

"You believe in destiny!" he said, a tinge of disdain in
his voice. "That would be the last thing I would believe in. I
believe in man. Man creates his own destiny. You're rather
more of an ideologue, are you not, doctor?"

"What can you do, it's one of my weaknesses," confessed Murlich with a somewhat flippant composure. "My
scientific experience and speculations do not preclude me
from believing that there may exist forces which eclipse human will. Take, for example, what the great Hetking called the
supra-vital vortex, except that where Hetking's theories only
apply to the evolution of the races, I would extend the influence of the supra-vital vortex to a sequence of events; I give it
a subjective significance."

Darembert replied:

"While I will submit myself to your authority in such
matters, I do not agree with you. I believe that in our era we
must throw off all moral constraints, as we have shed all our
material ones, and the day will come when man will be able to

239

be on an even footing with Nature. We can produce rain, hail, storms on demand, so what would stop our children from altering the course of our seasons, and thus, at their whim, modify the balance of forces which has so far dictated our climatological and, consequently, our societal conditions throughout the world. They shall be masters not only of physical phenomena, but also of their own destinies. This is why we needn't worry ourselves regarding their fate, for, after us, they will know how to rejuvenate the Earth, such that it will last forever, with no unforeseen circumstances!"

"You believe this, doctor?" interrupted Murlich, fastening his penetrating eyes on him, through his tinted glasses. "Well then, I'll further surprise you," he went over to some book-filled shelves at the back of the room, and showed Darembert a small pamphlet, "by telling you that I have made this the cornerstone of my life." And he read the title on the grayish cover: *A Christian's Revelation.*

"A Christian's!" the doctor blurted out in a low voice. "Is this something modern? Are there still Christians around?"

Murlich smiled:

"Oh! Christians, I'm sure there're still some around, just like there must still be some devotees of all the religions which have existed. I'm not acquainted with any myself...as for this pamphlet, it is roughly a century old. I obtained it from my father's library, it has always been in my family. It is most curious, this account of an ecstatic state which the author, who goes by the name of Florian, Catholic abbot, presents."

"Yes, a pamphlet! There were tons of them in that era."

"Wait...in this ecstatic trance, God appeared to him to announce the coming of a deluge comparable to that which had devastated the Earth in the earliest Antiquity. Of course, this in and of itself is not so extraordinary, but what is, is that with regards to a coming deluge, the visionary in question agrees with Hetking: and the American scientist only expressed this opinion many years after the probable publication date of this pamphlet."

"So what then?" asked Darembert. "Is this why you admire it so much?"

"Primarily for that reason…because the idea set forth corresponds closely to my conception of our planet's future, and especially because of the philosophical pleasures its reading has afforded me. Yes, I admit, I sometimes like to unwind from my work by wandering into a less materialistic field. This is where we butt heads, doctor, is it not?"

The doctor objected:

"My dear professor, you have just now cited Hetking. You have named, if you'll allow me to point out, one of the greatest of materialists…For you to have adopted his doctrine of the supra-vital vortex would seem to preclude any such metaphysical leanings in your views. Have we not heard you, at the Museum of Natural History no less, declare the religious practices of yesteryear…"

"Oh! I'm not talking about the rites themselves, for I would be the first to proclaim their vanity. History has shown us that the exterior manifestations of a cult of divinity have always been inversely related to freedom of thought. Truly, a God who forces you to remain under his yoke, rather than drawing you to him with love, must be rejected. However, were I to tell you that I did not aspire towards a certain spiritual ideal greater than the current state of humanity, I would be lying. Would you reproach me espousing Hetking and his law, rather than pure materialism? Did our ancient cosmogonies offer no more grandiose a view than that presented us by species after species, linked one to another, through endlessly mutating matter!… How do you see this leading irrevocably to atheism?"

"But," said Darembert, "Hetking's theory, an extension of Darwin's, closes the cycle of organic evolution. Now Darwin, showing the links which united all species since the Earth began, established not only the analogous nature of their physical constitutions, but also that of their emotional makeups. In so doing he demolished his era's fortress of dogmatism: the belief in the immortality of the soul. He proved that there reigns, over any emotional baggage any animal, including man, might have, the so-called 'universal law of the conservation of matter and energy.'"

"Every Biblical fable demolished, the mystical theories of Plato, of Christ, of Mohammad—all sapped. This is what Darwin did, and especially what Hetking, who extended his work, did…So you see, my dear professor, that from there to pure rationalism…"

Murlich shook his head:

"Rationalism, yes, a word that well describes an era of reasoning taken to extremes. Ah! Reason, we've got plenty of that, so much so that the tree has dried up to its very core from keeping its branches bent to earth. Well then," he raised his brow, and the light played upon the lens of his glasses, "I say that, far from driving me from the concept of a conscious finality having directed all the different transformations of Nature leading to our creation, Hetking's system forces me to such a conclusion!…Do you think our morals would be hindered by it?"

But Darembert, visibly annoyed, grumbled:

"How about we talk about our patient instead?"

Sadness immediately returned to Murlich's features, who, as was his custom, had lost himself for a moment, contributing all of his scientific earnestness to the discussion!

"You're right!" he said, his voice suddenly tinged with fear.

"Now," Darembert added, "you needn't give in to despair! I still have a few tricks up my sleeve! Let's deal with the fever first, that's what worries me most, as it brings on delirium."

And he prescribed, based on a new method which he had just inaugurated at his clinic at the National Homeless Shelter, febrifugal injections, coupled with the administration of a sedative. At the same time, an intravenously-administered physiologically-adapted serum would sustain the patient.

"I will come every day," he concluded. "Besides, I'll contact two colleagues for a consult. The days I am unable to come myself, I'll scnd one of my assistants."

"Thank you, thank you doctor," Murlich repeated, shaking Darembert's hand. The latter, crossly, but not spitefully, added:

"No need to thank me, the case interests me. And besides, even were it only for you!"

CHAPTER IX

Alix kept watch over Gulluliou. The delirium had held for a week. He was a reduced to a withered rag, now exuberant, now prostrate, a wretched ghost, spitting blood, torn by a horrible cough, swinging his arms about, haunted by visions translated in hiccups, a mishmash of words, of sobs, of laughs. He relived both his former years and the present in a nightmarish fog, his life in Borneo and his European life inextricably tangled, addressed his brothers from back home, his master, the crowd at the Museum of Natural History, shouted out his name, reenacted the scene in the Chamber, exerting himself to exhaustion. Then, fallen back on the pillow, calmed down by friendly hands, he whispered in a sibilant voice his doll's song:

Minnili, Minnili, the little
Bird, hops about the branches

One night, Alix was keeping watch over Gulluliou. The suite was quiet, enveloped in a sleepy calm, stagnant with the smell of stale medications. It was 9 p.m. Alix was waiting for Murlich to relieve her of her watch for the evening. Sitting near the bed, she daydreamed in the subdued glow of veiled light. Gulluliou had had a bad bout of delirium, and had just fallen asleep, short-winded, his emaciated body stretched out under the covers.

The young woman dreamed of vague things. In one corner the great palm leaf fluttered under invisible currents.

Suddenly, Gulluliou awoke and rose up on his elbow. With his disease-sunken eyes he stared at Alix. He remained this way for a moment. In the shadowy half-light, a worrisome fire rose in the depth of his stare: Alix recognized the same little flame of stifled brutality, coming to the surface. She had seen it once before, this shifty flame, and again she was afraid. Had she had any doubt of Gulluliou's enamored state, the ill-intentioned glow was back, reminding her.

In the white nightshirt, the white of the sheets and pillow, in all the white of this child's bed, the gray sunken-eyed face with its pouting lips took on an expression of hate. Man and beast, still fighting it out behind those shifting pupils.

The ape stirred. Words slipped from his mouth.

"Alix, you beautiful!"

She got up. His heart beat in anguish over this woman. Alone with Gulluliou, just like the other time! She forced herself to speak, softly:

"Come on Gulluliou, get some sleep!"

"No…you beautiful!"

"Are you thirsty? Do you want something to drink?"

"No, Alix…Love you!"

He drew himself up more. He was sitting now. He repeated: "Love you!" grinding his teeth. His face became haggard, as on the brink of a bout of fever-induced delirium. The beast was winning, a burst of energy was rising from the darkness of his primitive soul, from the vast forests of his native land, from the sap spurting from the torn vegetation.

He took one of his black legs out from under the sheets.

Alix did not want to cry out. She feared that such a cry would only further irritate the beast, and precipitate that which threatened her. No, she would defend herself if it came to that! Her virginity became tinged with virile courage.

A Malayan dagger was hanging on the wall, near the window.

"Love you, Alix, love you!"

Gulluliou had gotten down out of bed, standing, his arms extended, tottering for a few seconds. Then, he began to move towards her. Hideous, pitiful and terrifying, emaciated and hairy, his head wavering atop his bony frame, his coat the brown of an empty gourd. He kept going; he was now in the middle of the room, uttering the same words, with the same monomaniacal insistence:

"You beautiful, Alix! Love you! Love you! You beautiful."

Sometimes his voice took on a coaxing tone, at times full of sweet nothings, then it would screech, like a tight rope on a rusted pulley. His red eyelids blinked, drool hung in thin threads from the long hairs on his chin; with his fingers, he drew things out in air in crooked motions. From time to time, his chest hammered out deep coughs.

Previously screened from her by his nightshirt, what the light revealed for but a moment was so monstrous, so clearly detailed, that Alix no longer hesitated. She took a step, and extended her hand to the knife.

Gulluliou, wild with lust was going to reach her. With his own dark, frantic virginity he leapt forward to conquer this womanly virginity. In such a manner would his brothers, deep in a jungle awash in the vigor of the tropical flora, consummate their matings.

In disgust and terror, the memory of the creature's kiss kept coming back to her like a hiccup; had she not wiped it from her mouth as she had wiped it from her memory? Were those lips, those horrid lips of a wild beast, of a disease-riddled creature, once again going to assault hers, to drink afresh from the fruit she had kept from any further outrage?

It was a beast after all, and since the beast was not laying down his weapons, why spare him?

She drew the knife from its sheath and held it tightly in her hand.

But suddenly, before she moved any further, Gulluliou stopped and staggered, his hands searching across his chest. His joints collapsing he dropped into an armchair behind him.

He was taken by a fit, blood issuing from his mouth stood out in beads, staining his clothes. He moaned in pain.

Before this blood and this collapse, Alix was unable to hold back a cry, a single cry, issuing from her tight throat. And moved only by pity, she stayed the patient's collapse, forgetting both the danger she had been exposed to and her anger.

Quick steps on the stairs, voices in the hallway. The door opened, Murlich appeared along with Darembert who was coming for his nightly visit:

"What's going on? Did you fall?"

Pale, she had risen to her feet: any resentment she had harbored was once again stricken from her proud and independent character. She indicated Gulluliou, collapsed, exhausted, moaning plaintively:

"Doctor…a bout of delirium. He wanted to get up and I was unable to stop him…I only had time to stop him from going any further…He went and collapsed there, in that armchair. But I was afraid, that's why I screamed!"

"I understand, I understand," replied the doctor. "Damn, such accidents are awfully annoying!…He has a serious case of haemoptysis…We'll put him back to bed. Will you help me, Mr.Murlich?…I hope it won't be too serious."

They put Gulluliou back in bed.

Alix had remained stock-still, inside the ring of shadows cast by the light shade. He heart was still aflutter, striking the bars of her chest like a mad prisoner. She had not let go of the dagger.

Then, unassumingly, she hung it back on the wall, without a word to anyone.

CHAPTER X

This savage blow sank Gulluliou into a new bout of misery. He was no longer delirious, but he remained bedridden for several days, unconscious and motionless. At least, during this period, he was spared the coughing and spitting up of blood, and Darembert congratulated himself on this improvement.

Finally the ape regained consciousness. He could recognize those around his narrow bed: Darembert holding his wrist took his pulse, peering at the thermometer he drew from beneath the patient's armpit; Murlich, a sad smile on his face, his beard iridescent, his glasses reflecting the virginal decor; Alix, who had immediately hastened to his side at the news that he was going through a lucid interval. The patient saw the three familiar figures. His eyes, which were half closed in the daylight, fluttered with quiet happiness, the words he sought were translated into a little gurgle in his throat. He was too weak. On the doctor's instructions, the nurse who watched over him had had him drink something, a spoonful of a thirst-quenching wine. The patient coughed; they wiped his mouth.

His temples were hollow, the flattening of his skull made his ears stick out, his sunken cheeks emphasized his jaw:

"My little Gullu," Murlich said in pongo as he leaned over him, "can you recognize your master?"

The ape's thick lips, raised at the corners for an instant, sank under their own weight, and, buried in the pillow, his head moved in an affirmative sign while he continued to gurgle in a weak attempt to speak.

Alix in turn approached, her thin features tense with emotion, assuring herself of his conscious, fitful wakefulness.

Alas! She judged herself irrational and stupid, powerless before this near-human creature. She felt confused and wondered how she could be so cold and self-assertive towards men, yet freely forgive the vagaries of an ape? She did not know, and preferred not to look too deeply into the question, for each time she returned to it, it was with heartfelt pity for the poor, mysterious Gulluliou. Far from hating him, she shared, in a vague manner, his suffering.

Lucie, the chambermaid, knocked softly at the door, announcing that someone was still waiting downstairs to see Gulluliou: a journalist who wished to be invited in. Darembert

247

shrugged his shoulders: "Shall they never leave the poor beast alone?" It had gone on this way since the notorious events at the Legislature, since it became known that Gulluliou was bedridden. The newspapers constantly sent out reporters to get the latest news. Even the general public showed up and were ruthlessly tossed out. The door had remained strictly closed; Murlich no longer went out; helplessly watching the rapid, cruel collapse of so many years of work, of his greatest hopes, of the one who was the greatest recipient of his affections. However, the situation was not desperate yet, but had Darembert himself not voiced his fears? Such an expert's lack of certainty became almost a death warrant.

It was the end of April. The spring was rising up everywhere in its pale greenery, gracile as fine gauze stretched over the trees. Countless buds had burst forth in the Auteuil gardens at the sun's first caress. In front of the house the chestnuts were already covered in young leaves, in advance of the laburnum and birches, which were barely speckled with emerald. But this palette of greens extended to the shrubs along the grillwork of the fence to the privet, whose previous year's foliage darkly speckled the otherwise pale green of the new growth, and to the laurels and euonymus splaying out like mirrors the varnished leaves which winter had been unable to wither. Inside the curves of the sandy walkways the lawn was refreshing the soil with it fresh blanket. A border of irises, near the porch, displayed the speckled purple of its calyces. At the back of the garden, against Murlich's pavilion, a bed of pink hyacinths was beginning to flower, already giving off their lovely aroma. Along with these, a few tufts of violets and a bed of fire-red primrose accounted for the few flowers that were out.

Gulluliou fully regained his lucidity. In his bed he appeared as intelligent and familiar as before, but his gestures and the rare things he would say were tinged with melancholy. From his long body all nervous energy was gone; as thin as they were, his arms seemed heavy, only rising very slowly, his awkward-fingered hands emerging brown and limp from his white sleeves. Gulluliou would from time to time take some sugared wine, some egg yolks, some milk. He altogether refused any meat. He was given a number of toys, small musical instruments, cardboard animals, and dolls. He would amuse himself for a few moments, soon stopping to cough. His cough came in starts, very weakly, but repeatedly, and one sensed that they tore apart this worn out machine.

This went on for eight days. Darembert multiplied his visits, using all the resources in his arsenal to maintain in place the life-force which sought, at every moment, to desert Gulluliou. Meanwhile, the house remained gloomy, drowning in an atmosphere of expectancy and sadness. Murlich and Alix felt the vague hope they had so long entertained, vanish with every hour the decline in the poor creature's condition progressed. Besides, the doctor one morning himself anticipated Murlich's questions:

"Yes indeed! It's clear to me that it's over," said Darembert. "I was right, back in the month of January, the first time you called me, to warn you of the climate. They all wind up this way these poor creatures! They need to be in the Tropics."

"But," the naturalist objected, drawn, in spite of himself, to reply by his habit for controversy, "others have managed to make monkeys from Borneo and Africa survive in our cold latitudes. I've witnessed some cases. If Gulluliou dies, it is fate, it is not through any lack of vigilance on my part. Certainly it would be no exaggeration, in one way or the other, to say that being overly protective would have been to preclude any chance the poor little one would have had to acclimatize. But perhaps he was too young, yes perhaps I should have waited. Ah! We learn from everything, regardless of one's age!"

And Murlich, his head bowed, led the doctor through the pavilion's narrow hall, accompanied him across the spring garden awash in golden sunlight where the sparrows noisily chirped their happiness at the awakening of the light.

CHAPTER XI

One morning, towards eight, as Murlich still slept, tired from having stayed up long into the night, the nurse knocked on his door. Gulluliou wished to see him. She explained that the patient, having woken from a short sleep, had uttered a sentence in pongo in which Murlich's name had repeatedly come up. The ape had looked about the bed for the presence of his old master. Murlich, with a sense of foreboding, sent someone to warn Alix, who then very busy with the new season's fashions, was already up and in morning conference with her forewoman. She came quickly, finding her cousin already in the dying creature's room.

A half-daylight penetrated through poorly closed drapes, and the night-light still burned. Gulluliou had sat up in bed, his head held high and, smiling, he held the scientists' hands in his own. When Alix entered, he turned towards her with a deep shudder, and looked at her without saying a word. The young woman drew closer, her eyes questioning Murlich, who with a despairing nod of his head confirmed the worst. The nurse returned, and put out the night-light.

Gulluliou shifted his legs, his eyes on the window, and said in pongo:

"I want to see the daylight...the Sun shining!"

Murlich signaled that they open the drapes. Light flooded the room, bathing its white knick-knack-laden walls, the great palm leaf, balanced over the heating duct, continuing its endless, silent, rhythmic movement. Gulluliou surveyed all of this, his eyes dazzled for a moment. His hands painfully tore at his chest, he issued a soft plaintive moan, then whispered:

"I want to breathe the wind coming through the trees."

"Look," said Murlich, "how beautiful the trees are. Can you see the leaves?"

"No...I want to see the leaves...I want to get up, I am strong!"

"Get up! Oh! You mustn't my little Gullu, as you well know the doctor has forbidden it!"

But the ape shook his head, rising on his two fists, trying to get his long legs out from the covers where a last bit of energy was manifest. And since anything which might now upset him would likely be worse than the thing itself, Murlich cautiously offered no further resistance. Overcome with pity, they watched Gulluliou, rise to his feet, totter. The expression on his face showed no weakness, but rather a great happiness.

He moved like a drunkard as they covered him with a dressing-gown; the view of the trees from the bay-window was still hidden by the tulle drapes which the nurse now moved aside. Through the windows the view was awash with foliage, treetops. From among the large leaves of a nearby chestnut branch emerged fluffy pink and white cones about to flower. A long wisteria branch waved in the breeze, following the same rocking motion as the palm leaf in the corner of the room. Gulluliou dropped back into the armchair which had been pushed up behind him, remaining still a moment, his eyes wide. The cuckoo clock tolling the half-hour in the entrance hall downstairs surprised him a little. His teeth jutting out, he smiled weakly and said:

"The trees!"

Then, suddenly, he cried out unexpectedly:

"I'm hungry!"

Alix had sat down beside him. The ape drew his eyes from the garden to look at her, and it was the same worrisome look from the depths of his eyes, both piercing and soft, a look the young woman knew to be a silent avowal of his love. She was troubled, so overcome with sadness before this creature's dying moments, that she had to hold back her tears. The fierce independence she had cultivated would come to this: crying over the death of an ape. Memories unconsciously came back to her, flashing past but distinct, of what had transpired in the theater-box, the night of *The Triumph of Man*, when Maximin had undoubtedly elicited by the leaven of jealousy the love which already smoldered in Gulluliou. Then came, brutal, the attempts at savage passion, this bestial aberration which the mysterious conquering superiority of man over beast had overcome. O! what influence, what effluvia could measure the distance, often imperceptible between the two species, attesting, regardless of physical makeup, to the dominance of one over the other? Perhaps Gulluliou was dying of having guessed, in his animal consciousness, of this yet insurmountable barrier.

Murlich, having left for a moment, reentered with the chambermaid who was bringing in a small tray, upon which Gulluliou, his vision still clear, recognized some bananas. He smiled again, more cheerfully, and extended his hand. He held the plate between his knees which were bent into an acute angle beneath his dressing-gown, and ate slowly, peeling the yellow fruit in a long-accustomed manner. The ape's cadenced and labored breathing, while he enjoyed this small pleasure, was all that broke the silence. He had offered bananas to his two friends, who had declined. He ate them all up, with an appetite which belied his worn out body. He even drank a full glass of muscat, and began to repeat in pongo, with an increasing firmness which lit up the eyes in his ashen face:

"I am strong now, I am strong. Look Alix! Look, master!"

He was strong! With a nod of his head, Murlich now considered the decline of this individual on the threshold of adolescence, whose strength had no doubt exceeded that of an adult man, but who, now weaker than an old man, was in his death throes. For science would not be deceived, this seeming recovery was only a portent of an impending death, as if the grim reaper wished to first intoxicate those whom he would soon favor with the kiss of eternal sleep!

9 a.m. tolled; Murlich knew the doctor would not be long in arriving, that he would arrive in time, although, clear signs of collapse were already apparent. The ape no longer spoke, but watched Alix and Murlich. This life's end within the rebirth of spring was attended with a tragic yet gentle wait.

For a moment, Gulluliou's gurgling breath came with greater difficulty, and a series of coughs made him wince. He put his hand to his hollow chest, a pink froth rose to his lips, which the nurse immediately wiped away with a handkerchief. Murlich took the dying creature's arm, felt for a pulse: a frightful temperature; a man with such a fever would have long ago passed out. The battle Gulluliou's mortal frame kept up against the fatal incursion was no less than superhuman.

Almost another hour passed; the room was plunged into silence. Curled up in the back of his armchair, the ape continued to die, visibly weakening. He frequently closed his eyelids for prolonged periods of time, as if asleep, his life seemingly reduced to his wheezy breathing. From time to time, they made him swallow a spoonful of medicine or tonic. Alix, moving about noiselessly, prepared the medicine, and helped the nurse make up the bed a bit. Finally Darembert's arrival was announced; Murlich hurried down to meet him:

"Ah! Doctor, we've been waiting for you!"

Darembert, frowning, asked:

"He is worse?"

Quickly the naturalist brought him up to date. As he spoke, the other shuffled his rough shoulders, knitted his wide brow and clean-shaven face. It was over. There was no doubt about it.

"Nothing remains," said Darembert, "but to try to prolong what little time he has."

"Prolong it? Whatever for?" replied Murlich. "It's over, isn't it? Why then maintain a delusion from which we can only suffer when it will have disappeared? No, no, doctor, no more serums, they would only create an artificial state. Gulluliou is no more. He has played his role; nothing will be lost. Nothing is ever lost" he daydreamed aloud, his voice quavering. "Ah! How I would have enjoyed taking him all the way. I had an impact on this life of his."

In spite of his usual skepticism, Darembert was overcome, blurting out an avowal of his hidden admiration:

"Dear professor, your contributions to science are such that your name will be remembered amongst the foremost of your time. You have been able to convince many of your adversaries. Indeed, Hetking's theory, I myself long denied it! Anyhow!"

The two scientists looked upon each other in the full light of this bright morning. One glance had ended their revelatory exchange. Murlich had proved experimentally the great theory which assigned humanity a new destiny, less prideful, and more in keeping with the laws of Nature.

In the few moments of silence afforded them, Murlich and Darembert—the latter now shaken in his beliefs—could, with their ability to quickly reason things out, foresee all the implications of the mysteries hidden by the mere idea of Gulluliou, the near-human. The circle was widening. Based on the humanity of the present, they conceived that of the future, that of faraway times. When would the human race begin slipping, when would it be replaced by another?

And until then, through what phases would it pass, what modifications would it endure? Would it indeed, after a universal cataclysm, renew itself for another period of time, as the great American evolutionist had predicted? Would the new Deluge announced by Hetking, and, before him by friar Florian, ever take place? These questions were thrown together in a confused manner in these minds accustomed to quick and bold conclusions.

Murlich headed for the stairs, telling the doctor:

"Let's get up there quick, so you can see him."

Footsteps were heard on one of the garden's gravel paths, then a pause. The entrance hall was tinged with the light filtering through the green and blue-tinted glass panels of the door which opened on the vestibule. Maximin could be seen through the door. He entered:

"The ladies in the workroom have informed me," he said to the naturalist, after having acknowledged Darembert, "that Miss Alix is here at your patient's bedside."

"Yes," answered Murlich, "he is much worse, very, very much worse! It truly is the end! Would you like to come up with us?"

The poet hesitated, wondering if he should go in the room and show himself before the dying creature. Between him and Alix, whom he had seen once or twice since the ape's relapse, the creature had rarely come up in conversation: Maximin would ask of the patient's condition, in which he interested himself for appearance's sake, if not entirely sincerely, and she would invariably answer evasively.

He whispered:

"Perhaps seeing me, who am not entirely on familiar terms with her lately, would impress her? Ah! the poor creature, I did not think him in so serious a state. Well, I'll come with you, and stay off in the wings should it be necessary."

The doctor and Maximin followed Murlich, who had already reached the first floor and was signaling them to walk on their tiptoes. They entered Gulluliou's room.

10 a.m. tolled downstairs, it had been roughly two hours since the ape had risen from his bed. Alix, seeing the poet, approached him; Maximin silently sensed the need for an excuse, mumbling something about the scientist having led him there, and that he would only stay a moment. Already the young woman had joined the doctor, who was taking Gulluliou's temperature. The pongo had just fallen into a faint; a few drops of ether between the lips had revived him. Darembert, shrugging his shoulders, spoke softly to his assistants.

"Nothing, nothing we can do. Leave him here, he will pass any moment now, just like a lamp which is suddenly extinguished when the current fails. The most rapidly progressing case I've ever seen!"

Gulluliou had just opened his eyes, had drawn a long breath, his throat gurgling. Then with a jerking cough he spat out a large clot of blood.

Blood came forth from his nostrils, his temples and eyes even more hollowed out; a spoonful of muscat poured into his mouth was rejected. He began to mouth a series of unrelated syllables: Alix listened. Rhythmically, Gulluliou shook his right hand, weighed down on the arm of the chair. He spluttered out almost imperceptibly:

"Minnili, Minni…li!"

The young woman understood: she laid the doll on the ape's knees. Gulluliou took the fragile toy which in his weakened hands seemed as weighted down. With his despondent eyes he gazed upon Minnili. Evocative of his distant childhood, was the little forest-bird not still singing in the mind of this exile from a foreign race? Minnili, Minni…li! There was in the clear morning light which accompanied the death of this brother of a lower order, human beings who stood in silence, in the grip of a great sadness: Alix holding back her tears, Murlich his hand squeezing that of Son-of-Doves, Darembert seeking a miracle, Maximin, stirred to the very depths of his poet-philosopher's compassion.

For a moment, having moved closer to Gulluliou, Maximin saw the ape's eyes shift up, missing him, moving towards Alix's and locking on them for a time, before closing under the shock of the bright light. For a brief second the same shudder united these three individuals born of a common fiber. Alix and Maximin were filled with pity for one another, and for the one on the brink of death, who left them with the sadness of having loved.

Time crawled by, Gulluliou had been still. Darembert, taking on full responsibility, had vainly tried injections of caffeine and serum. The dying creature continued to weaken, burning up with fever, from time to time spitting up chunks of his lungs. The doctor took his temperature:

"40-2-5" he whispered to a frightened Murlich.

Around 11:30, Maximin felt it better to leave, knowing himself to be an outsider, and of no help in this prolonged deathwatch.

Gulluliou began to struggle against his impending death: he was perfectly conscious, for his eyes remained fixed, with an expression of suffering and affection, now on Murlich and now on Alix. His hands clamped down in irregular convulsions along the arm of the chair. The haemoptysis worsened, became a near constant retching up of blood. It was horrible; the ape's powerful death-rattle was impeded from emerging from his throat by a frothy gurgling. Twice more, he passed out, they thought it was over. Darembert had to check if his heart was still beating.

The naturalist tried to encourage Alix to leave, to avoid witnessing such a death, but she insisted on staying.

"No, no, I beg you, let me stay until the end, it's the least you can do, dear cousin, to allow me to be near you in this time!"

Highly agitated, she smothered her short sobs by biting into her handkerchief. Ah! what a horrible thing to see a soul perish; an inferior one perhaps, but one which loved her…Loved! Gulluliou loved her! But why then was she now crying? No! Impossible, monstrous, mad! No, she could not love Gulluliou.

Yet, nonetheless, she cried.

So as to no longer see, she turned and leaned her forehead against a window, looking at the sun-drenched garden.

At last, when the familiar old *coo-coo* in the entrance hall tolled noon, Murlich, Darembert and the nurse saw Gulluliou, who had been passed out for a time, open his eyes. He looked straight ahead of him. His face, somewhat contracted, relaxed, his features taking on a human-like resignation, and through the gurgling of a clot behind his teeth, a barely audible voice came forth from between his slightly parted lips. He whispered:

"Alix, Alix…"

Then:

"Boorli, Boorli !"[32]

Frozen in place, he nonetheless seemed to stretch himself out towards some unknown point which only his pupils could perceive, his mouth only stirring weakly, while his entire huge body had collapsed, as if folded back into the chair. Murlich,

---

[32] "The trees, the trees!"

tapping Alix on the arm, told her to open the window. Light flooded into the brightly-painted room, the freshness of clean air, the rustling of the birds superimposed on the patient's death-rattles. And Gulluliou, his face in an almost idealized smile, plumbed the spring sky, up there, with his troubled gaze. For a few moments he seemed to listen to the garden's thousand voices, repeating the soft and faraway song of Minnili, the little bird of the guava tress.

Then, a hiccup rose in his throat, he stopped moving, his suffering ended.

Darembert bent over, and raising his head, deeply moved, mumbled:

"It's over."

He held Murlich and Alix's hands.

His eyes full of tears, Murlich said, simply and truthfully:

"My poor child!"

And the man bemoaned the death of the one who had allowed him a glimpse at the mystery of the future: Gulluliou was gone, he was back in his land of warm humid light, where things were more beautiful, where his race would continue to ascend.

Before the mortal remains of this strange soul, human beings cried.

*Marie-Charles-Joseph de Pougens (1755-1833) was a diplo-
mat who was posted to Rome in 1776, where at age 22 one of
his paintings earned him entry into the local Art Academy. At
24, he almost died of smallpox, which left him partially blind.
Back in France, he started his own printing business and he
also wrote books on art, diplomacy, business, physics, botany,
geology, mineralogy, poetry, archeology, mythology, and the
history of criminal justice. He is, however, best remembered
for his novella* Jocko *(1824), which inspired a blatantly deriv-
ative and eponymous play by M. Gabriel and M. Rochefort,
staged at the Théâtre de la Porte Saint-Martin on March 16,
1825 before Madame la Duchesse de Berry. The portrayal of
the ape's behavior in the novel is supported by extensive foot-
noted "proofs" cited from numerous scientific sources of the
day.*

C. M. de Pougens: *Jocko*

I had been living for some years on the island of [...] but
as I don't wish to be identified, I will abstain from mentioning
its name or what post I held, thereby excising any details
which might reveal my identity to a capricious public which
might either not care a whit or react maliciously. I will, however, recount the following anecdote, because my memories of
it are dear to me, painfully dear...and also because it includes
a remarkable instance which in part accounts for my present
opulence.

It was the hottest portion of the summer; 5 p.m. had just
struck on the parish church's large clock. The Sun's rays still
pierced to the ground. Tired of the strain my duties imposed
on me, and naturally of a melancholy character, I left home
and went to wander about the [...] Forest, not far from where I

had resided since my arrival on the island. Barely 200 paces into the darkened alley, where a delightful coolness prevailed, I heard a small noise to my left. A living creature seemed to be fleeing and slipping through the foliage. I tended my ear, but soon heard nothing more; so I continued my walk and took up my former train of thought. Since I had left my guests, my so-called friends, boisterously crowded around a table loaded with exquisite wines, I was no longer alone, but was with my-self and my memories.

I heard a second rustling similar to the first. I stopped and made out, between a number of interlaced branches, a small, almost round head, two charming almond-shaped eyes gazing caressingly towards me,[33] a short though not stumpy

---

[33] According to don Felix d'Azara, some people say that the caraya, a monkey, which according to him belongs to the fam-ily of the howler-monkeys, when surprised far from their lair and finding no place of refuge, lay on the ground, join their hands and seem to plead for mercy. *Essays on the Natural History of the Quadrupeds of the Province of Paraguay*. ~This capacity to express through facial expressions and gestures its various emotions can also be seen in monkeys of smaller spe-cies: "When one has frightened a coaita monkey with a gun-shot," states Mr. Audebert, "he extends his arms towards his enemy, stares at him, shifting his jaws back and forth see-mingly begging for his life. Such gestures, and the intent gaze of a creature so similar to man, have often troubled the soul of hunters little accustomed to such game, this emotion being sufficiently strong that many have given up this type of hunt-ing...Indeed, let us imagine a monkey laying in the grass stained with its own blood, fighting to stave off death, extend-ing its little hands towards the one who has injured it, and turning towards him its almost human face; imagine the dying animal's eyes, which by their touching appeal seem to re-proach to its enemy the pain it experiences and its coming demise." *Histoire [Naturelle] des Singes*, Coaita. Such a scene convinced the traveler Stedman to no longer hunt these ani-

nose, two moist lips, and small milky-white teeth,[34] a figure, if not pretty, at least somewhat spicy. On first glance, the skin seemed a mousy yellow, highlighted by a light silvery sheen.

The figure moved, showing itself almost to the midriff. I stepped forward to catch it, but in a fraction of a second she had climbed, or rather launched herself, to the top of a coconut tree. Her limbs were supple and limber. I would add that, as best as I could tell, she was somewhere between 4'2" and 4' 3"[35]

Gracefully ensconced between several heavily leaf-laden limbs, she observed me attentively. I signaled to her to come to me and she imitated my gesture, inviting me to come to her. I would have been hard-pressed to comply, for if I was still quite lithe, my agility was far from equaling hers.

Naturally of a curious disposition, my many voyages had led to frequent opportunities to observe the different families of monkeys,[36] orangs,[37] jockos,[38] and pongos.[39] I quickly rec-

---

mals. The chevalier Foucher d'Obsonville in a note to Mr. de Buffon speaks with complaisance of how pleasantly disposed was a small loris he had raised. "The indications of his sensitive nature," he states, "consisted in taking the end of my hand and holding it tight to his breast while locking his half-open eyes on mine." *Nat. Hist.*, addition to art. Loris.

[34] "All of the orang-outang's teeth, even the canines, are similar to those of man." Buffon, *Nat. Hist.*, art. Orang-outang.

[35] Naturalists generally agree that the pongo or orangutan of the largest species is about the height of an average man. G. Cuvier, *Tableau élémentaire de l'histoire naturelle des animaux.*

[36] "There exists," states Linnaeus, "so little difference between apes and man that one has yet to find a sufficiently subtle observation to determine the border which separates them." *Syst. Nat.* Indeed, it would be rather difficult, at first glance, to differentiate between man and the monkeys of Guinea to which Peiresc assigns the name of *barris*, whose combed white beards and slow, measured pace lend a venerable air. See Gas-

sendi, *Vita Peiresc.* "Were one to judge strictly on the basis of the way they are formed," observes Mr. de Buffon, "apes could be taken as a variety within the human species." However Pliny adds that the ape differs significantly from man in its temperament. "Man," he states, "can live in all climates; he lives and thrives in those of the far North and under a Mediterranean climate; the ape has trouble surviving in the temperate zone and can only thrive in the warmest countries." *Nat. Hist.*, art. Monkeys.

[37] As is well known, the word "orangutan" meaning wild man is only a generic term. "This name of wild man," states Mr. Relian, "arises from their external resemblance to man, particularly with regards to the way they move about, and of a way of thinking which is specific to them and which one does not find in other animals. Letter to M. Allamand, Batav, 1770, cited by Mr. de Buffon, *Nat. Hist.*, addition to art. Orangoutang. One has long recognized this strong resemblance between the orangutan and man. "The different species of monkeys," states Pliny, "are, of all the animals, those which by their body's conformation most resemble man. They can be distinguished among themselves by their tails. Monkeys are of a remarkable agility... Mucianus writes that monkeys have even been seen to play chess, once taught to distinguish the different chess pieces." Pliny, *Nat. Hist.* Mr. de Buffon did not fear to state that "the orang-outang could be considered the greatest of apes and the last of men." *Nat. Hist.* art. Monkeys. "The orang-outang," states M. Ch. Bonnet, "is so similar to man, that the anatomist comparing the two, thinks he is comparing two individuals of the same species, or at least of the same genus; and struck by the strong and numerous similarities between the two, he will not hesitate to place the orangoutang immediately after the savage Hottentot." *The Contemplation of Nature.* It is not only in its outward conformation that the orangutan offers a striking resemblance to man, he approaches the latter no less by his gait and behavior. "I have seen," states Bontius, "a few individuals of each sex walking

ognized the individual before me belonged to the latter species; however, I later dubbed her Jocko, as it seemed a prettier
name.

I had the habit of always carrying a little bread in my
pockets, which it pleased me to distribute amongst the small
birds I encountered along the route of my long and solitary
walks. Seeing that she was still examining me with great attention, I threw a bit of the bread her way. She descended from
the coconut tree in which she had taken refuge, and leaping,

---

on two feet, particularly a female who in modesty would escape the stares of men she did not know by covering her face
with her hands (if one can term them such), shedding abundant
tears, moaning pitifully, indeed undertaking all the actions one
might expect to see from a human, such as one would have
thought her only lacking in speech… It is named orang-
outang, or man of the woods."

[38] This ape, known as a chimpanzee in some parts of Africa,
and jocko or enjocko by the inhabitants of the Congo, is according to the observations of Mr. Ans. Desmarets, much
more similar to man than the orangutan with respect to the
proportion of its limbs to its body. See *Dictionnaire raisonnée
universel d'histoire naturelle.*

[39] According to Andrew Battell and some other travelers, "the
pongos cover their dead with leaves and branches, which the
local human inhabitants view as a form of burial." The pongo,
which is as tall as the tallest man, is remarkably strong and
such that, if one believes travelers' accounts, capable of holding their own against ten men. Thus do they have the advantage against men which they meet in remote locations. Armed
with a club they will even attack elephants which they sometimes defeat. They are frequently seen to abduct villagers,
particularly women, but are treated well. Battell, whom I cited
above, speaks of a young boy in his employ who was abducted
by a pongo: this child spent an entire year [*sic* Battell says a
month] amongst these apes. Upon his return he assured him
that he had in no way been harmed.

quick as a flash, to the ground, she took up the small piece of bread, sniffed at it a few times,[40] looked at me, pondered over it with an expression of mistrust,[41] and refused to eat it. I knew of this natural hesitation among the jocko and pongo species: to put an end to it, I took a second piece of bread, ate half of it and tossed her the rest. With a remarkable dexterity, she caught it on the fly, and promptly ate it. Then, picking up the

---

[40] "Monkeys," states Mr. de Buffon, "will not eat anything without firsthand having smelled it." Mr. Virey has also made the observation that the sense of smell and taste are highly developed in the monkey. "These two senses," he adds, "take precedence over the others and direct their appetites." In his *Voyage en Afrique, vol. II*, Mr. Levaillant writes of a monkey he has celebrated under the name of Kees. "It was," states this traveler, "a monkey of a species extremely common on the Cape and known as *bawian* (baboon or papió). He was very friendly and became attached to me in particular. I made him my taster. When we found fruits or roots unknown to my Hottentots, we never touched them until my dear Kees had tasted them; if he discarded them we judged them to be unpleasant or dangerous and we left them behind." Mr. Levaillant cites a number of other instances of the sagacity and keen sense of smell of Kees, his monkey, amongst which the following: "The water," he states, "was getting low... I see Kees suddenly come to a stop, and turning his eyes and nose into the wind that came from the side, took off running, with all my dogs in tow, without any of them barking...How surprised was I to find them assembled around a lovely fountain, over 300 feet from the place they had run off from." *Ibid.*

[41] "Monkeys," states Linnaeus, "are generally suspicious; they remember being treated well or poorly, etc." *Syst. Nat.* Allamand observed that "a monkey named Rolloway, loving towards his master, was suspicious of strangers, and would take on a defensive posture when these tried to approach or touch him." *Addition to Buffon's Nat. Hist.*

first piece which had remained on the ground, she sniffed at it a second time, then avidly swallowed it.

As I remained motionless for a few moments, she thrust forward her little hand towards me, shaking it in a seemingly impatient manner. She seemed to invite me to repeat my gifts. Indeed, I tossed her a number of other small pieces of bread, which she continued to catch with great dexterity, but as soon as I took a step forward, she ran off at some distance, never letting herself be approached. I reversed my steps, walking backwards while still throwing her bits of bread from time to time. The lovely little paw remained constantly extended towards me. She would shake it slightly and draw it back towards her, also, from time to time, voicing soft, pearly, silvery cries,[42] which she varied across different scales, and which surely meant something. Finally, seeing I was no longer throwing her anything, she left, streaking off to the magnificent coconut tree, tearing off several nuts and letting them fall at my feet. I opened one up with a large knife I carried; I drank some of the milk and ate a piece of the flesh. I then moved off to give pretty little Jocko the liberty to acquire the rest for herself, which she was in no way loath to do, though in a manner which suggested this food was no less than old hat to her, and that this wasn't the first time she ate the flesh and drank the

---

[42] Monkeys express their affection by very quiet little cries, which among the capuchin monkeys (sapajous) resembles the sound of a flute; it is only when they are angry that their raucous screeching voice is heard." Audebert, *Histoire [Naturelle] des Singes*. This soft modulated cry is found in a number of other monkeys or analogous creatures, such as the tamarin, the *thévangue* or loris, etc. Mr. Foucher d'Obsonville states with regard to an animal of the latter species, "that he sometimes uttered a kind of modulated call or soft whistle. I could easily distinguish," he continues, "a cry of need, of pleasure, of pain, and even one of impatience." *Note sent to Mr. de Buffon.*

milk of a coconut.[43] As it was getting dark, I made my way towards the city. The charming little creature followed me, letting me hear from time to time that silvery cry I found so pretty. Seeing that I no longer responded to her calls, she turned around sadly and moved off slowly.

The next day I returned at about the same time. My dear little Jocko was waiting for me just inside the woods: lying in the middle of a tuft of young shrubs, she had parted the branches and was looking through the leaves. As soon as she saw me, she ran up to meet me with great demonstrations of joy. Her forward progress was so quick that she almost touched my clothes. Frightened by this somewhat involuntary approach, she ran off and took refuge atop a tree over 100 paces away. Fearing to further frighten her, I took on an indifferent mien and threw two or three small pieces of bread on the path. She came down slowly, sniffed at them, undoubtedly to ascertain if they were of the same nature as yesterday's, and ate them with gusto. I had brought an ample supply of soft biscuits. I threw her half of one,[44] which she caught on the fly,

---

[43] According to Inigo de Biervillas' *Voyages,* the monkeys of Calcutta know full well how to break open a coconut, to eat its seed and to drink the milk it bears. He recounts that the locals take advantage of these circumstances to capture these animals alive. Small holes are made in the coconuts; the monkey doesn't hesitate to stick his hand into them in order to finish opening the coconut, and the hunter then captures them before they have had a chance to get rid of the coconut.

[44] Monkeys, like almost all quadrumanous animals, are omnivorous. They happily consume nuts, acorns, bulbs, leaves, lettuce, bread, eggs, etc. However, accustomed to living in large trees in hot climates, fruit are among their favorite foods. They pick them and bring them to their mouth in the manner of men. Mr. Fréd. Cuvier, in his description of an orangutan observed in Paris in 1808, reports that "this animal ate almost indiscriminately of fruits, vegetables, eggs, milk, meat; he very much enjoyed," he added, "bread, coffee and oranges."

as she had done the day before, sniffed at it, appeared unde-
cided and did not eat it. I put part of the remaining half in my
mouth and threw the rest to her. She disposed of it in a wink,
along with the piece she already held. Her pleasure was then
made manifest by gambols and little leaps;[45] she spun like a
top and leapt from the ground with remarkable agility, de-
scribing lovely and graceful lover's knot patterns. She would
then take a couple of steps towards me, extending her two
little hands so I might give her more biscuits.

This scene repeated itself every afternoon: I arrived with
my pockets full and left with them empty. Every time I gave
her a new kind of cake, she showed the same hesitation, the
same doubts; she would not eat until she had witnessed me
doing so.

Attentive to my arrival in the forest, one day she came up
to meet me, placing before me, albeit at some distance, some
lovely coconuts, placing a kind of sharp stone beside them. I
admired her instincts. I broke open the two best nuts, took one

---

"When the orang-outang," states Ch. Bonnet, "can no longer
find fruit in the mountains or in the forest, he will go to the
seashore to find a large kind of oyster weighing several
pounds, which often remains open on the shore. However, the
circumspect ape, fearing that the oyster in suddenly snapping
closed will catch his hand, skillfully tosses a stone into the
shell, not allowing it to close, leaving him to eat it at his leisure. Among the true monkeys, there are females who will
place their long tails between the pincers of large crayfish, and
as soon as these pinch it they draw our their tail quickly, take
them off and go and eat them some way off." *The Contemplation of Nature*.

[45] It is a most amusing spectacle to witness," states M. Virey,
"to see, in those vast, ancient forests of the torrid zone, monkeys leaping from tree to tree, hanging suspended from
branches, jumping and frolicking, taking on thousands of ridiculous poses, annoying each other, fighting or having fun together, etc." Art. Singes, *Dict. d'hist nat.*

and moved some distance off, so she could come up and take the other. I drank the milk, ate part of the flesh; she imitated me. While she ate she gazed at me with a satisfied appearance and let me hear that lovely cry which had been pleasing to my ear from the first.

These occurrences suggested something to me for the morrow. Besides my usual provisions of biscuits, cakes and tarts, I brought a flask of excellent Calcavallo wine, which I had brought from Lisbon. I poured some in a glass and pretended to drink a portion of it. Then I put the glass down at my feet and I drew back a few feet. My little Jocko drew closer, took up the glass with great dexterity and drank the wine in several sips.[46] Looking at me then with a surprised and satisfied demeanor, she at the same time let her tongue slip back and forth across her tiny lips. When she had finished drinking, she put the glass down in the same spot she had picked it up from. I picked it up and went to wash it in a hollow which contained a bit of rain water.

I then filled it half-way, brought it up to my mouth, and left the rest to my small friend, who appeared to savor it with

---

[46] Orangutans and other monkeys such as capuchins, etc. will happily drink wine, brandy or other strong liquor. See Buffon, *Natural History.* Guillaume Rubruquis reports that to capture Cathay monkeys one places at the entrance of the cave where they sleep strong intoxicating liquor. "They come all together," he states, "to taste this beverage, calling out *chin-chin*, and get so drunk that they fall asleep, such that the hunters can easily capture them." A story translated by Bergeron in his *Voyages in Asia:* The orangutan of which Tulpius speaks drank quite competently from a vase he held with one hand on the handle and one hand underneath; and when he was done drinking, he never failed to properly wipe off his lips. The female individual seen in Paris in 1808 also drank from a glass held with two hands; she would then sometimes take a lady's companion's handkerchief to wipe off her lips and hand it back after having used it.

even greater sensuality than the first time. Then, still constant in her imitations, she went and rinsed off the glass and returned it to the same spot, hoping I would fill it again, which I did not do, hoping to spare her.

Indeed, the wine, however mild, had affected her senses. My Jocko's eyes were more animated, she was more expansive, more confident, and familiar to the point of drawing sufficiently near to me to touch the edge of my clothes with the tips of her fingers. I could easily have caught her, but refrained from doing so. I neither wished to distress her, nor force her back to her former mistrust.

In the days that followed, my Calcavallo wine, my Xerez wine, of which I poured her, at my discretion, small doses, always seemed to afford her the same pleasures. Finally, I decided to bring her some of the island's excellent liquor, of which I had an ample supply. Having allowed her to ingest somewhat more of my snacks than usual, I placed before her a small glass of crème de Créole. At first she seemed surprised and worried, but soon her enjoyment took the upper hand, and she stuck out her two little hands while dancing around me. It was her way of asking for something. I placed a second glass before her, but only half full, for I feared compromising the darling creature's health. Little Jocko avidly took hold of it, but only drank the liquor little by little and in moderate doses. She seemingly delighted in savoring it. A semi-drunken state followed which was made manifest in her eyes: her fears and hesitations vanished, she threw herself at me and rested her little head on my shoulder, rolling it as she snuggled against my chest. I continued my walk and she followed me, stamping her feet. From time to time I gave her small pieces of cake, which she ate without even looking at them. There was no longer any mistrust between us. I took her right arm, slipped it under my left arm and so continued walking for almost a quarter of a mile.[47] Sometimes she ran off to chase butterflies,[48]

---

[47] Everybody knows that the monkeys known as Barris (*simia troglodytes*, Linnaeus), orangutans, pongos and jockos are

269

sometimes she walked beside me and matched her paces to mine with an admirable accuracy.

As her arms, while not completely disproportionate, were a bit longer than those of a human being, I decided to take her two hands and cross them in front of her. I don't know what she thought of it, but was affrighted, moved a few steps away from me, and took on a sulky air. I then remembered what I had read in a number of traveler's accounts, and that I myself had observed on different occasions, regarding the natural modesty of the females of this species.[49] This along with re-

---

conformed such as to be able to stand upright with ease. "Dressed in a suit," states Gassendi, "the monkeys known as Barris will immediately begin to walk on two feet." However, according to the observations of Mr. Daubenton, "the orang-outang's heel resting more awkwardly on the ground than man, it runs more easily than it walks and would need artificial heels taller than those of our shoes if one wished to allow it to walk easily and for any length of time." *Encyclopédie méthodique*, art. Orang-outang. "I have seen," says Mr. de Buffon, "an orang-outang present its hand to lead someone in who had come to visit him, and to walk about with them in a staid manner, as with company."

[48] "The long-legged baboon eats beetles, flies and other insects which it catches most dexterously on-the-fly." Buffon.

[49] The most highly accredited travelers attest that the orangu-tan and apes of that family generally have a stronger sense of decency than other animals. One can read in Henri Grose's *Voyages aux Indes-Occidentales*, that two orangutans given to Mr. Horne, governor of Bombay, could not bear to be stared at by the curious, and would hide their privy parts with their hands. Mr. Relian, surgeon in Batavia, speaks of a pair of orangutans, one male, one female, which he had had a chance to observe. "They were all embarrassed when one stared at them too much. The female would then throw herself into the male's arms and would hide her face in his chest, which resulted in a truly touching spectacle." This natural sense of

tracing in my mind a number of incidents of ancient history led me to shudder in horror. However, glancing over to my little Jocko, I smiled at my indignation, and was tempted to credit as fabulous or to ascribe to the vagaries of Art certain Greek and even Roman depictions which I had seen in Italy, particularly in Portici, as well as on several ancient medals.

I drew her back by gesture and voice and presented her with a small piece of cake. She came back without showing any sign of satisfaction, and walked some ways in the same direction with me, but at some distance away.

We each had to go our own way. I amused myself by tipping my hat and bowing deeply to her. At first she seemed rather perplexed, but she soon decided what to do: she tore off several banana leaves and in no time skillfully fashioned herself a kind of hat, placed it on her head and in turn bowed and tipped her hat to me in the most profound manner, made all the more comical by her seriousness. Then we each went our own way, though not without, on a number of occasions, turning to look at each other.

The next day she came to me adorned with a hood of woven leaves, more artistically assembled than on the previous day. In her hand she held a staff bearing a few leaves similar to thyrsus.[50] I saw in this attitude a half innocent, half

---

decency was apparent in the case of the little Jocko seen in Paris in 1808. "She is," said the editors of the *Journal de Paris*, "covered with a *redingote* in the manner of our ladies, and when someone enters her room, she takes on an air of reserve, assuming a very decent posture, and covering her legs and thighs with the panels of her *redingote*."

[50] As one has seen above, the orangutan, the pongo, the chimpanzee or jocko walk on two feet like man. The most celebrated travelers agree that in order to stabilize their walking in such a position, they often carry in their hand a staff which serves them at the same time in defense and in attack. [In Greek Mythology a thyrsus is a staff usually made from the

wild demeanor which drew a smile from me. She had brought me several lovely coconuts. We ate of their flesh and drank their milk. I had given her pieces of biscuit, a bit of good wine; we were the best of friends, when something happened which led to our falling out. I will describe it briefly.

With no particular design in mind, I had equipped myself with a small mirror. I drew it from my pocket and suddenly showed it to her. At that very instant, surprise, fear and a terrible jealously was expressed in her features.[51] In a fit of rage

---

giant fennel bush, most commonly associated with the Dionysians. [Ed.]

[51] It is pointless to repeat here all that has been reported regarding the jealousy of monkeys, not only towards those of their own species and of the opposite sex, but also towards those of our species. "The baboons one sees in our menageries," states Mr. Audebert, "cry out horribly when a spectator pretends to caress a woman in their presence." ~"I saw in Martinique," states the late Mr. Moreau Saint-Méry, "a medium sized baboon who had developed a violent passion for his master's daughter...To this unfettered love was combined a furious jealously of any man who might approach her. He seemed to know that there was one amongst them whose advances she favored. One day, to put the baboon's discernment to the test, she allowed her hand to be kissed; the creature's screams tore through the air and it made every effort to break the double chain which held it back, showing such a frightful anger that he who had raised his ire was allowed to escape, and the decision immediately taken to sell the baboon to someone who wished to take it to France." D. Fél. d'Azara, *Essays on the Natural History of the Quadrupeds of the Province of Paraguay*. Mr. Edwards in a letter to Mr. de Buffon, tells how a man who had been with a young lady to see a baboon locked up in a menagerie, had given her a kiss to excite its jealousy; the animal became furious, picked up a pewter pot which was at hand and threw it at the young man's head,

she threw herself upon the figure, intent on tearing it limb from limb. Unable to take hold of anything, she turned about or rather she ran behind the mirror, came back in front, stretched an arm out on the opposite side, ran behind again, repeating this tiresome maneuver over 20 times. Now, let no one dare tell me that animals are incapable of abstract thought!...Wise Locke, what have you to say to that?[52]

Finally, breathless, agitated and trembling, she ran towards me, rolling her pretty little head frenetically against my chest, wrapping her arms around me and squeezing me with all her might, as if to draw me from the object of her worries and terror. I put the fatal mirror back in my pocket and caressed her, giving her a few of the snacks with which I was amply supplied. I let her drink a bit of liquor, and we had soon made up. But she gazed upon me with an extraordinary expression; one would have thought she wished to speak to me.

---

causing him a large wound. See Buffon, *Nat. Hist.* Female monkeys are no less jealous of women.

[52] A number of writers have no difficulty ascribing to the orangutan the faculty of thought. "If one is to believe travelers," says Linnaeus, "the wild man or orang-outang, makes a whistling sound which passes for speech amongst them: gifted with reason, he believes that the world was created for him, and that one day he will again be its master, etc." *Syst. Nat.* Indeed, monkeys have an excellent memory, remembering good and ill treatment for a long time. Mr. de Grandpré tells of a young chimpanzee, which was aboard a ship, where it proved to be of great intelligence, helping the baker to make bread, etc. etc., dying during the crossing, a victim of brutality at the hands of the second mate, who had unfairly and harshly mistreated him. This interesting creature meekly received the abuse targeted at him, showing a moving resignation, extending its hands to beg the blows that rained upon him to be stopped. From then on he continually refused to eat, and died of hunger and pain, mourned as a man might have been." *Voyage à la côte occidentale d'Afrique*, vol. I.

273

That night she could not leave me. Even though I indicated she should leave, and even pushed her aside with my hand, she held onto my clothes, moved off a couple of feet only to return constantly to my side. Having reached the last trees in the forest, she stopped suddenly, raised her arm towards the setting sun,[53] nodded her head sadly, crying out so painfully yet so tenderly that I could not but be touched. I must admit that this action, which had something solemn to it, greatly surprised me and got me to thinking. At that moment I recalled that a few Nature observers had suggested, without however spelling it out precisely, that they were not far from believing that individuals of this race had, in their own way, a concept, however vague, of a Supreme Being. That intellectual capacity of beasts which has been commonly termed animal instinct, has yet to be fully quantified or appreciated. O philosophy! what unknown regions have you yet to explore!

Unfortunately the next day circumstances which I cannot describe as anything other than terribly annoying kept me from our regular rendezvous. Various important affairs kept me at home without a single moment of leisure. I did not see my little friend again until the day after. Alas! I did not find her where we normally met. I called out to her, but in vain. I was extremely worried. I proceeded forward. "Jocko! Jocko!" I cried out, "where are you?" I clapped my hands together. Finally I found her stretched out on the ground at the same spot where I had shown her the mirror; she was almost motionless. The dear little creature opened her eyes and shuddered upon seeing me. I made her swallow a few drops of cordial I had with me. Her breathing seemed difficult, congested;

---

[53] The mococos, or mococo lemurs have a rather singular natural habit: it is to frequently take up an attitude of worship or pleasure before the Sun. They sit, as travelers tell it, gazing towards this celestial body with arms extended, repeating such demonstrations on several occasions each day, taking up hours of time, following the Sun's orientation as it rises or sets." Buffon, *Natural History*.

her entire frame was extremely weak. I gave her something to eat; she had trouble swallowing it. When she was somewhat recovered, it became clear from the avidity with which she took the food I offered her, that the poor creature had not eaten anything for at least 24 hours.

When her hunger was appeased and we had drunk the milk of several coconuts, we renewed our customary walk: I have mentioned how she would walk beside me. All of a sudden she stopped short, fell at my feet, kissed them and wrapped her arms around my legs. It was difficult to disengage her. I finally managed to get her on her feet again; she was shaking like a leaf. I had her sit down, wishing to have her eat. I presented her with marzipans which she greatly relished, but she returned them to me sadly, and when night began to fall, she herself took the path back to the forest outlet. All the way she seemed pensive and preoccupied. At last, she left me with such an expressive look, that I could not help but be worried about her to some extent.

I returned the next day at the accustomed hour, and again I could not find her. I called her and sat down to wait for her. Half an hour later I saw her running up to me with her usual lightheartedness. She was out of breath. I presented her with a biscuit and a bit of wine in a glass. She refused the biscuit, but fell upon the wine, finishing it in a single gulp. Taking hold of my hand she tried to draw me along with her into the thickest part of the forest. I must admit that I hesitated somewhat in following her, fearing to find myself amongst too great a number of her species to be able to defend myself. I knew that the males, quite dangerous towards women, were entirely vicious towards men.[54] However, after having considered things briefly, I fought back this involuntary urge for timidity, consi-

---

[54] Male monkeys' unbridled lust for women is a fact long attested to by naturalists and travelers of all nations. See Gassendi, *Vita Peiresc.* One has seen (above) how violent monkeys can become, even in captivity, towards men who incite them to jealousy.

dering it no less than pusillanimity on my part. Laughing, I followed her. She was excited and seemed impatient, which I could not understand. We proceeded close to a third of a mile through the brush, not without a great deal of difficulty on my part.

I could not avoid being surprised when I made out, among an elegant grouping of coconut trees, a pretty almost completed hut roofed with leaves.[55] However, I soon remembered that the existence of such rustic constructions had been witnessed by a number of famous travelers and by our best naturalists. My little Jocko was not at ease; she jumped about, clapped her hands, and uttered that delightful fine, silvery cry. A pall of sadness spread over her features, for she soon realized that I could not get in her hut without bending over awkwardly. She had made the door in proportion to her small stature and not to mine, her foresight not extending that far. She was taken with a kind of rage; she threw herself on the transverse beam which determined the height of the entrance, turned everything over, then took me off a few paces and having loaded me with a few branches she had stocked up, took an armful herself and signaled me to follow her. I obeyed, and the one-time pretender to the throne of Nature became a female pongo's laborer.

She immediately began remodeling the hut's entrance. It only took her a quick glance to render it proportionate to my stature. I helped her in all good faith, and the work was soon done. I found two long benches of moss arranged like beds,[56]

_____

[55] "More industrious than elephants, orang-outangs know how to build shelters out of woven branches, suited to their particular needs." Ch. Bonnet, *The Contemplation of Nature.* "One assures me," states Mr. Audebert, "that pongos build huts which they cover with leaves, and that the females and little ones live within these sorts of nests. *Histoire naturelle des singes.*

[56] "One is no less surprised," observes Mr. Ch. Bonnet, "to see the orang-outang settle down to sleep in a bed of his own mak-

276

and in one corner an ample supply of coconuts. The dear little creature, tired out, threw herself on one of these sites of repose. She seemed to invite me to follow her example by pointing out to me the one in front of her.

She watched me with a rather satisfied expression, she was quite proud to see me enjoy the fruit of her work. A few moments later I got up, went to pick some banana leaves, laying them out on the moss so that it would not stick to my clothes or to the limbs of my small frame. She seemed enchanted to see that I had thus improved upon her handiwork, and on 20 different occasions she jumped with great agility from one mossy bed to the other.

Having unhesitatingly indulged herself in these excesses of gaiety, her appetite returned; she sat on her bed and extended her two little arms towards me, shaking them with her usual grace. Along with nice tender biscuits, I gave her bread and hard-boiled eggs, items she had not eaten before; she de-

---

ing, much as we would, place his head at the top of the bed, tie a handkerchief around it, and adjust the covers over himself, etc." *The Contemplation of Nature.* H. Grose, speaking of a pair of orangutans, one male, one female, given to M. Horne, governor of Bombay, whom I mentioned already above, states that on the vessel on which they were embarked, they would prepare their bed with the utmost care. *Voyages aux Indes-Occidentales*, p. 329 et al. One finds similar details in the description of a female orangutan given by Mr. Fréd. Cuvier in 1808. "Our animal," he states, "was used to wrapping herself up in covers, and showed an almost constant need to do so. On the ship she would take to bed everything which seemed appropriate to her for doing so. Whenever a sailor had lost a few pieces of clothing, it was almost always possible to find them in the orang-outang's bed." *Description of an orang-outang.* Having arrived in Paris, she would go every day to retrieve her cover where she had left it, place it across her shoulders, and climb up into the arms of her keeper to be taken to her bed." *Ibid.*

voured them. The dear little creature must have spent all night and a better part of the day working. We drank some Madeira wine; I had taught her, for my own amusement, how to clink her glass against mine.[57] Then we had a truly delightful meal together.

We had to leave each other. I cannot depict to you how surprised and hurt Jocko was,[58] her anguish was at its peak. At first she appeared thunderstruck, rooted to the spot, then leaning towards me for an instant, though making no attempt to hold me back. However, when I left the hut she cried out so plaintively that I couldn't help but retrace my steps. I made every attempt to make her understand that I would return on

---

[57] "I have seen," states Mr. de Buffon, "an orang-outang pour his own drink into a glass, and clink it with others' when asked to." *Natural History.*

[58] The female of the orangutan of Borneo, of which Vosmaer has given us a detailed description, "enjoyed," he said, "the company of others, without distinction of sex, preferring however those who took care of her and did her no harm. Often when these people left, she would throw herself to the ground as if in despair, uttering cries and lamentations." *Feuilles de Vosmaer*, selected by M. de Buffon. An orangutan transported from Borneo to Paris in 1808 showed great affection to its master. If he was not at the table in his usual spot, he would cry out in pain, refuse to eat, and would roll on the ground and strike his head. "Such a need for affection," states Mr. Fréd. Cuvier, "generally led our orang-outang to seek out people he knew and avoid solitude, which he seemed to very much dislike." Mr. Fréd. Cuvier adds that this young animal sometimes used all the resources provided him by his instincts to avail himself of the pleasures of company. Closed up in a room separated from the conference hall by a door held secure with a bolt, and the lock of which was too high for him to reach, he went and got a chair, pushed the bolt, opened it, and thus managed to get into the hall. *Journal de Paris*, September 1, 1808.

the morrow. I don't know if she understood, but I could tell that in her little head she was convinced that we should never part. To this end she had built a hut, stocked it with fruit and coconuts, had set up a proper household in her own manner.

I found all this interesting if not surprising. I knew that members of the jocko and pongo races frequently built huts, that they most often lived two by two,[59] that the female was somewhat shy, and that they held in common with the human race the practice of kisses to the forehead or cheeks, when they met.[60] Accustomed to living in communities, or at least in family groups,[61] they knew how to use fire, knew full well how to light it, but did not know how to maintain it.[62]

---

[59] Monkeys, especially those of the larger species, are monogamous, that is to say that they generally are content with a single female, or at most with two. "Their relationship," states Mr. Virey, "appears to be a kind of marriage, requiring fidelity, and they are terribly jealous." *Histoire des moeurs et de l'instinct des animaux.* The male and female have a strong attachment to one another, which they express through caresses and mutual accommodation. I have already mentioned above the pair of orangutans, one male, one female, sent to M. Horne, governor of Bombay. "The female," states H. Grose, "died on the ship, and the male showing many signs of sadness, took to heart his spouse's death, refusing to eat and only surviving her by two days." *Voyage aux Indes Occidentales.*

[60] Such caresses are not limited to individuals of their species. "Such animals," states Mr. Lecomte, "appear to be of a very tender disposition; they kiss those they like with surprising transports of joy." *Memoir on the Present State of China*, vol. II. Mr. Levaillant speaks in great detail of such caresses as he received from his monkey named Kees. "Often," he states, "I took him hunting with me; what frolics and happiness upon our departure, how tenderly he would come and kiss his friend!" *Travels in Africa*, vol. I.

[61] "The orang-outangs," states Ch. Bonnet, "live communally in the jungle, and are strong and courageous enough to chase

279

away elephants with clubs. They even dare to defend them-selves from armed men." *The Contemplation of Nature.* ~The other families of monkeys such as the howler monkeys, the baboons, the red and blue monkeys of Gambia, the coaitas, etc. which also form more or less large societal groups made up of individuals of the same species, and headed by a leader who is generally the strongest member of the troop. At the slightest call of distress, or for pillaging, the various individu-als of a given family or societal group offer each other mutual support, either in attack or defense. They establish amongst themselves a certain pecking order, with subordinates and individuals involved in enforcing order during marches and other operations, as well as in punishing the negligent with a beating and sometimes even with death. Virey, *Histoire des moeurs et de l'instinct des animaux.* "We were often visited," states Mr. Levaillant, "in the middle of the day by large troops of bawains, monkeys of the same species as my friend Kees. These animals, surprised in seeing so many people, were even more so when they recognized one of theirs living peacefully amongst us, yet who answered them in their language." *Voyage en Afrique, vol. II.* As reported by D. Fél. d'Azara, the carayas, monkeys native to Paraguay, live in families made up of four to ten individuals, led by a single male. This chief al-ways places himself in the highest spot so as to ensure the safety of the family he leads, which family will only move once its leader is himself in motion. *Essays on the Natural History of the Quadrupeds of the Province of Paraguay.* I would point out that these monkeys are not the only ones to provide each other with mutual assistance. The large monkeys known as *Cochinchina monkeys* show the same courage and drive in saving, at the risk of their lives, animals of their spe-cies who have been wounded by hunters. Here are a few de-tails which are given in this regard by a modern traveler, Capt. Rey. "We began at 5 a.m.," he states, "to climb Taysons gorge, and before reaching the station where we intended to breakfast, we had killed over 100 individuals of the large species of monkey one finds only in this region, and are known only as *Cochinchina monkeys*...I dearly wished to capture alive a few youngsters, to bring them back to France. It was only with great difficulty that we were able to manage it, and it was necessary to kill a large number, for the more we wounded, the more came in response to the poor creatures' cries...What was most remarkable was that the uninjured ones always sought to carry off into the jungle the dead and injured. Three youngsters we captured were taken from the body of their father or mother, from which one had a great deal of trouble detaching them." I need not weigh in further here on the cruelty of hunters who, to satisfy their guilty greed, or often to stroke their poor self-esteem, don't think twice about immolating creatures so similar to man in their exterior conformation, their habits and the mutual goodwill they have for one another. All those who have studied monkey behavior know the sequence and types of tactics these animals follow when it comes to pillaging a garden, an orchard or a field of sugar cane. Before beginning their expedition, they assign one or two amongst them to climb up to a high point so as to establish that there are no men about to bother them. If these scouts do not see anyone, their calls inform the remainder of the troop, who then begin their marauding. Some pick the fruit, the sugar cane, etc., taste them and dispose of what does not suit them; others, arrayed in a chain pass the items along from hand to hand in order to more quickly have them stored in a safe place, while others, serving as sentries and entrusted to call out with a *whoop, whoop, whoop*, or whatever other warning call was agreed upon, at the approach of the enemy. Upon hearing this warning, the raiders, and even the mothers with their little ones, leap into the trees, or escape into the mountains. Sentries who, by their negligence allow their fellows to be caught by surprise are severely punished. Kolbe, *Description of the Cape of Good Hope*, even insists that they are put to death if any member of the troop dies during the raid. Such details have been attested to by a number of travel-

281

The next day I arranged to arrive earlier. I found it difficult to find her hut again. My little Jocko was stretched out on her bed. She gave a start upon seeing me, and gave me her usual delicate cry. I had brought along with me a saw, a hammer, some nails, a little case which was held closed by hooks

---

ers and naturalists. Stedman gives an eyewitness account of a case of sentries being posted to cover a group of monkeys' marauding. "These creatures," he states, "arrange sentries around the site of their pillaging in order to give the alarm, and I have seen with what precision and intelligence those which have been assigned this role have acquitted themselves. *Voyage à Surinam.* The same traveler mentions a species of monkey whose individuals live alone and do not gather in family groups. "I must speak of another monkey which I saw at the home of colonel P***, at which in Surinam is called wanacoe... This is the only monkey of its kind which is not social. This solitary creature is so despised by monkeys of other species, that they continuously assault them and steal their food." Thus the monkeys too have their pariahs! *Voyage à Surinam.*

[62] "The people of the country, when they travail in the woods, make fires where they sleep in the night; and in the morning, when they are gone, the Pongoes will come and sit about the fire, till it goes out: for they have no understanding to lay the wood together." Purchas, *Pilgrims.* When domesticated, monkeys can be taught to light a fire, feed it and watch it so as to avoid the accidents it might cause. The unfortunate chimpanzee whose sad end I have already reported (above) had, according to Mr. de Grandpré, "learned to warm an oven; she kept close watch that no live coals escaped that could set the vessel on fire, and judged accurately when the oven was sufficiently warm, never failing to inform the baker, who, confident of the creature's sagacity, depended upon it, and hastened to bring his dough as soon as the monkey came to get him, without the former ever leading him to error. *Voyage à la côte occidentale d'Afrique, vol. I.*

and bore various utensils; two cups, two drinking glasses, a few plates, a coffeepot, a flint and some tinder.

Seeking to put to the test the instincts and adaptability of these animals and finally confirm those singular facts I had read of in travelers' accounts and in writings on Natural History, but which I doubted to some degree, I gave all these treasures to my little friend; she was ecstatic, her eyes beamed with happiness.

Bringing new furniture to Jocko's pretty hut on a daily basis was a pleasure: a jug to draw water, some small tables, folding chairs, a small chest of drawers, which, not wishing to let anyone in on my secret, I carried piece by piece and reassembled as best I could afterwards.

One afternoon, intending to light a fire, I took it upon myself to teach her how to operate the flint, and could not help but laugh at her awkwardness: she would strike her fingers and was afraid of the sparks which sprang from the stone. I took it from her, and in one stroke lit the tinder. At the same time I used a sulphur-match to light a candle. Jocko was dumbfounded. She watched this spectacle, new to her with a mixture of admiration and fear, which brought an indescribable liveliness to her already expressive features.

I had prepared, at some distance from the hut, a sufficiently wide perimeter to set up a fire place. She did not appear surprised, but what she apparently did know, as I mentioned before, was how to feed and maintain the blaze, by throwing more wood on it or by carefully fanning it. I had brought fire tongs and a shovel. I taught her how to use them, and I must admit she had a remarkable capacity to understand and imitate what I did. I did however have to repeat my lessons on several occasions.

I sent her to draw some water,[63] filled the coffee pot and a small cooking pot, and I amused myself by teaching her to

---

[63] "The orang-outang goes to the fountain to get water, fills a jug, places it on its head and brings it back to the house."

make coffee, then tea in a Delft-ware teapot, which was part of Jocko's household effects. She found the tea and coffee much to her liking, particularly when I put lots of sugar in it. Using some small wooden spoons [64] with which I had equipped myself, she would stir it in such a pleasant manner, that I could not help but smile. Finally, she managed to cook some fresh eggs and to cut some sippets with a little box tree handled knife I had given her. However, I had a hard time teaching her the correct quantity of coffee so as to make a brew that was neither too strong nor too weak.

I had however managed to teach her to set a table in front of the hut, to cover it with large banana leaves,[65] to place two

---

Bonnet, *The Contemplation of Nature*. These facts are also reported by a number of other travelers.

[64] "I have seen," states Mr. de Buffon, "an orang-outang go and take a cup and saucer, bring it to the table, put sugar in it, pour some tea, let it cool to drink it, and all this without any encouragement or words from his master, and often of his own account...I have seen him sit at the table, spread out his napkin, wipe his lips with it, use a fork and spoon to bring food to his mouth." The female of the orangutan described by Vosmaer also knew how to use a fork and spoon. "When she was given strawberries," states the Dutch naturalist, "it was a pleasure to see how she would stab them and bring them one by one to her mouth with a fork." The female orangutan which I have already mentioned on several occasions, could eat perfectly well a hard-boiled egg in the shell, as long as one prepared some sippets for her. Fréd. Cuvier, *Descript.*, etc.

[65] "Trained to serve in the home, the orang-outang, at a single sign or at his master's voice...will rinse the glasses, serve drinks, turn meat on the grill, crush in a mortar what one gives him to grind, etc." Ch. Bonnet, *The Contemplation of Nature*. One can see that the barris (a type of chimpanzee), orangutans, and monkeys, learn to do different tasks, and to proffer their masters all the services one might expect from a domestic servant; they sweep rooms, clean boots, untie the bows in shoes,

seats opposite one another, to fill her little centerpiece with fresh leaves and flowers, to place her plate correctly across from mine, to arrange in a symmetrical pattern on little varnished-wood plates the fruit or dry preserves and little cakes I brought her from the city. She was so skilled and intelligent that she could prepare toast and jam and cut sippets as easily as any woman in Lisbon or London might have. Sitting across from one another at a small table, we would share small meals together almost every day. She would serve me with the greatest care, attention and a zeal which never slackened. The dear little creature always gave me what she deemed to be the best,[66] and the best in her opinion was the largest fruit, the biggest piece of cake, keeping for herself only the poorest, those of lesser value.

With continued attentions I managed to teach her how to smoothly open a bottle with a corkscrew, to clean the glasses properly, and to mix some water with her wine. She also well knew that the liquors were to be poured in lesser quantities than ordinary wine. Indeed these little banquets had an eleg-

---

etc. The female orangutan of which Vosmaer speaks knew how to behave at the dinner table. "After having eaten," states this naturalist, "she took a tooth-pick and put it to the same use as we do." *Feuilles de Vosmaer.*

[66] While I may be diverging from my subject matter, I cannot help but report the following anecdote, which I guarantee to be genuine. A man fallen into a most wretched state, and whose bitter disposition one too often criticizes in others, and which one should not be proud of, had a dog, his only friend. This poor creature, driven by his instinct, had developed the habit of stopping before the door of certain high class hotels; there he would most skillfully search the waste drain for the roots drawn into it by the water which escaped when the cooks drew out the plug from the sink. He would separate the chewed upon pieces from those which appeared to be more appealing, keeping the poor pieces for himself, and reserving the best for his master.

ance which might have surprised some, had they known that they had been laid out by a young animal which until recently had received no lessons but those of Nature.

As her nakedness bothered me, I liked to drape her with brightly colored shawls,[67] which I had obtained for her use, and which she would later put away in her chest of drawers. I almost always read or meditated upon things while eating the fruit and eggs she had prepared for me. As my little Jocko felt it her duty to mimic me in everything, she would pick up a book,[68] which, naturally she more often than not held upside down, which was all the same to her. When I turned a page, she would do so in turn; she would insert the bookmark when I would, close and place the book on the table. At the first sign of clearing the table, she would remove everything, wash the plates and cups thoroughly, then return every item to its proper shelf in her little hut without breaking anything. Even though these simple yet amusing events were repeated every day, I never tired of them. As soon as my business in the city was

---

[67] Mr. Allamand speaks of a female orangutan observed by Mr. Harvood. "She would willingly cover herself with pieces of fabric, but she would not suffer to be dressed in clothes." See Buffon, *Nat. Hist.* An individual which is discussed below liked to be covered; and, "in order to accomplish this," states Mr. Frédéric Cuvier, "she would take any piece of material or clothing which was near her." *Description d'un orang-outang.* Mr. G***, at whose home this interesting creature spent most of her time in Paris, from her coming off the ship to her death, wrote to me that the cold led this small jocko to allow herself to be clothed in a small woolen cardigan, a *redingote* and even a pair of pants; but often, when she was alone in the hall, she would get as close to the fire as she could and would take off all her clothes.

[68] "I saw," states Mr. Audebert, "a mangabey who would take a book, place it on a table and turn the pages with some skill, grimacing as if the book's contents excited his indignation." *Histoire [Naturelle] des Singes*, art. Mangabey.

done, I went off to be close to my dear little Jocko; there I would read and write as though I was alone. It was rare for me not to find something to eat waiting for me.

She did not touch any of the provisions I left in her hut until I formally turned them over to her by placing them before her. Besides, she was quite clear as to what belonged properly to her amongst the things we held in common. She had her own small clothing accessories, some jeweled glass rings, little boxes, shawls with which I was pleased to dress her in when I was about, and colored scarves with which I adorned her little head in the manner of the Creoles, and drop earrings. I remember that she cried out frequently and fidgeted a great deal before allowing her ears to be pierced. She put up a struggle and tried to escape; I had to get angry in order to subdue her.

As soon as I left she would undress, and would only resume wearing them when she expected or rather anticipated my arrival. I had brought her one of those wooden clocks termed cuckoo clocks, which are made in the Black Forest, hoping to get her used to counting the hours and knowing the time, but I was never able to manage it. I had however been assured that a number of members of different orang species had managed to count up to five.

When our little snack was finished or often when I took my tea or coffee with her, I daydreamed or composed poetry, which I afterwards wrote down. Jocko, my faithful imitatrix did not fail to take possession of the pens I had discarded, and to scribble most gravely on the small pieces of paper I let her have. What would a European have thought of this bizarre exchange. Well! Those incendiary pages, those passionate verses which the public received in so kind a manner, I wrote them beside the female of the wild and fierce pongo.

One afternoon when I thankfully arrived a few moments earlier than usual, I did not find Jocko at the entrance to the woods. I drew near, listened, heard moans and plaintive cries; followed suddenly by complete silence. I entered the hut and saw the poor creature stretched out on her bed. Her flesh was torn in a number of places, bore scattered spines, and seemed to be encrusted with small fragments of stone.

I picked her up; for a moment I thought her dead, but she had only fainted. I forced her to breathe and then to swallow a few drops of spirits. When she was herself again, I thought I understood that she had been knocked out of the top of a very tall tree, or that she had hurt herself falling off a cliff. Thanks to the advance preparations there remained some fire near the hut. I warmed up some wine in haste and washed the dear little creature's wounds. She opened her lovely gazelle-eyes and looked at me caressingly. I mashed some herbs between two rocks and made a kind of compress from them. I made it my duty to apply this to her wounds, which to my great surprise were already covered, at least in part, with medicinal herbs she had chewed up.[69] However, she had not pulled out all the spines and fragments of hard materials, undoubtedly because of how painful such an operation would have proven. I took care of it with as much solicitude and tenderness as I could; I securely tied the different compresses using ligatures made from the scarves I kept in Jocko's chest of drawers. I renewed the banana leaves with which I had covered her little bed, which was now stained with blood. I kept close by my little patient who moaned so softly, yet with such evident pain that I could not help but shed tears.[70]

---

[69] One should not be surprised at the skill with which monkeys, particularly the howler monkeys, probe and dress the wounds they receive. Here is what the eyewitness Oexmelin tells us: "The moment one of them is wounded, the others gather around him, put their fingers in the wound and act as though they are probing it. If they then see that a lot of blood is flowing, they keep the wound closed while others bring a few leaves which they chew and carefully place inside the open wound. I can claim to have seen this several times, and much admired it." *Histoire des flibustiers.*

[70] The young brown capuchin monkey raised by Mr. Moreau-Saint-Méry, being sick as a result of his gluttony, gave himself

I would have given anything to spend the night with her, but I feared worrying my people, and I did not dare give in to this initial impulse. The poor creature had a burning fever; I felt for her pulse on several occasions as she stretched out her arm with charming grace.[71] Finally, when I had to leave her, I

---

up willingly to the care being given him. "It was a touching sight," states Mr. Moreau-Saint-Méry, "that of the little animal, its cries rising above my own voice with the horrible agony it endured, opening its mouth and swallowing the oil I gave it."

[71] A male orangutan, closed up on a ship, fell sick. "He would let himself be treated like a man; he even twice had a bloodletting from his right arm. Every time he felt poorly he would show his arm so as to be bled, for he remembered that it had done him some good." *Extracts from the Voyage of Mr. de la Brosse* as reported by Buffon, *Nat. Hist.* The young jocko which arrived in Paris at the beginning of March 1808 was then 10 to 12 months old. "The fatigues of a long ocean voyage," states Mr. Fréd. Cuvier, "along with the cold the animal was subjected to in crossing the Pyrenees in the snowy season, put her life seriously at risk. Having arrived in Paris, she had several frozen fingers, suffered from a hectic fever caused by an obstruction in the spleen, as well as a cough which gave scant hope she would survive more than a couple of days." *Description d'un orang-outang.* Mr. G***, to whom this little jocko had been sent, and who had given her the name Maiden of the Forest, watched over her with the most scrupulous exactitude. A doctor would come to see her. As soon as she saw the doctor, she would look at him with soft eyes and extend her little arm so he could take her pulse. With a lot of care she was able to partly recover, but she finally succumbed after five months… On the day she died, M. G*** had been forced to go to the country with his family, and had left her with a servant he trusted. She of the forest, sensing her time had come, wandered on several occasions through all the rooms, looking for her friends with a sad, worried expression;

placed a folding chair near her bed, put out several glasses of diluted red wine. I prepared water in which I soaked toasted bread, and encouraged her to drink alternatively of the two beverages. I arranged some moss pillows covered in banana leaves. She held my hand and drew it towards her as if to tell me not to abandon her…then she licked the tips of my fingers with her little rose-colored tongue, hot with fever. When I left the hut she gave a deep sigh. The next day I was with her at the break of day.

I found poor Jocko without fever, but so weak that she could not rise from her bed. She had clearly understood what I had sought to make her understand; she had used all the drinks I had left on the folding chair to allay her powerful thirst, for not a drop remained. She herself signaled in a manner entirely unintelligible to me but which was made clear to me, as we shall see, some days later. She showed me her wounds, cried out painfully, the turned to look towards the little chest of drawers I had given her.

Not yet daring to remove the bandages for fear of making her suffer too much, and thus to contribute further to her extreme weakness, I gave her a bit of biscuit soaked in diluted wine. She kissed the tips of my fingers, it was one of her normal caresses when she was happy. Finally I left her, having filled her glasses with lightly sweetened water into which I had mixed a few drops of wine. I left, but it is needless to add that I returned that afternoon. She was sleeping. I let her sleep and when she did wake up she seemed very pleased and surprised to see me by her side.

Given that 24 hours had passed since the bandages had first been applied, I warmed up some water and wetted the compresses with it. Thankfully poor Jocko had only minor

---

finally, having given up finding them, she came to moan and die on her covers, which were spread out in the garden. Mr. Fréd. Cuvier states that "upon her autopsy, most of her intestines were found to be disorganized and full of obstructions." *Description d'un orang-outang.*

contusions to the head, and even though her flesh was cruelly torn, I found no fractures. I had brought cloth bandage and agaric with me. I applied the new compresses and made new ligatures. The fever had completely receded. I gradually adjusted her food; never any meat, I did not wish her to learn of this unpleasant practice; but vegetables, cooked fruit and small cakes she could have. She was dying of hunger; however, fearing I might harm her, I only half-satisfied her hunger. Who would have thought? Even when she was in the peak of health, I would leave a number of edibles inside the hut, making my usual interdictory signs to her, and the next day I found everything as it was, she had not dared to touch it.[72]

She seemed to improve imperceptibly and after a few days she could sit up. However, her weakness was still so great that having wished to rise, she fell back on her cot. I sat next to her. From time to time she rested her little head upon my shoulder while I read. When she was hungry, she would draw up close and shake her two little arms as she drew them back towards herself. The next day I decided, as much to entertain her as to see what effect it might have on her,[73] to bring

---

[72] Acosta, cited by Stedman, attests to have seen, in the Government House in Cartagena, a monkey which, when his master ordered him to, would go and get wine at the wine seller's, holding in one hand the bucket and in the other the money, which he never gave to the wine seller until he had received the wine. Sometimes, on his way back, he might be assailed by children throwing stones at him; he would then place his bucket on the ground, catch the stones which were thrown at him in his hand, and throw them back at his assailants so skillfully that they lost interest in repeating the attack. He would then pick up the bucket and bring it faithfully back to the house, and though he very much enjoyed wine, he would not drink a drop until his master gave him permission. *Voyage à Surinam.*

[73] Monkeys are in general closely attuned to melody. If one is to believe the illustrious Gassendi, the great barris monkeys of

a guitar with me. At first she was frightened, especially when she strummed the strings with her fingers. She drew them away quickly, looking behind the guitar with a curious but worried look, then inside, and, as she was wont to do, turned her questioning eyes towards me.

I took the instrument out of her hands and played along while I sang a Venetian barcarole, and then a lovely romantic piece by Raph.

Solitario bosc'ombroso A te vien l'afflitto more.

I cannot portray how surprised and enthralled she was. All her senses appeared paralyzed and she could barely breathe. She knelt down, crossed her little arms and raised them towards me, begging me to continue. Even after I had stopped singing, she continued to listen.

Suddenly, as if waking from a dream, she struck her forehead, ran to the little chest of drawers, opened a drawer she had some days ago drawn my attention to through her gesticulations. She brought me, O! ineffable surprise! several shells of different colors, and 29 or 30 of the largest diamonds that I had ever seen in my life.[74] They were like those found at the foot, and in the crevasses, of Mount Orisa.

Guinea can learn to skillfully play the flute, the guitar, and other instruments. "*Qui maximi sunt, et Barris dicuntur...ludere fistula, cithara, aliisque id genus.*" *Vita Peiresc.* Count Panoglorowski, exiled to Siberia by tzar Peter, and having only a dog and a monkey as companions, took up the task of training these two animals. The dog learned, it is said, to play chess, and the monkey to play the flute. *Journal de Paris*, September 1, 1808.

[74] Those who ask how the fascinating Jocko could have brought her friend such a quantity of diamonds must remember that, far from being buried in the mines of Raolconda, Coulour and Soumelpour, many diamonds are found on the soil surface. The scientist Mr. Werner notes that one finds at the base of the Orixa mountains of India diamonds which, he says, were originally formed within these mountains, and

Here the European's lust for riches prevailed over the man of Nature, exposing his base avaricious nature. I held Jocko between my arms, hugged her tight against my chest, and kissed her with abandon. I brought the diamonds one by one to my lips, to show her my satisfaction, thus imitating her favorite gesture. I held my hands out towards her while shaking them, as she did when she innocently asked me to give her biscuits or cakes. I then moved towards the door, holding her by the arm. She looked at me surprised, and seeing that I repeated the half-begging, half imperative gesture, she took on a sad expression, bent down her head onto her chest, showed me her wounds, sat on the floor, and with an expression which bespoke consternation, rested her forehead against the cot.

I raised her to her feet and gave her a few of the snacks she liked best and had her drink a little vanilla cream, to boost her strength. I had her sit down, and, notwithstanding how upset I was, once again took up singing her a nocturne and accompanying myself on the guitar. This renewed the naive creature's original attitude and enthusiasm.

Pillars of society, armchair philosophers, so-called friends of Nature, here is a man playing barcaroles to entertain a female pongo; how degrading! And yet I felt honored in taking care of her; I thought that in bringing a few minutes of calm, of innocent pleasures to my poor little sick friend I would expiate, at least in part, the urges of sordid avarice which I had been unable to repress.

---

which were separated from them afterwards. See *Nouvelle théorie sur la formation des filons* [New Theory of the Formation of Veins], etc. It is also known that the diamonds from the Soumelpour mine, which draws its name from a town located on the Gouel River, which flows into the Ganges, are not found in their original location, but often mixed through the river's sands, which stripped them from their matrix. ~It is thus quite natural to think that Jocko had found, either in a sandbank beside a river, or rather in the fissures of a rock, the diamonds which she presented as a gift to her friend.

Within a fortnight she had entirely recovered. We returned to our evening snacks, our walks, I might even have said our reading, for, as I mentioned above, when I took up a book, she ran off quickly to get hers and imitated my every move down to the minutest detail. Finally, having eaten some fresh eggs and enjoyed our sweets and small cakes, she watched me sadly, and at the least sign she ran off to fetch my guitar and held it out to me. I played, I sang a song or two, and her enjoyment was just as great as ever. As soon as I was finished she would come and kneel before me, licking the tips of my fingers. Then she would clear the table and put everything away with an admirable dexterity and cleanliness.

Persevering, as one might expect, in my avaricious motives, I would bring out the diamonds she had brought me, and, right in front of her, kiss and handle them lovingly, dangle them from my clothes, put them away in my pockets with particular care, hoping by my gestures to have my most avid desires known to her. The little creature clearly understood, for she tipped her head and took on an expression of consternation.

Finally, one day, even though I had come a bit later than usual, I did not find her in the hut; nothing had been readied outdoors. The table was almost always set; she would have made the effort to light the fire in the clearing a few paces from the hut, and to arrange our two seats in their usual spots. I was a bit concerned and waited at the edge of the woods, looking anxiously to right and left. After a half hour, I saw her running up; she was out of breath and seemed overwhelmed with fatigue. She fell senseless at my feet. Her left arm was weighed down with a parcel which appeared to be rather heavy and was wrapped in banana leaves. I grabbed it; the effort it took to pry it from her arms was enough to wake her; she fell upon it, tearing off the leaves. O! a new surprise! I almost fainted myself, when, after having presented me with magnificent multicolored shells, which this innocent creature still seemed to prefer above all, I glimpsed a quantity of diamonds three-fold that of the first set. I raised up my poor

Jocko, who was haggard and breathless, resulting either from the trials she had undergone, or due to the great rate at which she had sped through the forest. It was difficult to restrain myself. The past, present and future washed over my heart. O! reader, do you not already know of my emotional life? Might you be convinced that the greedy European played but a secondary role in the matter. Wait! These are not my memoirs I write, but a simple anecdote, a simple account of circumstances in my life, though ones truly of some importance, as they substantially contributed to altering my destiny.

When Jocko had interpreted my stare and read the great joy, might I say exaltation, expressed in my eyes, she shook her little arms and asked me for something to eat. Nothing was prepared, but I always had a good supply of dried fruits, jams, cakes and of the sweet wines she preferred even over the finest liquors. She ate and drank hungrily. On this occasion she was not injured, but upon examining her I found several contusions on her body; her flesh was wrinkled in several places. Finally, having sat herself down on a folding chair that was lower than mine, she rested her head on my chest and fell into a deep sleep; deep, I say, but not peaceful, for she appeared agitated and moaned softly.

Lost in my thoughts, I was sad and pensive; a few tears escaped from my eyes, dropping across the sleeping Jocko's brow. I had just received some letters from Lisbon which led me to believe that my recall was imminent; painful memories awaited me in my homeland. What was I to do with this dear little creature who gave such endearing signs of attachment to me? I had almost forgotten that Jocko only barely belonged to the human race; I thought of her as a young savage which I could only communicate with through gestures and signs, the only primitive tongue, not withstanding what our Hebraic scholars might tell us. It was not a creature similar to me, but rather an interesting copy thereof.[75]

The series of observations which her presence had suggested to me supported my views regarding animal instincts, that philosophical branch of Natural History. I had always considered such observations as important and as useful to anyone searching for the truth, as one of the objects most worthy of holding the attention of beings with conscience and thought, as well as one of the boldest chapters of the great book of Nature.

How often had I regretted that poor Jocko was deprived of speech,[76] and that she had no other language but her own ever so expressive features and a limited range of cries to express such varied truths. I had often examined and palpated the sort of inner mandible which formed a pocket on either side of the inside of her cheeks, and I tried to make her pronounce her name. She barely guessed at my intentions, and made incredible efforts, but all in vain; she was only able to proffer the vowel twice repeated and the two vowels in my name. I remember that this weak attempt nonetheless affected me powerfully, but this was short-lived.

Getting back to the diamonds and the scene where the dear little creature had collapsed exhausted: Jocko, once re-

---

[75] "If the orang-outang is not a man," states Mr. Ch. Bonnet, "he is the most perfect prototype thereof which walks the Earth." *The Contemplation of Nature.*

[76] None of the species of monkeys known to us have the ability to produce articulate speech or distinct words. ~"It is," states Mr. G. Guvier [*sic*], "physically impossible for the orang-outang to articulate any sound because of a sac which communicates with its larynx and renders his voice entirely silent." *Tableau élémentaire de l'histoire naturelle des animaux.* We know that Africans attribute the monkeys' silence to their laziness, and fervently believe that these creatures do not speak lest they would be put to work. Froger, *Relations du Voyage de Rennes.*

vived, remained sluggish for a few moments, seemingly suffering from pains in all her limbs. Finally she went as she usually did to get my guitar, watching me with a more touching expression than was usual; one would have thought she read my mind and that she knew the extent of her role in my sadness. Indeed, what could be done? How was it to be resolved? Abandoning her was a barbarity of which I felt myself incapable; taking her with me was undoubtedly the preferred solution. But how inconvenient! Back in Europe I would be unable to take care of her for extended periods of time. I would either have to close her up in my house in the city, or send her to the country where she would necessarily be neglected, were she not to become the servants' plaything. In the end I could only expect unhappiness or calamity to ensue, with the poor creature nonetheless being the source of the huge fortune which I would enjoy.

Who would have believed it? I admit to my shame that I tried every which way to make her understand that I wished to know whence she drew all these treasures; but I was unable to do so, and was so hard-hearted as to show my annoyance and allow threats to supplant caresses. O Europe! your cold poisons alter and dominate the heart's gentler emotions like the froth which rises to the surface.

My worries as to my poor Jocko's fate grew from day to day. I watched her, tenderly singing melancholy airs to her. For several days, for fear of what awaited me in my homeland, or perhaps the memory of the sadness which had led to my determination to leave her and take refuge in another hemisphere, I was so wracked with sadness as to be noticed by all.

Finally, on December 28, 18**, tormented by a secret uneasiness, I left my home earlier than usual; I had provided myself with cakes and candied fruit of those types most agreeable to my little Jocko. I walked quickly, being impatient to arrive. From a distance I heard a sound that was unknown to me…I pressed on. O terror! I spotted some traces of blood. I ran forward and saw an awful snake, which I first thought to be a boa, but later recognized to be one of the great Javanese adders, eight to nine feet long, and known as "yellow and blue" for its tiger-striped skin with transverse blocks of bright blue.[77] The monster was engaged in combat with the unfortunate creature, whose limbs were torn and whose body was covered in large wounds from which ran rivulets of blood. I never walked abroad without a two-shot pistol. I aimed straight for the awful reptile's head. I wounded it, it stopped, coiled up again and drew itself up to launch itself at me; my second shot put it to flight. It went off and died a quarter mile from where this deadly scene had occurred.

Jocko had fallen to the ground unconscious, not only as a result of her loss of blood, but also as a result of her fear of the pistol-shot, not to mention that which the very sight of snakes induces in individuals of her species.[78] I ran to her, took her to her hut, laid her down on her bed. She had, as was her custom, started a fire in the usual spot. I washed her wounds, they were horrendous. As I had the first time, I crushed medicinal herbs between rocks and made a sort of compress. I made bandage

---

[77] The Javanese yellow-blue adder often hides in rice paddies, and more commonly in shrubby woods. Its normal length is from nine to ten feet, but some have been seen so large as to be compared to large trees. This snake, whose strength makes it a dreadful foe, feeds on birds and even some fairly large animals. See *Mémoires de la socièté de Batavia* for 1787.

[78] Monkeys' horror of snakes is well known; the mere sight of the skin of one of these reptiles is enough to have them collapse. The traveler Levaillant had killed a large snake during a hunt. "I noticed in this instance the fear that these animals instill in monkeys. It was impossible to bring Kees anywhere near the snake I had just obtained, regardless of the fact that it was quite dead." *Voyage en Afrique*, vol. *II*, p. 258. This fear is quite natural, for monkeys, who by their light-footedness and their habit of sleeping in trees escape the predations of lions, tigers and other ferocious beasts, even those of man, have no more fearful enemy than these hideous reptiles, which can creep up and surprise them even in the tallest branches.

strips from my handkerchief and applied strong pressure to the poor wretch's wounds. I staunched the flow of blood. Slowly I brought her back by dint of cordials and salts. Her pallor was such that to her light tawny color had succeeded a whitish tinge[79] which made her resemble an adolescent girl of our species. She opened her eyes, closed them and uttered a few weak groans. No, no, I have no reticence to confess that my tears flowed abundantly. I felt for my poor Jocko's pulse and eagerly awaited every beat. By their quickening, their intermittence, I expected her to soon be consumed by a violent fever.

If only I had had some presence of mind; but alas! could I remain calm under such circumstances? If I could have focused on something other than my hopes and fears regarding the fate of this fascinating creature, what a host of curious observations might I have been led to make, while attentively examining what the poor creature endured: terror, hope, a terrible delirium. One refuses them a soul! Philosophers, rather let us say atheistic doctors, you dare limit and circumscribe the works of the Supreme Creator? Jocko, deprived of the power of speech, made no intelligible sound, at least to us, but how many different emotions were reflected in her features! I was crushed by it. She was suffering incredible pains, and her eyes, animated by the fever, thirsted for my presence, expressing unutterable fear when I drew away for a moment. How could I leave her? However, I was not without being anxious to the potential worry and despair of my people, of all my friends, if rather than returning at my usual time, I spent all night in the forest. Well then! Let them blame me for giving precedence to a pongo female; I only had a moment's hesitation and uncertainty with which to reproach myself.

I had taken a step towards the hut's doorway; a painful cry from Jocko drew me back. I gave her a few sedatives in

---

[79] If one is to believe Mr. Desfontaines (note sent to Mr. de Buffon), the complexion of different monkeys is prone to change when they are frightened. *Nat. Hist.* addit. to art. Pithèque.

the hope of diminishing the horrible pains she endured. For a moment I believed her saved, her convulsions ceased, she seemed to breathe more easily, the fever had dropped almost miraculously. "Jocko! Jocko!" I cried out. She turned her little head towards me, looked at me with a soft, caressing expression, made as if to rise, fell back upon her bed, and gave up her last breath.

Three days later, I left for Europe.

Léo d'Hampol: *The Missing Link*

Through the tinted windows of my work quarters, I distractedly watched the large trees stripped of their leaves, shaken roughly by the wind. The sky was menacing: large brick-hued clouds ran across a clear, bright, almost blinding background. The silence was almost complete. From time to time, however, the sound of steps was heard, muffled by the road's brown dirt. A shadow passed quickly, then all returned to the torpor of a hushed landscape.

I had spent the night with a patient, an old man who feared the hereafter and I was exhausted, completely exhausted, my legs were heavy, my head nodded. I diverted my eyes, stung by the unbearable glare of the winter sun piercing through the screen of clouds.

Mechanically, I scanned the newspaper which my butler had tossed, fully open, on the desk before which I was sitting.

In what possible manner could the news I had just come across in the society pages interest me? Nonetheless, I reread it twice. It concerned a duel, after a quarrel amongst a circle of friends, between Mr. de Videmar and Count Ladislas Wolsky. I was unacquainted with the latter; the other, Mr. de Videmar, I had crossed paths with years ago. He was simply mad about duels, and almost always successful. Like our military leaders, he had fought great hosts of pretty eyes, blue ones, black ones, gray ones and violet.

How long ago that was!

The wind rose, the big trees' branches creaked plaintively, exposing their winter scars to the white sun. I listened for what? I was not sure, I sensed someone was coming.

Often at night, I was prone to strange premonitions which unsettled my scientific training. My ears rang, so this time again, I believed it to be an auditory hallucination. Not at all, the bell at the gate sounded its long, desolate peal. Someone had rung at my door.

I was in a state I would qualify as one of telepathic receptivity. I was waiting for someone, before the bell rang my ears had perceived the sound of steps. I stood up trembling. At the garden gate, I saw the shadow of a human form stretch out. An old man was waiting for someone to answer his call. My butler would open the door.

The visitor, who refused to give his name, yet insisted on seeing "the doctor" was allowed in. Framed in the doorway, he stepped forward, wan, trembling, prey to a most violent excitement.

I designated a chair, which he failed to sit in. He waited impatiently for my butler to leave and the door to close behind him. We were alone.

My life experience, study of society, and strong common sense had taught me to quickly recognize someone's social standing. However, in the present case, my empirical science failed me. Who was the man before me? The future would tell.

The individual, straight as a picket, appeared to be roughly 60 years of age. There was snow on the roof and an abundant mass of hair spread over the collar of his vest. The face was pleasant, somewhat haughty, but his manner was timid, almost embarrassed.

His eyes scanned suspiciously around him. Finally, upon my assurance that he could speak without fear, he decided to say:

"Doctor, I have at home a wounded individual whose condition is worrisome come right away. The case is the result of an accident." He emphasized the last word of his incoherent utterance.

"No problem, if it isn't too far from here," I replied in a somewhat disillusioned manner. "Why so mysterious?"

The old man pondered for a few seconds, then, with sudden resolution, continued:

"I am not permitted to tell you who you will be treating. I cannot even tell you where the injured has been taken."

"This whole story sounds like something out of a dime novel," I exclaimed with a somewhat forced good humor.

"Please God it were so, but it is sad reality."

"However, for me to reach the one who sends you, you must give me their address, unless as in the novels I alluded to, you blindfold me."

The old man did not seem to notice the irony of my comments; but pronounced himself gravely:

"I won't blindfold you, but I will take the precautions I was instructed to. You will have to submit to them."

Though I remained polite, I frowned, annoyed at my interlocutor's enigmatic attitude.

"And if I accept your conditions?"

"Then my friend will pay any fee you care to ask for, we won't haggle."

I indicated by a gesture that I was not a man to take advantage of a situation. The old man did not seem to notice, saying in a lugubrious tone which sent a shiver down my spine:

303

"You must, should you choose to accompany me, swear not to attempt to uncover the mystery which envelops this entire affair."

"I swear!" I quickly replied.

"Then let's go. A carriage awaits us some 100 meters from here, I will drive."

"I'll follow you."

In less time than it takes to state, I slipped into my overcoat, put on my fur hat, and took up my cane. The old man was already outside when I caught up with him.

The road stretched out monotonously only to sink into the horizon, allowing me to immediately pick out the parked carriage my guide had mentioned.

We walked without exchanging a word. Having arrived near the carriage, I noticed that one of the horses had been tied to a tree by the road.

The old man ordered:

"Get in!"

So imperious had his voice become, that I hesitated. I attributed this tone to his eagerness to return to his friend and quite willingly settled into the carriage. I had barely sat down when I was plunged into complete darkness. Most likely thick blinds had been lowered from the outside. While I was not the least bit frightened, instinctively I wished to get out, but the doors resisted my efforts. I was a prisoner. Besides, in truth, these excessive precautions were nothing unusual, I had been duly warned.

The carriage sped off. The road was long, and by design, hesitant and seemingly random. I understood that one was trying to confuse me, in case my sense of direction was particularly well developed.

After a period of time, which I would estimate at an hour and a half, the carriage stopped, the blinds went up as if by magic, and before me, gray and morose, notwithstanding the melancholy caresses of the January sun, was the featureless landscape which extends across all of Paris' suburbs.

Where was I? Between you and me, I could not have cared less, dominated as I was by a natural curiosity which rendered me impatient in my wait for further developments in this adventure.

My guide opened the carriage's left-hand door, and most politely, this time, begged me to step down. I jumped to the ground and waited until he was ready to tell me where we were going, for I could not see any residence nearby.

He tied his horse to a tree, which led me to think that we still had some walking to do before reaching our destination. My predictions were confirmed; the old man asked me to follow him along a narrow path enclosed on either side by a thickset hedge.

This path penetrating into the darkness by degrees, led to a modest looking cottage, a residence admirably suited to cover up a crime or mask an adventure.

The cottage was located in the middle of a large wall-enclosed garden, a rather ordinary-looking gate allowing one a glimpse of the full property within, and particularly of how messy it was.

Before going in, the old man stated quietly, albeit not without betraying some deeper feelings:

"I forgot to mention that the injured person, not wishing to be recognized, will have his head covered with a thick veil. You will limit yourself to examining the wound he received full in the chest."

"But," I began, "to come to a firm diagnosis it is indispensable."

"I disagree," the old man abruptly interrupted, who took offense every time something did not go his way. "There's still time to pull out, to say no!"

I gave up.

Sighing and shrugging my shoulders I said, "I understand, I will do whatever it is you wish. Only by a sense of professional duty did I make such a valid observation." The stranger ignored me and opened the gate, crossed the porch and signaled me to stop.

"Wait for me here for a couple of seconds, I will come back and get you."

I took advantage of the fact that I was alone to more carefully look over the property that sheltered the mysterious patient. My survey was quite short, as the old man returned almost immediately.

"You may come now."

I followed my guide, who having crossed the vestibule, climbed a rather steep staircase leading to the room. To the left, an open door; we had arrived.

In a spacious and soberly decorated room, on a four-poster bed thickly enveloped in cretonne drapes, a creature was moaning. I say *creature* because I could not as yet see the injured person who had called for my expertise. The red sheet which covered him outlined a human form. It was all I could see of it.

I drew closer.

Even though I had been warned, I could not refrain from responding with surprise: the injured person had his head wrapped up in a thick shawl so it was impossible to see his features, only the hairy chest, abnormally large and powerful, could be seen, with a deep red wound gaping, resembling lips prepared to cry out. It was from a sword thrust, of this there was no doubt.

The injured person moaned softly as I probed the wound and nodded my head. There was no use deluding oneself, the wound was fatal.

Did he read in my features the inexorable end? Whatever the case may be, the old man was now livid, his hands convulsively shaking. He stumbled, overcome with grief, before collapsing into a chair.

Rather than going to his aid, I returned to the patient's bed, and naturally threw off the cover which hid the lower half of the body. My loud cry was answered by an angry outburst. The old man was in front of me, wild and threatening, a revolver in his hand pointed at my chest.

"Wretch!" he howled, "is this how you respect your solemn vow? You take advantage of my weakness to uncover
my secret, but you will not leave here alive, this house will be
your grave!"

And as I tried to protest, he added, even more vehement-
ly:

"I wished to have a colleague's opinion, for I too am a doctor, but I have no use for you now."

And still threatening me, he added:

"Walk in front of me. At the rear of the vestibule through which you came here, there is a staircase which leads to a cell where you will be at leisure to consider the dangers of not reining in one's imprudent curiosity. Make no attempt to resist, you understand. Do not attempt to escape, I will show no pity. I will gun you down like a mad dog."

I don't claim to be any braver than my fellows, but I must admit that I was little intimidated by these wild threats. Rather, I was overcome with thoughts brought on by the events I had witnessed. Reasonable prudence led me to obey my captor. Without turning around, I went down the steep staircase I had climbed before, with unfeigned calmness, still under the threat of the revolver whose barrel followed my every move. I found the cell and entered without putting up the least resistance.

Behind me the clash of metal on metal indicated that some large bolts had been drawn in order to prevent my escape. Notwithstanding the gravity of the situation, I could not help but smile when I considered that in a moment I would perhaps be called upon to undertake, for a brief moment, one of the most interesting endeavors of *mie prigioni*: escape.[80]

My prison was dark, receiving its only light through a vent covered with narrow steel bars. I ran headlong into a short step-ladder. The cell was less sinister than I had been expecting, and one could at least sit down. For a moment I forgot where I was, and pondered what I had seen: those powerful, hairy and oddly developed pectorals, and the lower extremities—for this patient had never walked upright, it would have been impossible. His skin was indeed that of a

---

[80] Allusion to *Le mie prigioni* (1832), a popularly celebrated prison journal by Silvio Pellico (1789-1854), an Italian writer, teacher and editor imprisoned for eight years between 1822 and 1830 by the Austrian invaders of Italy. [Ed.]

human, but his anatomy was that of an ape. It was some sort of monster whose features I had been barred from seeing. What a fearful mystery! Given the strange circumstances, perhaps I was the victim of a hoax, but no, I don't think so. Besides, if the old man's anger was any indication, I remained confused. This was all very nice, but I must escape this wasp's nest. I was strong and limber and little disposed to end my days in this cell.

My colleague had forgotten that I carried a small surgery kit on me, which could serve as well for a burglar as a doctor. The bars were nothing to fear, an athlete could easily have broken them, but I was content to dig them out.

With even greater precaution, I put myself to the task. The cracked plaster broke off and fell to the floor with a reassuring ease. Within an hour, if nothing came to interrupt me, my work would be done. I worked tirelessly, without a sound to disturb me. Night fell. I waited for the darkness to be complete. It was unlikely that I had been simply abandoned; my jailer must have been keeping watch, ready to shoot if I stuck out the tip of my nose.

By the glow of a match, I looked at my watch: 8 p.m. Night had indeed come—dark night, complicit night.

Would the vent be large enough? Could I get through? I was anxious. The time came to begin my escape. I climbed up the step-ladder, pulling myself through by the strength of my wrists. My head was through, I waited, waited for the bullet which would punish my temerity. Nothing. My body was through now. Did the pebbles crunch beneath my footsteps? No, I guess not. I was just about over the wall when a door opened, there was a sound of hasty steps. Oh well! I jumped down quickly as a shot rang out. I had been shot at, but felt no pain, I had not been hit. I ran, someone was speeding along behind me. I continued to run—the dark trees dancing by me in the dark sky—another shot, farther this time. I dropped exhausted. I perked up my ears, nothing, complete silence. He had lost my trail.

I got hold of myself, my strength returning bit by bit. I walked, notwithstanding my fatigue, I walked on and on. Suddenly I saw a glimmer of light, a vehicle's headlights: a vegetable farmer's truck.

I tried to steady my voice.

"Hey pal! Where am I?"

"On the road to Poissy,"[81] he answered rudely.

I have often asked myself whether I should have reported this adventure to the police, but my professional scruples prevented me from doing so. I was assaulted, that is true, but should I have spoken up about it? Besides, would anybody have believed me? The best thing was to forget about it.

I have returned to my usual occupations.

This morning not being so busy, I am looking as usual through the tinted window panes of my quarters, the white snowflakes falling haphazardly, turning my garden's flowerbeds to a cottony white.

Someone rings at the gate.

It is Dr. Debert, an old school friend who practices in Versailles. When he crosses the Vésinet, he never fails to come and visit me.

We are chatting of trivial things, when he suddenly exclaims:

"Ah! I forgot to relate a most interesting thing I did. A few days ago I was a witness at a duel, a serious duel, my dear man, between your old enemy Mr. de Videmar and a Polish gentleman."

"Well! I saw that in the newspaper, but your name was not mentioned."

"Could be the press has indeed not made much of it since de Videmar's adversary, count Ladislas Wolsky, is a strange individual, enigmatic and profoundly distasteful. The count was struck fully in the chest."

---

[81] Poissy is a town in the north of France. [Ed.]

My ears perked up. Debert continued:

"The wound seemed serious, but oddly enough the wounded man and one of the witnesses, a haughty and unpleasant-looking old man, refused my care."

"Go on," I said breathlessly.

"What's wrong with you?"

"For God's sake, go on!"

"I spoke again of this to Videmar, who seemed only mildly surprised and who passed on rather strange information regarding Wolsky. It seems this Polish count had moldered for some time in a Siberian prison, where he would have contracted a deforming type of rheumatism, which required him to almost always lie down or sit. However, he has a reputation as a swordsman which somewhat belied the condition which should rather have kept him bedridden."

"How is he physically?" I blurted out, prey to unutterable emotions.

"The count is ugly; of a simian ugliness. The forehead is low and retreating, the bright eyes lost in bushy eyebrows, the exceedingly narrow, razor-cut lips thrust forward in a queer prognathism. Overall he is massive, almost repugnant. The quarrel arose over a dropped glove. The count, no doubt to mock de Videmar, who is rather myopic, got down on hands and knees to find it. Videmar, who did not take well to the joke, wished to punish the Polish man, and without the intervention of several friends the scene would have degenerated into fisticuffs."

As Debert spoke, a veil was torn aside. I understood and was terrified.

"Do you not know the name of the old man who was his witness?"

"It was spoken before me wait."

"Was it not Bronzkowitch?"

"That's it!"

"Well then, your count Ladislas, the Polish aristocrat who crossed swords with Videmar, is not a man."

Debert's eyes opened particularly wide.

"No, it is not a man it is a monster or rather, an individual which stands between the ape and man."

"You're crazy!"

"No, I'm quite sane. I remember something told me in confidence by a Russian colleague regarding the son of one of his friends, Dr. Bronzkowitch. The latter, a great admirer of Lamarck, Huxley, Darwin and Haeckel, was passionately involved in discovering the 'missing link,' the link missing between the ape and man; he sought it frenetically, madly!

"Then, Nature, as if she wished to avenge herself of this man who sought to expose her most intimate secrets, recreated in a child which the brilliant doctor's wife bore, the archetype of the link Darwin had searched for.

"The friend who told me all this, described to me in such a manner that I would be hard pressed to duplicate, the horror of the situation. Bronzkowitch dedicated his life and his wealth to making a man out of his ape. Thankfully, like the missing link, even if an upright stance was painful to him, he only stood up long enough to mislead those around him, and he was capable of articulate speech. It is frightening! Do you understand now the story of the Siberian prison, why the center of attention was always tired, sitting or lying down— because he was only comfortable on all fours.

"If you aren't yet convinced, the story I'm going to tell you will dissipate your doubts," and immediately I gave him a complete account of my adventure.

When I was finished, Debert, who was deep in thought, said to me:

"We must get to the bottom of this affair."

Thanks to my recollections, I was able to find the path I had followed in escaping the homicidal bullets. There was the wall I climbed over in the wet soil, one could still see signs of my footsteps, and those of another, those of the old man, desperate to see me dead.

But where was the house? I could see only ruins. Nothing was left but a few unstable walls and some calcinated beams. The old man had kept his secret by blowing himself up with his son, the ape-man. Debert and I looked at one another.

"It is a shame," he muttered. "What a lovely presentation we could have made to the Academy of Sciences."

The old man kept his secret

Grégoire Le Roy (1862-1941) was a member of the Ghent group of Belgian Symbolist writers whose name is often encountered in connection with that of Maurice Maeterlinck. He is known especially for his collections of poems La Chanson du Soir *[Evening Song] (1887) and* Le Rouet et la Besace *[The Spinner and the Bag], which he illustrated, and which deals with the sufferings of the poor. Short story collections include* Contes d'après-minuit *[After Midnight Stories] (1913) and* Joe Trimborn *(1913).*

Grégoire Le Roy : *The Strange Adventure of Brother Levrai*

To my friend, brother Levrai,
among the incurables at the public lunatic asylum.

Sleep-walkers interest us; we flee from the insane. Nevertheless, the mysterious kingdoms of their subconscious are remarkably similar to one another.

As for me, I have always been keenly curious about certain forms of insanity and I remain the last friend of the poor brother who was locked up at Petites-Maisons.

This is his story.

I tell it as a composite of several talks we had together. If I do not present the story in the teller's own voice it is that I had to put some order amongst certain details and place in chronological order generally disjointed and episodic facts and remembrances, such as poor lunatics generally provide.

The words may be different, but I have maintained intact the meaning and intention, which represent the understanding of a story.

One may complain that the story is full of crazy and improbable things. How could it be otherwise?

Besides, wisdom can draw more than one lesson from lunacy, just as the man of wit discovers, in his neighbor, what makes him an idiot and from which he only differs in that he avoids allowing others the same perspective.

Rome had not yet admitted as orthodox the theory of evolution. She reserved judgment, in her obliging attention to all that relates to knowledge, and closed her eyes on the battles raging around the great principle.

Without having given safe haven to the working hypothesis that God had perhaps contented himself in creating the first cell, leaving in its care the perfection of his work, it neither encouraged nor discouraged anyone. Like a mother watching over her children's gambols, if ready to intervene at the first sign of danger, she measured the risks incurred, in such intellectual games, to those of hers who were following the new doctrine.

She was conscious of her authority and that she would know, at the appropriate time, to either draw them back to a respect of the doctrine or make it conform to scientific necessities, if the clear interests of the church required such a sacrifice.

In the favored shadow of this maternal tolerance, brother Levrai had given himself, body and soul, to questions of anthropology, and later, tempted by the example of the glorious adventurers who had exiled themselves to India in the hope of finding the vestiges of the putative ancestor, he had exchanged his secular priest's cassock for the earnest missionary's frock and had shipped out to the mysterious lands of the Malay archipelago.

Driven by his hankering for knowledge—to experience, as he put it, Truth fulfilled—and strong in the priest's vocational sacrifice which extends to the sacrifice of one's life, he scornfully ignored the already explored regions of Borneo, to

315

rush off, enraptured in faith and science, into the most fearsome jungles of a fearful land.

To say that in his scientist's soul he had forgotten God would be to misrepresent the sincerity of his faith, but it would be equally true to state that he did not choose the most inhabitable regions, when other regions could have, with greater likelihood, been presumed to house tribes in need of conversion. When the scientist and the believer are at odds over things which are so closely related, it is very rare that one does not come to lead the other on.

Furthermore, having met with truly isolated troglodytic races, consumers of raw roots and meat, which supplanted the less and less numerous hordes of Dayaks and Papous; having descended step by step the scales of barbarity, the brother had eventually lost all traces of humanity.

The mystery of the jungles deepened along with the rising dangers associated with wild beasts, these as much to be feared as were men. But Nature beautified herself so solemnly; the vegetation transformed the Earth into a marvelous world; the interlaced lianas and flowers formed such wild and fantastic arabesques; the clearings which suddenly opened up into fairyland chambers were the site of such fascinating silence that all notion of fear, all instinct of self-preservation was extinguished under the intoxicating influence to share in the multifaceted life of dominant and virginal Nature. And the brother had ever pressed forward, towards the heart of the mystery, untouched by any other emotion, living off the few roots which science helped him identify as being able to satisfy his hunger.

Only night was worrisome, for then the monkeys would chase him, their numbers growing daily, accumulating in living garlands hanging from the trees to the left and right of his path, advancing with him and only stopping at night, no doubt curious of his sudden stop, and then only to burst out in such a racket that sleep would not close his tired eyelids.

Thus, for many days was it an extraordinary existence in which even his consciousness dwindled as he distanced himself from humanity, as he left it behind, as he thought, much as one leaves a country behind.

Amidst this prodigious and incredible vegetation, he soon no longer conceived of his individuality from the rest of Nature. He ended up seeing himself, in a conceptualization that was only in part under his control, as only one more unit in this bewildering profusion of wildlife and vegetation.

Like his inferior fellows, did he not live at the whim of the Unknown? Like them, had he not lost his sense of self-preservation, only to find it again when suddenly face to face with impending danger? Yes indeed, it was their awe and wide-eyed surprise before all things, their continuous ecstatic state, softly slipping into an underlying unconsciousness, pushing him towards blissful animality.

On occasion he would remember his mission, which he somewhat neglected; but in absolving himself he reasoned that perhaps God would one day show him the marvelous things which bear within them the science behind all creation. Then, having beheld such a thing face to face, he would draw from his soul lyrics worthy of the loveliest hymn to God, words which would proclaim his Truth.

This one thought, almost a hope, was enough to retemper his will; he would move on again fresh and renewed, like the greatest seekers of knowledge, against all odds, even ready to undergo a missionary's martyrdom, for, in the end, were he not the one to bring truth to others but rather he who seeks it unto death, would he be any less a missionary of Truth?

Thus discovering in his passion the very justification for his passion, he once again considered the other goal of his mission: to find the mysterious link which ties man to his un-known ancestor, the pithecoid, in a word, that which represents the Holy Grail of the anthropologist's science, the yet inviolate tabernacle of revealed truth.

The brother, lifting his eyes to those accompanying him on his way, cried out: "A bit more than you, a wee bit more! I couldn't even express what, but, well…that something, that nothing which nonetheless differentiates you from us…"

317

Upon this, the monkeys afforded him their sympathy and forgot their nightly carousing. Who knows, he thought, perhaps they are angels which the Lord has sent to lead me as he once did Toby; they are perhaps to me what the star was to the Wise Men! In his simplicity, it had never occurred to the brother that he could have guessed so accurately.

A few days later, as he proceeded on his way, following his supernatural guides, these—as the Wise Men's star did when they were in sight of Bethlehem—suddenly stopped; their raucous cries were muffled; soon there was only a great whispering as if the wind, unknown in this thick jungle, had begun to blow the reeds and palms.

The brother stopped. What did his angels want? Left and right, all there was were thousands of glittering, apprehensive eyes. The monkeys, oscillating in counter-point the garlands of their intermingled bodies and interlaced tails, slowly, very slowly drew back and disappeared, one after another, in the direction whence they had come.

The brother felt abandoned, alone, terribly alone, as if his guardian angel had forsaken him. What could he do, it was not time to retire to sleep; definitely, he would not go back. Besides, some vague prescience warned him that great things were going to happen.

Night was not yet complete; he went on, less assuredly perhaps, hesitating as to which direction to take. Finally a sort of winding passage among the lianas opened up before him. It was almost a path, but a path arched over by the tree canopies. Surprisingly, the leaf litter showed signs of trampling! But now, a few paces farther, a clearing opened up, where, for reasons known only to Nature, the vegetation had reined in its exuberant growth. It was a veritable green-walled and roofed crypt whose twilight sparkled with myriads of phosphorescent insects. The smells of moist soil and succulent flowers thickened the warm air.

The brother stopped, intimidated, composing himself as when he entered a church. A greenish half-light obscured the clarity of things—his eyes were acclimating to it—he soon was able to distinguish, along with the walls and columns the jungle simulated, a few raised beds upon which were strewn sets of bones. It was a cemetery, the catacomb of a new species. He moved forward a step at a time, dumbfounded.

His anthropologist's eye could not deceive him.

This cranium! These femurs! These jaw-bones! He began to measure them, to estimate their volumes, and who knows what else? His heart was pounding, his hands clenched the bones; he held truth! And suddenly he trembled. Was it not a sin to know so intimately what God had seemingly wished to keep hidden for so many eons, that which he had so carefully hidden! Truth! Was this not God's treasure, and did man truly have the right to appropriate it in this manner, through patience and perseverance?

Ah! How difficult it was to distinguish good from evil!

How clearly he comprehended the huge import of the parable of the forbidden fruit! God and the devil were right; the Lord because it was true that man in eating of the fruit of science transgressed upon the mysteries which surrounded him; the devil because it was true that through science man attained absolute wisdom.

What was he to do? And, like Hamlet, he held a skull in his hand; and, like Eve, he thought he held the forbidden fruit in his hand; he hesitated.

Hamlet won out. Besides it was too late, since he already knew. He had measured and estimated the volume of everything. He was convinced; he even wondered if he would go further, for this cemetery led to the unavoidable conclusion that a colony of pithecanthropes was present.

He would go on! But which way? His angels were no longer there. It was only a passing hesitation; a mysterious certainty drove him as if, having so distanced himself from humanity and come closer to his less evolved fellows, an innate sense of direction had been added to his other faculties. Besides, the path took up again on the far side of the clearing, and as he straddled roots monstrously twisted and knotted like the coils of a giant serpent, how his soul took flight! His attention was soon entirely devoted to the silence which, in these impenetrable jungles, was of an unusual nature: it is not the silence of the plains or mountains, where the slightest sound expands infinitely through space or echoes and dies out; it is a living silence, alive with thousands of imperceptible sounds which an innumerable, invisible fauna creates through the efforts of their hidden but continuing life.

However, a remarkably regular series of blows, muffled by their distance, broke through the silence. The brother went on. The blows became more distinct, and, had it not been for the improbability of such a supposition, Levrai would have taken them to be the sound of a hammer or axe.

This was also the call of the Unknown, echoing through the missionary and scientist's heart. Was he going to find himself among an unknown people? How would the first meeting unfold? Bloody visions of martyrdom clouded his eyes.

The blows had suddenly stopped. The brother took a few quiet, tentative steps, careful not to disturb the cover of silence which spread out around him. And again he found himself in front of a clearing; frozen, he tried to peer in. No one! Had they fled at his approach? And notwithstanding his earlier visions of torture and death, he was wracked with regret. The words gorilla, orangutan trembled on his lips.

But here it was that his eyes suddenly stopped, awe-struck, on some sort of huge nest built of screw-pine leaves and woven branches, a genuine hut supported on the main limbs of a tree and reaching to the upper limbs for support as it circled about the trunk.

O! What minutes of anticipation! The anticipation of the big game hunter who sees the tiger's head emerge from the jungle like a blossom suddenly bursting open. The nest's leaves were suddenly thrust apart; a sudden leap, and an extraordinary creature, half-man, half-beast was standing there erect, right in front of the brother. A tragic moment, for ape or man, it held a great club in its hand.

Their eyes met and the anger burning in the ape's eyes died out while it observed the brother's humble, not to say pitiable aspect.

On his side, the brother, seeing the gradually mellowing mood of the…man and wishing to ensure his goodwill, said to him in his most fawningly sympathetic voice, nonetheless tinged with his overwhelming emotion:

"Good day, my friend…"

He would have preferred something better suited to the solemnity of the occasion, but nothing had come to him.

The ape, on his part, replied with an inarticulate grunt, which nonetheless indicated his seemingly great forbearance for the inoffensive and hang-dog look of the one engaging him in an exchange.

The brother was already saying to himself that he had here, at hand, the celebrated mystery of human history, the truth regarding creation. His emotions overwhelmed him; the large ape appeared beautiful to him, particularly in terms of moral beauty, for, when all was said and done, if he had wanted to, he could have sent the brother sprawling ten feet away with one blow of his club.

How shameful to think that a man would have acted thus! He was so overwhelmed that had the brave anthropologist dared, he would have given the ape a great big hug, but he did not even risk a handshake. But such moments cannot last forever, as impressive and eternal as the first meeting between man and his ancestor might appear in the eyes of Levrai. Again he would have liked to have something grand, unforgettable to say, words which would have consecrated this unique instant of Eternity but he was too awestruck to be inspired.

"Good day, my friend…" he repeated with a smile.

The ape affectionately took hold of his arm, and drawing him towards the tree, made a soft little cry. His mate showed herself.

Levrai, for all that he was a priest, could not help but find her somewhat attractive. She was not overly hairy—for that matter, her husband was not either—more so than ordinary women, certainly, even those with the most abundant hair, the bushiest eyebrows, the most shadowed lips, but this detail only proved a greater attraction to him. The brother was going to look her over in even greater detail when he remembered his youth and saw himself on the slippery slope of covetousness, or worse, even perhaps adultery!

He nonetheless had some difficulty during the days which he stayed with his new hosts, to avoid, without offending her with a blunt rebuff, to the ever mounting attentions of his hostess. He thought, more than once, he could read in his friend's eye a small glint of jealousy. He was wrong; everything pointed to the male being above such feelings, but the brother saw with bitterness that the sins of lust and adultery were older than man, and that no bloodline went back far enough, for these sins sank their roots even into our ancestral animality. How well he now understood the inefficacy of laws and religions in proscribing physical love!

It was only these matters of the flesh which troubled the fortnight he spend among his hosts—like those cold, nasty winds which sometimes mar a lovely spring morning. Besides, he quickly regained his composure, and, his missionary's conscience regaining the upper hand, he tried, at every appropriate opportunity, to draw the exchange into the domain of his apostolate. It was rather difficult; they understood each other so little, not to mention the difficulty in discussing the divine in a place yet so close to primeval nature.

To the brother, however, they were men, rough and uncouth, but men! He even had to admit, to his disarray, that they understood him better in all things than he did them. But every time he had said to himself: "now is the right moment to broach the great question," and had begun to talk, by gestures as much as by words, of the Infinite, while his hosts' eyes had indeed followed the mysterious signs of the *Absolute* he traced out in the air, when, carried away with his subject, he tried to have them understand the great questions of the faith, he had found his listeners distracted, dozing off, just like peasants during a Sunday sermon. His flock even had the unfortunate habit, at the most solemn moments, for example when he extolled the supreme importance of only considering one's salvation in the hereafter, of scratching with their fingers the sores which plagued the brother's neck.

He had to face the facts; these people were not yet at the stage of considering God. Beyond food and drink and letting Nature provide for them, the only thing which worried them was the extinction of their race.

They had managed to explain quite clearly that they were the last of their species, and that notwithstanding their diligent efforts they had not borne any children, and that their name, which for them was the equivalent of their species, was going to be forgotten and lost in nothingness. It was through a feeling of pride, born from the remarkable things they believed they had done, that pretty much inexplicable instinct, which pushes our middle-class to wish for a boy in order to perpetuate the family name but which only really manages to perpetuate their misery.

When, finally, the missionary became disillusioned as to the efficacy of his zealous preaching and he saw, more clearly than ever, the dangers of this *ménage-à-trois*, he resolved to part from his friends. The anthropologist took the upper hand; he foresaw a mission to accomplish, that of going to announce to the scientific world what he had seen, that is the very truth regarding the theory of evolution. His self-esteem was excited by the importance of such a mission, and with all the tenderness one can convey in gestures, he opened up to his friends.

The woman was greatly saddened, a rather human emotion, for one knows that a man will most regret the departure of his mate's friend, while the woman will rather more cry over the departure of her own friend.

On the day of their separation, the goodbyes were touching and even, miraculously, at certain moments, tears wetted his hostess's eyelids; the man was awestruck, he had never seen the likes of it, neither he, nor his mate, nor any of his species had ever cried.

It was the first sobs of the race and it was love which had brought them on! The poor unfortunate went sadly back to her nest and then only his friend remained to escort him back out.

They followed each other in silence, but already the split had occurred in their hearts. The steps they took together tread on the ground of parting, the ground which separates, the ground which draws apart; memories interposed between them as one made his way back to the land of men and the other, in spirit, turned back to the lonely place where his mate waited for him.

In such a manner they reached the crypt. The wild man stopped and the brother understood that this was the spot which he had tacitly chosen as the farthest point he would go. The brother made it understood with friendly gestures that he would have been well pleased were he to walk along farther with him, but in vain. By other gestures the primitive man made him to understand that this cemetery represented the ends of the earth to him, and that none of his race would ever consent to go beyond the territory where his ancestors had settled for eternity, that it was an intangible law not to see beyond the death, and it would have shown a lack of respect for them to go on.

Thus the cult of the past and the sadness of love which had been recently manifest in the spouse, these two characteristics of our civilization, the brother realized, the great apes knew and were subject to already.

There was nothing that could be done, the reasons were among those one does not discuss; the moment of parting had arrived. Friend held out a hand to the friend who placed his in it; the priest lifted ceremoniously his right hand and was going to make the sign of the cross over the ape's head, when the latter, taken by who knows what fear, turned suddenly and disappeared into the jungle.

After much trials and tribulations and yet more dangers, the brother had finally reached Pontianak.

His spiritual headquarters was the Capuchin convent where he found Father Palud, his director of conscience, in flourishing health. He had been anxious to see him again, especially since such great but fearful things had occurred in his shaken soul, and that he felt the need to retemper his faith in the strong, perhaps somewhat sectarian faith of his confessor, and to draw from it that blind confidence in God that one loses too easily when alone with Nature.

He had just given a truthful account of his incredible adventure, increasingly apprehensive of Father Palud's obstinate silence, when the latter, in a curt, cold voice which cut like a knife, cried out in irritation:

"What you have done is a crime. You have betrayed the Church's eternal truth for the adulterous love of worldly truth. You have picked the forbidden fruit and I understand that you would wish other men to bite into it.

"For the sake of simple scientific curiosity you would abandon all your spiritual learning. This will not happen! Even if it is the death of me, I will save the eternal truth. Follow me!"

"But."

And without further delay, the monk, shoving in front of the sad and discouraged missionary who dared not further disturb Father Palud's stubbornness, left the convent in tow and headed into the jungle, retracing step by step the unbelievable and dangerous route the brother had already covered twice, full of hope upon leaving, with the scientist's pride of having discovered upon his return.

It would take too long to tell of this expedition. Every day they got lost, the brother could barely make out where he was going now that the monkeys were no longer there.

What was it then which cried betrayal from the bottom of his heart? Yes, he was committing an act of betrayal, and though it wasn't clear to him if it consisted in the great ape or science, he understood that he had not behaved in a loyal manner. But his soul was that of a child and the hard, severe monk was pressing upon it with the fierce ardency of his faith.

The few times Father Palud broke the silence it was to utter harsh rebukes:

"What exactly drew you to that damned couple?"

"It is said that we descend…"

"Ah! I know! Common ugly traits have led atheists to believe…But it is rank falsehood! It contradicts the Scriptures."

"I believed I was drawing near to the Truth, that is God himself."

"Shut up! God cannot contradict the Church, and that truth, differing from that of the Church, can only be in opposition to God!"

"But, Father, can there not be two truths?"

"Indeed! There is the devil's truth; and there is that of God! Mere physical appearances can be deceiving, but the latter is nothing before the one, clear, eternal truth of the Church. This truth is simple, well ordered, complete; it forms a system which has passed all the tests the best scholars have put it to. And what are your scientific observations, those hunches of the intellect, those dispersed crumbs, compared to the bastions of theology, built upon the greatest minds?"

"Father, I thought that the eternal truth was made up of thousands of small truths that one gathers up along the way like little white pebbles, as Tom Thumb did in order to find his way, and that these small truths, they too, were eternal; that they fill the world and surround us, but that we don't always perceive them, undoubtedly because of their very smallness."

"Blasphemer! Those are material truths, truths of the flesh, truly pebbles compared to pure crystal; in a word, the devil's work! God's truth cannot be found on the open road, but in the soul; not in Nature, but in the purely spiritual."

"Yes, but, Father, it is precisely that I perceived the soul of my two friends being in some many ways akin to the human soul. Thus, when I preached to them…"

"Eh! What? You dared bring the word of God to such creatures?"

"Did not St. Francis preach to the animals?"

"Yes but they were birds, chickens, ducks, geese, all sorts of inoffensive lower forms of life, simple farmyard animals, and not huge, vile apes, barely covered with hair, abominable brutes, entirely abnormal creatures which resemble man!"

"This is true," the brother had to agree, in spite of his scientist's hopes.

"But I am thankful that I am mistaken," added the monk, "how could you have spoken to apes?"

"I admit it was difficult; but through gesture…"

"Oh! gestures, they are meaningless…"

"That's to be seen, to my mind, it was through gestures that they best understood me. In this regard, I often wondered if it is not rather with gestures than words that one should try to convey the Infinite. This is to some degree what people do anyway, for have you not noticed how quickly one reverts to gestures in exchanges of this sort? Thus is it not clear that the symbol and image are but thoughts which make motions and would well love to be understood? When I want to convey by speech what transcendent inspirations reveal to me of the absolute, I first realize that the words' meaning changes as they flow from my mouth; my sentences obscure the precision of my thought and in the end come to express the opposite of that I thought myself to be revealing. Thankfully the arms got involved and at least indicated the general direction of my thought; were one to simply add a few images and symbols which, in turn, display gestures, things would be much clearer."

He is insane, thought the monk. *He is a simpleton. God will pardon him!*

The brother put a finger to his lips; the monk understood.

The moment grew in solemnity; the time was coming; they were coming to the end of their expedition.

Though they had not crossed through the crypt—the brother had more than once lost his way—the bower, the famous bower opening on the clearing was only a few steps away. They took them, these steps, but how slowly and carefully

327

were they taken, and in what silence! Both their hearts were beating and a light sweat cooled the monk's brow.

Suddenly, a shot went off, over the brother's shoulder and the pithecanthrope which had just appeared between the parted branches of its suspended home, dropped, face forward, at the foot of the family tree.

The brother caught the monk's arm, wishing to protect the female he believed was still hidden, but not another leaf stirred.

"Father, what have you done?" the brother asked sadly.

"I have saved God's creation."

It was only after a long search that they found his mate, but she was dead and lying on a bed of leaves, her head resting against a tree, still holding tightly in her hand the tiny crucifix which the brother, naive as he was, had left her upon his departure after explaining to her as best he could the salvation that would come to her through it.

"A profanation!" Father Palud screamed, while the brother, in his simple way, was rather proud to see that his mission had not been entirely in vain.

There was nothing further for them to do there, but make their way back.

And so, there followed the return to Pontianak, a mournful, silent, lugubrious journey, during which the brother saw the strength of his apostle's faith dwindle little by little. No longer knowing where his duty lay, in doubt as to whether he had sinned or acted meritoriously towards God, having lost from his soul that clarity which calls and guides vocations through great sacrifices, like the little light in the woods which brings hope to the lost, the brother wept more than once over himself, the fruitlessness of his work, on his shattered faith and on the growing antipathy between his conscience and science.

Disillusioned, wishing only to rest, like aged sailors after their last trip, he asked to be repatriated and donned once again the robes of a parish priest, hoping to find, as a country vicar in some remote provincial place, forgetfulness of his adventure and aspirations.

Unfortunately, his sufferings were not over, and the last trial would be the hardest.

Barely disembarked in Marseilles, he found out that an anthropological congress was to hold an extraordinary session and that brother Buissonnire would be the speaker. That was enough for him to wish to attend.

When the day arrived it was clear that the assembly was prey to an extraordinary excitement. An unforgettable day was to be inscribed in the annals of anthropology. So, when brother Buissonnire rose, a stirring of attention, like a wave on the sand, expired into silence; the very air of the hall seemed steeped in solemnity.

Having quickly reviewed his previous discoveries, after saluting the authors which led him to them, brother Buissonnire began the description of his own finds.

Levrai was worried. He wondered if the speaker had indeed remained the orthodox brother which he had known, or if, like so many others, he had ended up falling into the Darwinian abyss. His worry was short-lived; Buissonnire, as if he had sensed it, quickly dissipated it.

"But before I tell you what my discovery was, I feel I must clear up a certain amount of ignorance, which while absent from those assembled here, nonetheless merits attention and is worthy of the respect of a priest, such as I am.

"Some overzealous polemists, neglecting to keep up with the new teachings of Rome, go from door to door spreading their hatred and contempt for evolutionism.

"It is time that they learn that this theory is now nothing less than highly orthodox, and that it is the opinion amongst our best theologians that God might well have contented himself in creating the first cell, foreseeing in his wisdom and eternal will, the successive stages through which his creation would evolve over the passage of time.

"I wished to bring this up to restore things to their proper perspective and avoid that, in the future, God's ministers, such as myself, do not pass in the eyes of certain among the faithful as impious or renegades and become victims of an underhanded persecution when they undertake the noblest function of their calling, which is the preaching of the truth."

Levrai was crimson! So, his perilous travels in the jungle, the pithecanthropes' cemetery, the days spent among his hosts, all that was not the devil's truth, as Father Palud had stated. Instead it was his second expedition and the ensuing massacre which were affronts to the truth?

Levrai thought he would choke.

"Are you feeling poorly?" asked his neighbor.

"It's nothing, just a little dizziness."

"This isn't all," continued the orator, "and if I thought it necessary to admonish rather severely those on my side, I have a few words for those—in the other camp—who make themselves out to be the virtuosos and cultivators of doubt.

"Certain scientists are averse to any new theory, simply because it is new, or because it too closely describes factual observations and Nature. They will gladly accept a philosophical principle as long as they believe it to be a simple witticism, that is to say doubtful, but they rebel as soon as they are asked to admit as genuine, facts and phenomena whose recognition would make a scientific truth of the theory to the exclusion of all other systems. Oh! then they retreat in orderly, serried ranks.

"Thus was it that, at first, they found evolutionism rather to their liking; however, they added that such a theory would not be of value until specific facts came to confirm it.

"And they dozed off, convinced that such facts would not be forthcoming, since nothing of the sort had been seen in centuries.

"Man, one might say, fears the truth; his instinct is to avoid any knowledge of it; he avoids it as much as he can with the excuse that doubt is the scientist's top attribute. He denies like someone on the stand, demanding proof and more proof, only giving up when he senses himself caught in the web of truth, like a fox in a trap or the starling in a snare.

"Truth be told, truth envelops us on every side in a huge net of which natural phenomena form the mesh. However, this mesh is not so tight that the rankest stupidity cannot escape. Must we have counted one by one all the elements of the mesh before agreeing that the net exists?

"There are theories before which one is struck by a sense of their truth, just as one has feelings of love when presented with Beauty. Indeed, such feelings are not sufficient to consecrate theories, for, in such a case, the faith of a coal-miner would be a sufficient criterion, but it is not rash to assert that, without this sense, no intellect is capable of understanding, completely and in its universality, a concept of such scope. The entrenched sectarian doubt is a form of mental short-sightedness which bars one from distinguishing simultaneously the whole and the details of a concept.

"It has been said that to believe or to deny everything are equally easy, for they dispense with thought. They are the two subterfuges of the lazy—and, it is time to state it—man bears in his inherited traits the monkey's main fault: laziness.

"But let me return to my subject.

"We were told: 'Show us vestiges of the intermediate race, and we will believe.' Until then nothing will fill the abyss which separates man from the beast, and this abyss is as unbridgeable as the faults which split open entire mountain ranges, forming with their debris the continents between which, today, the Oceans circulate. And the scientists dozed off again with the conviction, the great number even with the hope, that the absence of proof would wear down with time the grandeur and the attraction of the Darwinian principle.

"To better circumscribe the problem, with the ulterior motive of rendering it unsolvable, they went as far as outlining in advance the conditions of their surrender.

"You know these conditions: walks upright—*erectus*— cranial volume, etc.

"And the faithful disciples began to look. They scratched through—one after the other, so far as to wear down their nails—the geological strata, which for so many centuries had come to accumulate on the primitive Earth."

The brother outlined chronologically the remarkable discoveries made in the last 50 years, a half-century of heroic patience.

"But," he added, "all these skulls, all these sets of bones, as convincing as they might be, had the defect of presenting themselves completely naked, without any accessories which might denote some progress towards civilization, as, for example, a tool, a weapon, in a word, an irrefutable vestige of comfort and intellect.

"Well, I won't hesitate to state, I believe I have found it.

"It is in the mysterious Corrèze cave, near the *Monkey's Chapel*, that I discovered the venerable remains which are now before your eyes!

"For years I had been searching, I dug carefully with my hands in the sands and silts which the tides of the seasons had brought there, when, O tragic moment! I saw the remains and that in circumstances of remarkable interest.

"In a long rectangular trench, clearly dug by a human being, rested a skeleton lying on its back, oriented in an east-west direction, the head raised up against the wall of the grave, which proves overwhelmingly that, following a custom still alive among some races, one had placed the deceased facing the east, as if one had wished to signify by doing so that another sun, the sun of a new life, would rise before the deceased's soul. Flint and quartz tools, those which he had no doubt used to sustain and protect his life, were arranged around him, as is still done today, with the weapons and medals of honor of our dead. Besides this, the abundance of bones told of the diverse fauna which has been partaken of in the funerary banquets which the anthropoids gave, as we do, in honor of their departed parents.

"As you can see, these are the hints of a budding civilization. Like us they avoided solitude and silence; like us, they ate and pondered things in a group; like us, they called upon their dead to preside over the principal actions of life.

"But they were men, you will say! Eh! well, no! For there to be no possible doubt, one need only carefully consider these remains from a morphological point of view. The features of the skull are bestial; all the traits of simians are present together; the cranium was flattened, the prominent brow, and beneath the superciliary arch, the nose was separated from it by a deep depression resembling the notch of an axe. To all of this, add a facial prognathism even more hideous as among the descendants of Charles Quint.[82] So tell me, does there remain any doubt on the simian identity of our precious subject?

"You see gentlemen, our searching has paid off. Our ancestors after 10,000 or 20,000 years of sleep and waiting seem to be rising from their graves to claim from their descendants the recognition of their paternity."

Brother Levrai thought he was dreaming. He would not have described it otherwise if he had had to give an account of what he had recently seen in Borneo. What to do? Would he speak of his own discovery? His faith no longer stopped him. But how could he confess to his pointless crime? Also, he thought, the question is resolved, and it would be rather poor manners, not being registered as a speaker, to get involved in a discussion wisely organized in advance.

Already the illustrious Dr. Moyen had reached the podium.

This professor enjoyed a most envied reputation as a prudent scientist, resistant to immoderate enthusiasm regarding bold theories, faithful to the wisdom of learned men of the old school.

---

[82] Charles V (Quint means "five" in Middle French), ruler of the Holy Roman Empire, also known as Charles of Habsburg, Archduke of Austria (1500-1558). Members of the Habsburg royal family, Charles Quint included, suffered from mandibular prognathism (protrusion of the lower jaw), thought to be genetically determined by inbreeding. [Ed.]

"I shall begin by paying homage," he said, "to my eminent colleague; it is our duty to encourage the researchers whose discoveries are the very spring from whence science drinks. However, let us not be carried away in our desire to attain certainty. Truth is not so simple. As long as it was only a theory, one could close one's eyes and let young minds get heated through its contact, but today, when events appear to confirm their thesis, we must see things in another light. Besides, it would be unworthy of a scientist to believe for an instant that truth could let itself be captured.

"But, especially consider the noble and genuine monuments of intellect, which such a truth would undermine to their ultimate collapse. What would become of the admirable inventions of the philosophers and creators of the book of Genesis? Let the members of this assembly take hold of themselves and return to a wiser conception of things.

"Why, then, would these discoveries that one cannot deny not incite us to proclaim that these half-simian, half-human remains, those of a lost species, a species which would stand—I would propose officially—as the happy medium between man and ape, an inferior race not ascending but parallel, and which would be to the human being what the curate is to the priest, the clergy to the bishop, or in a well-structured society, the poor to the rich.

"Man would thus remain the center of the universe.

"This is a new theory, you will say, yes, but a theory which leaves the question open and does not rattle too forcefully the doors of the sanctuary within which we must leave truth inviolate.

"Nothing," he added, "would allow us to settle the question today. The proof has not been made. What have been brought are, I will admit, suggestive hints, but doubtful, incomplete hints. I believe I express the opinion of the majority in affirming that true scientists will only face the facts when one among us will come and tell us: I saw him with my own eyes, I touched with my own hands *Pithecanthropus erectus*."

"I am the one," Levrai cried out, no longer able to silence the truth which leapt from his heart to his lips. "I have seen it, I have touched it, I have spoken to it, I have even killed it..."

The rest was lost in the general din and indignation.

The most charitable among them thought him mad.

The ushers drew around him quietly; they took him away; he allowed himself to be taken, already regretting the scandal he had caused. It was only in the cabin where the Brothers of Charity locked him up that he finally understood the reality of things.

The kindest care, the most persuasive treatments were never able to overcome his insanity, and, many years later, his keeper, more in compassion than in irony, would still tell visitors who felt sorry for the meek and taciturn man:

"That one, he's the man who has seen truth."

Marcel Roland: *The Missing Link*

From the village where they had set up the center of their explorations, they had left with the rising sun and had already been walking for three hours. The part of Borneo through which they made their way was mountainous, and divided by deep, dark valleys. Rocky peaks alternated with almost impenetrable jungles. Accompanied by a native guide and carrying their plant presses, the two naturalists had just climbed halfway up a precipitous outcropping. After stopping in the shade of one of the rare trees growing on this gravelly slope, they went on their way. Suddenly, they found themselves in a natural hollow, carved out of the rock.

"A cave!" cried out Mounier.

"No, a tunnel!" answered the other.

In saying these words, the second European, Steiner, pushed aside a curtain of dried lianas which half covered the opening. A narrow circle of pale daylight appeared at the other end. It was indeed a passageway which extended at both ends into open air.

"Let's go in!" Mounier offered resolutely. "I'll go first!"

They silently made their way down the passage, their rifles at the ready, followed by the native whose supple tread barely brought a crackle from the granitic debris strewn across the floor. They could walk upright, but sometimes the ceiling would abruptly drop or bristle with sharp spikes, forcing them to bend over. Large bats, hanging upside-down from the roof, their serenity disturbed, took wing with cries that spun through the oppressive air. They finally reached the end of the straight passageway

Steiner, who had taken the lead, lifted a sort of blind of twigs such as hung at the other end, but suddenly stepped back.

"Just in time," he grumbled, "I was going to take quite a tumble."

Indeed, the ground dropped off abruptly in front of the cave floor, sloping down sharply, almost perpendicularly to heaps of boulders. The three companions stopped and took in the scene which presented itself to them. They saw an extremely deep, funnel-shaped cirque, at the bottom of which, amongst fearful shadows, one could hear the roar of an invisible torrent. The edges of this deep granite basin were lost at a dizzying height, far above their heads, and the light from the sky, falling on the chaotic assemblage of irregularly-shaped boulders, contrasted areas of light with black pits.

The corridor from which the explorers were emerging, continued on the other side of the cirque, but to reach it one had to follow an extremely narrow platform, created by a freak of Nature, which ran all along the wall.

"It's dangerous!" pointed out Steiner, "but if we want to know what this underground passage leads to, there's no hesitating!"

"Let's go!...You don't suffer from vertigo, do you, Sikoula?" said Mounier.

The native smiled. Vertigo, pah! He was well acquainted with peaks, and experienced in the most awkward of balancing acts!

They continued their perilous hike. Here and there the suspended walkway widened and the piles of boulders beneath made any possible fall much shorter.

Then, mere meters away, Steiner made out, upon a crag, a bunch of pale mauve flowers.

"*Velamina Sigillata*!" he cried out triumphantly, his face glowing with happiness. "Finally! I knew I would succeed in finding it!"

This *Velamina Sigillata*, was an extremely rare plant, a genuine jewel of Botany, of which only one living example existed in cultivation and which he had searched for in vain for years! He had come to Borneo with the hope of perhaps finding, in the midst of its abundant vegetation, the coveted specimen, which he counted upon to cement his professional reputation. This expectation had not been a disappointment! On the edge of the walkway, his eyes sparkling, he contemplated the object of his dreams.

He extended a finger. "There, Sikoula...Ten dollars for you if you bring me back that plant with its roots!"

In a flash, the native had slipped down a granite rib to a spot a few feet below the walkway, and began to leap from boulder to boulder to where the *Velamina* opened its mauve corollas.

Suddenly, there was a stifled cry and his arms flailed out: he had lost his footing. The Europeans, who had been following him, saw him waver and drop, head first, over the precipice. But at the very moment he was to disappear, from behind a rocky outcropping emerged a huge, muscular black arm, bearing a crooked hand. This hand grabbed the man as he fell, and held him still, suspended over the abyss like a gesticulating puppet. Slowly, something fearful, a gigantic, hideous creature, was revealed before the explorers' eyes.

They had enough time to make him out clearly, to notice his body's long fawn-colored hair, his spindly legs, bending under the weight of the torso, the head's flattened skull, the sunken brow, the prominent cheeks and forward-jutting jaws that made up its features. Buried beneath the beetling brow, gleamed a set of furtive, yellow eyes. Still holding Sikoula at arm's length, the marvelous creature had turned towards the strangers and was looking them over. They too looked him over, frozen in fear and amazement. This was no orang, for it was much bigger, better proportioned and missing the pair of lateral cranial protrusions characteristic of the Asian anthropoid. There was, all told, over his features a singular, indefinable expression, less bestial than human. The features of this creature would not allow it being assigned to any species of ape. The two naturalists, accustomed to all forms of the simian race, of which the island had supplied them with numerous examples, had no doubt whatsoever of this. What they were seeing was a new, unknown life-form.

Struck by a sudden thought, Mounier leaned over and whispered:

"Steiner! Could it be...It...the ape-man?...You know of course, the pithecanthrope, the missing rung in the ecological ladder between the gorilla and us! There are claims it is not extinct. Travelers have met it in certain old-growth forests. I myself didn't believe it, however..."

But already, his partner, driven by his haste to save the native had shouldered his rifle. Before his partner could stop him he had shot at the monster without further thought.

It jerked, threw down its stick and put its free hand to its chest, over its heart. With its other arm it still held Sikoula, suspended motionless over the abyss. It had but to open its fingers and the poor wretch would have been splattered over the bottom. At this thought the two explorers shuddered. Furious at his own thoughtlessness, Steiner muttered,

"What an idiot I am!"

But, rather than perpetrate the act of vengeance they feared, to their amazement the creature put the native softly down on a boulder from which he could easily regain the platform. Then in a look which gave away its suffering it seemed to say: "Go back to your own kind, go...You are safe now!"

And while a still trembling Sikoula returned to his companions, the mysterious creature, leaned tottering against a boulder. His hairy hand pressed against the thorax from which a red stream flowed. It moaned, and turning its head several times towards the men, towards those who had just condemned him to death, he moved off towards the underground passage. Helping himself up by way of great masses of stone, he climbed the fairly steep slope leading to it. Having reached the tunnel's entrance, he called feebly. The travelers immediately saw a long-haired female and her agile children emerge and busy themselves around him...One last look back and the creature disappeared.

"I feel like I've committed murder," Steiner admitted.

Perplexed, almost anguished, they turned back. A few days later they returned to this spot with a large escort. The tunnel, the cirque, the neighboring areas were searched, but no trace was found of the family of anthropoids.

Had they come face to face with a human ancestor, which remained the matter of legends, or had they simply encountered an orangutan of superior instincts? None was ever able to solve this enigma.

SF & FANTASY

Guy d'Armen. *Doc Ardan: The City of Gold and Lepers*
G.-J. Arnaud. *The Ice Company*
Aloysius Bertrand. *Gaspard de la Nuit*
Richard Bessière. *The Gardens of the Apocalypse*
Félix Bodin. *The Novel of the Future*
André Caroff. *The Terror of Madame Atomos*
Didier de Chousy. *Ignis*
C. I. Defontenay. *Star (Psi Cassiopeia)*
Charles Derennes. *The People of the Pole*
Georges Dodds/Paul Wessels (anthologists). *The Missing Link*
Harry Dickson. *The Heir of Dracula*
Jules Dornay. *Lord Ruthven Begins*
Sâr Dubnotal *vs. Jack the Ripper*
Alexandre Dumas. *The Return of Lord Ruthven*
J.-C. Dunyach. *The Night Orchid; The Thieves of Silence*
Henri Duvernois. *The Man Who Found Himself*
Henri Falk. *The Age of Lead*
Paul Féval. *Anne of the Isles; Knightshade; Revenants; Vampire City; The Vampire Countess; The Wandering Jew's Daughter*
Paul Féval, *fils. Felifax, the Tiger-Man*
Arnould Galopin. *Doctor Omega*
Nathalie Henneberg. *The Green Gods*
V. Hugo, P. Foucher & P. Meurice. *The Hunchback of Notre-Dame*
Michel Jeury. *Chronolysis*
Octave Joncquel & Theo Varlet. *The Martian Epic*
Gérard Klein. *The Mote in Time's Eye*
Jean de La Hire. *Enter the Nyctalope; The Nyctalope on Mars; The Nyctalope vs. Lucifer*
André Laurie. *Spiridon*
Georges Le Faure & Henri de Graffigny. *The Extraordinary Adventures of a Russian Scientist Across the Solar System* (2 vols.)
Gustave Le Rouge. *The Vampires of Mars*
Jules Lermina. *Mysteryville; Panic in Paris; To-Ho and the Gold Destroyers*
Jean-Marc & Randy Lofficier. *Edgar Allan Poe on Mars; The Katrina Protocol; Pacifica; Robonocchio; Tales of the Shadowmen* (anthologists; 7 vols.)
Xavier Mauméjean. *The League of Heroes*
John-Antoine Nau. *Enemy Force*

Marie Nizet. *Captain Vampire*
C. Nodier, A. Beraud & Toussaint-Merle. *Frankenstein*
Henri de Parville. *An Inhabitant of the Planet Mars*
J. Polidori, C. Nodier, E. Scribe. *Lord Ruthven the Vampire*
P.-A. Ponson du Terrail. *The Vampire and the Devil's Son*
Maurice Renard. *The Blue Peril; Doctor Lerne; The Doctored Man;.
A Man Among the Microbes; The Master of Light*
Albert Robida. *The Adventures of Saturnin Farandoul; The Clock of
the Centuries.*
J.-H. Rosny Aîné. *Helgvor of the Blue River; The Givreuse Enigma;
The Mysterious Force; The Navigators of Space; Vamireh; The
World of the Variants; The Young Vampire*
Brian Stableford. *The New Faust at the Tragicomique;The Empire of
the Necromancers (The Shadow of Frankenstein; Frankenstein and
the Vampire Countess; Frankenstein in London); Sherlock Holmes &
The Vampires of Eternity; The Stones of Camelot; The Wayward
Muse.* (anthologist) *The Germans on Venus; News from the Moon*
Han Ryner. *The Superhumans*
Jacques Spitz. *The Eye of Purgatory*
Kurt Steiner. *Ortog*
Villiers de l'Isle-Adam. *The Scaffold; The Vampire Soul*
Philippe Ward. *Artahe*
Philippe Ward & Sylvie Miller. *The Song of Montségur*

MYSTERIES & THRILLERS

M. Allain & P. Souvestre. *The Daughter of Fantômas*
A. Anicet-Bourgeois, Lucien Dabril. *Rocambole*
A. Bisson & G. Livet. *Nick Carter vs. Fantômas*
V. Darlay & H. de Gorsse. *Lupin vs. Holmes: The Stage Play*
Paul Féval. *Gentlemen of the Night; John Devil; The Black Coats
('Salem Street; The Invisible Weapon; The Parisian Jungle; The
Companions of the Treasure; Heart of Steel; The Cadet Gang)*
Emile Gaboriau. *Monsieur Lecoq*
Steve Leadley. *Sherlock Holmes: The Circle of Blood*
Maurice Leblanc. *Arsène Lupin vs. Countess Cagliostro; Lupin vs.
Holmes (The Blonde Phantom; The Hollow Needle)*
Gaston Leroux. *Chéri-Bibi; The Phantom of the Opera; Rouletabille
& the Mystery of the Yellow Room*
William Patrick Maynard. *The Terror of Fu Manchu*
Frank J. Morlock. *Sherlock Holmes: The Grand Horizontals*

P. de Wattyne & Y. Walter. *Sherlock Holmes vs. Fantômas*
David White. *Fantômas in America*

SCREENPLAYS

Mike Baron. *The Iron Triangle*
Emma Bull & Will Shetterly. *Nightspeeder; War for the Oaks*
Gerry Conway & Roy Thomas. *Doc Dynamo*
Steve Englehart. *Majorca*
James Hudnall. *The Devastator*
Jean-Marc & Randy Lofficier. *Royal Flush*
J.-M. & R. Lofficier & Marc Agapit. *Despair*
Andrew Paquette. *Peripheral Vision*
R. Thomas, J. Hendler & L. Sprague de Camp. *Rivers of Time*

NON-FICTION

Stephen R. Bissette. *Blur 1-5. Green Mountain Cinema 1*
Win Scott Eckert. *Crossovers* (2 vols.)
Jean-Marc & Randy Lofficier. *Shadowmen* (2 vols.)
Randy Lofficier. *Over Here*

HEXAGON COMICS

Franco Frescura & Luciano Bernasconi. *Wampus*
Franco Frescura & Giorgio Trevisan. *CLASH*
L. Bernasconi, J.-M. Lofficier & Juan Roncagliolo Berger. *Phenix*
Claude Legrand, J.-M. Lofficier & L. Bernasconi. *Kabur*
Franco Oneta. *Zembla*
L. Buffolente, Lofficier & J.-J. Dzialowski. *Strangers: Homicron*
Danilo Grossi. *Strangers: Jaydee*
Claude Legrand & Luciano Bernasconi. *Strangers: Starlock*

ART BOOKS

Jean-Pierre Normand. *Science Fiction Illustrations*
Raven Okeefe. *Raven's L'il Critters*
Randy Lofficier & Raven OKeefe. *If Your Possum Go Daylight...*
Daniele Serra. *Illusions*